S0-AZO-671

The Surgeon's Mate

Patrick O'Brian

The Surgeon's Mate

Thorndike Press • Chivers Press
Waterville, Maine USA Bath, England

This Large Print edition is published by Thorndike Press, USA and by Chivers Press, England.

Published in 2001 in the U.S. by arrangement with W. W. Norton & Company.

Published in 2001 in the U.K. by arrangement with HarperCollins Publishers Ltd.

U.S. Hardcover 0-7862-1936-X (Famous Author Series Edition)
U.K. Hardcover 0-7540-1662-5 (Windsor Large Print)
U.K. Softcover 0-7540-9076-0 (Paragon Large Print)

Thorndike Press Large Print Famous Authors Series.

The tree indicium is a trademark of Thorndike Press.

The text of this Large Print edition is unabridged.
Other aspects of the book may vary from the original edition.

Set in 16 pt. Plantin.

Printed in the United States on permanent paper.

British Library Cataloguing-in-Publication Data available

Library of Congress Cataloging-in-Publication Data

O'Brian, Patrick, 1914–
The surgeon's mate / Patrick O'Brian.
p. cm.
ISBN 0-7862-1936-X (lg. print : hc : alk. paper)
1. Great Britain — History, Naval — 19th century — Fiction.
2. Maturin, Stephen (Fictitious character) — Fiction. 3. Aubrey, Jack (Fictitious character) — Fiction. 4. Large type books.
I. Title.
PR6029.B55 S87 2001
823′.914—dc21 2001027335

MARIAE SACRUM

Author's Note

Great men can afford anachronism, and indeed it is rather agreeable to find Criseyde reading the lives of the saints or Hamlet going to school at Wittenberg; but perhaps the ordinary writer should not take many liberties with the past. If he does, he sacrifices both authenticity and the willing suspension of disbelief, and he is sure to receive letters from those with a greater love of precision than himself. Only the other day a learned Dutchman reproached me for having sprinkled eau de Cologne in the forepeak of HMS *Shannon* in my last book: the earliest English reference to eau de Cologne, said he, quoting the Oxford Dictionary, is in a letter of Byron's dated 1830. I believe he was mistaken in assuming that no Englishman ever *spoke* of eau de Cologne before that time; but his letter made me uneasy in my mind, all the more so since in this present book I have deliberately kept Sir James Saumarez in the Baltic some months after he had taken the *Victory* home and struck his flag. In the first draft I had relied on the Dictionary of National Biography, which maintained the Admiral in command for my chosen period: but then, checking in the memoirs of one of his subordinates, I found that in fact another man had taken his place. Yet I did want to say something about Saumarez, an outstanding example of a particular type of sea-officer of that time, deeply religious, extremely capable, and a most effective diplomat, so as I really could not rearrange the calendar any more I decided to leave things as they were, although out of some obscure feeling of respect for that noble ship I omitted all reference to the *Victory*. The historical sequence, therefore, is not quite exact; but I trust that the candid reader will grant me this amount of licence.

The sails of a square-rigged ship, hung out to dry in a calm.

1	Flying jib	12	Mainsail, or course
2	Jib	13	Maintopsail
3	Fore topmast staysail	14	Main topgallant
4	Fore staysail	15	Mizzen staysail
5	Foresail, or course	16	Mizzen topmast staysail
6	Fore topsail	17	Mizzen topgallant staysail
7	Fore topgallant	18	Mizzen sail
8	Mainstaysail	19	Spanker
9	Maintopmast staysail	20	Mizzen topsail
10	Middle staysail	21	Mizzen topgallant
11	Main topgallant staysail		

Illustration source: Serres, Liber Nauticus.
Courtesy of The Science and Technology Research Center,
The New York Public Library, Astor, Lenox, and Tilden Foundations

1
2
3
4
5
6
7
8
9
10
11
12
13
14
15
16
17
18
19
20
21

Chapter One

The long harbour of Halifax in Nova Scotia on a long, long summer's day, and two frigates gliding in on the tide of flood under their topsails alone: the first, since she had belonged to the United States navy until a few days before, wore the Stars and Stripes under a white ensign; the second showed no more than her own shabby colours, for she was HMS *Shannon*, the winner in that short and bloody action with the *Chesapeake*.

The *Shannon*'s crew already had some notion of the welcome they should receive, because news of the victory had spread and dories, yachts, privateers' boats and small craft of all kinds had met them beyond the distant harbour's mouth, sailing along with them, waving their hats and bawling out 'Bravo — huzzay — well done, *Shannon* — huzzay, huzzay!' The Shannons took no great notice of the civilians, apart from a distant acknowledgement, a discreet wave from the watch below; but the small craft took great notice of them, and although the casual observer saw little to exclaim at in the *Shannon* herself, with most of her rigging new set up, a fresh suit of sails bent to her yards, and her paintwork at least as trim as it was when she set out from this same port some weeks ago, the more knowing eye of the privateersmen saw the deep wounds in her bowsprit and her masts, the mizen fished with capstan-bars, the shot still lodged in her side and the plugs where they had gone through: yet even the most unobservant could not miss the gaping void in the *Chesapeake*'s stern and larboard quarter, where the *Shannon*'s full starboard broadside had raked her again and again, sending some five hundredweight of iron hurtling clean through her length at every blast. They did not of course see the blood of that savage conflict, the blood that had poured thick from the scuppers, for the Shannons had cleaned both ships and they had priddied the decks as far as they could; but even so, from the state of the masts and the yards and of the *Chesapeake*'s hull, any man who had seen action could imagine the slaughter-house look of the ships when the battle ended.

The Shannons, then, knew how they would be received, and the watch below had already contrived to slip into their best shore-going rig of glazed broad-brimmed hats with *Shannon* embroidered on the ribbon, bright blue jackets with brass buttons, loose white trousers with ribbons in the seams, and very small shining black pumps; but even so they were astonished by the prodigious volume of sound that met them as they neared the wharves — by the overlapping waves of cheers and then by the even louder, even more highly-valued, exactly-ordered cheering as they passed the men-of-war that lay in the harbour, each one with her yards and rigging manned all over, roaring in unison '*Shannon*, huzzay, huzzay, huzzay!' so as to make the air and the sea under it tremble while the frigate slipped along on the height of the tide to pick up her familiar moorings. The whole of Halifax had turned out to greet them and their victory, the first victory in a war that had started so disastrously for the Royal Navy, with three proud frigates taken one after another by the Americans in single-ship actions, to say nothing of the smaller vessels: obviously the sailors were the most ecstatic — and their bitter pain at all these defeats could be measured by the hoarse enormity of their present joy — but the thousands and thousands of redcoats and civilians were delighted too, and young Mr Wallis, in command of the *Shannon*, could scarcely be heard when he gave the order to clew up.

Yet although the Shannons were pleased and astonished, they remained for the most part grave, gravely pleased: their deeply-respected captain lay between life and death in his cabin; they had buried their first lieutenant and twenty-two of their shipmates; and the sickbay, overflowing into the berth-deck, held fifty-nine wounded, many of them very near their end and some of them the most popular men in the ship.

When the port-admiral came up the side, therefore, he saw a sparse crew, togged to the nines but with a restraint upon them, and a thinly-peopled quarter-deck — few officers to greet him. 'Well done, by God,' he cried above the wail of bosun's calls piping him aboard, 'well done, the *Shannon*.' And then, 'Where is Captain Broke?'

'Below, sir,' said Mr Wallis. 'Wounded, I regret to say. Very badly wounded in the head. He is barely conscious.'

'Oh, I am sorry for that. Damme, I am sorry for that. Is he very bad? The head, you say? Are his intellects in trim — does he know about his famous victory?'

'Yes, sir, he does. I believe that is what keeps him going.'

'What does the surgeon say? Can he be seen?'

'They would not let me in this morning, sir, but I will send below and ask how he does.'

'Aye, do,' said the Admiral. A pause. 'Where is Mr Watt?' — referring to the first lieutenant, once a midshipman of his.

'Dead, sir,' said Wallis.

'Dead,' said the Admiral, looking down. 'I am most heartily sorry for it — a fine seamanlike officer. Did you suffer a great deal, Mr Falkiner?'

'We lost twenty-three killed and fifty-nine wounded, sir, a quarter of our people: but *Chesapeake* had above sixty killed and ninety wounded. Her captain died aboard us on Wednesday. May I say, sir,' he added in a low voice, 'that my name is Wallis? Mr Falkiner is in command of the prize.'

'Just so, just so,' said the Admiral. 'A bloody business, Mr Wallis, a cruel business: but worth it. Yes, by God, it was worth it.' His eye ran along the clean, orderly, though scarred deck, the boats, two of them already repaired, up to the rigging, and lingered for a moment on the fished mizen. 'So you and Falkiner and what hands you had left brought them both in between you. You have done very well indeed, Mr Wallis, you and your shipmates. Now just give me a brief, informal account of the action: you shall put it in writing presently, if Captain Broke don't recover in time for the dispatch; but for the moment I should like to hear it from your own mouth.'

'Well, sir,' began Wallis, and then paused. He could fight extremely well, but he was no orator; the Admiral's rank oppressed him, so did the presence of an audience that included the only surviving American officer fit to stand — though even he was wounded. He brought out a lame, disjointed tale, but the Admiral listened to it with a glowing, visible delight, for with what he had heard before it fell into perfect shape, even more perfect than the rumours that had already reached him. What Wallis said confirmed all that he had heard: Broke, finding the *Chesapeake* alone in Boston harbour, had sent his consorts away, challenging her captain to come out and try the issue in the open sea. The *Chesapeake* had indeed come out in the most handsome, gallant manner: they had fought their battle fair and square, evenly matched, broadside to broadside, with no manoeuvring; and having swept the *Chesapeake*'s quarterdeck clear, killing or wounding almost all her officers in the first few moments, the *Shannon* had raked her, boarded her, and carried her. 'And it was just fifteen minutes, sir, from the first gun to the last.'

'Fifteen minutes, by God! That I did not know,' said the Admiral; and after a few more questions he clapped his hands behind his back and paced up and down, silently digesting his satisfaction.

His eye caught a tall figure in a post-captain's uniform standing by the Marine officers and he cried, 'Aubrey! Why, it must be Aubrey, upon my life!' He stepped forward with his hand outstretched: Captain Aubrey whipped his hat under his left arm, edged his right hand from its sling, and gave the Admiral's as hearty a shake as he could. 'I was sure I could not mistake that yellow hair,' said the Admiral, 'though it must be years . . . a wounded arm? I knew you was in Boston, but how come you here?'

'I escaped, sir,' said Jack Aubrey.

'Well done,' cried the Admiral again. 'So you were aboard for this noble victory!

That was worth an arm or two, by God. Give you joy with all my heart. Lord, how I wish I had been with you. But I am most damnably grieved for poor dear Watt, and for Broke. I must have a word with him, if the surgeon . . . Is your arm bad?' — nodding towards the sling.

'It was only a musket-ball in the *Java* action, sir. But here are the doctors, sir, if you wish to speak to them.'

'Mr Fox, how d'ye do?' said the Admiral, turning to the *Shannon*'s surgeon, who had just come up the main hatchway with a companion, both of them in their working clothes. 'And how is your patient? Is he fit to receive a visit, a short visit?'

'Well, sir,' said Mr Fox with a doubtful shaking of his head, 'we dread any excitement or mental exertion at this stage. Do you not agree, colleague?'

His colleague, a small sallow man in a blood-stained black coat, dirty linen and an ill-fitting wig, said, 'Of course, of course,' in a somewhat impatient tone. 'No visits can possibly be allowed until the draught has had its effect,' and he was moving away without another word when Captain Aubrey took him by the elbow and said in a private voice, 'Hold hard, Stephen: this is the Admiral, you know.'

Stephen looked at Aubrey with his strange pale eyes, red-rimmed now after days and nights of almost incessant exertion, and said, 'Listen now, Jack, will you? I have an amputation on my hands, and I would not pause to chat with the Archangel Gabriel himself. I have only stepped up to fetch my small retractor from the cabin. And tell that man not to talk so loud.' With this he walked off, leaving nervous smiles behind him, anxious looks directed at the Admiral: but the great man did not seem at all put out. He gazed about the ship and over the water at the *Chesapeake* and his deep delight showed clear beneath his immediate concern for the *Shannon*'s captain and her missing officers and men. He asked Wallis for the muster-roll of the prisoners of war, and while it was being fetched he stood by an improvized hood over the cabin skylight with Jack Aubrey and said, 'I know I have seen that face before; but I cannot put a name to it.'

'He is Dr —' began Captain Aubrey.

'Stay. Stay. I have it. Saturnin — that's the man. Admiral Bowes and I were calling at the palace to enquire after the Duke, and he came out and told us how he did. Saturnin: I knew I should get it.'

'The very same man, sir. Stephen Maturin was called in to doctor Prince William, and I believe he saved him when all else had failed. A prodigious physician, sir, and my particular friend: we have sailed together since the year two. But I am afraid he is not quite used to the ways of the service yet, and he sometimes gives offence without intending it.'

'Why, he is no great respecter of persons, to be sure; but I am not at all offended. I don't take myself for God the Father, you know, Aubrey, although I have my flag; and anyhow, it would take a great deal to put me out of humour on such a day — Lord, Aubrey, such a victory! Besides, he must be a great man in the physical line, to be called in to the Duke. How I wish he may save poor Broke. Your servant, ma'am,' he cried, gazing with respectful admiration at an extraordinarily elegant young woman who suddenly appeared from the temporary hood, carrying a basin and followed by a weary, blood-spattered surgeon's assistant. She was pale, but in these surroundings her pallor suited her: it gave her a quite remarkable distinction.

'Diana,' said Captain Aubrey, 'allow me to name Admiral Colpoys: my cousin Mrs Villiers. Mrs Villiers was in Boston, sir, and she escaped with Maturin and me.'

'Your most humble, devoted, ma'am,' said the Admiral, bowing. 'How I envy you, having been in such a brilliant action.'

Diana put down her basin, curtsied, and replied, 'Oh, sir, I was kept below stairs all the time. But how I wish,' she said with a fine flash of her eye, 'how I wish I had been a man, to board with the rest of them.'

'I am sure you would have struck them dead, ma'am,' said the Admiral. 'But now you are here, you must take up your quarters with us. Lady Harriet will be delighted. Here is my barge, at your pleasure, if you choose to go ashore this minute.'

'You are very good, Admiral,' said Diana, 'and I should be most happy to wait on Lady Harriet, but what I am about will keep me some hours yet.'

'I honour you for it, ma'am,' said the Admiral, for a glance at the basin showed the nature of her occupation. 'But the moment you are ready, you must come up to the house. Aubrey, the moment Mrs Villiers is ready, you are to bring her up to the house.' His beaming smile faded as a high quavering shriek, almost inhuman in its agony, came up from the sickbay, piercing the noise of cheering like a knife: but he had seen a great deal of action — he knew the price there was to pay — and with little less good humour he added, 'That is an order, Aubrey, d'ye hear me?' Then, turning to the young lieutenant he said, 'Now Mr Wallis, let us go to our business.'

The hours had passed: Captain Broke had been carried to the Commissioner's house and his wounded shipmates to the hospital, where those who were not out of their minds with pain lay peacefully enough by the wounded Chesapeakes, sometimes exchanging quids of tobacco and smuggled rum; the American prisoners of war had been taken out of their ship, the few surviving officers paroled and the men sent to the barracks; and the most wretchedly miserable of all, the British deserters captured in the *Chesapeake*, had been taken to prison, with no likelihood of leaving it except for a journey to the gallows. At present the cruellest face of war was no longer to be seen: joy and lively anticipation began to overcome thoughtfulness and grief in the frigate as neighbouring captains sent over parties of volunteers, men enough to provide a harbour-watch so that the Shannons might have a run ashore; and the newcomers' gaiety, combining with the continuing shouts and yells from the wharves, made the younger liberty-men laugh aloud as they stood, treading on one another's toes on the gangway, while their companions, moving carefully not to get tar on their gleaming ducks, hoisted out the boats.

'Cousin Diana,' said Jack Aubrey, 'should you like to go ashore? I will hail *Tenedos* for her captain's gig.'

'Thank you, Jack,' said she, 'but I had rather wait for Stephen. He will not be long.' She was sitting on a small green brass-studded trunk, the only thing she had brought with her in their hurried flight from Boston, and she was gazing out at Halifax over a shattered nine-pounder gun. Jack stood by her and gazed too, one foot on the carriage; but he gazed with no more than the shallowest surface of his attention, while the rest of his mind floated free. His whole being was suffused with deep happiness, for although this victory was none of his, he was a sea-officer through and through, wholly identified with the Royal Navy from his childhood, and the successive defeats of the last year had weighed upon him so that he had been hardly able to bear it. Now the burden was gone: the two ships had met in equal fight; the Royal Navy had won; the universe was restored to its true foundations; the stars had resumed their natural march; and as soon as he reached England there was every likelihood that he should have a command, the *Acasta* of forty guns, that would help to make their march more natural still. Then again, as soon as he was ashore he would run to the post for his letters: he had not heard from Sophie, his wife and Diana's first cousin, all the time he had been a prisoner of war in Boston, and he longed to hear from her, longed to hear how the children did, longed to hear of his horses, the garden, the house . . . yet beneath all this there was a point, and more than a point, of anxiety. Although he was an unusually rich commander, an officer who had made more prize-money than most captains of his seniority — more indeed than many admirals — he had left his affairs in a highly complicated state, and their unravelling depended upon the honesty of a man whom neither Sophie nor his friend Maturin trusted at all. This man, a Mr Kimber, had promised Jack that the disused lead-mines on his land could be made to produce not only more lead but also a surprising amount of silver by a process known to Mr Kimber alone, thereby yielding a very handsome return indeed upon the initial outlay; yet the last letters that Captain Aubrey had ever received from his wife, far away in the East Indies, before he was captured by the Americans on his return voyage to England, had spoken not of yield, not of profit, but of obscure unauthorized doings on the part of Kimber, of very heavy new investments in roads, mining-equipment, a steam-engine, deep-sunk shafts . . . He longed to have this clarified; and he was tolerably confident that it would be clarified, for whereas Sophie and Stephen Maturin understood nothing of business, Jack had based his opinion upon solid facts and figures, not mere intuition: in any case, he had a far greater knowledge of the world than either of them. But more than that he longed to hear of his children, his twin daughters and his little son: George would be talking by now, and the want of news had been one of the hardest things to bear during his captivity; for not a single letter had come through. And most of all he wanted to see Sophie's hand and to hear her voice at one remove: her last letters, dated before the American war, had reached him in Java and he had read them until they cracked at the folds, had read them again and again until they, with almost all his other possessions, had been lost at sea. Since then, no word. From a hundred and ten degrees of east longitude to sixty degrees west, almost half the world, and never a word. It was the sailor's lot, he knew, with the packets and all other forms of transport so uncertain, but even so he had felt ill-used at times.

Ill-used by fate in general rather than by Sophie. Their marriage, firmly rooted in very deep affection and mutual respect, was far better than most; and although one of its aspects was not altogether satisfactory for a man of Jack Aubrey's strong animal spirits, and although it might be said that Sophie was somewhat possessive, somewhat given to jealousy, she was nevertheless an integral part of his being. She was no more faultless than he was himself, and indeed there were moments when he found his own faults easier to excuse than hers; but all this was quite forgotten as his inner eye contemplated the parcel of letters that he would find waiting for him over the smooth water there in Halifax.

'Tell me, Jack,' said Diana, 'did Sophie have a hard time of it, with her last baby?'

'Hey?' cried Jack, brought back from a great way off. 'A hard time of it with George? I hope not, by — I hope not, indeed. She did not mention it at all. I was in Mauritius at the time. But I believe it can be very bad.'

'So they tell me,' said Diana: and after a pause, 'Here is Stephen.'

A few minutes later the boat was alongside, and they made their farewells to the *Shannon* rather than her people, for they would all meet again on shore in the course of the festivities that would follow the victory — the Admiral had already spoken of a ball. Diana refused Wallis's offer of a bosun's chair and ran down after Stephen as lithe and nimble as a boy, while the boat's crew stared woodenly out into the offing, lest they should see her legs; but she did call out to beg that those on deck might take great care of her trunk. 'It is my all, you know, my little all,' she said, smiling up into Mr Wallis's enchanted face.

They made a curious group there in the stern-sheets as the boat pulled for the shore, a group bound together by strong, intricate relationships; for not only had the two men competed for her liking in the past so that it had very nearly broken their friendship, but Diana had been the great love of Stephen's life, his prime illusion. She had thrown him over in India in favour of an American, a very wealthy man called Johnson, whose company she found increasingly unpleasant on their arrival in the States and, after the declaration of war, quite intolerable. It was when Maturin reached Boston as a prisoner of war that they came together again and that he found that although he still admired her spirit and beauty, it was as though his heart were numb. What changes in her or in himself had brought this about he could not tell for sure; but he did know that unless his heart could feel again the mainspring of his life was gone. However, they had escaped together, reaching the *Shannon* in a boat; and they were engaged to be married, an engagement that Stephen felt to be her due, if only as a means of recovering her nationality, and one that to his astonishment she seemed to welcome, although up until this time he had thought her the most intuitively perceptive woman of his acquaintance. Indeed, but for the battle they would already have been man and wife by the law of England if not by that of the Catholic church (for Maturin was a Papist), since Philip Broke had been about to exercise his powers as a captain and marry them at sea, and Diana would have been a British subject once more, instead of a paper American.

Yet in spite of these currents of feeling beneath the surface they talked very cheerfully and calmly all the way to the landing-place and up to the Admiral's house, where they parted like old friends, Jack to report to the Commissioner and then to see about his post and their lodgings, and Stephen to an unnamed destination with a sailcloth parcel under his arm, his only baggage, while Diana remained with the short-legged, good-natured Lady Harriet Colpoys.

Stephen did not name his destination, but if they had reflected neither of his companions would have had much difficulty in guessing it. In the course of their long service together it had necessarily come to Captain Aubrey's knowledge that although Dr Maturin was certainly an eminent medical man who chose to sail as a ship's surgeon for the opportunities of making discoveries in natural philosophy (his chief passion, second only to the overthrow of Buonaparte), he was also one of the Admiralty's most prized intelligence agents; while immediately before their escape Diana had seen him remove the papers that his parcel contained from the rooms that she and Mr Johnson occupied in Boston, explaining his action by the statement that they would interest an intelligence officer he happened to know in Halifax. Stephen was perfectly aware of this, but the long-established habit, the second nature of extreme discretion to which he owed his continuing existence made him non-committal in all circumstances; it also caused him to take a roundabout way to the office of his correspondent, looking in shop windows and taking full advantage of those that showed the street behind him. It was an automatic precaution, but here it was an unusually necessary one, for as he knew better than any man in Halifax there were several American agents in the town; and Johnson's fury at being robbed of both his mistress and his papers would urge him to make extraordinary efforts in the way of revenge.

However, he reached the office unfollowed, with an easy mind, and sent in his name. Major Beck, the Marine in charge of intelligence on the North American station, received him at once. They had not met before and Beck looked at him with lively curiosity: Dr Maturin had a great reputation in the department as one of the few wholly voluntary agents who were also wholly effective, wholly professional; and although Maturin's mixed Irish-Catalan parentage meant that he was primarily an expert on Catalan affairs, Beck knew that the Doctor had recently accomplished the feat of decimating the ranks of the French service by means of false, compromising information conveyed to Paris in all good faith by the Americans. Seeing that this concerned his own field, Beck was officially acquainted with it; but he had also heard vaguer, less official accounts of other equally remarkable coups in Spain and France, and he found that he was most illogically disappointed by the meagre, shabby, undistinguished man who sat on the other side of the desk, slowly undoing a sailcloth parcel. Against all reason Beck had expected a more heroic figure: certainly not one who wore blue spectacles against the sun.

Stephen's reflexions were equally unflattering. He observed that Beck was an obscurely misshapen fellow with watery goggling eyes, spare sandy hair, no chin, a prominent Adam's apple, and, in spite of an intelligent forehead, the settled look of a man who fitted nowhere. 'Are we all, always, so distorted?' he wondered, thinking of some of his other colleagues.

They talked for a while about the victory, Beck speaking with an enthusiasm that brought colour to his unhealthy thin-skinned yellow face and Stephen steadily disclaiming any particular knowledge of the action: he had been below from the first gun to the last: he knew nothing of the evolutions, nor was he able to speak to the number of British deserters serving in the American ship or of the means employed to seduce them. Beck seemed disappointed.

'I received your warning about the Frenchmen in Boston,' said Stephen, struggling with a knot, 'and I thank you for it. I was able to meet them with a mind prepared.'

'I trust there was no unpleasantness, sir? Durand is said to be a most unscrupulous, determined officer.'

'Pontet-Canet was worse: a busy, troublesome fellow that gave me real uneasiness for a while. But, however, I clapped a stopper over his capers.' Dr Maturin was proud of his nautical expressions: sometimes he got them right, but right or wrong he always brought them out with a slight emphasis of satisfaction, much as others might utter a particularly apt Greek or Latin quotation. 'And brought him up with a round stern,' he added. 'Would you have a knife, at all? This string is really not worth the saving.'

'How did you do that, sir?' asked Beck, passing a pair of scissors.

'I cut his throat,' said Maturin, shearing through the string. Major Beck was used to bloodshed in open and in clandestine war, but his visitor's everyday, unemphatic tone struck a chill to his heart, the more so as Maturin happened to take off his spectacles at this moment, glancing at Beck with his expressionless pale eyes, the only remarkable thing about him.

'Now, sir,' said Stephen, the documents unwrapped at last, 'you are no doubt acquainted with Mr Harry Johnson's role in American intelligence?'

'Oh yes, indeed.' Beck could not be unaware of his chief opponent's activities in Canada: from the first days of his appointment he had been struggling against Johnson's well-organized, well-supplied network of agents.

'Very well. These are papers that I took from his desk and strong-box in Boston. The Frenchmen were consulting them when I put an end to their machinations.' He laid them one by one on the major's desk: a list of American agents in Canada and the West Indies, with comments; ciphers to be used on various occasions; letters to the Secretary of State containing a detailed account of the past and present relationships between the French and American intelligence services; remarks on his French colleagues' characters, abilities, and intentions; projects for future operations; a full appreciation of the British position on the Great Lakes . . .

By the time the last document took its place on the desk Dr Maturin had reached and surpassed the heroic stature expected of him. Major Beck gazed over the heap of papers with deep respect, with something not far removed from awe. 'It is the completest thing,' he said, 'the completest thing that ever I heard tell of. A clean sweep, by God! This first list alone will keep a firing-squad busy for weeks. I must digest the whole mass. These will be my bedside companions for many a night.'

'Not these documents themselves, sir, if you will allow me. Sir Joseph and his cryptographers must have them —' the Major bowed at Sir Joseph's name, '— and I propose carrying the greater part to London by the first ship that offers. Copies, by all means, although that raises certain problems too, as you know very well. However, before we discuss the copying or indeed anything else, I have an observation to make: an observation and a request. Have you heard of Mrs Villiers?'

'Diana Villiers, Johnson's mistress, a renegade Englishwoman?'

'No, sir,' said Stephen, with a cold, unwinking look. 'No, sir. Mrs Villiers was not Johnson's mistress: she merely accepted his protection in a foreign land. Nor is she in any conceivable way a renegade. Not only did they disagree most bitterly when he attempted to enlist her in the war against her own country, but it was owing to her that I came into possession of these documents. I should be sorry to hear her name used lightly.'

'Yet, sir,' said Beck after a moment's hesitation, 'and I speak under correction, without intending the least disrespect to the lady, it appears that she took out papers of naturalization in the States.'

'That was a thoughtless act, one that she regarded as a trifling formality without the least real effect upon her natural allegiance. It was very strongly represented to her, that the process would facilitate Mr

Johnson's divorce.' Stephen observed a certain knowingness or fellow-feeling or even connivance in the Major's eye; he frowned, and went on in a colder tone, 'But since she is technically an enemy alien, sir, I wish to observe — I wish to state it as my considered opinion, that the usual certificate should be made out in her favour, as to one of our people; although at the same time I may point out that she has little or no notion of my connexion with the department. I have brought her with me, and apart from all other considerations it would not be fitting that she should be molested, or made uneasy in any way.'

'Directly, sir,' said Major Beck, ringing a bell. 'I am glad you told me,' he said, 'Archbold would certainly have laid her by the heels before nightfall. We have had any number of females — however, the lady in question belongs to quite another category.' His assistant came in, a man quite as ugly as Major Beck, with rather more of that indefinable appearance of hidden deformity, but with much less of his apparent intelligence. 'Mr Archbold,' said the Major, 'an X certificate in the name of Mrs Villiers, if you please.' The paper came, Beck completed it with an official wafer and his signature and passed it over, saying, 'But you will allow me to observe, sir, that this is valid only for my own region. If the lady were to return to England, there might be very considerable difficulties.'

Stephen could have retorted that he intended to do away with these difficulties by marrying Diana and making her a British subject again; but he preferred keeping his own counsel. In any case, he was very, very tired, both from the extraordinary exertions at the time of his escape and from his almost continual surgical activity aboard both ships ever since the battle. He made no reply, therefore, and after a short silence Beck said, 'I believe, sir, you mentioned a request?'

'I did. It is that you will authorize the paymaster to accept a draft on my London banking-house. I have an immediate and pressing need for money.'

'Oh, as for money, Dr Maturin,' cried Major Beck, 'I beg you will not trouble with the paymaster and his seven and a half per cent and all the paper-work. I have funds here at my disposal that can deal with any difficulty of that kind at once. They are intended to procure information, and for a single one of these documents, I should be fully justified in . . .'

'You are very good, sir,' said Stephen, 'but I must tell you that from the very beginning of my connexion with the department I have never accepted a Brummagem ha'penny for anything that I was able to do, or to produce. No. A note to the paymaster will answer perfectly, if you will be so kind. And perhaps you would let me have a couple of discreet able-bodied men: the frontier is no great way off, and until you have dealt with the agents named in Mr Johnson's list, I should not choose to wander about Halifax alone.'

Preceded by one discreet man, six foot tall, followed by another, and accompanied by a third, Stephen walked to the paymaster's office, transacted his business, came out with a comfortable bulge in his pocket, and stood for a while in thought. Then, followed by his companion, he took a few irresolute steps down the street before stopping at a corner. 'I am at a stand,' he said.

'Sir?' said his guardian.

'I am at a stand. I do not know where I lodge.'

The street was almost empty, since all those who could get away were down at the harbour, staring at the *Shannon* and the *Chesapeake*: in this virtual desert the two other men did their best to be inconspicuous, loitering in negligent attitudes, quite detached; but they soon caught their colleague's nod, and joined him on the corner. 'The gentleman is at a stand,' he said. 'He does not know where he is staying.'

They all looked at Stephen. 'Has he forgot the name of his hotel?' suggested one.

'Have you forgot the name of your hotel, sir?' asked the first man, bending down to speak in Stephen's ear. Stephen ran his hand along his bristly jaw, deep in thought, trying to overcome his weariness of mind.

'He is probably staying at Bailey's,' said another. 'That is where most of the physical gentlemen put up.'

'Is it Bailey's, sir?' asked the first, bending again.

'White's? Brown's? The Goat and Compasses?' said the others, addressing not Dr Maturin but their companion.

'I have it,' cried Stephen. 'I have the solution. Pray conduct me to the place where the officers receive their letters.'

'We must hurry, then,' said the first man. 'We must even run, sir. They will be closed, else.' And some minutes, some few hundred yards later he said, panting, 'There. I was afraid of it. The blinds are drawn.'

The blinds were drawn, but the door was on the jar; and even if it had been tightly shut Captain Aubrey's strong sea-going voice would still have spread far out into the street. 'What the devil do you mean with your "after hours", you idle young hound?' he was asking. 'As God's my life . . .'

When Stephen opened the door the sound increased, and he perceived that Jack had the young man by the frill of his shirt, that he was shaking him to and fro and calling him 'an infernal b—.'

The shirt frill came adrift and Jack turned to Stephen. 'He says it is after hours,' he cried.

'It is not only that, sir,' said the clerk to Stephen, as to a saviour, 'but Mr Gittings has the keys. There ain't nothing in the waiting rack and I can't open the strong-box without I have the keys, it stands to reason.' He wiped his tears on his sleeve and added, 'And there's nothing in it for Captain Aubrey neither, I could pledge my sacred word: though always willing to oblige any gentleman that treats us civil.'

Stephen contemplated the strong-box. It was an old-fashioned affair with a common tumbler lock and it would probably not resist his solicitations more than a few minutes; but this was neither the time nor the place to display his talents. He said, 'I am happy to find you, Captain Aubrey. The name of our inn, or hotel, has escaped my mind, and I am mortally fatigued. I would give all I possess to go to bed.'

'You certainly look uncommonly fagged,' said Jack, dropping the shirt-frill. 'Quite done up. We are at the Goat, and I will take you there directly. Harkee, sir,' to the clerk, in a last burst of disappointed fury, 'I shall be here first thing tomorrow, d'ye hear me, there?'

In the street Stephen thanked his escort, sending him back with his best compliments to Major Beck, and he and Jack walked on alone.

'A miserable goddam afternoon,' said Jack. 'Disappointments at every turn — a heroes' welcome, truly. The town is crammed with soldiers, and I could only get one room between us at the Goat.'

'That is bad,' said Stephen, who had often shared a cabin with Captain Aubrey, perhaps the most resounding snorer in the service.

'Then when I went up the hill to report, the Commissioner was not in the way. There were a good many men waiting for him: we gossiped for a while and I learnt a damned unpleasant thing or two. Harte is back on the Board of Admiralty, and that fellow Wray is made acting second secretary.'

'Mother of God,' said Stephen to himself, and well he might: Jack, as a lively bachelor in Minorca, had cuckolded Mr Harte repeatedly, and cuckolds were likely to use their horns even long after their receipt; while Jack had also publicly, justly, accused Mr Wray, a person even then high in Government employ, of cheating at cards. It was an accusation that Wray had not seen fit to resent in the usual manner at the time, but it was not likely that he would stomach it for ever.

'I waited as long as I could, but then when I reached the office at a brisk run — and I can tell you, Stephen, that brisk running, at my age, ain't what it used to be — all I found was another disappointment. A miserable goddam afternoon.

'Ooh-hoo, husband,' said a pretty whore in the twilight. 'Come with me and I will give you a kiss.'

Jack smiled, shook his head, and walked

on. 'Did you notice she called me husband?' he said after a few paces. 'They often do. I suppose marriage is the natural state, so that makes it seem less — less wrong.'

The word marriage reminded Stephen that he had meant to take Beck's certificate, that necessary document, to a priest and arrange for his wedding with Diana; but he could at present scarcely drag himself along — all the weariness of the last few days was rising in him like an overwhelming fog, now that the interminable crisis was past. All that survived was the spirit of contradiction. He said, 'Not at all. On the contrary, as one of your great men of the past age observed, it is so far from natural for a man and woman to live in a state of marriage, that we find all the motives which they have for remaining in that connexion, and the restraints which civilized society imposes to prevent separation, are hardly sufficient to keep them together.'

'Hark,' said Jack, pausing in his stride. Down by the harbour a band had begun *Heart of Oak*, and a great concourse of people were either chanting the words or cheering. Smoke and the rosy glow of torches could be seen above the roofs, and suddenly the flames themselves came into sight, crossing the far end of their street — an unofficial procession of seamen and civilians, leaping and capering as they passed the narrow gap, and on every hand more people were hurrying down to join it, among them the pretty whore.

Good humour came flooding back into Aubrey's face. 'That's more like it,' he said. 'That's more like a heroes' welcome. Lord, Stephen, I am so happy, these little vexations apart. And tomorrow, when I have Sophie's letters, I shall be happier still. Listen. There is another band striking up.'

'All I ask,' said Stephen, 'is that they should welcome their heroes at a decent distance from the Goat — that they should not strike up within a furlong of the inn. Though the Dear knows, I believe I should sleep through ten bands playing in the corridor.'

They may well have played there, or at least outside his window, for the Shannons celebrated their victory as whole-heartedly as they had won it, and Halifax rocked with the sound of their merriment until dawn and beyond; but Dr Maturin lay like a log until a sunbeam, darting through his bed-curtains, teased him into wakefulness at last. His body was beautifully limp, perfectly comfortable; his mind was rested, calm, relaxed; he would have moved out of the beam and lain there browsing among his thoughts, perhaps dropping off again, if he had not heard a somewhat artificial cough, the cough of one who does not wish to wake his companion but rather to advertise his presence if waking has already taken place.

He pushed the curtains aside and met Jack's eye, his surprisingly sombre eye. Jack was standing by the window, looking unnaturally tall, even taller than usual, and Stephen observed that this was because he had taken off his sling and the arm hanging down by his side changed his proportions. He smiled on seeing Stephen, wished him a good morning, or rather afternoon, and said, 'I have some letters for you.'

Stephen considered for a moment. At least some part of Jack's sad appearance arose from the fact that he was wearing a broad black band of crape on his arm; but there was more to it than that. 'What's o'clock?' he asked.

'Just turned of noon, and I must be away,' said Jack, giving him a small bundle of letters.

'You have been up a great while, I make

no doubt,' said Stephen. He looked at the covers without much interest.

'Yes. I was at that God-damned office the moment they opened their doors. Their chief was away, but even so I made them rummage the place from top to bottom — such disorder you would not credit — but never a word for me.'

'Several packets have been taken by the Americans, or lost at sea, brother.'

'I know, I know,' said Jack. 'But even so . . . however, whining will do no good. Then I reported to the Commissioner. He was very civil, very welcoming, and he gave me good news of Broke — had been sitting up for an hour, talking quite rationally, and may be able to write his own dispatch. And he asked me to dinner after the funeral: but I noticed he felt uneasy, and after a good deal of backing and filling out it came. I am not to have *Acasta*, but am to go home. I was away too long, and she has been given to Robert Kerr.'

The *Acasta* was a particularly fine forty-gun frigate, one of the few that could be considered a match for the heavy Americans, and Stephen knew how Jack had looked forward to commanding her in these waters. He looked for some words that might soften the blow, but finding none he said, 'I am grieved for you, Jack. But listen, if you feel the least pain or throbbing in that arm, you are to put it up — you are to put it in your bosom.' He stretched, gaped, took off his nightcap, and said, 'You spoke of a funeral?'

'Yes, of course. You are not awake, Stephen. We bury poor Lawrence of the *Chesapeake*.'

'Should I come too? I can be ready in a moment. I should be very willing to show the respect I feel, if it is usual.'

'No, the custom is only men of the same rank, apart from those detailed to attend and his own officers. Stephen, I must go. Tell me, did you get any money? I shall not have time between the funeral and the dinner, and I should like to do the proper thing as soon as possible.'

'It is in my coat-pocket, hanging behind the spence.'

Jack plucked out the roll of bank-notes, peeled off what he needed, called out 'Thankee, Stephen,' buckled on his sword and ran down the stairs.

All the post-captains in Halifax were gathering on the gun-wharf: he knew most of them, but he only had time to greet one or two before the clock struck; exact to the minute the coffin came ashore with its escort of Marines, and the cortège formed behind it, the few American officers who could walk, the soldiers, the captains two by two, the generals and the Admiral.

They marched to the sound of a muffled drum, and the cheerful streets fell silent as they came. Jack had taken part in many processions of this kind, some of them very poignant indeed — shipmates, close friends, a cousin, his own officers or midshipmen — but he had never regretted an enemy commander as he regretted Lawrence, a man quite after his own heart, who had brought his ship into action and had fought her in the handsomest manner. The steady beat, the marching steps in time, caused his bitter disappointments of this morning to fade from his mind; and the exactly-ordered ceremony, the chaplain's ritual words, and the rattle of earth on the coffin, made him very grave indeed. The firing party's volley, the last military honours, jerked him from his thoughts, but not from his gravity. Although death was so much part of his calling, he could not get rid of the image of Captain Lawrence standing there on his quarterdeck just before the first devastating broadsides; and he found the reviving cheerfulness among his companions particularly jarring. It was not that their respect for the dead man was feigned, nor that their formal bearing until the time the gathering broke up was hypocritical, but their respect was for an unknown, though certainly brave and able commander — respect for the abstract enemy, for officerlike conduct.

'You knew him, I believe?' said his neighbour, Hyde Parker of the *Tenedos*.

'Yes,' said Jack. 'He came to see me in Boston. He had captured one of my officers when he took the *Peacock*, and he was very kind to him. He commanded their *Hornet*, you know: a fine, gallant fellow. As gallant as you could wish.'

'Ay,' said Hyde Parker, 'that's the devil of it. But you can't make an omelette without breaking eggs, you know; you can't have a victory that counts without a butcher's bill. And this is a noble victory, by God! I doubt I have ever been so happy as when I saw *Shannon* bringing in her prize; certainly I have never cheered so loud or long in all my days. I am as hoarse as a corn-crake still.'

The general happiness that filled the naval base was even more evident at the Commissioner's splendid dinner; it flowed into Jack once again as he sat there after the cloth was drawn, going over every move in that memorable action, showing his enraptured fellow-sailors each sail set, each piece of rigging carried away, each movement of the two frigates, with the help of a pair of models brought up from the dockyard.

It was equally apparent at the port-admiral's, with a gay and sprightly Colpoys who sang as he went up the stairs, and a cheerful, talkative mistress of the house, intensely pleased with life in spite of the anxieties of the great ball she was to give at such short notice. The universal lightness of heart had infected Diana too — few women loved a ball more than she — and she greeted Stephen most affectionately, kissing him on both cheeks. 'I am so glad you are come,' she said. 'Now I can give you your card instead of sending it. I have been helping Lady Harriet write them since breakfast time. Half the Navy list, and countless soldiers.'

'My card?' said Stephen, holding it at a distance, with a suspicious look.

'Your card for the ball, my dear. The ball, you know: a vast great party where people dance. You can dance, Stephen, can you not?'

'After my own fashion. The last time I danced was at Melbury Lodge, during the peace. You were good enough to stand up with me, and we walked through a minuet without disgrace. I hope you will be so kind again.'

'Alas, Stephen, I cannot come. I have nothing to wear. But I shall watch from the gallery; you shall bring me an ice from time to time, and we can abuse the dancers.'

'Did you bring nothing in your little trunk?'

'Oh, there was no time to choose, and I did not have my wits about me. Apart from jewels, I just threw in some shifts and stockings — whatever came to hand. And anyhow, I could not have told that I should be invited to a ball.'

'There are mantua-makers in Halifax, Villiers.'

'Halifax mantua-makers,' said Diana, laughing heartily — the first time he had heard her laugh since they met in America: It moved his heart strangely. 'No. In this desert there would be only one hope. Lady Harriet has a very clever Frenchwoman who smuggles things from Paris: she brought a whole mass this morning, and among them there was a blue lutestring we both admired. Lady Harriet could not wear it, of course; it has sleeves to here and precious little back or front and as she said herself, she would look like a monument. She chose a wicked merde d'oie muslin, but at least it covers her entirely, and they are letting it out for her at this minute. I should have bought the blue, but Madame Chose asks the earth, and I must make the five cents I brought with me last and last. Do you know, my dear, I positively darned a pair of stockings last night. If this were London or Paris or even Philadelphia I should sell a couple of pearls: the rope is unstrung. But there is nothing but pinchbeck and filigree in this desert. The one thing I really do understand is jewels, and it would be desperate nonsense to sell any of them in Halifax. The Nawab's pearls in Halifax! Can you conceive such a thing?'

In any other woman her words would have been a flat demand, and a tolerably coarse one at that; with Diana this was not the case. She had, and as long as Stephen had known her she always had had, a perfectly direct way of talking to him, with no reserve, nothing devious about it, as though they were people of the same kind or even in a way confederates; and she was genuinely surprised when he said, 'We are in funds. I drew upon London, and you must certainly have your lutestring gown. Let us send for it at once.'

It came; it was approved; and Madame Chose retired with her swingeing price. Diana held the dress in front of her, peering intently into the looking-glass over the fire. She was not in looks, but the frank delight in a new dress, almost entirely unaffected by years of an unusually wealthy life, gave her a fine animation. Her eyes narrowed, and she frowned. 'The top is sadly uninspired,' she said, nodding at the mirror. 'It was meant to be set off with something: pearls, I dare say. I shall wear my diamonds.'

Stephen looked down. The diamonds, a rivière of diamonds with an astonishing pale-blue pendant stone in the middle, had been given to Diana by Johnson in their early days: by some mental process of her own she had entirely dissociated them from their source; Stephen had not. His pain was not the piercing thrust of jealousy but rather a certain grief at hearing her say something crass. He had always taken it for granted that whatever Diana might actually do, her tact was infallible and that she could not, without intending it, say anything that would give offence. Perhaps he had been mistaken: or perhaps this long stay in America, living only among the loose, expensive set of Johnson's friends, together with her distress, had coarsened her for the time, just as it had given her a hint of a colonial accent and a taste for bourbon and tobacco . . . a refuge in coarseness, as it were. But then again, he reflected, Johnson had certainly taken the diamonds back, and Diana, recovering them and escaping with them at great risk, might well feel that she had thereby established an independent title to the jewels, much as one pirate overcoming another pirate would appropriate his goods with a tranquil mind, whatever their provenance. He looked up, and said, 'Might they not look a little excessive in what is, after all, a provincial gathering?'

'Not at all, Maturin,' said she. 'There are several women of fashion here, apart from the rest. Many of the soldiers' wives have followed them — I saw at least half a dozen names I knew when I was addressing the cards — and there are some among the sailors: Mrs Wodehouse, for example, and Charlotte Leveson-Gower, and Lady Harriet herself. She may be no Aphrodite, but she has emeralds as big as soup-plates and she is determined to wear 'em all, together with everything else her bosom can contain; which is not inconsiderable.'

The first stab past, Stephen did not care one way or another: in any case, Diana no doubt understood these things better than he did; she had kept very good or at least very fashionable company in London and India. He felt in his pocket and brought out some papers: the first was not the one he was looking for, but he smiled when he saw it and instead of putting it back he said 'This came for me this morning, and whimsically enough I had been dreaming of Paris not half an hour before.' He passed the letter over.

'They ask you to address the *Institut de France* — Lord, Stephen, I had no idea you were such a great man. They want you to tell them about the extinct avifauna of Rodriguez. What is an avifauna?'

'Birds.'

'What a pity you cannot go. You would have enjoyed it so. I suppose they took you for a neutral, or an American.'

'Yet perhaps I shall go too. As you see, the date is well ahead, and if we can take a reasonably expeditious vessel, I believe I shall go. This is their second invitation, and the last time I regretted not being there extremely. It is perhaps the most flattering honour I have received, and I should meet some of the most interesting men in Europe. The Cuviers are sure to be there, and I have some remarks on the antarctic cetaceans that will amaze Frédéric.'

'But how can you possibly go? How can you possibly go to Paris in the middle of a war?'

'Oh, as for that, with the proper consent and safe-conducts, there is no difficulty. Natural philosophy does not regard this war, or any other, with very close attention, and interchange is quite usual. Humphry Davy went and addressed them on his chloride of nitrogen, for example; and he was much caressed. But that is not what I meant to talk about.' He took up the second cover and laid it on the table before her, saying with some embarrassment, 'This is for pins.'

'Pins, Stephen?' cried she, astonished.

'I have always understood that women required a reasonable sum for pins.'

'Stephen,' — laughing with pleasure — 'you are blushing. Upon my word and honour, you are absolutely blushing: I never thought to see you blush. No. It is infinitely kind of you, but you have been far too kind already. I have a hundred and twenty-five dollars, plenty for pins. Keep it, Stephen dear, and I promise I will tell you when I am quite penniless.'

'Well,' said Stephen, taking up his third paper. 'Now here is a certificate for you, stating that although you are an enemy alien you may be admitted to Canadian soil and that you may remain upon it while of good behaviour.'

'Oh, I shall behave quite beautifully,' she said, laughing again. 'But what nonsense it is, Stephen: I am on Canadian soil already. I have always thought papers and legal formalities great nonsense, but I have never seen such a simple one as this. *During His Majesty's pleasure,*' she read, 'and his poor dear old Majesty has not the least notion I am here. Oh, what stuff!'

'No, but his servants have, I tell you in all sad sober earnest, Villiers, this is an important document. Without it you would have been taken away, Admiral or no Admiral. It is known that in law you are an American citizen, and as such you would ordinarily be placed under restraint: perhaps sent back again.'

'Who cares for the law and quibbles of that kind? Anyone can tell that I am perfectly English and always have been and always shall be. But tell me, how did you get it?'

'Sure, I went to the proper quarters, to

the officer that deals with things of this kind.'

'It was so kind of you to think of it,' she said: then she cried, 'Oh, Stephen, I had quite forgot,' — and he could have sworn the thought passed from his head to hers — 'were they pleased with the papers you brought from Boston? I remember you told me they were for an army intelligence officer here. How I hope they were useful to him.'

'Alas, it appears that they were more in the political than the military line. They are not without a certain value, I am told, but it seems that I could have chosen much better. I should not make much of an intelligence-agent, I am afraid.'

'No,' said Diana, laughing. 'I cannot imagine anyone less suited for it. Not that you are not intelligent, dear Maturin,' she added with a kind look. 'In your way you are one of the most intelligent men I know, but you would be far happier among your birds. To think of you as a spy — oh, Lord!' Amusement turned her a fine rosy pink. He had rarely seen Diana so gay.

'Will you give me the certificate, now?' he said. 'I must show it to the priest. He cannot marry us without it. Would Friday suit you, Friday morning, quite early in the day? You would not wish much ceremony, as I suppose; but Jack can give you away, and then you will be a British subject once more.'

All the gaiety was gone from her face, completely gone, leaving it pale: an ill-looking, somewhat earthy pallor. She started up, walked to and fro, and then stood by the long window looking out into the garden, twisting the paper as she stood.

'But now I have the certificate, what is the hurry?' she said. 'What does it matter, all these formalities? Do not think I don't want to marry you . . . it is only that . . . Stephen, make me one of your little paper cigars, will you?'

He took out a cigar, cut it in two, and made two small rolls in a fine leaf from his pocket-book, one for her and one for himself. He held up an ember for her to light it, but she said, 'No. I cannot smoke here. Lady Harriet might come in. I do not want her to think — to know — that she is harbouring a dissolute dram-drinking tobacco-smoking creature. Light yours and come into the garden: I will smoke it there. You know, Stephen,' she said, opening the french window, 'ever since you told me about bourbon and complexion, I have not drunk a drop of anything but wine, and precious little of that; but by God I could do with a drink now.'

In the secluded shrubbery they paced side by side, and a thin cloud of smoke followed them. She said, 'With all this hurry — the business of the ball — gossiping with Lady Harriet — worrying about what to wear — I was quite out of myself. I forgot where I was. Maturin, do not be disappointed when I say I should like to wait.' A pause. 'You are the only man I have known who never asks questions, who is never impertinent even when he has the right to be.' She was looking at the ground, her head drooping; and although he had known her many years, in many states of temper and mind, he had never seen her in such distress or confusion. She was standing with the sun full on her and his penetrating, objective eye examined her downcast face; but before he had time to say 'Not at all' or 'As you please, entirely' a footman came stumping into sight at the end of the gravel walk and called out in a strong voice, 'The Honourable Mrs Wodehouse and Miss Smith to see you, ma'am.'

Diana threw Stephen a quick, apologetic glance and ran into the house. She might be in a strange hurry of spirits, but she moved with the perfect, unconscious grace that had always touched him, and he felt a wave of tenderness, allied to his former passionate love; perhaps its ghost.

The footman was still standing there, his wooden leg firmly planted in the gravel, waiting for Stephen: that is to say, a person dressed as a footman in the Admiral's hideous orange and purple livery was waiting there; but his independent attitude, his long pigtail, his pleasant battered old face made his true nature and origin obvious at a cable's length.

'I hope I see you well, sir?' he said, touching a crooked forefinger to his eyebrow.

'Very well, I thank you,' said Stephen, looking at him attentively. The last time he had seen that face it had been bloodless, glistening with sweat, tight-clenched not to cry out beneath his knife, as the *Surprise* limped westwards to Fort William, cruelly mauled by a French seventy-four. 'But you were not an amputation,' he said.

'No, sir: Bullock, forecastle-man, starboard watch, in the old *Surprise*.'

'Of course,' said Stephen, shaking him by the hand. 'What I mean is, I saved that leg. I did not cut it off.'

'Nor you did, sir,' said Bullock, 'but

when I was in *Benbow* off the Cays, I copped it something cruel with a bar-shot; and our surgeon not being Dr Maturin, off it came, without so much as by your leave.'

'I am sure it was necessary,' said Stephen.

The remark, the support of his colleague, at least was necessary: but it seemed to carry no conviction at all, perhaps because the surgeon of the *Benbow* was nearly always drunk, and when sober, notoriously unskilful. The footman looked affectionately at Dr Maturin and said, 'And I hope Captain Aubrey is well, sir? I heard he come ashore off of *Shannon* as pleased as the Pope and twice as tall.'

'Prime, Bullock, prime. I shall be seeing him at the hospital directly.'

'My duty and very best respects, sir, if you please. John Bullock, forecastle-man, in the old *Surprise*.'

As prisoners of war in Boston, Aubrey and Maturin had been very kindly treated by their captors; they were penniless, they had no cold-weather clothes, and the officers of the USN *Constitution* had seen to all their needs. Neither intended to be behindhand in an action of this sort, and as he expected, Stephen found Jack with a wounded American lieutenant.

'Do you remember a man called Bullock, in the *Surprise*?' he said, as they walked away.

'Yes, I do,' said Jack. 'Forecastle-man, and a very good hand.'

'He sends his old captain his best respects.'

'Why, that's kind,' said Jack. 'John Bullock: he laid a gun as true as you could wish — dead on the mark, though rather slow. He was captain of the starboard bow-chaser. But I tell you what, Stephen: *old captain* is dead on the mark too. What with funerals and the blue devils and natural decrepitude, I feel like Methusalem's grandad.'

'You eat too much, brother, you drink too much, and you allow yourself to brood. A brisk ten-mile walk in the damp but interesting forests of the New World, outpacing the blue devils, will set you up — will renew your animal spirits. Ponce de Leon was of the opinion that the Fountain of Youth was to be found in these parts. And you are to consider, that a packet may arrive from England at any minute.'

'I dare say you are right about the Fountain of Youth, Stephen, but you are out as far as the packet is concerned. None sails before the thirteenth, and with these everlasting westerlies, we cannot hear for a great while yet. And anyhow, I could not take a walk today, even if there were a dozen Fountains of Youth and a tap-room too at the end of it. I have a damned unpleasant job at the prison, trying to identify the English deserters taken in the *Chesapeake*: they nearly all of them ran from our men-of-war. But before that I am going to see their master's mate, the one that was not knocked on the head. Shall you come?'

'No, Sir. The combatant officers are your natural province, the non-combatant mine. My particular concern today is their surgeon, an unusually learned man.'

The unusually learned man was sitting with a mug of spruce-beer in the empty operating-room, looking careworn, sad and weary, but resolute. He accepted Stephen's offering gracefully, and they talked about some of their cases for a while, taking alternative sips at the mug. When the spruce-beer — 'a dubious anti-scorbutic, sir, but a grateful beverage on such a day, and no doubt mildly carminative' — was done, Stephen said, 'I believe you told me, sir, that before you took to the sea, your practice lay chiefly among the ladies of Charleston?'

'Yes, sir. I was a man-midwife; or, if you prefer it, an accoucheur.'

'Just so. Your experience in these matters is therefore very much greater than mine, and I should be grateful for your lights. Apart from the obvious classical symptoms, what do you find to be the earliest signs of pregnancy?'

The surgeon pursed his lips and considered. 'Well, now,' he said, 'there is nothing wholly reliable, of course. But I believe the general facies rarely deceives me — the thickening of the skin; the pasty complexion in the very first stages, rapidly clearing; the cerous appearance of the eyelid and orbicular folds; the pallor of the caruncula lachrymalia; while the old wives' method of inspecting the nails and hair is not to be despised. And where the physician is familiar with his patient's ordinary behaviour, he can often form an opinion from variations in it, particularly in the case of younger women: abrupt, apparently causeless changes from gloom and anxiety to a high flow of spirits, even to exultation, will tell him much.'

'Sir,' said Stephen, 'I am much indebted to you for these remarks.'

Chapter Two

In the course of his service in the Royal Navy Stephen Maturin had often reflected upon the diversity among sea-officers: he had sailed with men of great family and with others promoted from the lower deck; with companions who never opened a book and with poetic pursers; with captains who could cap any classical quotation and with some who could scarcely write a coherent dispatch without the help of their clerk; and although most came from the middle rank of society, this species had such a bewildering series of sub-species and local races that only an observer brought up among the intricacies of the English caste-system could find his way among them, confidently assessing their origin and present status. There was also a very great difference in wealth, particularly among the captains, since when merchant ships were thick upon the ground it was possible for an enterprising or a lucky commander to make a fortune in prize-money after a few hours' eager chase, whereas those who had to live on their pay led a meagre, anxious life, cutting a very poor figure indeed. Nevertheless they were all marked with the stamp of their profession: rich or poor, loutish or polite, they had all been battered by the elements, and many of them by the King's enemies. Even the most recently promoted lieutenant had served all his youth at sea, while many post-captains as high on the list as Jack Aubrey had been afloat, with few breaks, ever since 1792. They all had a long, long naval war in common, with its endless waiting in the wastes of ocean and its occasional bursts of furious activity.

None of this applied to their wives however, and here the diversity was greater still. Some sailors, perhaps guided by their apprehensive families, married in their own class or sometimes higher; but others, home after the long and dangerous tedium of the Brest or Toulon blockade or a three-year commission in the Indies, East or West, sometimes flung themselves into the strangest arms. And although in many cases these unions proved happy enough, sailors being excellent husbands, often away and handy about the house when ashore, it did make for a curious gathering when the spouses were all invited to a ball.

Stephen contemplated them from among the potted plants: in spite of their differences in size and shape, the sailors' uniform made them a single body; much the same, though with more variation, could be said about the soldiers; but the women had chosen their own clothes, and the results were interesting. He had already recognized a former barmaid from the Keppel's Head in Portsmouth, now swathed in pink muslin and adorned with a wedding-ring; and there were some other ladies whose faces were vaguely familiar, perhaps from other inns, or from the stage, or from tobacco shops.

There was a clear distinction between the dresses, between those women who could both choose and afford good ones and those who could not, a distinction almost as clear as that between the jewels the ladies wore: and these ranged from the garnet pendant round the neck of a child who had married a lieutenant with nothing but his pay of a hundred a year to Mrs Leveson-Gower's rubies, which would have built a thirty-two gun frigate and provisioned her for six months, and Lady Harriet's thumping great emeralds. But it was not this that interested Stephen as he stood watching the crowd: he was more concerned with the ladies' bearing and behaviour, partly as a lesson in female social adaptability in a society so strongly aware of rank, overt or implied, and partly because he had a theory that the more free or even wanton a given past might have been, the more reserved, correct, and even prudish would be the established present.

His observation, interrupted from time to time by a glance at the top of the staircase to see whether Diana would ever finish dressing, did not bear his theory out and the only conclusion he could draw was that those with style retained it whatever their origins, while those who had none were lumpish or affected or both; though even these were already enjoying themselves. The general gaiety, the universal delight at the *Shannon*'s victory, so filled the entire gathering that nearly all the women were in good looks, and the ordinary worries of dress and consequence and husband's rank counted far less than usual. In short, that shared happiness and a strong fellow-feeling abolished distinction for the time being, in spite of the sometimes conflicting but always powerful hierarchies of service rank, social origin, wealth, and beauty.

This was not a discovery that warranted

any very prolonged seclusion among the plants — an uninteresting set, filicales and bromeliads for the most part — and Stephen moved out into the mainstream, where he almost immediately met Jack, accompanied by an equally tall but far bulkier man in the uniform of the First Foot Guards, a blaze of scarlet and gold. 'Why, there you are,' said Jack. 'I have been looking for you. Do you know my cousin Aldington? Dr Maturin, Colonel Aldington.'

'How d'ye do, sir,' said the soldier in the tone he thought suited to the subfusc garments of a naval surgeon. Stephen only bowed. 'This is going to be a prodigious fine ball,' said the Colonel to Jack. 'I can feel it in the air. The last I was at — oh, and I forgot to tell you, Sophie and I stood up together — was at the Winchester assembly, a miserable affair. Not thirty couple, and never a girl worth looking at. I took refuge in the card-room, and lost four pound ten.'

'Sophie was at the assembly?' said Jack.

'Yes, she was there with her sister, looking very well: we danced together twice. I flatter myself we — by God, there's a damned fine figure of a woman,' he exclaimed, staring at the head of the staircase. Diana was coming down in a long blue dress and a blaze of diamonds that eclipsed all the other jewels in the large, beautiful, and well-filled room: she always held herself very well, and now as she came slowly down, straight and slim, she looked superb. 'I should not mind dancing with her,' he said.

'I will introduce you, if you like,' said Jack. 'She is Sophie's cousin.'

'If she is your cousin, she is mine, in a way,' said the soldier. And then, 'Damn me if it ain't Di Villiers. What on earth is she doing here? I knew her in London, years ago. I don't need an introduction.'

He set off at once, pushing through the crowd like an ox, and Stephen followed in his wake. Jack watched them go: he was extremely hurt by the thought of Sophie dancing at the assembly. At any other time he would have been pleased to hear that she was not moping at home, but now it came on top of his bitter disappointment at having had no letters and of losing *Acasta*, and although he was not much given to righteous indignation his angry mind thought of her dancing away, never setting pen to paper, when, for all she knew, he was languishing, a prisoner of war in America, wounded, sick, and penniless.

She had always been a wretched correspondent, but never until now a heartless one.

Colonel Aldington reached Diana. He gave Stephen a surprised, disapproving glance, and then, changing his expression entirely as he turned to her he said, 'You will not remember me, Mrs Villiers — Aldington, a friend of Edward Pitt's. I had the honour of taking you in to dinner at Hertford House, and we danced together at Almack's. May I beseech you to favour me tonight?' As he spoke he gazed now at her face, now at her diamonds: and then with even more respect than before, at her face again.

'Désolée, Colonel,' she said, 'I am already engaged to Dr Maturin, and then I believe, to the Admiral and the officers of the *Shannon*.' He was not a well-bred man: at first he did not seem to understand what she said, and then he did not know how to come off handsomely, so she added, 'But if you would fetch me an ice, for old time's sake, I should be most eternally obliged.'

Before the soldier could come back the music had begun. The long line formed, and the Admiral opened the ball with the prettiest bride in Halifax, a sweet little fair-haired creature of seventeen with huge blue eyes so full of delight and health and happiness that people smiled as she came down the middle, skipping high.

'I would not have danced with that man for the world,' said Diana while she and Stephen were waiting for their turn. 'He is a middle-aged puppy, what people used to call a coxcomb, and the worst gossip I know. There: he has found a partner. Miss Smith. I hope she likes ill-natured tattle.' Stephen glanced round and saw the Colonel taking his place with a tall young woman in red. She was rather thin, but she had a splendid bosom and a fashionable air, and her face, though neither strictly beautiful nor even pretty, was extremely animated — dark hair, fine dark eyes, and a rosy glow of excitement. 'Her dress is rather outré and she uses altogether too much paint, but she seems to be enjoying herself. Stephen, this is going to be a lovely ball. Do you like my lute-string?'

'It becomes you very well indeed; and the black band about your thorax is a stroke of genius.'

'I was sure you would notice that. It came to me at the very last moment; that is why I was so late.'

Their turn came and they went through the formal evolutions required by the dance. Diana with her customary heart-moving grace, Stephen adequately at least; and when they came together again she said, above the ground-swell of countless voices and the singing of the band, 'Stephen, you dance quite beautifully. How happy I am.' She was flushed with the exercise and the warmth of the room, perhaps with the glory of her jewels and the excellence of her dress, certainly with the general heady atmosphere, the intoxication of victory: yet he knew her very well and it seemed to him that at no great depth beneath the happiness there was the possibility of an entirely different kind of feeling.

They were moving up the dance again when Stephen noticed Major Beck's assistant, talking to the Admiral's aide-de-camp, and to his astonishment he saw that the ugly little man was drunk already. His face was irregularly blotched with red, a red that clashed sadly with his uniform, and he was swaying: his bulging watery eyes rested on Stephen for a moment, and then moved on to dwell on Diana: he licked his lips.

'Everybody seems wonderfully happy,' said Diana. 'Everybody except poor Jack. There he is, standing by that pillar, looking like the Last Judgment.'

But more evolutions were called for at this point, and by the time they and the dance were over, Jack had abandoned his post. They walked off companionably together and sat on a love-seat near the door, where the pleasantly warm, sea-smelling air wafted in upon them.

Jack had moved to a long table spread with bottles and glasses, not much frequented yet. Having drunk a certain amount of champagne he said, 'That's very well. But I tell you what, Bullock, just you mix me a glass of bosun's grog, will you?'

'Aye, aye, sir,' said Bullock, 'a glass of grog it is. What you want, sir, is something with a bite in it: a man can blow himself out like a cow in grass with that poor thin fizzy stuff.'

There was certainly a bite in Bullock's mixture, and Jack wandered off with fire spreading through his middle parts. He spoke to a few officers through the din, putting on a proper smiling party face as he did so, and came to a halt near the band. It was quieter here, and he clearly distinguished the slightly too sharp A that a fat musician was giving his companions to tune their instruments: it was long since he had had a fiddle under his chin, he reflected, and he was wondering how nimble the fingers of his wounded arm would prove to be when he heard a clear voice behind him say — 'Who is that very handsome man over there by the window?' He looked towards the window, but there were only two gangling spotted midshipmen, too big for their uniforms, giggling together; and then, when the voice said 'No, nearer to the band,' he realized with a shock that it might be referring to him.

This was instantly confirmed by Lady Harriet's more discreet but still audible 'That is Captain Aubrey, my dear, one of our best frigate captains. Should you like me to introduce him?'

'Oh yes, if you please. He was on board the *Shannon*, was he not?'

At this point a stream of people passed between them in a persevering struggle to reach the sorbets that had just appeared, and Jack studied the band attentively. He *was* a handsome man, but no one had ever told him so and he was unaware of the fact; now he was delighted, frankly delighted to hear the news — charmed to learn that anyone could find him good-looking. He was handsome, that is to say, in the eyes of those who did not look for the bloom or the slenderness of youth, who admired a big broad-shouldered man with a high complexion, bright blue eyes and yellow hair, and who did not object to a face that had the mark of a cutlass-slash from one ear right across the cheek-bone and another scar, this one from a splinter, along the line of the jaw to the other ear. It was clear that Miss Smith did not, for when he turned and the introduction was made, she looked at him with an eager admiration that would have satisfied the vainest soul. He was strongly prejudiced in her favour; he returned her look with a particularly attentive, complaisant deference; and in fact he saw a fine lively young woman, brimming with spirits, quite to his taste — he particularly noticed her bosom.

He at once asked her for this dance and the next, and when, half way through the second, she said 'Is not this a splendid ball?' he replied, 'The best I have ever known,' with real conviction.

The atmosphere was no longer oppressive; the noise was not the mindless cackle of fools but the reasonable gaiety of a very agreeable set of people celebrating a victory — and such a victory! The full glory of it came to him again with an ever greater force. A remarkably good band, too: their phrasing of the minuet was uncommon pretty. And his partner danced well; he loved a spirited partner who could dance and enjoy it. A splendid ball.

There was only one cloud in their evening, and that was when Miss Smith, pointing out Diana and Stephen, asked, 'Who is she, in the blue dress and magnificent diamonds?'

'She is Diana Villiers, my wife's cousin.'

'And who is the little man dancing with her? He seems very particular — they have danced together several times already. And what is his uniform? I do not recognize it.'

'That is a naval surgeon's coat, but he must have forgotten the regulation breeches. He is Dr Maturin, and they are engaged to be married.'

'But surely,' she cried, 'surely such a fine woman cannot throw herself away on a mere surgeon?'

In a decided voice, but not unkindly, he said, 'No woman that I have ever met could throw herself away on Stephen Maturin. We have sailed together for years — we are very close friends — and I value him extremely.'

As he finished they had to dance up to the head of the line, holding hands. She gave his a firm pressure, and when they were in their places she said, 'I am sure you are right. I am sure there is much more in him than meets the eye. Naval surgeons must be far superior to those on land. It was only that she is so very, very elegant — I cannot tell you how I admire beauty in a woman.'

Jack instantly replied that he too admired beauty in a woman — that he was very happy to have a most perfect example as his partner — by far the most perfect example in the room. Miss Smith neither blushed nor hung her head; she did say 'Oh fie, Captain Aubrey,' but when he took her hand again to whirl her round there was no reprobation in her clasp.

By the time he took her in to supper he knew a great deal about her: she had been brought up in Rutland, where her father had a pack of hounds — she adored fox-chasing, but unhappily many of the men who hunted were sad rakes — she had been engaged to be married to one, until it was found that he had an unreasonable number of natural children. She had had several seasons in London, where her aunt lived in Hanover Square; and from what she said Jack learnt, to his surprise, that she must be thirty. She was now keeping house for her brother Henry, who, though a soldier, was so short-sighted that he had been put into the commissariat; he was away now, looking after the army stores at Kingston, an inglorious employment. But even the real fighting soldiers were not much better; they marched and counter-marched and accomplished little; they were not to be compared with the Navy. She had never been so excited in her life as when she saw the *Shannon* bring in the *Chesapeake*. She was filled with enthusiasm for the Navy, she cried; and Jack, looking at her flushed and eager face and hearing her tremulous, enraptured tone, quite believed her.

At the supper-table itself she begged him to describe the battle in every detail, and he did so with great good humour: it was a comparatively simple single-ship action, lasting only a quarter of an hour; she followed it with the utmost eagerness and, it seemed to him, with unusual good sense and understanding. 'How glad you must have been to see their colours come down. How proud of your victory! I am sure my heart would have burst,' she exclaimed, clasping her hands over her bosom, which yielded to the pressure.

'I was delighted,' he said. 'But it was not my victory, you know. It was Philip Broke's.'

'But were you not both in command? You are both captains.'

'Oh no. I was only a passenger, a person of no consequence.'

'I am sure you are being too modest. I am sure you rushed aboard, sword in hand.'

'Well, I did venture on their deck for a while. But the victory was Broke's and Broke's alone. Let us drink to his health.'

They drank it in bumpers. Their neighbours joined them: they were redcoats, but full of good will. One of them had obviously wished Captain Broke a happy recovery many times already, so many that a few minutes after this fresh toast his friends led him away, leaving them alone at the table. Miss Smith returned to the Navy. She showed the keenest interest in the service: she knew almost nothing of it, alas, having always lived so far from the sea, but she had adored poor Lord Nelson and she had worn mourning for months after Trafalgar. Did Captain Aubrey share her admiration, and had he ever met the great man? 'Yes, I do, and I did,' he said, smiling with great benevolence, for there was no shorter way to Jack's heart than a love for the service and an adoration of Nelson. 'I had the honour of dining with him when I was a mere lieutenant: the first time he only said "May I trouble you for the salt?", though he said it in the kindest way; but the second time he said "Never mind manoeuvres; always go straight at 'em".'

'How I honour him,' she cried enthusiastically. ' "Never mind manoeuvres; always go straight at 'em": that is exactly what I feel — that is the only way for anyone with spirit. And how well I understand Lady Hamilton.' And after a pause in which they both ate cold lobster she said, 'But how did you come to be a passenger on the *Shannon*?'

'That is a long story,' said Jack.

'It could not be too long for me,' said Miss Smith.

'A trifle of wine?' suggested Jack, advancing the bottle.

'No more, I thank you. To tell the truth my head is turning a little already. But perhaps it is the dancing, or the music, or the closeness, or sitting next to a hero: I have never sat next to one before. But when you have quite finished your lobster, perhaps we might take a turn in the fresh air.'

Jack protested that he had done eating; he had only been toying with his lobster; he too found the room insupportably close.

'Then we can go out by this glass door. I am so glad: I had half promised that odious Colonel Aldington the next dance, and now I shall be able to escape him.'

In the garden she took his arm and said, 'You were going to tell me how you came to be a passenger on the *Shannon*. Please start from the very beginning.'

'The very beginning would take us back to the *Leopard* — the old *Leopard*, you know: fifty guns on two decks. They rebuilt her, more or less, and gave me the command, with orders to take her out to Botany Bay and then to proceed to the East Indies. It should have been a straightforward passage, but there was bad luck aboard. Plague broke out when we were in the doldrums; then a Dutch seventy-four ran us down into the high southern latitudes, far south and east of the Cape; and then we contrived to run foul of a mountain of ice in a thick fog and beat off our rudder. We were obliged to bear away, half-sinking, for some islands still farther south and east; and it was nip and tuck whether we should fetch them or no, with all hands pumping day and night. But, however, we did; and not to be long-winded about it, we patched the *Leopard* up, hung a new rudder, and carried her first to New Holland and then through the Endeavour Strait to rendezvous with Admiral Drury off Java.'

'Java! That is in the East Indies, is it not? How romantic! Spices and people in palanquins! Elephants too, I dare say. How you have travelled, and what a great deal of the world you have seen! Were the ladies of Java as beautiful as they say?'

'There were some pretty creatures, to be sure; but none to touch those of Halifax. The Admiral was very pleased about the Dutch seventy-four —'

'Why, what happened to it?'

'Oh, we sank her: a lucky shot can do wonders in those seas, with a following wind. I am speaking of the forties, you understand, with a full gale and more right aft. She broached to and sank the moment her foremast carried away. But he was not so happy about the *Leopard*'s statement of condition: her guns had been obliged to be heaved overboard, and in any case the ice had given her frame such a wrench that she could not carry any weight of metal — no good to man or beast: only fit for a transport. However, that did not concern me. I was already appointed to another ship, a frigate called the *Acasta*, so he packed me off home in *La Flèche*. We had a beautiful passage —'

Miss Smith uttered a shrill scream and recoiled into his arms. A toad was walking deliberately across the path, glistening in the light from the windows. 'Oh, oh,' she cried, 'I nearly touched it.'

Jack helped the toad gently on to the grass with his toe, somewhat hampered by her clinging arm. When it was gone she said she could not bear reptiles, nor spiders: they made her feel quite ill. Then she laughed in a way that Jack would have thought unsteady had she been a plain woman, and suggested that they should find a seat in the shrubbery. But as it happened, victory, wine, good food, and perhaps the warmth of the ballroom had suggested the same thing to so many other guests that there was not an empty seat to be found among the clustering laurels; while at the secluded summerhouse they started back only just in time to avoid a very grave indiscretion. They were obliged to be content with a bench near the sundial; and there, as they sat down in the warm night air, filled with the smell of greenness and summer and night-scenting flowers, he glanced up at the guards of the Bear for a notion of the time; and seeing that they were dimmed by wafts of low haze drifting in from the sea he observed 'I dare say we shall have a shower, presently.'

But she, taking no notice of his remark, said 'You were saying you had a beautiful passage.'

'So we did, logging at least two hundred miles from noon to noon, day after day of sweet sailing, until we had rounded the Cape and crossed the tropic line. But then a damned — an extremely untoward thing fell out. She took fire, burnt to the water-line, and blew up.'

'Heavens, Captain Aubrey!'

'Then the boats separated in the darkness, and seeing they were not provisioned, we had a sad time of it until we were picked up by *Java*, some way off Brazil. But even then our troubles were not over, because some days later *Java* fell in with the American *Constitution*, and as you remember, the Americans beat her into a cocked hat.'

'Oh, how well I remember: people absolutely wept when they heard the news. But they said it was not fair — that the American was not really a frigate at all, or that they had more guns or something.'

'No: she was a frigate without any kind of doubt, a heavy frigate; and it was a fair fight, I do assure you. She would have been a tough nut to crack in any case, and in the event she used her guns better than we did: and we were taken.'

'But the dear gallant *Shannon* has set that right,' she said, laying her hand on his knee.

'So she has,' said Jack, laughing with pleasure. 'And now I find it hard to remember how hipped we all were at the time. Well, the Americans were very good to us once it was all over: they sent most of *Java*'s people home in a cartel and carried those of us who were knocked about back to Boston. Maturin very handsomely volunteered to come with me and his other patients —'

'You were wounded?' she cried.

'Oh, only a musket-ball in the arm,' he said. 'But it went bad, as these things will, and I should have lost it but for him. So there we were, do you see, prisoners of war in Boston. Our exchange was delayed for one reason or another, and finding the situation did not suit, Maturin and I took a boat, together with Diana Villiers —'

'What in Heaven's name was she doing there?'

'She had been staying with friends, before the war was declared. And we sailed out to meet *Shannon* as she stood in to look into the harbour. Broke was kind enough to take us aboard and give us a passage to Halifax, and that is how —'

The rain he had promised, the rain foreseen by the toad, began to fall quite fast, and they ran in. Their entry was not particularly remarked: they were only one couple out of several, and they were preceded by a young lady who attracted far more comment, her white dress being liberally scattered with moss behind and even stained with the green of grass. Even so, they were not quite unnoticed. Colonel Aldington gave them a sullen, resentful look; and when Jack was drinking rum-punch to ward off the damp, Miss Smith having retired for a moment, he said 'Look here, Jack, this is all very fine and large, but you took my partner. I saw you steal away just as I came to claim her — I saw you — and I had to stand there like a fool all through that dance and the next. It ain't right: no, it ain't right.'

'None but the brave deserve the fair,' said Jack: and pleased with the thought he began to sing in his deep, surprisingly tuneful voice

'*None but the brave*
None but the brave
Deserve the fair ha, ha, ha! What do you

say to that, Tom?'

'I don't know what you mean to imply about the brave,' said the Colonel, exceedingly cross, 'but if that is your idea of the fair, well, all I can say is, your idea is not mine. That's all. I could say more: I could say that after what I heard just now it is no more than I might have expected. I could say something about reputations, and warn you not to burn your fingers, but I shan't. And I could advise you to put your glass down and drink no more — you have had quite enough — but I shan't do that, neither. You always was a self-willed —'

Miss Smith's reappearance checked any retort that might have been forming in Jack's mind: the music began again, and as he led her into the dance he observed that it was strange how differently wine took different men — some grew glum and fault-finding, some quarrelsome or tearful; for his part he found it did not affect him at all, except perhaps to make him like people rather more, and to make the world seem a more cheerful place. 'Not that it could be much more cheerful than it is already,' he added, smiling at the throng, where the greenbacked girl, dancing away totally unconscious of her betrayal, was adding much to the gaiety of nations.

'Surely, Maturin,' said Diana, as the night wore on, 'Jack and Miss Smith are making themselves very conspicuous? Except when they vanish into corners, they are dancing together all the time.'

'Let us hope they enjoy it,' said Stephen.

'No, but really, Stephen, as a friend, should you not tell him what he is at?'

'I should not.'

'No: I suppose not. But upon my word, that woman makes me feel quite indignant: seducing poor Aubrey is like taking pennies from a blind man's hat — see him beaming all over his face and figuring away like a young buck! If it had been that jolly girl with the green back I should not say anything; but with a wrong 'un like Amanda Smith . . .'

'A wrong 'un, Villiers?'

'Yes. I knew her in India when I was a girl. She came out with the fishing-fleet — stayed with her aunt, a woman with just the same long nose and just the same idea of laying on the paint with a trowel. They come from Rutland, a raffish set: slow horses and fast women. She tried too hard there and she has tried too hard here; but the army is pretty cautious when it comes to actually marrying, you know; not at all like the Navy. And now her reputation is

— well, not much better than mine. Jack really should take care.'

'Certainly she seems unusually complaisant. But is she not perhaps a trifle silly, a little given to enthusiasm?'

'Don't you believe it. She may be an hysterical, flighty, unbalanced ass, but she has a pretty clear head when it comes to the main chance. He is known to be very well off: all the sailors call him Lucky Jack Aubrey. I tell you what, Stephen, unless the roof falls in, he will end the night in that woman's arms; and then he may find himself in a pretty pickle. Could not you give him a hint?'

'No, ma am.'

'No. Perhaps not. You are not your brother's keeper, after all; and I dare say it will be no more than a passade.'

'Tell me, my dear,' said Stephen, 'what has happened to ruffle your spirits?'

She paused — three steps to the left, three steps to the right, true to the time — and gave him the direct answer he expected. 'Oh, it was nothing,' she said. 'It was only that I was talking to Lady Harriet and Mrs Wodehouse when Anne Keppel came up. She gave me a broad stare and pretended to admire my diamonds — she did not remember having seen them in

London — could never have forgotten such a rivière nor such a pendant — had I come by them in America? What had I been doing all this time? Impertinent woman. And I had noticed a chill before that. Colonel Aldington or some other old woman has been talking, I swear.'

Stephen made some remark about diamonds and jealousy, but she pursued her own line of thought, saying 'Oh, on such a night as this even the most virulent prude — though God help us, Anne Keppel has no stones to fling — could not be very unkind. But how I do hope we get a ship soon. Lady Harriet is a dear good woman, but even so, life in a station like this, with scrubs like Aldington and Anne Keppel spreading their ill-natured *ragots* right left and centre, would be hell after a very little while. Oh, bah,' she said. 'Come on, Stephen.'

They danced up the middle; and as he handed her across and received her again he saw that her mood had changed. The dangerous gleam, the raised head of defiance had given way to joy in the dance, to pleasure in the ball and its happy crowd bathed in music and the sense of victory. She was looking as handsome as ever he had seen her, and again he wondered at his own insensibility: and when she cast an eye over the turning dancers and said, with an intensely amused look 'I love that girl with the green on her back,' he wondered even more, for Diana amused — and it was not a usual expression with her — was entrancing. Perhaps his insensibility was no more than a now habitual protection, a way of making the inner void more nearly tolerable: he certainly felt his heart move, as it were involuntarily. Then again, he too was enjoying himself very much more than ever he had expected: the void was still there, certainly, a blank like the white pages of a book after the word Finis, but it was far down, far beneath his consciousness of the moment. The band was deep in a minuet, a Clementi minuet in C major that Jack and he had arranged for violin and 'cello, one that they had often played together; and now that he was in it, in it for the first time as a dancer, the familiar music took on a new dimension; he was part of the music, right in its heart as one of the formally moving figures whose pattern it created — he lived in a new world, entirely in the present. 'I love that girl with the green on her back,' she said again over the deep throb of the 'cello, 'she is having such fun. Oh Stephen, how I wish this night would last for ever.'

In fact it lasted only a very few hours more, only just long enough for Captain Aubrey to fall deeply asleep in Miss Smith's predictable bed. The east was lightening when she shook him awake, saying in a low urgent tone 'You must go. The servants are moving about already. Quick — here is your shirt.'

His head was hardly clear of it before he observed to his consternation that she was in tears. She clung to him, saying, 'We must never, never do it again.' Then calming herself she said 'Here are your breeches.'

His arm was still awkward and he had some difficulty with his neckcloth. She tied it for him, laughing in a way that surprised him, laughing unsteadily and making not altogether coherent remarks about Lady Hamilton doing the same for Nelson: and again she repeated 'Never mind manoeuvres: always go straight at 'em, ha, ha, ha!' His coat was on; his hair was tied up; she whispered 'Go by the garden gate: it is only bolted. I will leave it open tonight.'

Stephen saw him creep into the room they shared, and in spite of the creaking of the boards, almost impossible to ignore, he would have let him reach his bed unnoticed if, in an excess of caution, Jack had not flung down the primitive basin in which they had to wash. It rang like a bell, trundling in a wide spiral until it came to rest against the small table at Stephen's side. This could not credibly be overlooked, and he sat up.

'I am truly sorry to have woke you,' said Jack, smiling at him with a fine glowing face. 'I went for a walk.'

'You look as though you had found the Fountain of Youth, brother. But it is to be hoped that you took a cloak, or at least a flannel waistcoat: with your wound, and at your time of life, the morning dews can have a very dismal effect. The natural humours of the body, Jack, are not lightly to be disturbed. Show me your arm. Exactly so. Tumor, rubor, dolor: there has been inconsiderate exercise, I find; and you are to put it up in a sling again. Do not you feel it — do not you feel a stiffness in the joint?'

'It is a little painful,' said Jack. 'But apart from that, I am astonishingly well. I feel as young as I did when I was first made commander, for all your harping on age and flannel waistcoats, Stephen: even younger. A morning walk sets you up amazingly; that is your Fountain of Youth, for sure. I dare say I shall take another tonight.'

'Did you see many people abroad?'

'A surprising number, walking about in all directions — several officers I knew.'

'What you tell me confirms my supposition: Halifax is an early-rising town. I formed this opinion first from the noise in the street and then from the coming of a little puny boy — a marked case of scoliosis, poor child — with this note for you from Mr Gittings.'

'Who is Mr Gittings?'

'He is the person in charge of the post.'

Jack ripped open the note, carried it to the window, and read, *'Most regrettable mistake . . . Captain A's mail set specially aside . . . subordinates misinformed . . . packets await his pleasure.* God bless my soul: God strike me down: I had never . . . Stephen, I shall step round at once.'

'Before you leave,' said Stephen, 'I will sling your arm anew. And may I suggest that before I do so, you should wash? In the broad daylight people might think you had been in a battle of some kind.'

Jack looked at the glass. In the dimness of Miss Smith's bedroom neither had seen the ludicrous smear of rouge on his face: painfully ludicrous, now that he looked so grave. He washed vigorously, stood silent with what patience he could command while Stephen slung his arm, and ran out of the inn.

It seemed hardly a moment before he was back pounding up the stairs with two canvas-wrapped packets and a number of later covers. 'Forgive me, Stephen,' he said, 'nearly all of these are from Sophie, and I cannot read them in a public room.'

He was deep in the pile, busily sorting and arranging so as to read them in order, by the time Stephen had dressed to go to the hospital: his look of startled guilt had changed to one of eager, happy anticipation. By the time Stephen returned, the heap had been reduced to an exact sequence and read over twice; the letters lay under a water-carafe, with several sheets of accounts beside them; and Jack's face showed an odd mixture of deep contentment and worry.

'Sophie sends you her dear love in all of these,' he said. 'And all is well at home, apart from that damned fellow Kimber. George is breeched, and the girls are learning deportment and French. Lord, Stephen, to think of those turnip-headed little creatures learning French!'

'Had she received any of your letters from Boston?'

'Yes: two. Admiral Drury's duplicate dispatches had already told her *Leopard* was safe, and that good fellow Chads travelled down to Hampshire as soon as the court-martial was over to tell her how *Java* had picked us up and about *Java* and *Constitution*. He was very tactful about my wound: said it was nothing that would put me out of action for long, but it was thought better I should go to America with you and be exchanged from there rather than risk the hot southern passage in a crowded cartel. I am very much obliged to him: she believed it implicitly, and did not worry.'

'I am sure she did. I am sure she believed it.'

'Would the gentlemen like their breakfast now?' asked a chambermaid, bawling through the door.

'If you please, my dear,' said Stephen. 'And listen, child, beg them to make the coffee twice as strong, will you now?'

'I am sure she did,' he said, as he sipped his thin brew. 'There is a Latin tag you are no doubt familiar with, to the effect that men are usually seen to believe what they wish to believe. I was reflecting upon that only the other day,' he went on, staring out of the window at Diana Villiers and Lady Harriet, who were walking along the far pavement, followed by a footman carrying parcels. 'I was reflecting upon that, and upon its corollary, to wit, that often men do not see what they do not wish to see. In all good faith they do not perceive it. I was reflecting because I had a most striking instance of it in myself. For weeks I had the evidence of a given physical condition in front of my eyes, and yet I did not see it. The physician in me must at least have noticed some of the symptoms; and however fleeting and inconclusive each severally may have been he must have seen that the sum, the convergence, was at least significant: but no, the man would have none of it, and was genuinely amazed when the state of which I speak was forced upon his attention. *Gnosce teipsum* is very well, but how to come to it? We are fallible creatures, Jack, and adepts at self-deception.'

'So my old nurse used to tell me,' said Jack: Stephen could be prosy at times, and Jack's attention had wandered to the accounts next to Sophie's letters.

'You mentioned that damned fellow Kimber,' said Stephen.

'Yes. He is still at his capers — keeps pressing her for money — swears that a few more thousand will save our stake and turn a dead loss into a handsome profit —

talks of thousands now, as though they were the natural unit — I cannot make head or tail of the accounts he has shown her, though I am pretty good at figures — wants her to sell Delderwood — I do not think that goddam paper I signed just before we came away can have been a power of attorney, you know, or he could do without her consent.'

'What were the terms of your marriage-settlement?'

'I have no idea. I just agreed to whatever Sophie's mother — or rather her man of business — proposed, and signed my name where I was told: J. Booby, Captain, RN.'

Stephen knew Mrs Williams of old; he drew some comfort from the fact that as one of the most grasping women of his acquaintance she would probably have tied up Jack's property as tight as the most adamantine, Rhadamanthine law, double-twisted, would allow; and he said, 'My dear, long, long ago, when you first heard of this man's doings in the far eastern seas, I begged you to turn your mind deliberately from the question until *La Flèche* should have carried us home. I urged you not to waste your time and your vital energy in vain conjectures and recrimination, but to set the matter to one side until you might usefully consider it with the necessary data at hand — until you could obtain skilled legal advice, and confront the fellow in the company of a man as adept in business as he. That was sound advice, and now, sir, it is sounder still. There are only a few days or weeks to go, and to spend them in a state of impotent fury, so that you arrive in England with your intellects disordered, would be simple indeed. Only a few days: Captain Broke's dispatch will certainly be sent the moment it is written. The news will be infinitely welcome to Government.'

'Yes, by God!' cried Jack, his face lightening as the recollection of victory blazed up afresh. 'And happy the man who carries it. Stephen, I shall follow your advice: I shall be an old Stoic: I shall preserve an equal mind, and I shall not worry about Kimber. Besides,' he added in a low tone, the light in his eye diminishing, 'I may have enough worries here in Halifax.'

A truer word he never spoke; for although the sling that Stephen insisted upon, and the wound, the low diet, and the physic, excused him from nightly attendance on Miss Smith, her claims upon his company by day, if not upon his person, were painfully insistent. She seemed to take a perverse delight in compromising herself and in advertising their liaison; she would come openly to the inn when he took refuge on his sickbed, and read to him; and when he sought air and exercise, unable to bear any more of *Childe Harold* in an emphatic, enthusiastic tone, she walked, hanging on his arm, in the more public parts of Halifax, or drove him, inexpertly, round and round the town in her brother's dogcart. He saw that other men, especially his cousin Aldington, did not envy him; and he was obliged to admit that the company of a flighty, histrionic, unsteady, headstrong, extremely active and ill-judging young woman was not particularly enviable — that Miss Smith had an opinion of her value warranted neither by her charms nor her understanding — and that there were times when he wished Lord Nelson had never, never met Lady Hamilton.

At no time did he wish it more ardently than the day he took her to visit the *Shannon*, when she spoke of the pair with such eagerness and glee that it seemed to him that not even the dullest could fail to take her meaning. None of the *Shannon*'s officers was dull, and he saw a look of intelligence pass between Wallis and

Etough. In spite of her protests, her piercing cry that she longed to see where the hero had lain, he took her straight back to the shore. On shipboard some of his natural authority returned; by land he was pitiably weak. For although he was not unacquainted with women, and although he was very far from indifferent to them, so much of his life had been passed at sea that he was comparatively defenceless: he could not bring himself to be deliberately harsh or unkind. In spite of the reputation he had earned in the Mediterranean during his younger days, he was not at heart a rake; he had never worked out any form of strategy for this kind of encounter and he was surprised, concerned and surprised, when it appeared that strategy was called for.

They met quite often at the dinners he was obliged to attend, and she made him wretched and conspicuous with her mistimed solicitude; so much so that he actually cried off from the Commissioner's ball, although this was a grave breach of naval etiquette. There was also the growing likelihood of Major Smith's return; and although few men had more physical courage than Jack Aubrey, he did not relish the idea of an explanation with the soldier at all, not on his present moral footing.

Day after day went by: the *Diligence* packet came in from England, with a fresh batch of letters and some warm stockings. And day after day she lay at single anchor next to HMS *Nova Scotia*, and still poor Captain Broke's dispatch remained unwritten.

'He wanders sadly after a few minutes of painful concentration,' said Stephen. 'The wound in his head, the depressed fracture of the skull, is even worse than we had feared, and it would be very wrong, very cruel, to urge him to give a considered statement of his victory for a great while yet.'

'I wonder they don't ask young Wallis to write it,' said Jack.

'They have done so, but he begs to be excused: he does not wish to lessen his captain's glory, nor to encroach upon it, in the least degree.'

'Very right, very honourable in him, I am sure,' said Jack in a discontented tone. 'But there is such a thing as being too scrupulous by half. However, I dare say the senior officer and the Commissioner will fadge up something between them, if Broke don't recover in the next day or so. They must be on fire to send the news home: I know I am. I am with child to be aboard the packet — see her there in the fairway, swinging to the tide, and the wind as fair as you could wish. I wonder they hang about so long.'

'Why the packet, for all love? She is only to carry the duplicate and the mails: Wallis or Falkiner is to go in the *Nova Scotia* sloop with the original, and in the nature of things the dispatch must arrive before its echo.'

'You would think so, would you not? But the packet is a flyer, and the sloop is not. What is more, *Diligence* is not one of your established Falmouth packets; she is a hired packet, and she goes to Portsmouth, right on our doorstep, and I lay you three to one she gets there first, although I dare say Capel will give the sloop a tide or so, if only for the look of the thing.'

'A lady to see you, sir,' said a servant.

'Oh my God,' muttered Jack, and he hurried into the bedroom. Now that the outlying people had all seen the *Chesapeake* the inn was not so full: they had a sitting-room, and it was into this sitting-room that Diana was shown.

'You look blooming, my dear,' said Stephen.

'I am glad of that,' she replied: and as their eyes met he knew what was in her mind. He had observed this silent transference often, but never so often as with

Diana: it came irregularly — there was no commanding it — but when it did come, it was wholly conclusive. It worked in both directions and once it had happened there was not the least possibility of a lie, which could be embarrassing to him both as a physician and as an intelligence agent: he thought it was helped if not positively caused by the interaction of the two gazes and for this reason he sometimes wore blue- or green-tinted spectacles. However, Diana's first words were that they were to sail almost immediately. 'Lady Harriet told me, as a great secret, that Captain Capel and the Commissioner between them have written Captain Broke's dispatches, and they are to go off at once, one set in the *Nova Scotia* and the duplicate in the packet. But since everyone will know as soon as the orders are sent out, I thought no harm in telling you.'

Her second piece of news was that Miss Smith had overturned her dogcart, taking an awkward corner too fast. 'I came by soon after,' she said, 'and there it was, lying in a heap, with a man sitting on the horse's head. How I despise a woman who cannot take a tumble without flying into hysterics.'

'Was there much damage, so?'

'No. A wheel came off and she tore her

petticoat, that is all. I walked her home — tell me, Stephen, who is this Dido?'

'As I recall, she was Queen of Carthage: she granted Aeneas the last favours, and she was much concerned when he left her — when he *slung his hook,* as we say.'

'Oh. Well, that is a change from Lady Hamilton, at all events. She was in the secret too, and she kept on saying "I shall be a second Dido". How Jack came to be so simple, I cannot tell. Really, upon my honour, a girl like Amanda Smith! I could have told him how it would end.'

'That would have been a great satisfaction to you, Villiers.'

Before she could reply Jack walked in. 'How d'ye do, cousin?' he said. 'I heard your voice, and I thought I would just give you good day before going out. You are looking very well — peaches and cream ain't in it.'

'Thank you, Jack. I was just telling Stephen that Miss Smith has been overset in her dogcart; and that we are to sail directly, either in the *Nova Scotia* or in the packet.'

'Are we, by God?' cried Jack: and then, 'I hope she was not hurt? No arms or legs broken, or anything like that?'

'No. She was quit for the fright and a torn petticoat. But since we are to go so soon, now is the time to make your farewells and pack your belongings.'

'Oh, as for that, I have nothing but what I stand up in. I shall step round and ask for orders for the packet and then pull across and make sure of decent berths for us.' He hesitated for a moment, wondering if he should ask whether they would like a cabin between them: they had wished Captain Broke to marry them aboard the *Shannon*, and although the battle and Broke's wound had put an end to that, Jack had understood that the ceremony would take place in Halifax. But as neither had ever uttered a single word since, he felt a delicacy about raising the matter now: he said nothing.

A silence fell when he had gone: at last Diana said 'What is that?' pointing at the remains of their late breakfast.

'It is technically known as coffee,' said Stephen. 'Should you wish for a cup? I cannot recommend it, unless you particularly like ground acorns and roast barley, infused in tide-water.' After another silence he went on, 'We spoke of our marriage some time ago. My dear, since the ship is to sail so very soon, should we not walk round to the presbytery now? It is still before twelve: I am well with Father Costello, and he would pronounce the conjugo without any difficulty.'

She changed colour at this, stood up and walked nervously about the room. Passing by the table where his cigars were laid out she picked one up. He lit it for her, and out of the cloud of smoke she said, 'Stephen, I love you dearly and if ever I were to ask any man's charity it would be yours. But my dear I know very well that you do not want to marry me in the least; I have known it ever since I recovered my wits after that appalling time in Boston. I should have known it at once, the minute I saw you again, if I had not been so utterly destroyed, and terrified of that man. No: do not lie, Maturin. It is infinitely kind in you, but it is no use. No use at all. And in any case,' she said, looking at him defiantly while a great flush mounted in her cheeks, 'I would not marry any man when I was in child by another. No, by God, not to save my life. There. Give me a drink, Stephen: these confessions are perfectly exhausting.'

'There is nothing here but rum,' said Stephen, looking round for a clean glass, 'And that is the very last thing for you. I had meant to mention it to you some weeks ago: no spirits. Strait-lacing too is to be avoided, and tobacco.'

'You knew?' she cried.

He nodded, and said, 'You exaggerate

the importance of this, my dear, you do indeed. But it is not unnatural that you should; for you are to consider, that not only is your present physical condition well known to warp the judgment — and here I speak as a physician, Villiers — but that the recent turmoil of spirits, the escape, the rescue, the battle with the *Chesapeake*, must necessarily carry the process much farther, and cause your mind to make grave mistakes. You are mistaken, for example, in your estimate of my feelings. I may not appear as the trembling suppliant of former days, of my almost-youth; but that is the effect of age, no more. An outward display of emotion is indecent when one's hair is grey; but upon my honour, my essential attachment is unchanged.'

She laid her hand upon his sleeve without a word and gave him such a sad, disillusioned smile that he faltered, took a turn to the window and back, put on his blue spectacles, and lit a cigar for himself before going on, 'But even if you were right, which I deny entirely, there is the question of expediency — there is the question of your civil status. A marriage, even a nominal marriage, at once restores your nationality: perhaps even more important, it gives your child a name. Reflect, my dear, upon the condition of a bastard. His state is in itself an insult. He is born with heavy disadvantages under all the codes of law I know; he is penalized from birth. He is debarred from many callings; if he is admitted to society at all, he is admitted only on sufferance; he meets the reproach at every turn all through his life — any tenth transmitter of a foolish face, any lawfully begotten blockhead can throw it in his teeth, and he has no reply. I believe you are aware that I am myself a bastard: I speak with full knowledge when I say that it is a cruel, cruel thing to entail upon a child.'

'I am sure it is, Stephen,' she said, deeply moved. She pressed his hand, and they sat for a while without speaking. Then she said in a low voice, 'But that is why I have come to you, the only friend I can rely on. You understand these things; you are a physician. Stephen, I could not bear to have that man's child. It would be a monster. I know that in India women used to take a root called holi . . .'

'There, my dear, there is a certain proof that your judgment is astray: otherwise you would never have thought of such a course, nor would you ever have said such a thing to me. My whole function is to preserve life, not to take it away. The oath I have sworn, and all my convictions —'

'Stephen,' she said, 'I beg of you not to fail me.' She sat, twisting her fingers together, and in a low, pleading voice she murmured 'Stephen, Stephen . . .'

'Diana,' he said, 'you must marry me.'

She shook her head. Each knew that the other was immovable, and they sat in a miserable silence until the door burst open and a very young officer, pink and white, extremely cheerful, cried 'There you are, ma'am; there you are, sir. I have found you both at the same time. I can deliver both my messages at once.' And then, very rapidly, as by rote, and in an official tone he said, 'Admiral Colpoys presents his best compliments and respects to Mrs Villiers; has the honour to acquaint her that the packet sails directly, and begs her to repair aboard at her earliest possible convenience.' He drew breath and went on, 'The Commander-in-chief informs Dr Maturin that *Diligence* sails on the next tide but one, and directs him to proceed to the man-of-war's hard with the utmost dispatch. There she lies, sir,' he went on in a natural voice, pointing out of the window, 'the brig just beyond *Chesapeake*. She has the blue peter flying.'

Chapter Three

The *Diligence* tided it down the long harbour during the night, and before daybreak she was clear of the Little Thrumcap: by the time the dim sun began to whiten the eastern sky she had made a good offing, and with a moderate breeze on her starboard beam she was steering a little north of east under all plain sail, to leave Sable Island well to the south. Astern there was nothing to be seen: even if the weather had not been so hazy, she had long since sunk the high land of Cape Sambro. But six points on her starboard bow there lay a vessel dark against the light, a tall schooner, not five miles away. Not a sloop, not a man-of-war, but unmistakably a schooner: and in any case the *Nova Scotia*, given a whole tide's start, was at least forty miles beyond the horizon.

She was lying there with no way on her, breasting the swell under her reefed fore-and-aft mainsail; yet it was clear that she was no fisherman, since she had no dories anywhere around her, and in any case no skipper making a voyage for cod would have brought a long slim rakish schooner with little room for his catch to a place where there were even fewer fish.

The second mate, who had the watch, saw her as soon as the lookout on the forecastle, and after one hard stare across the lightening sea he stepped below to the cabin, where the Captain and Jack Aubrey were eating steak. 'I believe we have the *Liberty* to windward, sir,' he said.

'Is that so, Mr Crosland?' said the Captain. 'And how far off might she be?'

'A matter of five mile, sir.'

'Then bear up, Mr Crosland, and set the foretopgallantsail. I shall be on deck presently.'

Mr Dalgleish, the owner — literally the owner — of the *Diligence*, emptied his cup deliberately, took his spyglass from the rack, and walked up the companion-ladder, followed by Jack.

The stranger had already filled and worn on the same course, and as they watched, gazing over the starboard quarter, a signal broke out at her masthead: she fired a windward gun.

It was clear to Jack, as he considered her, that there was a strong possibility of her being an American privateer — no one else would lie there in the middle of the main shipping-lane between England and Canada — and he was not particularly surprised when Dalgleish, passing the telescope, said, 'Yes. She is the *Liberty*; and I see Mr Henry has given her a new coat of paint. Tom,' — to a nimble youth, his son — 'jump to the masthead and tell me whether Mr Henry's signal means anything or whether it is just another wicked falsehood. Mr Crosland, flying-jib . . .'

While Dalgleish was giving orders for more sail Jack studied the *Liberty*: a long low schooner painted black, about seventy-five feet in length and twenty in beam, a vessel of perhaps a hundred and fifty tons, built for speed. As far as he could see she carried eight broadside guns, probably twelve-pounder carronades, and something in the way of a bow-chaser. Her deck was crowded with men. She had set a square foretopsail and she was coming down goosewinged; but no schooner could show her best paces before the wind, goosewinged or not, and during his long study of her it did not appear to him that she gained much, if indeed she gained at all.

'Good morning, sir,' said a voice by his side.

'Good morning, Mr Humphreys,' said Jack rather coolly. Humphreys was the officer chosen to carry the duplicate dispatch rather than any of the master's mates who had fought in the action with the *Chesapeake*. In the opinion of the service it was a vile job, designed to secure Humphreys' advancement. There was no possible doubt of the *Shannon*'s officers being promoted, and Falkiner was in fact aboard the *Nova Scotia*, heading straight for a commander's commission; but even so it was felt that one of the younger men should also have shared in the glory at home.

'What do you see, Tom?' called Mr Dalgleish.

'Well now, Dad,' said Tom, 'I believe I make out a sail, hull-down, two or maybe three points abaft the beam. But it is cruel hazy there in the eye of the sun, and it may be an ice-mountain.'

'What away to leeward, Tom?'

'Nothing to leeward, Dad, bar a pod of whales — there she blows again! — and north I see clear to the horizon.' A pause; and then from on high, 'Harkee, Dad, that *is* a sail to windward. A schooner, too.'

'Thanks be,' murmured the master of the packet; and turning to Jack he said, 'I am right glad I said we should go south about Sable Island. With t'other beating up from leeward, they would have pinched us between them like . . .' With one eye to his glass, and that glass trained on the *Liberty*, he sought for some likeness that might strengthen the idea of two vessels gradually closing in upon a third from either side over an enormous stretch of sea, found none, and repeated 'Pinched us between them, like . . .' his hand imitating the movement of a lobster's claw.

'You think they had intelligence of your sailing, then?'

'Bless you,' said Mr Dalgleish, 'in Halifax you can scarcely piss against a wall, without the Yankees know next day. While we were waiting for the dispatches I was in the King's Head — a roomful of people — and I just happened to remark that I should go south about as soon as I had the bag aboard, ha, ha!'

'So you were not altogether surprised to find them waiting for you, on the southern course?'

'No, sir, I was not. Not *Liberty*, at all events. Mr Henry there,' — nodding over the miles of sea — 'has laid for me many and many a time, hoping to come up from leeward — for she lies uncommon close to the wind, and sails uncommon swift — to carry us by boarding. Which was how she took *Lady Albemarle* and *Probus*, both neat, fast-sailing packets; to say nothing of other prizes. A pretty good seaman, Mr Henry: I knew him well before the war. He was a packet-captain too, before he took to privateering. But t'other, his friend, I am surprised to see. They never hunt in pairs unless there is a fat merchantman to be looked for; and there ain't no merchantman, fat or thin, due to sail or to come in this fortnight and more. And a packet — why, 'tis a feather in their caps, to be sure, and one in the eye for King George, but it don't hardly answer the expense, if you have something like a hundred men aboard, at American rates of pay, eating their heads off; to say nothing of the wear and tear and the risk of carrying away a spar. And to say nothing, neither, of the clawing you may get in the last moments before you board.'

'I believe you could give him a rare old clawing, Captain Dalgleish,' said Jack, looking at the brig's array of carronades, five twelve-pounders to a side.

'So I could,' said Dalgleish, 'and so I shall, if he comes alongside. But never you fear, Captain, we have the legs of her, before the wind; and I have not even set my studdingsails yet. With this nip in the air there is sure to be fog on the Middle Bank or the Banquereau; we will shake them off there, and carry on with our course as before, if they don't give over first, as I dare say they will. A packet is no great prize; no cargo, and no market for the hull in the States; nothing worth cracking on for regardless all day, let alone by night, with all this summer ice coming down.'

After a silence Jack said, 'Have you ever thought of the lame-duck caper, Captain Dalgleish? Starting your sheets a trifle — steering rather wild — slipping a drag-sail over the blind side — sending half your people below? If you could lure her up in the next hour or so, you could deal with her long before her friend came up. You could *take the Liberty,* as one might say, ha, ha!'

Dalgleish laughed, but Jack saw that he might as well have been whistling psalms to the taffrail: the master of the packet was quite unmoved, was perfectly satisfied with his role — a strong, self-reliant man, confident that his was the right conduct. 'No, sir,' he said, 'that would never answer with Mr Henry. I know him and he knows me;

he would smell a rat directly. And even if he did not, Captain Aubrey, even if he did not, it is no part of my business to take the *Liberty*, as you put it so wittily. I am not a man of war, and my brig is not a man-of-war neither, but an unestablished temporary packet — temporary these last twelve years and more: a contract-vessel, as we say. For you gentlemen in the glory-line it is quite different: you are answerable to King George, whereas I am answerable to Mrs Dalgleish, and they see things in quite a different light. Then again, you can go to the dockyard and indent for half a dozen topmasts, any number of spars, nay, a whole new suit of sails, any day in the week you choose. But if I went to the Postmasters General and asked them for half a bolt of number three canvas, they would laugh in my face and remind me of my contract. And my contract is to provide a vessel at my own charges for His Majesty's mails, and to carry them, as per contract, as fast as is consistent with their safety: for the mails are sacred, sir. The mails and dispatches are sacred: particularly this blessed dispatch about the victory.' Here he looked significantly at Mr Humphreys, who gave a solemn nod; he did not say anything, however, for Jack was very much superior to him in rank, an awe-inspiring figure; and Humphreys, although he would not have relinquished it for the world, was conscious of his position, painfully conscious that he might be looked upon as a well-connected intruder, even perhaps as a scrub. 'What is more,' added Dalgleish, 'this brig is my livelihood, and no one will give me another if she is taken.'

'And a very handsome brig she is,' said Jack. 'I doubt I have ever seen finer lines.' He could not dislike Dalgleish: although his whole being was alive with the prospect of an action, laid on with cunning, ending with extreme violence, and very probably the capture of the *Liberty*, he found the packet-captain's calm, assured attitude convincing and indeed respectable.

He said as much to Stephen when they met in the middle of the morning for a private pot of coffee. 'I never thought I should like a fellow who ran so openly — who ran like a hare, without beating about the mulberry bush, or making any bones about it, although he has a neat little broadside, quite enough to make the schooner cry peccavi if he knows how to ply it.'

'Brother,' said Stephen, 'you speak of hares — of bones and mulberries — of a schooner, and I am none the wiser.'

'Why, don't you know we are being chased?'

'I do not.'

'Where have you been all the morning?'

'I have been sitting with Diana. At one time I came on deck, but they were arranging the sails, and desired me to go below again; so seeing that you and Mr Dalgleish were in conversation I returned to her side.'

'How is she?'

'Utterly prostrated. She is without exception the worst sailor I have ever known.'

'Poor Diana,' said Jack, shaking his head. But it was thirty years since he had felt a qualm of seasickness, and that only a slight one; his sympathy could be no more than remote and theoretical; and after a moment he went on, 'Well, the fact of the matter is, that we sighted an American privateer, a schooner, at daybreak, five miles off, with another, hull-down, far to windward: Dalgleish bore up, and now we are running for it: like a hare, as I said. I dare say we are making close on eleven knots. Should you like to come on deck and see how things lie?'

'If you please.'

At a casual glance the position seemed scarcely to have changed. The *Liberty* still lay on the packet's starboard quarter, and far over the grey heaving sea the other schooner still bore east-south-east. But there was a different feeling aboard the *Diligence*, a greater tension, and Mr Dalgleish's expression was more grave by far. The brig had already spread her studdingsails alow and aloft, and she was running beautifully, the water singing down her side so that there was a fine half-heard, half-felt urgent resonance in her hull. But the *Liberty* had spread much more canvas and she had gained perceptibly, while her distant consort had done better still; she was now hull up and she was about to cross in front of a long, indented iceberg that gleamed over there in the greyness like a close-packed squadron of ships of the line.

Dalgleish was talking to his first mate and to Mr Humphreys, who was now measuring the angle subtended by the pursuers with the utmost concentration. 'I never saw Mr Henry so determined,' said Dalgleish, turning to Jack. 'He is cracking on as though sailcloth and spars were free. Or as if we were a goddam Spanish galleon. Pray take my spyglass, sir, and see what you make of t'other.'

Jack fixed the distant schooner, steadying his hand on the aftermost shrouds, and he studied her as she crossed in front of the ice. 'She has spread drabblers,' he observed, 'boomed out on either side. I have never seen that before, with such a rig. She must be in a hell-fire hurry.'

'I thought so too,' said Dalgleish. 'I thought I picked them up. In all the time I have commanded this packet, to and fro scores of times, I have never seen the like, since war was declared. A man would think we were ballasted with gold.'

Stephen watched some gannets fishing away to leeward — the white flash of their headlong plummeting dive, the splash — and he listened vaguely to the sailors. There was some question of the wind dropping, of its chopping round into the north-west — of the state of the barometer — of skysails and kites: nasty frail wasteful things, costing the eyes of your head, in Dalgleish's opinion, and certain to carry away in this breeze — of a method, employed by Captain Aubrey in an emergency, of sustaining them by means of doubled travelling backstays, led through a block aloft, snubbed well aft, tended by a sharp hand, and only shifted at the last moment, if at all. He heard Dalgleish say 'that unlike some packet-captains he was not above learning from gentlemen of the Royal Navy; that however old you were, you might still learn something new every day; and that he should try Captain Aubrey's method.'

Here Stephen's attention was wholly taken up by a school of whales, of right whales, that appeared on the larboard bow; he borrowed a telescope and watched them as their steady course converged with that of the brig — watched them until they were so close that the glass would no longer focus and he could distinctly hear not only their vast steaming spout as they surfaced but even the indraught of their monstrous breath. At some point he felt a change in the brig's progress, a greater thrust that raised her general music by half a tone, and when he looked up he found that she had set flying kites, that the *Liberty* was distinctly farther off, and that all hands were very pleased with themselves.

'Now we can eat our dinner in peace,' said Dalgleish with great satisfaction. 'A very pretty notion of yours, sir, very pretty indeed. But even so, I believe I shall set up a couple of beckets, with an in-and-out turn *over* the hounds . . .'

The whales had gone, in one of their long, mysterious travelling dives; the sailors were deep in their hooks and thimbles, the advantages and disadvantages of hooks and thimbles with a selvagee strop as opposed to lashing-eyes, where backstays were concerned; Stephen returned to Diana. He was a great believer in the alcoholic tincture of laudanum, and this time she had retained his draught long enough for it to have an effect: she lay there, exhausted, but at least no longer racked, in a state between sleeping and waking.

She murmured when he came in, and he told her about the whales. She did not seem to be with him, but nevertheless he added, 'It also appears that we are being pursued by two privateers: remote and ineffectual privateers, however. Mr Dalgleish is quite happy; he is confident we shall shake them off.' Diana made no reply. He contemplated her. Lying there flat in her cot, her damp hair straggling, her face green and yellow, set in incipient nausea and general suffering, beyond all care for appearances, she was not a pretty sight: no spectacle for an ardent lover. He tried to put a name to his feeling for her but he found no satisfactory word or combination of words. It was certainly not the passion of his younger days nor anything related to it; nor did it resemble friendship — his friendship for Jack Aubrey, for instance. Affection entered into it, tenderness, and even a kind of complicity, perhaps, as though they had long been engaged in the same pursuit. Possibly the same absurd pursuit of happiness. This evoked some memories too painful to dwell upon, and he continued in a low voice, not to wake her if she was asleep, 'It seems that these schooners were lying on the course we were expected to take. They were to the south of some island, whereas the prudent Mr Dalgleish sailed to the north: their presence can hardly have been the effect of hazard.' It might have been the effect of intelligent guesswork on the part of the Americans: or it might have been that the list of their agents in Canada was defective — he doubted that a man like Beck would have left any hole unstopped. Yet on the other hand there was Beck's staff, and he was thinking about the drunken fellow at the ball when Diana suddenly spoke out of her apparent coma. 'Of course it was not just chance,' she said. 'Johnson would do anything, spend anything, to get us back. He is perfectly capable of hiring privateers, whatever they cost: he would spend money like water, he would move heaven and earth to get hold of me. And my diamonds,' she added. She turned uneasily, throwing the bedclothes about. 'They are all I have,' she muttered after a while: and then 'I shall never escape from that dreadful man.' And after still another pause 'But he shall never have them, not as long as there is breath in my body. No, by God.'

Stephen observed that she was clasping the case tightly against her. He had always known that she valued them extremely, but to this extent . . . He said 'I really do not believe you need feel concerned. We are a great way ahead, and Mr Dalgleish, who knows these waters extremely well, assures me that we shall meet with fog upon the Banks: there they can neither see nor follow us. I shall be heartily glad of it. If there is anything I dislike more than violence on land, it is violence at sea; since the peril is even greater, and apart from that, it is always wet and very often cold.' She had dropped into a heavy laudanum sleep; tears were still welling from behind her closed eyelids, but she herself was not there.

Almost certainly she was right, he reflected: Johnson was powerful, rich, and influential; his pride had been cruelly wounded and he was a revengeful man. Diana knew him intimately — who more so? — and she could not be mistaken in his temper. And surely it was significant that the privateers should let the *Nova Scotia* go by and pursue the *Diligence* alone? She might even be right about the necklace. It was a splendid bauble, so splendid that its central stone had a name, the Nabob or the Mogul or something of that kind; and he had noticed that even very wealthy men were extraordinarily attached to particular possessions. It was, after all, this attachment that gave their price to such diamonds as the Pitt, the Sancy, the Orloff . . . suddenly the name of Diana's came to his mind: it was the Blue Peter, a pear-shaped stone of a most surprising colour, like a pale, pale sapphire but with much more life and fire. An impious sailor had taken it from a temple in the time of Aurangzeb and it had kept the name he gave it ever since, a name that Stephen particularly liked, for not only had it a fine round sound but it was also that of one of the few flags he could recognize with certainty, the flag that ships flew when they were about to sail, and it had the pleasing associations of fresh departure, new regions, new creatures of the world, new lives, perhaps new life.

As Mr Dalgleish had predicted, they ate their dinner in peace, with the packet drawing slightly ahead in spite of the slackening breeze and the pursuers no more than a very distant threat. And as he predicted there was fog on the Middle Bank. When Stephen came on deck he saw it a great way off as a smooth low curve on the northern horizon, like distant land: he also saw that there were at least four ships scattered about the sea, some no great way from the packet and moving slowly on the same northward course. For an instant it seemed to him that Mr Johnson had mobilized the greater part of the United States Navy and that the packet was surrounded; but then he noticed the haphazard appearance of the ships in question, the absence of gunports, the presence of a lateen on the mizenmast, and although he was no great seaman he was convinced that these were not men-of-war. In any case no one seemed at all concerned — the *Diligence* was even exchanging civilities with the nearest — while Jack and Mr Dalgleish and the bosun were high in the rigging, like a group of apes, intent upon some immediate purpose of their own. 'What is

Captain Aubrey doing up there?' he asked the second mate.

'They are changing the beckets for grommets,' said the second mate. 'We should be man-of-war fashion from stem to stern, if Captain Aubrey had his way.'

'He must take care of his arm. Shirt-sleeves is madness in this biting cold: I have a mind to call out. However . . . Those — vessels over there, sir: a curious rig, is it not?'

'They are bankers, sir, bankers out of Portugal: terranovas, as we call them. You will see plenty more of them on the bank. If you can see anything at all: it looks mighty thick over there, as the Owner said.'

'Terranovas. I have heard of them. And that, I suppose, is the Newfoundland itself?'

'Not exactly, sir. That is the bank; or rather the fog over the bank. But being there is nearly always a fog over the bank, we sometimes call the fog the bank, if you understand me.' The second mate had a low opinion of Dr Maturin's understanding — a man capable of confusing bonnets and drabblers could hardly be expected to distinguish good from bad, right from wrong, chalk from cheese — but he was a good-hearted youth and he answered Stephen's questions kindly: why the fog? why did it not blow away in this wind? why did the Portuguese congregate in it? In the simplest words he could find he explained that the Portuguese went where the cod were, and this year there were even more cod on the Middle Bank than on the Saint Pierre or even the Grand Bank itself: the Doctor knew what a cod was? A gurt fish with a barbel under its chin, that loved almost any bait you could name, but squid and caplin most. The Papists were obliged to eat it, dried and salted, on Fridays and all through Lent; they went to Hell else. That was why the Spanish and the Portuguese, and the French too in time of peace, came to the Banks every year: they being Papists, upon the whole. But there were Blue-Noses and Newfoundlanders too. They came where the cod were, and the cod were on the Banks, where the bottom of the sea rose up quite sudden, sometimes to fifteen fathom, no more — the second mate had seen ice-mountains grounded on them many a time — but usually say forty or fifty fathom. And the Portuguee would anchor and send away his little dories with a couple of men in them to fish with the cod-line. As a boy the second mate had been out with his uncle, a Blue-Nose from Halifax, and he had caught four hundred and seventy-nine codfish in eleven hours, some of them fifty pounds in weight. As to the fog, it was caused by the cold Labrador current setting south, then rising over the Banks and meeting the warm air of the Gulf Stream — the Doctor had heard tell of the Gulf Stream? — and so brewing up a fog almost continual. Some days you would say the whole sea was steaming like a pot, it brewed so fast: and that was why the wind did not blow it away — it was brewed afresh continual. To be sure, there were some times in the year when the current set more easterly, and there was no fog; it might be clear as clear for days or even weeks; but for all that you always knew where the Banks were, even without taking soundings, because of the birds. There were always birds, particular birds, on the Banks, thick or clear.

'What kind of birds?' asked Stephen.

'Murres, dovekies, guillemots, razorbills, kittiwakes, sheerwaters, fulmars, skuas, all sorts of gulls, puffins, penguins —'

'Penguins, my dear sir?' cried Stephen.

'That's right, Doctor. A very old-fashioned bird, that can't fly but only swim. Some call them garefowl, but we call them penguins. It stands to reason, if a bird can't fly, it is a penguin: ask any whaler that has been far south.'

'Does it stand about a yard high — black and white like a prodigious razorbill?'

'That's the very bird, sir; but it has a white patch between its bill and its eye.'

Without the shadow of a doubt this was the Alca impennis of Linnaeus, the Great Auk of some vulgar authors, a bird Stephen had longed to see all his life, a bird grown so rare that none of his correspondents but Corvisart had ever seen a specimen; and Corvisart was somewhat given to lying. 'And have you indeed seen your penguin, sir?' he asked.

'God love you, many and many a time,' said the young man, laughing. 'There is an island up that away,' nodding towards Newfoundland — 'where they breed by wholesale, and my uncle the Blue-Nose used to go there when he was fishing the Grand Bank. I went with him once, and we knocked them on the head by the score. It would have made you laugh, to see them standing there like ninepins, to be bowled over. We cut them up for bait, and ate the eggs.'

'Blue-nosed hell-hound,' said Stephen

inwardly, 'Goth, Vandal, Hun.' Aloud, and with as much amenity as he could summon, he asked, 'Is there any likelihood of seeing one on this bank?'

'I dare say there is, Doctor, if you keep a sharp lookout. Do they interest you? I will lend you my glass.'

Stephen kept a sharp lookout, in spite of the cold that misted his telescope and deadened his blue extremities; and by the time the packet glided into the mist on the southern edge of the bank, far, far ahead of the schooners, he had seen not only murres and dovekies, but two great auks. The mist thickened; the *Diligence* was completely hidden from her pursuers; Mr Dalgleish took in his kites, royals, topgallants, courses, everything but the foretopsail lowered on the cap and a jib, just enough to steer by in that swirling obscurity; evening came on, and still Stephen stood there, shivering, in the hope of a third.

The *Diligence* ghosted along, her bell tolling continually, with double lookouts fore and aft, her best bower cleared away and poised a-cockbill from her starboard cathead, for as Mr Dalgleish said, he had no notion of carrying on by night with all these craft about and the danger of summer ice coming down. From far and near came the answering drums or whistles, and on every hand the howl of conchs from unseen dories. From white the fog grew grey and greyer still: the riding-lights and stern-lantern of a ship showed hazy gold two hundred yards away — a ship with a peculiarly thin and piercing whistle, worked by a crank.

'*Leviathan* ahoy,' hailed Mr Dalgleish.

'What ship is that?' asked *Leviathan* out of the fog.

'*Diligence*, of course. William, what's your ground?'

'Thirty fathom.'

Mr Dalgleish put his helm a-lee. The packet made a smooth sweep, brought her head to the wind, took on a little sternway, and dropped her anchor. 'Mr Henry is on the rampage again,' he remarked in a strong but conversational voice.

'Bugger him,' said *Leviathan*, now on the packet's starboard beam.

'How does the cod come in, William?'

'Tolerable, tolerable, Jamie,' said *Leviathan* with a fruity chuckle. 'No caplin, but they are taking squid. Send a boat over, and you shall have a bit of fish to your supper.'

The boat shoved off with the second

mate and came back, laughing as it pulled across the steaming water, with two cod as long as a man and the second mate clasping a very large, very damp, dead, black and white bird to his bosom as he came up the side. 'There, Doctor,' he said, 'they were going to use it for bait, but they have plenty of quid, and I thought it might please you.' Mr Dalgleish's predictions had been right up until this point; but over their supper of the best codfish in the world, gently poached in a bucket of sea-water, he foretold that *Liberty* and her consort would give over in the night; Mr Henry could not afford to stay out day after day with all those men aboard; a mere packet would not answer the outlay; he was not really a blue-water privateer but an offshore dasher, a snapper-up, and he would now be beating up for Marblehead as fast as he could fly, for the wind would not change until the moon began to wane. Mr Dalgleish was right about the wind: it hung in the south and west, bearing the *Diligence* cautiously across the Middle Bank, through hooting Spaniards, Portuguese, Nova Scotians and Newfoundlanders in the dim daybreak and the pallid day itself. But he was wrong about Mr Henry. They were scarcely clear of the mist before the schooners were seen, unmistakable with their raking masts, but fortunately still well to the south.

'Such obstinacy I have never seen,' cried Mr Dalgleish; again he said that the packet might be ballasted with gold, the way they carried on; and again the *Diligence* fled north-east for the Misaine and the Artimon banks, under a great press of sail.

Yet whatever ruses Dalgleish might conceive, and he thought of many, the devilish Mr Henry divined them. When they cleared the Misaine, there he was again; and on the Artimon, in spite of a night's lying to, the morning showed him stark and clear, within three miles. The only thing he could not do was to change the wind. It kept aft, so that the square-rigged *Diligence* had an advantage over the schooners. But it was an advantage that she maintained only by incessant attention to her trim every moment of the endless race — jibs, studdingsails and kites flashed in and out, and the meagre crew grew more and more exhausted, until Dalgleish determined to shape a course for the Grand Bank itself and its notorious, even thicker fog. And in the long haul eastward for the Grand Bank the advantage disappeared: with the wind a little abaft the beam the schooners sailed as fast as the brig in spite of the sheets hauled iron-tight aft and the owner at the wheel, trick after trick. They tore along, the three of them, their lee catheads rarely rising from the white racing water, their decks sloping like the roof of a house, the masts complaining, the wind sweeping in over the starboard rail, singing high and loud in the rigging, all tense and taut to the edge of the breaking-strain.

No fog on the Grand Bank: no refuge there. Birds by the hundred thousand, bankers by the score and countless dories hauling in the cod, but no fog. Some freak of the currents left the vast area as clear as the Mediterranean: and the moon was coming to the full — no refuge in the night either. Mr Dalgleish cursed the day he had not put into St John's, Newfoundland, and he put the brig before the wind again, a strong, irregular, gusting wind. As he did so the foretopmast gave a great rending creak and a lengthwise fissure appeared in its upper third. In such an eager chase they could not possibly lie to long enough to send up a spare, so they fished it at once with capstan-bars, wringing them tight against the wound with turn after turn of woolding; but a mast so badly sprung could not bear a great press of sail, and their advantage was gone. Now, even directly before the wind, the packet was on no more than equal terms in a light breeze; and when she had to reef her topsails the schooners gained.

So they ran, north and east — more north than east most of the time — through the clear light-blue day and the sparkling night, lit from horizon to horizon by an enormous moon. Jack and Humphreys, and Humphreys' servant, an old Marine, had long since attended to the packet's guns and small-arms, and they had put what few hands could be spared from the arduous driving of the brig through the great-gun exercise; but Jack had no illusions about the *Diligence*'s armament. With these poor little inaccurate short-range carronades her bark would be worse than her bite; and although the hands were good willing men, they were quite untrained and very few in number.

On Thursday night the breeze dropped almost to a calm, and from the dropping glass, the clouds astern, and the much greater swell there was a strong probability that the wind would veer into the west, if not well to the north of west, and blow very, very much harder. In the uncertain airs they caught the smell of ice; and towards the end of the first watch, when the moon was near its height, they saw a towering mountain, undermined by the warmer current, overturn completely, sending vast blocks flying into the sea, so that the spray flew high, a hundred feet and more, flashing in the moonlight; and some seconds later they heard the long deep thunderous crash, infinitely solemn and portentous.

On the Banks the *Diligence* had shipped ice fenders, spars over the bows to deaden the shock of drifting ice; but they also deadened her fine point of speed, and since the springing of the mast they had been taken in, the more so as she was now out of the ordinary track of summer ice. 'Unnatural,' was Mr Dalgleish's only comment as he ordered them to be shipped again: a necessary move, though possibly fatal from the point of view of capture, since any of these jagged blocks, almost entirely beneath the surface, scarcely to be seen, could pierce through a ship's bows even if she were only running at five knots, let alone the breakneck fourteen and two fathoms the packet had attained; and there were at least three more icebergs in their field of vision, gleaming to northwards.

Dalgleish had scarcely left the deck since the full hard chase began; he was unshaved; he looked very old and very tired; and now, with the prospect of a wind that must favour the privateers, he seemed almost crushed. But there was a fine gleam in his red-rimmed eye on Friday morning, when a sail appeared in the east, a blazing golden east, with the high nimbus blushing flamingo-red and every promise of a hearty blow. Stiffly he climbed to the crosstrees with his telescope, and when he came down he said to Jack, 'It sounds wicked to say so, but I believe she may be our salvation. Take my spyglass aloft, sir, and see if you think the same.'

Jack mounted to the masthead like a boy — a heavy boy — and from there, since the rising sun made it difficult to see the stranger, he first studied the *Liberty* and her companion, the one a little abaft the beam and the other on the packet's quarter. They had come up during the night, and although they were still far beyond the extreme range of long gunshot they had already felt the first gusts from the north-west that came with the sun; they knew what o'clock it was; and both had cleared away their bow-chasers: as far as he could judge, Mr Henry's was a long brass nine-pounder; and a very deadly weapon that could be, in good hands. Then he turned to the stranger, now clear of the blinding glare. She was a ship, close-hauled on the starboard tack: she was deep-laden, fat-bellied, certainly a merchantman of considerable size and value, and at this stage of the war certainly a British ship: and in her leisurely comfortable way, under courses and reefed topsails, she was steering a course that would lead her straight into the jaws of the privateers. They had only to shift their helms a little and they would take her on either side, board her and carry her before she was awake.

But they would have to change course quite soon. On her present tack, and with the strengthening, veering breeze, the merchantman would be to windward of them before long; and then, however close they could lie, they would surely lose her.

Those on board the packet watched with the closest attention. Three bells: four bells: not a telescope but what was trained on the *Liberty*, to catch the first sign of her bearing up for the merchantman. In the clear light they could see her people, Mr Henry among them no doubt, lining the starboard rail — it was black with men —

and staring out at the stranger, the answer to a privateer's most fervent prayer. She for her part seemed still asleep. She stood on and on, as though into an empty sea. Jack had often seen an indifferent lookout kept in merchantmen, but never anything to equal this. 'Give her a gun,' he said in strong indignation. 'With your permission, sir, I will give her a gun.'

'Give her a dozen, if you like, Captain Aubrey,' said Dalgleish with a bitter laugh. 'But believe me, she's in no danger. Mr Henry don't mean to touch her.'

Jack gave her two, happy to warm the carronades: he was almost sure that Dalgleish was right — so fine a seaman, so keen a privateer as Mr Henry, would never have let those precious miles go by, glass after glass, not with such a prize in view. No: he preferred the packet to the merchantman, and presently the guns would be used in earnest. At the first report Stephen ran up on deck: the situation was clear enough to the most unskilful eye, with the schooners manoeuvring like racing-yachts in the veering breeze, and in any case the first mate made it plain in one coarse phrase. After the second gun he stepped across to Jack and said 'What may I do?'

'Go down to the magazine and fill powder with Mr Hope,' said Jack. 'And then you can fight this carronade with me.'

Some minutes passed. The merchantman woke up, replied with a single gun, displayed her colours, lowered them in salutation, and hoisted them again. The privateers at once replied with a leeward gun apiece, and showed British colours. Jack gave her the remaining carronades of the starboard broadside: surely that must make them see that something was amiss? The well-remembered powder-smell eddied about the deck; the stumpy guns ran smoothly in and out; their breechings gave a comfortable twang. He and his mates reloaded with grape and round-shot.

The merchantman shook the reefs out of her topsails and stood on, as into the bosom of her friends. The *Diligence* had early thrown out a signal warning her of her danger, but she seemed to make nothing of it; and in fact she was in no danger at all.

The privateers might look wishfully at her, but it was now certain that the packet was their quarry, the packet alone. They had hauled their wind and they were forereaching on the *Diligence* diverging from the stranger's course; the crucial moment had almost passed, and presently the stranger would cross their wake into safety.

'Never say die,' said Dalgleish with a ghastly smile; he gave orders for topgallants and royals in spite of the wounded mast, and took the wheel himself, luffing up as close as ever she would lie and then easing off a trifle. He loved the *Diligence* and he knew her through and through; he called for all that she could give, and she answered superbly. But once the breeze had steadied and the chase had settled down to this new phase it was apparent that she could not possibly outsail the schooners on the wind: nor could she put before it now, since the change had set the privateers to leeward before ever they left the merchantman. They were coming up hand over fist, making a good seven knots to the packet's six; and by about noon the chase must end in a trial of force. The mails had already been brought on deck, and there they lay, three long, thin leather portmanteaux, each lashed to two pigs of iron so that they would sink when they were heaved overboard at the last moment.

Hour after hour they ran over the grey heaving sea. Heavy cloud gathered in the west, obscuring the whole horizon; both swell and wind increased, and many and many a time the hands glanced up at the fished topmast. In spite of the strong woolding they saw the hideous cleft gape and close on the heavier rolls. The bosun clapped on more bands, but even so Dalgleish could not tack against a head-sea to get more to windward of the schooners, not with a mast so wounded; and wearing would deliver him right into their hands.

'I will leave the glory-side to you, sir,' he said to Jack, his eye fixed on the maintop-sail's weather-leech. 'Once they open fire I mean to bear up sharp and steer between them.' There was a savage look on his grey, lined, hairy face as he added, 'We will touch them up handsome, if it is the last thing we do.'

Jack nodded: it was the only course open to them, short of striking, and although the probability of success in broad daylight was almost infinitely remote it was better than a tame surrender: anything was better than that.

Methodically he and Humphreys and their small party cast loose the carronades on the larboard side, fired them off and reloaded: Jack loved a clean, heated gun with fresh powder in it. He fired the last, and as it leapt in on the recoil a great howling roar from aft made him jerk round. Men were capering about the deck, clawing one another on the back, bawling and cheering. Someone let go the maincourse bowline with a run. The *Diligence* paid off and the *Liberty* appeared broad on the beam; her foremast was gone, broken off short at the partners, and together with its vast spread of sail it was lying over her starboard bow. As he looked her maintopmast followed it, and the schooner shot up into the wind, her slack mainsail beating madly.

But here was Dalgleish's furious voice, damning them all for lubbers, roaring 'Royal halliards, royal halliards, let fly! Tom and Joe, round in those fucking weather braces. Clew up, there, forward. Bunt-lines, bunt-lines, you poxed set of whoreson sods. Start them, Mr Harvey. Kick the buggers, oh! You, Joe, will you start that bloody sheet before I break your head?'

A wild turmoil, in which Jack received two kicks and one blow from a rope's end — the first since his voice had broken — and the *Diligence* was under plain sail, the strain on her wounded mast reduced, order restored. Mr Dalgleish handed over the wheel, and he and Jack inspected the *Liberty* at their leisure: she had run straight on to ice with all her force, impaling herself and, since she was already very much by the head, apparently shearing away her stem below the waterline. Her people were trying to get her boats over the side, and the other schooner was standing towards her, directly away from the packet, losing an hour's gain in five minutes.

After another board northwards the packet put before the wind and the schooners dropped astern. 'Will the single vessel continue to pursue us, do you think?' asked Stephen.

'No, sir,' said Dalgleish, yawning. 'You can go to your cot and sleep easy: I am sure I shall. She will cram all Mr Henry's men aboard, if she possibly can — look at the vast number of them going across, for God's sake — there is a silly bugger has thrown himself into the sea, ha, ha, ha! It is as good as a play. Then she will go home. And a weary time they will have of it, beating to the eastward day and night; they will be eating their belts and their shoes before they see Marblehead again, with all those hands aboard, and no stores saved out of the *Liberty*.'

'There is something in the misfortunes

of others that does not altogether displease us,' said Stephen, but nobody heard him in the general cry of 'There she goes' as the now distant *Liberty* slipped beneath the grey surface of the ocean.

'No, sir,' said Mr Dalgleish again, 'you can sleep easy now. And so can Mrs — so can your betrothed, your financy. I forget the lady's name. I hope she has not been disturbed by all the banging and calling out.'

'I doubt it,' said Stephen, 'but I will go down and see.'

He was mistaken. Diana was very much disturbed indeed. The first discharge of artillery had wiped out her already waning seasickness; she had misinterpreted the later gunfire and the uproar on deck, and Stephen found her dressed, sitting on a locker with a cocked pistol in either hand, looking as fierce as a wild cat in a trap.

'Put those pistols down at once,' he said coldly. 'Do not you know it is very rude to point a pistol at a person you do not mean to kill? For shame, Villiers. Where were you brought up?'

'I beg your pardon,' she said, quite daunted by his severity. 'I thought there was an action — that they had boarded.'

'Not at all, not at all. The most inveterate privateer, the *Liberty*, has undone herself entirely; she ran upon ice and sank not five minutes since; and the other, loaded like Noah's ark, is going home. Give you joy of your escape, my dear. You are looking better, I find,' he said, taking her pulse. 'Yes: you are far better. Should you like to take some fresh air, and see the discomfiture of our enemies?'

Stephen led her on deck, a deck still full of wild hilarity — no sense of hierarchy at all — and her appearance was greeted with a spontaneous, friendly cheer. Busy hands supported her to the rail, pointed out the distant schooner, now standing west; tight against her elbow the cook gave her a detailed account of the movements since sunrise in a hoarse whisper, almost drowned by the explanations of the two mates and a little stunted boy who wished her to know that he had foreseen it all from the start. Mr Dalgleish came up, took off his hat, and welcomed her with some ceremony: 'We are all very happy to see you on deck, ma'am,' he said, 'and hope we may be so honoured every day for the rest of the passage, when fine. Not that there will be so many days, if this wind holds true: those villains pushed us east so fast and far, I should not be surprised to raise

Rockall on Wednesday.' And seeing that Rockall meant nothing to her he said, 'I should not be surprised if we were to make the quickest passage ever known, bar *Clytie*'s in ninety-four. And how glad they will be to see us, ma'am, with the news we bring. I fairly laughed aloud when first I heard the *Shannon* had took the *Chesapeake*.'

Chapter Four

Having sent up the new topmast at last, the *Diligence* headed south and west with as fair and sweet a breeze as a sailor could pray for; it came in over her starboard quarter, often bringing rain, but always steady and strong, as constant as the Trades day after day; and although strictly it was a topgallant breeze, Mr Dalgleish spread his royals as well at the least slackening, for he was determined not to lose a yard of its thrust. In spite of their lying-to on the Banks there was every likelihood of their making an extraordinarily rapid passage, the privateers having pushed them eastwards so fast and far; he was perfectly convinced that the *Diligence* must be a very great way ahead of the dull-sailing *Nova Scotia* on her southern route — that they would be the first home — and like every soul aboard he was bursting to tell the news.

The wind held true; Dalgleish cracked on; the packet logged 269 sea-miles from one noon to the next; on the seventeenth day out of Halifax they struck soundings; and in the chops of the Channel he told his news to a homeward-bound Guineaman, bawling '*Shannon* has taken *Chesapeake*' through the driving western rain as he passed to windward, leaving her cheering like a ship of fools. He told it to a Cornish pilchard-boat and a pilot-cutter off the Dodman, to a frigate near the Eddystone, and to some others, mostly outward-bound.

By all sound reasoning the news, if it had reached England at all, should have been confined to the south-western tip of that damp island; and in any case the *Diligence*, racing up the Channel with a screeching south-wester and a following tide for the last stretch to Portsmouth, should certainly have outpaced it. But not at all. She was standing in with the signal for dispatches flying, Haslar on her larboard bow, Southsea Castle on her starboard beam, when the Admiral's barge, double-banked and pulling hard, came out to meet her. 'Is it true?' cried the flag-lieutenant.

'Yes it is,' answered Humphreys, one foot already on the quarterladder, the dispatch buttoned into his bosom. The barge rounded to, he made a spring, lost his hat in the breeze, landed asprawl, and was borne off laughing to the post-chaise and four that was to whirl him up to the Admiralty at ten miles an hour — a post-chaise hastily adorned with oak-branches, laurel having been in short supply since the beginning of the American war, for want of demand.

Yet even now that the news was public the packet did not moor in any atmosphere of anticlimax: the rumour's confirmation rather served to heighten the excitement, to strengthen the furious desire to know every detail. The passengers had to endure the eager questioning, though not the inspection, of the customs officers; and when at last they came ashore they were surrounded by people who begged to be told how, where, and when. The streets were crowded; work was at a stand, with all Portsmouth hurrying out of doors; and on the Common Hard liberty-men and dockyard mateys were already piling up the material for an enormous bonfire. Shopkeepers and their apprentices pushed through the mob to add crates, barrels, and strange offerings such as a three-legged sofa and a one-wheeled gig to the heap; there was cheering in every public-house — it was as though Portsmouth had just heard the news of a great fleet-action, a victorious fleet-action.

It was of course a measure of the country's profound dismay, of its painful astonishment, frustration and resentment at the series of defeats inflicted by the Americans, and perhaps of its love for the Royal Navy; yet even so Jack found it somewhat excessive. For one thing, it delayed him in the tedious round of formalities that he had to make before he was his own master: he was all alive with a lover's desire to see his wife, he longed to be in his own house and to see his children and his horses, and these obstacles brought a superficial annoyance over his deep happiness. The spirit of contradiction formed no great part of his character, but what there was of it came to life as he shouldered his way along to the port-admiral's office: the sailors might bawl and roar as much as ever they pleased — they knew what such a battle meant — but the triumphant civilians did not please him, nor did their shouting about the 'Yankees — we'll thump them again and again.' As he passed the Blue Posts a band of excited girls obliged him to step into the gutter, and there he found himself face to face with a pawnbroker by the name of Abse, a greasy acquaintance from very early days, when first Mr Midshipman Aubrey had anything worth pawning. Abse had scarcely changed; still the same pendulous cheeks like ill-shaved Bath chaps, still the same bulbous nose; and now both cheeks and nose had an unnatural purple flush. He recognized his old customer at once and cried 'Captain, have you heard the news? The *Shannon* has taken the *Chesapeake*!' They were borne past one another, but Jack still heard him call out 'We'll thump them again and again!'

By the time he came out of the office, having reported himself and having recounted the action in detail for the hundredth time, the bonfire was blazing high and the general din of rejoicing had grown louder still. 'I did not mind the hullaballoo in Halifax,' he reflected. 'Indeed, I enjoyed it — I thought it natural: right and proper. But then they were on the spot; they suffered from the Americans; their ships were taken; and they actually saw the *Shannon* and the *Chesapeake*.' It also occurred to him that when first he went ashore in Halifax he had not missed his dinner: now in the extreme excitement of reaching land, of telling the glorious news, and of seeing his sweetheart again (a Gosport woman), the packet's cook had completely lost his head. There had been no dinner, and Jack's empty stomach cleaved to his backbone: the case was altered. He made his way across the road to the Crown and called for bread and cheese and a quart of beer. 'And harkee,' he said to the waiter, 'send a sharp boy round to Davis's for a horse, a weight-carrying horse. He is to say it is for Captain Aubrey, and if he is here before I have finished my beer he shall have half a crown. There is not a moment to lose.'

No common boy could have earned the half-crown, the crowd being so thick and Captain Aubrey's thirst for beer so great — his first honest English stingo for a long, long while — but the Crown's boy, fed on heel-taps and nips of gin and what he could pick up, was preternaturally sharp, though wizened. He brought Davis's big mare by back ways, leapt the gate into Parker's Close and the other gate out of it, at infinite peril, left the huge snorting beast staring in the stable-yard and walked casually in to announce its presence just as Jack raised his tankard for the last time.

'You will excuse me, gentlemen,' said Jack to the group of officers who had already gathered round him, 'I have despatches for home, and must not linger.'

Davis's mare had carried a good many heavy sea-officers in a hurry — the task had aged her before her time, spoiling her temper entirely — but none so heavy nor so urgent as Captain Aubrey, and by the time they had climbed Portsdown Hill she was thoroughly discontented; her ears were braced hard aft, there was a nasty look in her eye, and she was sweating profusely. He paused for a moment to let her draw breath while he admired the telegraph, its arms whirling twenty to the dozen, no doubt sending further details of the victory along the chain to London. The mare chose this moment to get rid of him by a surprisingly nimble caper in a creature of her size, a frisk, a twist, and a lively imitation of the rocking-horse; but although Jack was not an elegant horseman he was a determined one. The enormous pressure of his knees drove most of the breath and some of the wickedness out of her; her iron mouth yielded to his ever stronger heave; she returned to her duty, and he rode her hard over the green down. Then, turning right-handed from the high-road, he galloped her along grassy lanes, the short-cuts he knew so well. Up hill and down dale, until on the last rise he came to his own land, his own plantations — how the trees had shot up! — and on through Delderwood, that lovely copse, on by Kimber's new road, where the mare nearly stumbled, on, holding her hard, past raw mine-workings, a tall, gaunt chimney, stark buildings, all uninhabited. But he had no eyes for them as he flew along, guiding his horse as instinctively as he would have steered a cutter through an intricate tide-way: for there, through a gap in the trees, was the roof of his house, and his heart was pounding like a boy's.

He had approached Ashgrove Cottage from the back, the quickest way, and now he rode into the broad stable-yard, unfinished when he had left it but now already quite mature, established, and even elegant with its clock-tower over the coach-house, its rosy brick, its rows of whitewashed boxes, and its archway leading into the garden. As he reined in a quick glance all round showed the same pleasant mellowing on every hand: the new wings (the reward of a successful campaign in the Mascarenes and the recapture of several East-Indiamen) that had transformed the cottage into a fair-sized country house now merged with the older building; the creepers that he had planted as miserable straggling wisps now made a brave show above the lower windows; and his apples topped the orchard wall. Yet everything was as still and silent as a dream. No horses' heads peered out of the half-doors — in any case, the half-doors were all shut — and no groom, no living soul moved about the spotless yard nor yet behind the shining windows of the house: not a sound but for a distant cuckoo, changing his tune far beyond the apple-trees. For a moment a strange premonition checked his joy, a hint of another world in which he did not belong; but then the stable clock gave a click and a whirr as it prepared to strike the quarter. There was life here, and he was sitting on a horse in a muck-sweat that must be looked to at once. He raised his voice and hailed the house: 'Ahoy, there!' the echo came back from Delderwood, 'Ahoy, there,' faint but clear.

Again the strangest pause, as though either he or this visible world were an illusion: his look of excitement and happiness faded, and he was just about to dismount when two little girls, with a small fat boy between them, marched past the archway in file, carrying flags and crying 'Wilkes and liberty, huzzay, huzzay. Right wheel, huzza, huzza.'

They were long-legged girls with ringlets, quite remarkably pretty; but Jack's loving eye could still make out traces of the turnip-faced, sparse-haired, stumpy little creatures he had left, his twin daughters: they were still remarkably alike, but the slightly taller one, the leader, was almost certainly Charlotte; and in all likelihood the fat boy was his son George, last seen as a pink baby, much the same as all others. His heart gave him a most unaccustomed wring and he called out 'Hey, there.'

It was an entirely one-sided wave of affection, however. Charlotte only glanced round and cried 'Come back tomorrow. They are all gone to Pompey,' and continued her pompous, fanatical march, followed by the others, all chanting 'Wilkes and liberty.'

He slipped from his horse and tried several boxes, all of them swept clean, scrubbed and bare, until he found one in use; there he unsaddled the mare, rubbed her down and covered her with a rug. The clock struck the quarter, and he walked across the yard, into the house through the kitchen door, through the empty kitchen with its gleaming copper pans, and into the white corridor beyond. In the silence, the clean, light-filled silence, he hardly liked to call, although the house was so familiar, so intimately well known that his hand found the doorknobs of itself: he was not an imaginative man, yet it was as though he had returned from the dead only to find still, sunlit death waiting for him. He looked into the dining-room: silence there, no more. The breakfast-room: neatness, clarity, no sound, no movement at all: automatically his eye glanced at the regulator, the austere clock by which he checked his astronomical observations. It had stopped. His own room, and there was Sophie sitting at his desk with a sea of papers in front of her; and in the second before she looked up from her sum he saw that her face was sad, worried, thinner than before.

Radiant joy, a delight as great as his own — innumerable questions, almost all unanswered, incoherent fragmentary accounts on either side, interrupted by kisses, exclamations, enraptured or amazed. 'And is it true?' she cried as she led him into the kitchen, for somehow it had become apparent that he had not dined. 'Oh, Jack, I am so glad to have you home.'

'Is what true, sweetheart?' said he, sitting at the white-scrubbed table and looking eagerly at the ham.

'That the *Shannon* took the *Chesapeake*.

There was a rumour this morning — the postman stopped to repeat it — and Bonden and Killick begged to go to Portsmouth; so I let them take the cart, with the others. I wonder they are not back yet: they have been gone for hours.'

'Yes, perfectly true, thank God. That is what I was trying to tell you. Stephen and Diana and I were aboard — as neat an action as you could wish, fifteen minutes from the first gun to the last — and we all came home in the packet together. Such a passage, once we had got rid of the privateers! Is there any more bread, my love?'

'Dear Stephen,' cried Sophie, 'how is he? Why is he not here? Do eat some more ham, my darling. You are dreadfully thin. I am so sorry there was none of the pasty left: the children ate it up for supper. Where is he?'

'He is still in Portsmouth, but he is to post up to town tomorrow, and he may look in. There was some difficulty about Diana, about her nationality, and she is not to move until they hear from the Secretary of State's office. She is staying with the Fortescues; and Fortescue, Stephen and I have gone bail in five thousand apiece that she don't wander off. Not that she will. She and Stephen are to be married at last.'

'Married?' cried Sophie.

'Yes. I was astonished too. The first I heard of it was when he asked Philip Broke to perform the ceremony — a captain can marry people, you know, aboard his own ship — and although Broke could not very well do so that day, seeing that *Chesapeake* was standing out of Nantasket roads, I know he would have done so after the action, if he had not been so badly wounded he could not even write his own dispatch. Yes, they are to be married, and perhaps it is all for the best: he has longed for her these many, many years. And certainly she behaved very well during our escape and then after the action — a rare plucked 'un, upon my word. Diana has never wanted for spirit; and I shall always be grateful to her for having sent you news of the *Leopard*.'

'So shall I,' said Sophie. 'And I shall call on her first thing tomorrow. Dear Diana: how I hope they will be happy.' She spoke with real feeling, and if Jack had reflected he would have applauded her heart's victory over what might be called her moral judgement or perhaps her principles: Sophie belonged to a quiet, staid, provincial family untouched by scandal of an amorous nature as far as it could trace its origins, a family that had been rigidly Puritan in Cromwell's time and that even now regarded the least irregularity with extreme abhorrence. In spite of her mother's upbringing she was too kind and too good-natured to be a prude; but on the other hand she had not the least intuitive understanding or sympathy for those who strayed on to the wilder shores of love — in its physical aspects even the domesticated strand was of no great interest to her — and Diana's irregularities had not been of the least, far from it. They had excited comment even in the very liberal society of London, where she had maintained a certain position only by her beauty, her spirit, and the friendship of some of the Prince of Wales's circle. But Jack did not reflect; his mind, in its delightful whirl, had caught up on the mention of Bonden, his former coxswain, and of Killick, his steward. He said, 'How in God's — how on earth did Bonden and Killick come here?'

'Captain Kerr sent them with a very polite note. He said since he was to have *Acasta* instead of you, it was but fair you should have your own people for your next command.'

'That was handsome in Robert Kerr, upon my word, very handsome indeed. My next command . . . ha, ha, Sophie. I tell you what — before I go to sea again, I shall fill the house with clocks. There is no life in a room, without there is a clock ticking away in it. There are some that go a twelve-month without winding.'

'Your next command,' began Sophie: but she knew she must not go on to wish that he might never have a next command, that he might never, never go away from home again, nor be exposed to storms, battles, shipwrecks or imprisonment; she knew that an implied condition of their marriage was that she should sit there waiting while he was exposed to all these things; so she ended, 'but I hope, dear Jack, that the clocks will not have to go a year, not a whole year. I am so sorry about the regulator: Charlotte's dormouse got into it, and is having babies.'

'Oh, as for a ship,' said Jack, 'I am in no great hurry unless they offer me *Belvidera* or *Egyptienne* on the North American station. What I hope for is one of the new twenty-four pounder frigates now building; and I do not think it would be asking too much — after all, it is not every day a fourth-rate sinks a seventy-four. That would give me some months ashore, seeing that she is ordered just to my liking and dealing with things at home.' A cloud came over their happiness, for *things at home* must necessarily include the wretched Mr Kimber: they understood one another perfectly, however; Kimber might mean endless complications and perhaps very heavy financial loss, but for the present Charlotte's dormouse was more important by far. He went on, 'Yet my time in frigates is pretty well over. A ship of the line is much more likely, and I shall be in no hurry for that.'

There was so much to say, so many crossed letters to disentangle, such news of the jasmin and the wonderful success of the espaliered apricot-tree, that after a while they lapsed into a delighted silence, holding hands over the kitchen-table like a pair of simpletons, looking at one another with infinite pleasure. Through this silence came the sound of Wilkes and liberty, often repeated and coming nearer. 'That is the children,' said Sophie.

'Yes,' said Jack, 'I saw them marching about like thrones and dominions. But what are they at?'

'They are playing Westminster elections. Your father is standing.' She hesitated for a moment and added apologetically, 'In the Radical interest.'

'Good God!' cried Jack. General Aubrey's snipe-like political career, now seeking to expose corruption, now to participate in it, had often carried him into opposition to Government, but never so far as this. Ever since the General had first been returned for the rotten borough of Gripe, the property of a friend, he had contrived to be a Tory when the First Lord of the Admiralty was a Whig, and some one of the many varieties of Whig when the First Lord was a Tory. The General, a man of demoniac energy that increased with age, with an unquenchable flow of soldierly, unpolished eloquence in the House, had been a thorn in the ministry's side as an opponent and a cruel embarrassment as a supporter. His occasional efforts at helping his son by political influence had always been ill-judged and sometimes nearly disastrous; it is true that the General rarely thought of him, but even so Jack would have reached post rank far earlier if it had not been for his father.

'Shall I call them in?' asked Sophie.

'Yes, do, my dear,' said Jack. 'I should like to make George's acquaintance.'

'Children,' called Sophie, dreading a want of recognition, 'come in and bid your father welcome home. He is come back from America.'

For all her precautions, they stared at him without the least knowledge and looked about the room for some other, more recognizable man: for a moment it was exquisitely painful, but then they remembered their manners, advanced gravely side by side, curtsied, and said 'Good afternoon, sir. Welcome home,' with a quick glance at their mother to see if that were adequate.

'George,' she murmured, 'where is your leg?'

The little boy blushed and hung his head, but gathering his courage he came forward from the door, made a jerky bow, and holding out his hand said, 'I hope I see you well, sir.'

'Welcome home,' whispered his sisters.

'Welcome home,' said George, staring with all his might, and then, with no transition, 'They will be here directly. I heard the cart in the lane. If the news is true, Bonden has promised to bring me an iron hoop. An *iron* hoop, sir!'

'I dare say you will get it, George,' said his father, smiling.

Charlotte, feeling that the silence which followed might be painful, said politely,

'Grandpapa was here the other day with Sir Francis Burdett, and he explained to us about the Westminster election and Wilkes and liberty. We have been voting for him ever since. Don't you wish he may get in?'

'Children, children,' said Sophie, 'you must change your shoes and wash your hands and faces. Fanny and Charlotte, put on clean pinafores. We are going to sit in the drawing-room.'

'Yes, Mama,' they cried, but at this moment the cart could be heard coming into the stable-yard and they rushed out in a body. A few seconds later they rushed back, cried 'It's true! There has been a famous victory! *Shannon* has taken *Chesapeake*! Huzzay, huzzay!' and vanished. They could be heard shouting barbarously, their piercing voices high above the men's deep rumble; and Jack noticed that in the yard they used the broad accent and the broader expressions of the lower deck. Fanny referred to Bonden as 'a goddam swab', but cheerfully, without the least injurious intent; and Charlotte was heard to say that 'although Worlidge was as drunk as Davy's sow, any crew of grass-combing b—s could have harnessed the pony better than that.' True enough: of the four men that made up the household at

Ashgrove Cottage, three had been bred to the sea from childhood — they knew nothing of horses; and although the fourth, the weak-headed Worlidge, had been a farmer's boy before the press-gang caught him twenty years ago, he was lying speechless in the bottom of the cart, incapable of moving a finger since before they started back. The others, faced with the mute, immobile, paralytic Worlidge and the loss of the collar had seized the pony to the shafts in a most seamanlike manner; there was not the least possibility of its coming adrift; but since the running bowline round the creature's neck choked it every time it advanced, they had been obliged to push the cart all the way from the Hand and Racquet, where they had celebrated the victory.

However, the exercise had sweated them sober, or at least sober enough to meet the not very exacting naval standards; and when Bonden (the strongest head of all) reported to the drawing-room for orders, his happiness owed little to dog's nose, flip, or raspberry shrub. He gave his captain joy of his return and joy of the victory, and listened with keen attention to Jack's account of the battle, following every move with total understanding. 'If it had not been for poor Captain Broke,' he said, 'it would have been perfect. I served under him in the old *Druid*, and he was a rare one for the great guns even then. Will he recover, sir?'

'I hope so, Bonden, I am sure,' said Jack, shaking his head at the recollection of that shocking wound. 'But the Doctor will be able to tell you better than I can. He may look in tomorrow, so let his room be priddied to the nines, in case he stays; and then just step round to Mr Kimber with my compliments, and I should be glad to see him early in the morning, before I set off.'

'Aye aye, sir,' said Bonden. 'The Doctor's room it is, and Mr Kimber to report immediately after breakfast.'

'Before you set off, my dear?' cried Sophie, the moment the door had closed behind him. 'But surely you do not have to go to the Admiralty at once? Surely the Admiral gave you leave?'

'Oh yes, he was most obliging — did everything that was proper — and he sent you his love. No: it is not the Admiralty I am worrying about, it is Louisa Broke. She must be told how her husband is as soon as possible, and if I travel up early tomorrow, I can take the Harwich Flyer there and back, and be home on Friday.'

'A letter, an express letter, would do just as well — you are so tired, dear Jack, and as thin as a rail — you must have some rest, and four and twenty hours in a stage-coach would quite knock you up, to say nothing of the ride to town — and anyhow as you told Bonden you cannot say anything about poor Broke's wound — an express letter, with every sort of good wish and comfort and Stephen's opinion — that would be far better in every way.'

'Sophie, Sophie,' he said, smiling at her: in her heart she was obliged to admit that in the service it was usual for men to travel great distances to comfort their shipmates' families, and that several times she had been most infinitely relieved by such kindness — only a few months ago the first lieutenant of the *Java* had come from Plymouth to assure her that she still possessed a husband; but even so she could not help rebelling against this sudden flying off. She muttered 'Louisa Broke' in a discontented, somewhat jealous tone, and several fresh reasons occurred to her: she did not utter them, however, for there was something in Jack's eye, the set of his head, that convinced her they would be useless, however sound; and presently their perfect happiness came back. They wandered into the garden to look at particularly valuable plants, above all those nearest the original cottage, those they had planted themselves. Neither had much genius in that line, nor indeed much taste, and the survivors (a small proportion) stood about in stark, unrelated clumps; but these flowers, such as they were, were peculiarly their own, and they loved them dearly. When she had to go in to attend to the children he went in with her, and she heard his strong, familiar step as he moved about the house. Presently he reached the music-room, and her piano, rarely used but fortunately retuned for the girls' lessons, gave out a great series of crashing chords, rising and rising with a splendid gaiety before they dropped to a deep, meditative thunder that merged quietly into a Hummel sonata that Jack often played and that she herself had learnt long ago. Then he took his fiddle, a fiddle far above his station, an Amati no less, bought from the spoils of the Indian Ocean, and played the same piece again, transposed for the violin. He did not play well; it was long since he had had a fiddle in his hands and in any case the fingers of his injured arm had not yet recovered all their nimbleness, but it would have been all one to Sophie if he had been Paganini — the house was alive again: it was fully inhabited.

She had been right about Jack's immovable determination, however: he and Stephen stepped into their post-chaise immediately after dinner next day and bowled away as fast as four horses would draw them, lurching and rumbling over the side-road from Ashgrove Cottage.

'I should not really be travelling in this style,' observed Jack, when they reached the highway and conversation was possible again. 'The common coach is more my line; or even the waggon.'

'You refer to Kimber, I make no doubt?' said Stephen.

'Not exactly. Kimber did not choose to come: he was just leaving for Birmingham, he said. But he sent a gang of what he called new associates in our venture, and rum cullies they were, some of them. A couple of little attornies in dirty neck-cloths, who kept taking notes . . .'

'Tell me, brother, are things very bad?'

'Well, the only thing that is clear is that Kimber has exceeded my instructions a thousand times over, with enormous workings, deep-shaft mining, and all sorts of machinery; and the association, as they call it, has taken interests in other concerns, including a navigation canal.'

'The canal alone was wanting,' said Stephen to himself. 'Now, apart from perpetual motion and the philosopher's stone, the picture is complete.'

'. . . and it is an odd thing,' continued Jack, 'on the one hand they say the losses and the debts are enormous — one fellow showed me a sum that was roughly twice what I possess, though he admitted it was only an estimate — and on the other they urge me to press on. Dig just a little deeper, they say, and turn a dead loss into a princely fortune. But in either case they want fresh money, or fresh security; and I saw one of the attorney coves looking round the room pricing the furniture. You would have admired me, Stephen: I was as cool as a judge, and I let them talk. They were importunate to know my holdings in Government stock — asked me straight out, God damn their impertinence — and the nature of my marriage settlements, and what was Sophie's fortune, and what was my father's estate. That was coming it a little high — they must have thought they had a fine pigeon to pluck, a fellow that had no notion of business and that could be persuaded or frightened into any kind of ruinous foolishness. But I cut them short, said I did not mean to put down another penny, and wished them good day. Lord, Stephen, there are advantages in growing older. Ten years ago, even five years ago, they would have ended in the horse-pond, and I should have had a suit for assault and battery on my hands, as well as all the rest.'

'How did they respond to this?'

'They made a good deal of noise, some hectoring, some conciliating — carrot and stick, rope's end and soft soap. They did not expect a gentleman to withdraw from his undertakings — it was useless to attempt to do so in any case, as they had a lien upon my property — in my absence the association had been obliged to take up money at an exorbitant rate of interest — they had every right to pledge my credit — Kimber had delegated his full powers to them — ready money would have been far cheaper than discounting bills, but unfortunately Mrs Aubrey had not seen fit to produce it — they meant no criticism: ladies could not be expected to understand business — the only way to proceed was to push on, to satisfy the more pressing creditors, to raise fresh capital, and push on. Now that I was back everything would be easy: they could find fresh capital on the security of my name alone — my signature, a mere formality. If I declined they would most reluctantly be compelled to take measures to safeguard their own interests.' A pause. 'God knows how I shall come out of it,' he said. 'It looks precious like a lee-shore to me.'

They changed horses at Petersfield, and as the chaise ran clear of the town Jack said, 'Lord, Stephen, I am so glad Sophie clapped down when she did. The moment she found Kimber was playing fast and loose she wrote and told him to stop, and from that moment on she refused to sign anything or to give him any money. And when things grew worse, she laid up the carriage, sold off the horses, and told the servants to look about for new places, all but Dray and Worlidge, who have only one sound leg between them. There is still a good deal in the stocks and at Hoare's, if only I can contrive to hang on to it. I believe she has a better head for business than you or I. She was against it from the start, you know — against that fellow Kimber and his whole goddam scheme.'

Stephen might have observed that he too had been against the whole goddam scheme from the start — that it had seemed to him a typical snare laid for Jack ashore, or at least for the richer kind of officer — but he did not, and Jack went on, 'A good woman is a — there is something in the Bible I don't quite recall, but it hits the nail on the head, as you might put it.'

'I am sure you are right,' said Stephen. 'Tell me, what happened to Killick's wife, the one he bought in the market with a halter round her neck, when we were last in England?'

'Oh,' said Jack, laughing, 'she went off again with her first husband within a few days of our sailing — it appears they make quite a practice of it, going from market to market along the coast — and when Sophie's mother searched her box she found all poor Killick's property, as well as a couple of our silver plates. I should never have allowed the rummaging if I had been at home, but I am just as pleased now: I value those plates.'

'Mrs Williams is now exercising her ministry in Ulster, I believe.'

'Yes, thank God: she is looking after Frances while she has her baby. It would have been the very devil if she had been here while Sophie was cutting down the establishment.'

‘I am afraid it has deprived her of a very real enjoyment,’ said Stephen, remembering Mrs Williams’ delight in economy, her triumphant saving of a candle-end, and her profound pound-foolishness.

Jack began, ‘Mrs Williams,’ in a strong voice, thought better of whatever he had been going to say, coughed, felt in the pocket of the chaise for a parcel wrapped in a napkin, and said, ‘Have one of these. Sophie made them, and I had to promise they should all be ate. She will never be happy until I am as fat as the Durham ox.’

They finished the sandwiches a little after Guildford, when dusk was falling; and Jack, having shaken the napkin out of the window, folded it up and said, ‘I believe I shall take a caulk.’ He composed himself in his corner; his chin dropped on to his chest; and as quickly, as definitively, as the setting of the tropical sun, he went to sleep. It was a gift common to most seamen, the result of many, many years of keeping watch; and Stephen, an insomniac, watched him enviously. The hedges sped by, growing dimmer; cottages, haystacks, villages; the Portsmouth coach, its lights already blazing and the guard tooting away on his horn; Jack slept on. He slept even through the next change of horses, and it was only when they were crossing Putney Heath that he sat up and said 'What is a garnishee?'

'A garnishee?' said Stephen, and considered for a while. 'Sure, it is a legal term; but what it signifies I cannot tell. I know nothing of the law, except that whenever a plain man comes into contact with it, he is likely to suffer extremely in his purse and spirit, however sound his cause: so I do conjure you, my dear, to take the very best advice you can, and at once. This is no time for half-measures, no time for your provincial lawyers. You must fee the finest talent in London; you must armour yourself with the highly-trained intelligence of an eminent counsellor, accustomed to meeting these scoundrels on their own devious ground, another Grotius, a second Pufendorf.'

'Yes, but where am I to find my second Pufendorf?'

'Where indeed? But at least I know a discreet intelligent person in town, a gentleman perfectly conversant with the reputation of those most in view, perfectly qualified to point out the shrewdest legal talent. Will I ask him?'

'That would be very kind, Stephen, if it don't put you out.'

It did not put Stephen out by so much as a yard: his whole purpose in going to London was to carry the spoils of Boston to his chief, Sir Joseph Blaine, the discreet intelligent person to whom he had referred. These spoils, these papers, he carried with him, wrapped in sailcloth; and since he had once left secret documents in a hackney-coach, he now took a chair, where he was obliged to hold the packet on his knee: it had cost him pains enough.

The chairmen carried him through the drizzle and the sparse, umbrella'd streets, past several transparencies of the victory, already much the worse for wear, though their guttering lights still showed a recognizable pair of ships, labelled *Shannon* and *Chesapeake* in enormous letters, together with as much in the way of wit or verse as space or invention would allow. They stopped at a discreet small house behind Shepherd Market; the leader thundered on the door, and there was Sir Joseph himself, holding a candle. 'My dear Maturin,' he cried, looking attentively at the packet as he brought Stephen into the hall, 'this is a delightful surprise. Welcome home at last!'

They walked upstairs to the library, a thoroughly comfortable bachelor's room — Turkey carpet, very easy chairs, a great many handsomely-bound books, mostly on entomology, some unusually accomplished erotic pictures and bronzes, a fire winking in the brass fender, a green-shaded lamp. 'I must beg your pardon for asking to come here, sir,' said Stephen, 'but I have been away so long that I no longer know how things stand at the Admiralty: I collected that there had been changes, so I thought it better there should be no possibility of misunderstanding or delay.'

'Not at all, not at all. Nothing could give me more pleasure. I ordered a fire as soon as ever your message came through; you always were a chilly mortal — pray pull your chair a little closer. No, I do assure you, I take it most friendly; and as you say, there have been changes at the Admiralty. Poor Warren is no longer with us — but that you knew before the *Leopard* sailed. Oh, what a stroke that was, Maturin! My congratulations did reach you at last, I believe?'

'In Java itself: you were too kind, too kind entirely.'

'There for once we must disagree: it was the completest thing in my experience — a model of its kind. And then Admiral Sievewright has gone, together with some others; but then again there are half a dozen new faces, very able young men, some of them; and we have a new second secretary, Mr Wray, from the Treasury. Or more precisely an acting second secretary, though I have little doubt he will be confirmed unless poor Barrow makes a most unexpected recovery. He is a man with a wonderful grasp of detail and a very great deal of energy. I wish I had half as much. He works harder than any of us, and yet he finds time to lead a very active social life: I never go anywhere without I see him. Perhaps you have met Mr Wray, Mr Edmund Wray?'

Stephen had met Mr Wray, but on a somewhat unfortunate occasion, when Jack Aubrey had accused the gentleman, in only very slightly veiled terms, of cheating at cards: Wray had not seen fit to ask for the usual explanation — perhaps he considered the veil sufficiently obscure — and with Jack's long absence the affair had blown over. But this scarcely seemed the time to elaborate on the acquaintance, particularly as Stephen was aware that Sir Joseph had not the slightest interest in the matter; his bright, knowing eye was fixed upon the sailcloth parcel.

'These I acquired in Boston,' said Stephen, unwrapping it at last. 'On the first sheet you will find a succinct account of the manner in which they came into my possession, and on the next a summary of their contents. Most are only of local significance, and Major Beck in Halifax has already dealt with them; but I flatter myself that some are of wider, more general importance.'

Sir Joseph put on his spectacles and sat at the library table, the lamp by his side. 'My God,' he cried, after a moment, 'these are Johnson's private papers.'

'Just so,' said Stephen. He got up and stood with his back to the fire, his coat-tails hitched forward, so that his meagre hams should grow really warm, and he contemplated Sir Joseph, intent on his reading in that silent room, wholly concentrated in that disk of light, tearing the heart out of the matter with an almost shocking eagerness. There was not a sound but the turning of sheets, and an occasional low exclamation: 'Ah, the dog . . . the cunning dog . . .' After a while Stephen turned to the bookshelves: Malpighi, Swammerdam, Ray, Réaumur, Brisson, the most recent Frenchmen, including the elder Cuvier's latest essay, which he had not yet seen. He read the first chapters, sitting on the arm of his chair, and then moved over to Sir Joseph's cabinet to find the insect in question. Drawer after drawer filled with creatures, lovingly killed, pinned down and labelled: in the second drawer he saw that great rarity a true gynandromorph, a Clouded Yellow, male one side, female the other, and beneath its scientific name he read *The Gift of my esteemed Friend Dr P. H.* Those were the letters he had been using for departmental communications at the time he gave Blaine the butterfly: Sir Joseph was always prepared for the unexpected, and no one but himself could decipher the initials appended to so many of the specimens throughout the great collection, particularly to the more exotic beetles, some of which Stephen recognized as coming from Java, the Celebes, India, Ceylon, and Arabia Felix, no doubt the gift of far-flung agents, all as nameless to him as he was to them. He found his insect, an ill-looking weevil, and returned to the text, tipping the book and the case so that they came within the rim of light. Sir Joseph read on.

Stephen was deep in Cuvier's argument; it was persuasive, it was elegantly put, yet somewhere there was a fallacy: he turned back two pages, keeping his finger on the weevil's rostrum, but the references to the illustration were obscure. The error might perhaps have become evident if he had not had a long day's travelling, and if part of his mind was not so taken up with Diana. It was an ill-regulated mind and if it were not carefully watched it would mourn Diana's death, or at least the death of his infinitely cherished myth; a dark, bitter, monotonous grieving. Yet the mourning was not pure — it no longer invaded him entirely, perhaps because often and often, in the most unexpected ways, the old myth and the new reality tended to coincide. Perhaps, he reflected, this had a certain relationship to marriage: they had been together a very long time and although they might essentially be strangers they were inextricably entwined. Diana Villiers: he stared into the declining fire, and Cuvier receded, faded, became infinitely remote.

Sir Joseph gave a sigh, bringing Stephen back into that pleasant room: he put the papers back into their folder and came round the table. 'Dear Maturin,' he said, shaking him by the hand, 'I am at a loss. I used all my superlatives when I wrote to you about the *Leopard* coup, and now I can only say them over again. You have done magnificently, sir, magnificently. Yet I shudder, yes upon my word I literally shudder, when I think of the risks you ran, to bring these papers away.' His praise ran on, handsome, generous and sincere; and then, 'You do not in principle object to suppers, my dear sir? There is a bottle I should like to share, to celebrate your return, a bottle in fact nata mecum consule Buteo, the last I possess. How I wish it may have survived.'

It had survived, a noble port, and as they drank it after their buttered eggs and devilled bones and Stilton cheese, Sir Joseph tapped the folder. 'Mr Johnson must be an unusually interesting man,' he observed. 'These records show his progress from the gifted amateur to the professional; a most strikingly rapid progress, as though he and his colleagues had condensed generations of experience into a few years. To be sure, he was overreached by the Frenchmen, but that might happen to anyone; and his network in Canada does him great credit. What kind of a man is he?'

'He is fairly young, and he has a superabundance of mental energy and animal spirits. I think he would be called a good-looking man; certainly he has easy, genteel, insinuating manners, and although in fact I believe that love of power is by far and away his strongest characteristic, he does not present anything of the unamiable outward appearance of an ambitious, dominating, masterful creature. He was born to a very considerable fortune; and he has strong natural parts. I do not pretend to say that there is a necessary relation of cause and effect, but he is exceedingly impatient of contradiction or of anything that thwarts him; and since he is a clever, remarkably tenacious and determined man, and one who can draw on great private wealth when secret funds are inadequate or delayed, he is a dangerous opponent. I am persuaded, for example, that he hired two privateers to waylay our packet: I am persuaded that he offered them a very great reward for seizing us. They lay in the path of the sloop bearing the original dispatches; they let it pass. Yet they pursued us with an inveteracy that can only be explained by the prospect of enormous gain. It is true that in this case Johnson had an unusually powerful motive.'

'Yes,' said Sir Joseph: but whether he meant that he thoroughly understood Johnson's motive or whether it was no more than an ordinary civil assent there was no telling. He filled their glasses, gazed at the candle through his wine, chuckled, and said, 'Such a coup, by God: such a coup . . .'

'It *was* a lucky stroke,' said Stephen. 'That I will not deny: and although it was forced upon me by circumstances rather than by any real merit of my own, I am not sorry to finish my career with a success, however fortuitous.'

'Finish, Maturin?' cried Sir Joseph, in a startled voice. 'What can you mean by that?' Sir Joseph possessed all the qualities required to make an excellent chief of intelligence, but he had never had much sense of fun at any time, and his dismal, anxious trade had smothered what little there was in his original composition. He did not perceive that Stephen spoke with a certain levity, yielding to the temptation of rounding out a phrase, and he went on with great earnestness, 'Maturin, Maturin, how can you be so weak? In your remote exile you have been reading our bulletins and communiqués, intended for neutral and above all for Russian opinion, and you have come to the conclusion that the war is virtually over, that because Wellington has overrun so much of Spain that Napoleon is defeated, and that because we hold your beloved Catalonia your occupation is gone. But I must tell you that Spain, particularly

Mediterranean Spain and Catalonia, is very lightly held — a few battalions of invalids and Portuguese — and a French movement there, an incursion from the Roussillon behind Wellington's right flank, would cut his immensely extended lines of communication. No, no: even there the situation is perilous to a degree, to say nothing of the north. Wellington has to be supplied by sea — command of the sea is the absolutely crucial point — and consider our Channel squadron alone: here is Lord Keith's latest statement. *The enemy has twelve sail of the line besides the Jemmapes in perfect readiness for sea and fifteen frigates* — fifteen, Maturin — *besides smaller vessels; and the force at present under my orders numbers fourteen of the line, eight frigates, six sloops, two gunbrigs, one schooner and two hired cutters, eleven either in port or on their way to refit.* A third of them useless, the French all ready for action; and it is the same with all the other squadrons. As you see, a successful sortie by the French would leave Wellington hanging in the air, and completely change the face of the war: even as it is we have continual complaints from him about naval protection and supplies. No, no: I do assure you, Maturin, the war is in its most dangerous stage. We are at our last throw; we have no reserves left; and if Napoleon achieves a victory by land or sea I doubt we can ever recover it. You have been away a great while and perhaps you cannot fully appreciate the immense decline in this country's resources since you left. Taxes are as high as they can possibly be, perhaps even higher, and yet the money does not come in: we can scarcely fit out the fleet. Government's credit is very low. You could paper your room with Treasury bills, the discount on them is so shockingly great. Trade is almost at a standstill; gold is not to be had — paper money everywhere — and the City is deeply depressed. The City is morose, Maturin, morose!'

Stephen was indifferent to the City's mood, but otherwise he abounded in Sir Joseph's sense: he did not possess his chief's wealth of immediate, detailed information, but he had helped in the drawing-up of too many fallacious documents to have been deceived by much of what he had read, and he knew very well that the situation was critical, that the alliance against Buonaparte was fragile in the extreme, and that with both sides exhausted a single victory, well followed-up on the part of the French might mean a wholly disastrous end to the war and the establishment of tyranny for generations to come. Sir Joseph was preaching to the converted, and Stephen regretted his remark: he regretted it all the more because with the years Sir Joseph's tendency to prolixity had grown. He was being prolix now, about the Stock Exchange.

'I do not suppose,' he said, 'there are many things that men think about with such deep, careful, zealous attention as money, and the Stock Exchange is an infallible index of their thoughts, the collective thoughts of a large number of intelligent, informed men who have a great deal to lose and win. Even this Heaven-sent victory of yours, and Wellington's at Vitoria, have scarcely moved the City to anything more than bonfires and illuminations and patriotic addresses. These gentlemen know that we cannot go on alone much longer, and at the first stroke of ill-fortune our allies will desert us, as they have so often deserted us before. No, sir: if I were half as sanguine about Napoleon's downfall as you, I should go down into the City tomorrow and make my fortune.'

'How would you do that, for all love?'

'Why, I should buy Government stock, India stock, and any sound commercial shares whose value depends on foreign trade: I should buy them at their present dirt-cheap rate, and then as soon as Buonaparte was knocked on the head, or peace was declared, I should sell them at a perfectly enormous profit. Perfectly enormous, my dear sir. Any man with foreknowledge could do the same: any man who could command a considerable sum, or whose credit was good for a considerable sum, could make his fortune. It would be much like betting on a horse-race if you knew the winner in advance. That is how fortunes are made on the Stock Exchange; although I must confess that the issues concerned are rarely so great.'

'You astonish me,' said Stephen. 'I know nothing of these things.'

'I never supposed you did,' said Sir Joseph, smiling at him affectionately. 'Allow me to pour you a little wine. But, however,' he went on, 'I shall not make my fortune, alas, for the very good reason that I thoroughly agree with the gentlemen in the City: I believe they are perfectly right. Napoleon is still a very great commander, and although he got into a sad pickle in Moscow, he has astonishing powers of recovery. He has just shown us what he can do at Luetzen — Berlin is in the greatest peril at this very moment. I dread another of his sudden brilliant strokes, dividing the allies and destroying them piecemeal: he has done it again and again, and he still has something like a quarter of a million men in Germany, all living off the country; and fresh divisions are being trained in France. And in any case, his fleet is quite untouched. There they lie in the Scheldt and in Brest and Toulon — do you know, Maturin, that there are no less than one and twenty ships of the line and ten heavy frigates in Toulon alone? — beautiful, well-equipped, well-manned ships that we try to blockade with old worn-out squadrons, crazy with keeping the sea in all weathers right round the year. No, no, Maturin: take the Stock Exchange for your barometer, and rest assured that there is a great deal of work for us to do before Boney is brought down.'

'Then let us drink to his ultimate confusion,' said Stephen.

'Confusion to Boney,' said Blaine, savouring his port. After a moment he continued, 'Only a little while ago the First Lord and I were lamenting your absence most bitterly. Although the Mediterranean is your natural field, had you been here we should have begged you to accept a peculiarly suitable mission in the Baltic. There is an island there, a very strongly fortified island mounting a great number of heavy guns, that is held by a Catalan brigade in the French service, a remnant of the great Spanish garrisons that were placed all along the Pomeranian shore until the rising. They have been led to believe that their presence is of the first importance for the independence of their country, a necessary condition for Catalan autonomy. What misrepresentations, what downright lying was used to convince them of such transparent humbug I cannot tell, but there they are, in defiance of all common sense and historical fact; and they are likely to be a cruel thorn in our side, if operations in the north follow their probable course — we have great hopes of the King of Saxony: Napoleon is not alone in having unreliable allies,' observed Sir Joseph in an aside. Then returning to his Catalans he said, 'They have been kept in the strictest isolation — easy enough on an island, after all, ha, ha — and it appears that they have no idea of the happenings in the outside world except for what the French choose to tell them. And when a man of your intelligence, at a distance from the theatre of war, can form what you will allow me to call so erroneous and superficial view of the position, I wonder less at their conviction that Napoleon is carrying all before him and that he will restore their country to its pristine independence: or at their determination to blow his enemies, to blow us, out of the water if our men-of-war and transports work down the coast from Memel and Danzig, supplying the armies and landing behind the enemy's lines, as we hope to do.'

'Are they a coherent political body, a single organization? Did they form a unified movement in Catalonia? What were their aims, with regard to Madrid?'

'There you have me,' said Sir Joseph. 'I could have given you a tolerably exact account some days ago, but this wonderful new haul,' — patting Johnson's papers — 'has driven the details out of my mind. My memory is not what it was: the files are at the office. But I do remember very clearly that the First Lord held this up as one of the most striking instances of a situation where five minutes of explanation, éclaircissement, persuasion, call it what you like, could do more than a powerful squadron, with all the loss of life and ships and treasure an action may entail, and that with no guarantee of success against such a fortress, in such dangerous waters: an action not unlike a somewhat smaller Copenhagen, without the benefit of surprise and without the presence of a Nelson. Five minutes of plain, truthful statement would open their deluded eyes, and save a very costly, bloody, and uncertain battle. Of course, very, very few men could do it: the emissary would have to be a man they knew and trusted and believed, and your name instantly occurred to both of us. You would have been the perfect choice. And I am sure, from your previous form, that you would not only have convinced them, but that you would have induced them to turn their guns against the French.'

'Much would depend on the leaders, in such a case,' said Stephen. There were many currents in the general Catalan movement for autonomy, many shades of opinion, many separate organizations, each with its own chief, sometimes bitterly opposed to one another. He knew nearly all of them, some from his childhood; many were friends he had worked with, and although others seemed to him wrong-headed they were men he respected; but some he did not trust at all.

'Yes,' said Blaine. 'Certainly, I wish . . .

but you shall have all the details tomorrow, as soon as I can consult the files. Obviously, you will have to know them; yet I hope and trust that the knowledge will be of no more than historical importance — that the mission will have been successfully accomplished in the next week or so, if indeed it has not already been settled. Since we could not lay our hands on you, and since speed was essential, we confided it to Ponsich.'

'Pompeu Ponsich?'

Sir Joseph nodded. 'He went into the matter very thoroughly; he studied all our information; and in spite of his age he agreed to go. He said that he was confident of success.'

'If En Pompeu was confident, then I am quite happy,' said Stephen. 'You could not have chosen better.' Pompeu Ponsich was a poet, a scholar and a philologist known throughout Catalonia, a universally respected patriot.

'I am relieved to hear you say that,' said Sir Joseph. 'There were times when I doubted the wisdom of sending an elderly man of letters, however eminent. Though indeed for the right man the thing in itself is simple: it requires no extraordinary feats, such as you accomplished aboard the

Leopard and just now in Boston, but merely a convinced, convincing statement of the truth, supported, if necessary, by the documents we have provided. There was no lack of them, God knows, to prove Buonaparte's total bad faith with regard to Catalonia: or to any other country at all, for that matter.'

'I am glad the matter is in such good hands,' said Stephen. 'And although I should have been happy to go, I am just as pleased you have found a better man. I have been invited to address the Institut on the seventeenth, and unless there is any particularly urgent need for my presence here, I should very much like to do so.'

'To address the Institut, indeed? There's glory for you, upon my word: Pray what is your subject?'

'The extinct avifauna of Rodriguez; but I may diverge a little. I may just touch upon the ratites of New Holland.'

'Certainly you must go: we had not thought of asking you to leave for the Mediterranean before Fanshaw returns. Certainly you must go. Apart from anything else you will meet so many interesting men — pray remember me very kindly to the Cuviers and to Saint-Hilaire — and you will have the most perfect, most

Heaven-sent opportunity for entering into direct contact with —' He caught Stephen's cold, pale eye, realized that port, enthusiasm, and professional zeal had very nearly hurried him into a grave indiscretion, a serious error of judgment, and searched quickly for a way to come off with some degree of credit '— with former acquaintances,' he ended, lamely enough.

'With former scientific acquaintances, certainly,' said Stephen, fixing him still. 'I particularly look forward to seeing Dupuytren again, for although he sees fit to accept Buonaparte as a patient I love him; to hearing Corvisart on auscultation, that interesting probe, and the artificial anus; and to making many fresh acquisitions of a purely scientific nature.'

In spite of their mutual esteem, even their mutual affection, there was a slight awkwardness for a moment; but then, in an entirely different tone, Blaine broke the silence by saying, 'And yet even though the purpose of your voyage is entirely innocent, as of course it will be, might not there be some danger of your being recognized? You have done them great damage, and it would not be wise to place any very great reliance on a safe-conduct: not many men concerned with intelligence possess your scruples.'

'I have considered that, but it appears to me that at present the danger is negligible. The only Frenchmen who knew me for certain, by name and by appearance, were Dubreuil and Pontet-Canet; and as you know, both are dead. Their followers, who might possibly have some vague notion of my identity, are still in America; and even in the most unlikely event of their having been recalled at once, our brave packet made such an extraordinarily rapid passage that they cannot be in France until several weeks after my return to England.'

'That is true,' said Blaine.

'Furthermore,' said Stephen, 'I also look upon this journey as a kind of insurance: if any suspicions attach to my name, they are likely to be done away with by a public assertion of my scientific role — and I think I may venture to say without excessive vanity, that no man in Europe knows more of the anatomy of Pezophaps solitarius — and by my placing myself in the enemy's power, in the lion's mouth, of my own free will, and by my conscious innocence of any evil intent.'

'True again,' said Sir Joseph. 'And I have no doubt that your paper on the solitaire will make a great deal of noise, establishing you, if that were necessary, as the foremost authority on the subject. Still, I shall be glad to have you back as soon as may be, before there is the least possibility of any agent's return from America. And in any case I dare say you would like to go without delay. Brisk action is called for. Should you wish me to take the necessary steps for official permission, and for transport? We have a cartel sailing on the twelfth, which should answer very well.'

'If you please,' said Stephen. 'And since you are so very kind, I will allow myself to make two other requests.'

'I am delighted to hear it,' said Sir Joseph. 'There is little enough that you have ever allowed us to do for you; and what with the *Leopard* and now this Boston coup, we are so very much in your debt.'

Stephen bowed, hesitated for a moment, and said, 'The first concerns Mrs Villiers. As you will have seen from my report, it was largely by her means that I acquired these papers: yet at the same time she has remained in ignorance of my connexion with the Department. For obvious reasons she accompanied me in the packet. But since she is technically an enemy alien she was detained on our arrival.' 'Yes?' said Sir

Joseph, his head on one side. 'As you may remember,' said Stephen deliberately, 'the last time we spoke of her you were not altogether happy in your mind about her relationship with Mrs Wogan.'

'I remember,' said Sir Joseph. 'And I remember the lady too. I remember her perfectly. I had the pleasure of meeting her at Lady Jersey's, and again at the Pavilion. But if I do not mistake, you were no easier in your mind than I, at the time of her sudden departure for the States.'

'I was not, and I am very happy indeed to say that I was wholly wrong. Her loyalty to this country was entirely unaffected by her passing connexion with Mr Johnson, or by any papers she may have signed. That I will guarantee unconditionally. My request is that she may be released.'

'Very well,' said Sir Joseph, writing on a slip of paper. 'I shall attend to it myself: there will be no difficulty. The lady may set her heart at rest.' He paused a moment, but finding that Stephen did not intend to go any farther he continued, 'You mentioned a second request, I believe?'

'So I did, too. But this is a purely personal matter; it has nothing to do with the Department. I have a friend, a sea-officer, who was on shore for a while between commands and who succeeded in getting himself into very deep waters there. During a prolonged absence the water grew deeper still, and now I am very much afraid that it may close over his head, unless expert legal advice can extricate him. May I therefore beg you to tell me the name of the most eminent lawyer now in practice?'

'Would you be prepared to let me know the nature of your friend's trouble? Upon that depends the kind of adviser I should recommend. For a dispute over prize-money, it would be Harding, of course, unless he already acts for the other side; for criminal conversation or anything in the matrimonial line, for example, no doubt he should consult Hicks.'

'I will lay the case before you, as far as I understand it. My friend fell into the hands of a projector, a man more modest than the usual run, since he promised to turn my friend's lead not into gold but only into silver — there are disused lead-mines on my friend's estate. He was delighted with the scheme, delighted with the man, and in his simplicity he signed papers without reading them.'

'Signed papers without reading them?' cried Sir Joseph.

'I am afraid so. He had been appointed to a ship. It seems that he did not wish to lose the tide.'

'Good God! Yet really I should not be surprised: the imbecility of your sailor ashore passes all belief. I have seen countless examples of it, in all ranks, even in very able men, capable of leading a fleet and of conducting difficult diplomatic negotiations with real finesse. Only last week a distinguished officer I know assigned his half-pay for a lump sum: with this sum in his pocket in the form of negotiable bills he walks into a coffee-house. There he falls into conversation with a stranger: the stranger proposes an infallible scheme for multiplying capital by seven and a quarter without the slightest risk: the officer hands over his bills, and only when the stranger has been gone for some time does he realize that he does not even know the fellow's name, far less his dwelling-place. But to return to your unhappy friend: has he any clear notion of the import of these papers?'

'He fears that one may have been a power of attorney: though on the other hand he had already given his wife just such a document. But at all events, on his return he found that the projector, the thaumaturge, had plunged into wild expense, carrying out vast operations, even digging the traditional canal.'

'Yes, yes, of course, the canal,' said Sir Joseph, and Stephen, seeing the knowing look in his eye, said, 'It would be idle to pretend that I am not speaking of Jack Aubrey. I dare say you have seen the monstrous ditch in Hampshire?'

'I have, indeed,' said Sir Joseph. 'It has caused a deal of comment.'

'And that is not all. This reptile Kimber, for Kimber is the projector's name, now conceals himself behind a cloud of confederates, or rather of accomplices, to whom he has conveyed his ambiguous powers. Some of them are lawyers of the vilest kind, and they threaten proceedings. I am exceedingly concerned for Aubrey. I am very much attached to him and to his wife, and as you know I am under very great obligations to him.'

'You have nearly always sailed with him, I recall.'

'Ever since I took to the sea: and what is more, what is infinitely more, he plucked me from the hands of the French when I was taken at Mahon — a brilliant raid, carried out at great personal risk.'

'Certainly he has every claim on my

gratitude,' said Sir Joseph. 'I have never met the gentleman, though you have often mentioned him. I know him by reputation, of course: a most dashing resourceful commander, the very type of fighting captain. Lord Keith thought very highly of him. And very fortunate by sea: indeed, they call him Lucky Jack Aubrey in the service. He must have made a vast deal of money at Réunion and the Ile de France. How such a man, whose parts enable him to bring a long and difficult campaign to a successful conclusion, can play ducks and drakes with his hard-earned fortune, launching blindfold into chimerical schemes, signing unread documents, trusting his fellow-men, is beyond my comprehension.' Sir Joseph shook his head, trying to enter into the mind of one who trusted his fellow-men without long and repeated proof of their integrity: he could not manage it, and he went on, 'Lucky at sea, perhaps: less so by land. He was certainly not at all fortunate in his choice of a father. Have you met General Aubrey, Maturin?'

'I have, alas,' said Stephen.

'Now that he has espoused the Radical cause, it is worse than ever. He and his disreputable friends are a grave embarrassment to the ministry, and after his speech at Spitalfields there was some question as to the wisdom of appointing his son to a command. And in fact *Acasta*, which was designed for Captain Aubrey, was given elsewhere: as Mr Wray pointed out, there are so many distinguished officers unemployed, whose appointment would strengthen the Government side. Much the same applies to honours. It was in contemplation to recommend a knighthood or even a baronetcy in acknowledgement of your friend's sinking the *Waakzaamheid* when he had the *Leopard*; but I very much fear that it will come to nothing. If you value Aubrey, pray do tell him to keep his father quiet, if it is at all possible. But that is neither here nor there. Our present task is to decide upon the lawyer who is to preserve Captain Aubrey from the consequences of his folly. He must be a keen fellow, thoroughly accustomed to dealing with clever rogues, and not over-nice . . .' Sir Joseph turned the legal talent of the town over in his mind, and as he did so he sang 'Coll' astuzia, coll' arguzia, col giudizio, col criterio . . . con un equivoco, con un sinonimo, qualche garbuglio si troverà,' in a fruity, knowing undertone. 'Yes,' he said at last, 'Yes, I believe I have our true London Bartolo, the sharpest of them all. His name is Skinner, Wilbraham Skinner, and he lives in Lincoln's Inn.'

'Sir Joseph,' said Stephen, rising, 'I am deeply obliged to you.'

'Will you dine with me tomorrow?' asked Sir Joseph, lighting him down the stairs. 'I will ask Craddock and Erskine, and then we could look in at Covent Garden: there is a most exquisite young person singing Cherubino — a truly angelic voice.'

With great reluctance Stephen was obliged to refuse — he had to take the Holyhead coach, having some business to transact in Ireland: and when he proved inflexible, Sir Joseph said, 'Then I shall send the papers round before you leave. Where are you staying?'

'At the Grapes, in the Savoy.'

'Your old haunt,' said Sir Joseph, smiling. 'The permit and the Transport Commissioners' docket for your journey to Calais will be there before eleven o'clock. A couple of servants, I suppose?'

'If you please,' said Stephen: he paused at the door, and then said, 'It may be that I will take Mrs Villiers to Paris: there are circumstances that may render it desirable. Would there be any objection?'

'None at all,' said Sir Joseph. 'None at all on our side, and certainly none on the other. A lady with American papers will always be welcome in Paris. I shall just leave a blank in the docket for your servants and any eventual companion, and you will write in whatever you choose.'

'That would be most obliging in you, my dear Blaine.'

'Not at all, not at all. A very good voyage to you, dear Maturin, and pray give the Cuviers my warmest regards.'

Chapter Five

'Lord, Maturin, I am so glad to see you back,' cried Diana, running across Mrs Fortescue's drawing-room and taking him by both hands. 'Did you have a good journey? Come into the garden and tell me about it — Mrs Fortescue will be down any moment with all her loathesome brood. No: you look quite fagged. We will sit down.' She led him to a sofa. 'Well, my dear, and how did it go?'

'Much as these things usually go,' he said. 'A great deal of hurry, a great deal of delay, and at last the discovery that it could all have been done as well or even better by the post. I left my toothbrush in Tuam or Athenry, and a valuable pair of list slippers in Dublin itself, and then on the way back an American privateer brig chased us into Holyhead, and we trembling in every limb.' Use had accustomed him to the present Diana, and he mourned for her earlier manifestation only when he was alone. In a quiet way he was pleased to be sitting there by her; they were very easy together; her affection was like a home-coming; and once again he had the feeling that this might be very like marriage. She was looking well, physically well, he observed; the pure complexion often associated with pregnancy gave her a fine brilliance — clearly there was none of the costiveness which was to be feared in that interesting state. But a knowing eye also perceived that beneath Diana's present animation, her immediate pleasure, not all was well: far from it. The traces of deep unhappiness might be impossible to define, but they could not be mistaken; nor could the signs of more recent distress and vexation of spirit.

The reason for this became apparent a few moments later, when Mrs Fortescue came in with her children. There were five of them, and to Stephen they seemed no more loathesome than the ordinary brood: squat, commonplace, low-browed little creatures with colds, apt to stare and put their fingers in their mouths, but not absolutely criminal. Their mother, on the other hand, was one of those naval wives who had so often caused him to reflect upon the sailor's condition. She was a big, plain, coarse-complexioned woman, rather masculine, and although she ornamented her person with a large number of pins, ribbons and brooches, she had also adopted a breezy, confident manner which made them seem even more incongruous. She used a good many nautical expressions: rather more, perhaps, than most sailors. After a short while it became evident to Stephen that she was on terms of covert hostility with her guest, and that she was afraid of Diana. He was not called upon to take any part in the conversation: Mrs Fortescue had a strong sense of the naval hierarchy and of her own position in it as a senior post-captain's wife, and when she heard that he was a surgeon she had little or nothing to say to him; furthermore he rarely paid much attention to his clothes, and now, arriving from a long journey, he was more than usually shabby and unkempt, not to say dirty and unshaved.

His mind drifted off to Paris, to Pezophaps solitarius, and to the silent battle that two little Fortescue boys were waging in the far corner, by a flower-stand: they were striving for some object that he could not make out, possibly a handkerchief, egged on by their sisters. At the same time Mrs Fortescue and Diana were in fairly civil disagreement on some subject that escaped him. He would certainly include some remarks upon the Ratitae of New Holland . . . He was aware that the dispute had come to an end; that Diana had presumably gained her point; and that Mrs Fortescue, unwilling to continue the engagement directly, had conceived the plan of making Diana uneasy by attacking him. 'Tell me, sir,' she said, with a look of commiseration, 'is it true that in the Prussian service, surgeons are required to shave the officers?'

'Only too true, ma'am,' he replied. 'And in our own it is worse by far. Dear Lord, how often have I not been set to black Captain Aubrey's shoes?'

She reddened with anger, but before she could reply Captain Fortescue walked in, and Stephen was interested to see a look of pure love on her face, followed by a glance of anxiety and suspicion at Diana, and then with barely a second's pause by renewed anger (the one flush doing for both) as the flower-stand came crashing down, one boy, petrified by his father's entrance, having released the object, so that the other fell sideways. The room was filled with noise, with accusation, blame, denial, and shameless informing; and when the children were led away to be whipped, howling as they went, Stephen and Diana walked into the garden.

'How have you been coming along, my dear?' he asked, as they paced by the Captain's lilies, his pride and joy.

'Very well, Stephen, thank you,' she said. 'I have obeyed you in everything: I have been incredibly good — only one glass of wine at dinner, though there are always vast crowds of people here, which incites one to drink, and no tobacco at all, not even snuff. Stephen, you would not light a cigar, would you, and give me a waft when we are quite out of range of the house?'

'I might,' said Stephen; and after some other physical enquiries he said, 'Have you seen Jack?'

'Oh yes! Except when he was in town he and Sophie were here almost every day until he was called down to Dorset, because his father was ill. Since then Sophie has come over as often as she could — she is a dear, dear creature, you know, Stephen — and we have sat together as mumchance as a couple of gib cats, with our men far from home. You never told me why you went, by the way.'

It was rare that Stephen could answer such a question with complete candour and he did so now with a pleasant feeling of ease. 'I went for a formal riding of the bounds, the bounds of a demesne in Joyce's Country that belonged to my cousin Kevin. It was confiscated, forfeited, after the ninety-eight rising, but since he was killed in the Austrian service, fighting against Buonaparte, it is to be restored. I shall have good news for his father when I see him in France. And I have good news for you too, Villiers,' he said, feeling in his pocket. 'Here is your order of release. It is still conditional, since you may only live in London or the home counties, but I cannot conceive that you should wish to live anywhere else. You are not pleased, Villiers?'

'Oh but I am, Stephen. Delighted. And it was so good of you to take so much trouble. I am infinitely obliged to you, my dear; the idea of getting out of this revolting house, with all these repulsive children . . . Stephen, light your cigar, for God's sake.' She took a deep draught, breathed out the smoke, turned pale, and leant on his arm. 'I am not used to it any more,' she said; and then, turning a haggard face to his, 'I cannot live in England, Stephen. It is bad enough having to support tales of what happened in India: what will it be like when gossip starts coming back from Halifax? I know so many people.

Scores of them here, hundreds in town. It is hard enough for me to keep my head high in Hampshire; imagine what it would be like in London in a few weeks' time — Diana Villiers with a great belly and no husband. You know how very small our world is — cousins, acquaintances, connexions at every turn. I could not go to a theatre or the opera or a decent shop without running into someone I know. And can you imagine me mewed up in some forbidding farmhouse, not daring to meet any civilized being, not even the parson, for fear of discovery? Or in some back street on the Surrey side? I should run melancholy mad.'

'Sure, a creature of your social temper requires company.' It was true: without it Diana would pine away. 'But you are to consider,' he went on, 'that a purely nominal ceremony would do away with these inconveniencies. As Mrs Maturin you would be brought to bed with your friends around you, in a decent part of town.'

'Stephen,' she said in a stronger voice. 'I will be damned to Hell before I marry a man when I am with child by another. You would not rid me of it when I asked you, and I promised to do nothing myself. I respected your wishes: respect mine, dear

Stephen. Dear Stephen, pray take me to Paris.'

'Would not the same objections apply in France? And could you live easy in an enemy country?'

'Oh, nobody has ever thought of Paris as enemy country. We are at war with Napoleon, not with Paris. See how everyone flocked over there as soon as they could, during the peace. I was there myself with poor Cousin Lowndes — the one who took himself for a teapot, you remember: they thought a mesmerist could do something for him — and Paris was filled with English. That was just before we met. Anyhow, I know quantities of people there, émigrés who went back, and dozens of friends from before the war, when I lived there with my father. In Paris it would not matter — nobody knows or cares exactly what has passed — I am a widow, and in any case a liaison is neither here nor there in Paris — the atmosphere is quite different. Besides, the war will be over presently: the King will be back — d'Avaray presented me to him at Hartwell, you know — and it will be the old France again. I do beg of you to take me with you, Stephen.'

'Very well,' said he. 'I will come for you

in the morning, at half past ten o'clock. Here is Captain Fortescue. How do you do, sir?'

'I am so sorry for the infernal din just now,' said Captain Fortescue, 'but such things are inseparable from family life; and since it is our duty to increase and multiply I suppose we must put up with it. You are admiring my lilies, I see. Ain't they splendid? This one will interest you, Doctor, a great rarity brought me from Canton by my nephew in the Company's service. Oh God, they are at it again,' he cried, narrowing his eyes and leaning towards the lily, where several red beetles were copulating in his sight, increasing and multiplying. 'The dogs, the vile French vermin! And this is inseparable from gardening, too. Forgive me while I fetch my little spray.'

Paris was in all its charming splendour, the trees full-leaf under a gentle smiling sky, the Seine almost blue, the streets filled with moving colour. Much of this colour was provided by the countless uniforms, and these uniforms were those of the enemy; but the difference between what the troops of Buonaparte and his allies really wore in the wet and muddy field and the full dress that delighted the Parisians' eyes was so great that there was no hostile, and very little truly warlike, effect — rather one of a superbly managed, superbly lit stage of enormous size, filled with actors dressed and sometimes mounted with unparalleled magnificence. Diana contributed to this colour in a pervenche-blue gown from Madame Delaunay's, a striking hat only a few hours from the Place Vendôme, and a slim black Cashmere scarf-like shawl — garments that brought many a look of respectful admiration from gorgeous gentlemen in brass helmets with horsehair plumes, silver breastplates, clashing swords and spurs, sabretaches, bearskins, little jackets, mostly gold lace, worn on one shoulder alone, curious hats with square tops or round with jelly-bags, scarlet, amaranth, or cherry-pink. Splendid figures in gleaming boots and sidewhiskers beamed upon her or twirled their moustaches with a killing air as she and Stephen wandered about the city, showing one another former haunts, dwelling-places, or even play-grounds.

'Here,' said Diana on the Ile des Cygnes, 'here I first learnt to play marelle, with the Penfao girls. We used to trace the lines from the balustrade to this bush — Lord, how it has grown! It has quite hidden the last square, that we used to call Heaven. Stephen, what is marelle in English?'

'I cannot tell,' he said after some reflection. To escape notice they had been speaking French ever since they landed from the discreet vessel that went to and fro at quite frequent intervals, ostentatiously ignored by the authorities and the navies on either side, a vessel that was neither a full-blown cartel (since Buonaparte would not exchange prisoners) nor yet a neutral, but that often carried hemidemisemi-official negotiators, communications about prisoners of war, distinguished literary men or natural philosophers, and, in the Dover direction, the beautifully-dressed dolls without which Englishwomen would not have known what was in fashion — ever since they landed they had been speaking French, and already there were English words, rarely-used words, that tended to escape them.

They walked across the bridge and looked at a tall thin high-shouldered house in the rue Gît-le-Coeur in whose garret Stephen had lodged as a student. 'Dupuytren lived just below,' he observed. 'We used to share our corpses. Now, my dear, if you are not too tired, I should like to carry you to the faubourg Saint-Germain; I have a friend there, Adhémar de La Mothe, who has a vast great place with no one in it, and it occurs to me that you might like to live with him. He looks forward to it extremely, and he will invite you to accept one of the upper floors: his aunts will be able to recommend reliable maidservants.'

'Is Madame de La Mothe an amiable woman?'

'There is no Madame de La Mothe. That is the whole point, Villiers. Adhémar is not a marrying man at all. He did make an attempt long ago, but it did not answer, and the poor lady obtained a decree of nullity in Rome: labour lost, alas, since she was led to the guillotine within five minutes of its delivery — virgin martyrs are always depicted carrying a palm, you know. But he is a civilized creature; he lives for music and painting and he is fond of women, as friends, handsome women that know how to dress. I believe you will like him.'

'I am sure I shall, if you do,' said Diana in a doubtful voice.

'His acquaintance would certainly make your life more entertaining; he knows everyone with any sort of taste or style in Paris, and he is still quite rich. And quite apart from that, although he has no official position of any kind, and no political activity whatsoever, men of his tastes form as it were an occult society, almost a freemasonry; they know one another, and they can sometimes find a sympathetic ear where others might seek in vain; it was to this that he owed his life in ninety-four, when most of his family went to the scaffold — that is one of the reasons why his house is so empty. So in the unlikely event of any difficulty, any unpleasantness, his protection might be of value. I tell you this, Villiers, because I know I can rely upon your discretion. It would never do to show the least awareness: although in some ways he is more than usually quick, he believes he is quite undetected. He is very much afraid of scandal, and to beguile the world he professes a passion for the chaste Madame Duroc, the banker's wife. What is it, Villiers? Why do you stop?'

'I beg pardon, Stephen: I just wanted to show you the house where I lived when I was a child.'

'But it is the Hôtel d'Arpajon,' said Stephen, looking at it attentively, a grave building on three sides of a courtyard, well back from the road. 'I have always known that you spoke excellent French, but I had no idea that you had learnt it in the Hôtel d'Arpajon — the Hôtel d'Arpajon, for all love.'

'I suppose it never came up — I suppose you never asked. You never ask, much, Stephen.'

'Question and answer has never seemed to me a liberal form of conversation,' said he.

'I will tell you, then, without being asked. We lived here a great while — my father had to leave England, you know, because of his debts — years and years. It seemed to me for ever, though I suppose it was only three in fact: I was eight when we came, and eleven when we left. He loved Paris: so did I. That was my window,' she said, pointing. 'The third from the corner. We had all that wing on the left. But Stephen, what is so odd about my having learnt French at the Hôtel d'Arpajon?'

'Only that my cousin Fitzgerald lived there too — Colonel Fitzgerald, Kevin's father, the gentleman we are to see tomorrow. And yet it is not so very strange, after all; your father was a military man; so was my cousin; soldiers tend to flock together, and what more natural than that one should pass his quarters on to another?'

'Did I ever see him, I wonder? Scores of English officers came to visit my father, and they generally wore their regimentals: I knew all the facings.'

'You may well have done so. A tall thin man with one arm and a face more cut about than Jack Aubrey's. A long face: you could mistake him for a horse, except for the missing arm. But he would not have been wearing English regimentals, because he was in the Irish Brigade, in the French King's service — Dillon's regiment.'

'I did see some of them; I remember their uniform. But they all had two arms. What happened to him?'

'He was too old and sick to go off to Coblentz with the others when the brigade was disbanded — the Irish would not fight against the King, as you recall — and he retired into Normandy. He lives there still, breeding horses. You will like him too.' A battery of field-artillery came down the rue de Grenelle. 'I hope those are none of his horses,' said Stephen in her ear, through the thunder of wheels. 'He hates the bloody tyrant as much as I do.' They walked on, and he said, 'You will like him too. For, do you see, I have divided up your days without the least reference to you: a town life at the Hôtel de La Mothe

— and apart from the friends you already possess, there is always a great deal going on there: Adhémar gives a concert every week — and when you are sick of town, there is the Colonel in his rural cot, with green acres, nymphs and swains. And as for your lying-in, I have consulted Baudelocque: he is certainly the best accoucheur in Europe; we are old friends, and he will wait on you as soon as you are installed — you could not be in better hands. I am sadly ignorant of midwifery, and often worry when there is no cause.'

This was not a welcome subject, and the light, the fine glow died out of Diana's face, which had been alive with the happiness of freedom recovered, the excitement of Paris regained and of new clothes. She said, 'That was a very curious coincidence, the Hôtel d'Arpajon, was it not?'

'Prodigious,' said Stephen. 'And yet in a way one might say that the whole of life is a tissue of prodigious coincidences: as for example that at the very moment we attempt to cross the road this particular coach and six should come by; yet though extremely unlikely, it is a fact. And the glabrous face within belongs to Monsieur de Talleyrand-Périgord.' Stephen took off his hat: the glabrous face returned his bow. 'It is a most improbable coincidence that as we enter La Mothe's courtyard, and it is just here, on the right — take care of the excrement, Villiers — some merchant should walk into his counting-house in Stockholm, or that Jack Aubrey should mount his horse to pursue the fox. Though now I come to think of it, Jack would scarcely pursue the innocent fox at this time of the year: yet the principle remains. You may object that the overwhelming majority of these coincidences are undetected, which is eminently true; but they are there for all that, and as I raise this knocker, some man in China breathes his last.'

Jack was not in fact pursuing the fox, but he was mounting a horse, the powerful grey mare belonging to his father that was to carry him to Blandford and the post-chaise for home. General Aubrey appeared briefly, flanked by two swag-bellied men with red faces; others stared vacantly from the billiard-room. 'Not gone yet, Jack?' he said. 'You must cut along. Good-bye to 'ee, and don't jag the mare's mouth.' The General had never had much opinion of his son's horsemanship. 'Come on, Jones, come on, Brown,' he cried eagerly to his companions. 'We must get to work.' Then remembering himself he half turned and called over his shoulder, 'Give my love to — give my love to your wife and the young 'uns.' Mrs Aubrey, Jack's step-mother, did not appear at all: when the General married her out of the dairy the sprightly young woman had vowed that now she was a lady she would never rise before noon; and this oath at least she had kept most religiously.

Jack rode off without looking back. He was profoundly sad: it was not his father's health, for the old gentleman had recovered as quickly as he had fallen sick, his vigour unimpaired, but rather the odd, cunning, foxy look that had come over his face; and his companions. They were City men or politicians or both combined; he did not know exactly what they were at, although obviously money was their one concern, their talk being all of consols, omnium, and India stock; but even if he had not had his recent experience of money-men he would still have distrusted them. Woolcombe House had never been famous for propriety, particularly since the death of the first Mrs Aubrey, Jack's mother; the General's acquaintance including many fast-living, hard-drinking, high-playing men and the more careful village mothers did not send their daughters into service there; but Jack had never known the like of Jones and Brown admitted to the place. It was not only that their Radical politics were odious to him, but they were also flashy, loud-voiced, pushing fellows; they had no notion of the country; their confident, familiar approach was unlike anything he had experienced at home. Of the politicians some appeared to love humanity, but they were harsh and unfeeling to their horses, brutal to their dogs, rude to the servants; and there was much more in the way of voice and clothes that he felt but could not name. Certainly the General had profited from his association with them; it was years since he had borrowed any money from Jack, and he had recently set about altering Woolcombe on an ambitious scale. It was perhaps that which saddened Jack most. The house in which he was born had no doubt been a raw and staring edifice when it was first built, two hundred years ago — highly-ornamented red brick with a great number of gables and bays and high corkscrew chimneys — but no Aubrey since James's time had sprung up with Palladian tastes or indeed with any tastes at all in the architectural line, and the place had mellowed wonderfully. Now it was beginning to stare again, with false turrets and incongruous sash-windows, as though the vulgarity of his new associates had infected the General's mind. Inside it was even worse; the panelling, old, dark, and inconvenient to be sure, but known for ever, had been torn out and wallpaper and gilt mirrors had taken its place. Jack's own room had already vanished, and only the unused library, with its solemn rows of unopened books and its noble carved plaster ceiling, had escaped; he had spent some hours there, looking, among other things, at a first folio Shakespeare, borrowed by an earlier Jack Aubrey in 1623, never read and never returned: but even the library was doomed. The intention seemed to be to make the house false — ancient outside and gimcrack modern within: at the top of the hill, where he had always taken a last look back (for Woolcombe lay in a dank hollow, facing north), he directed his gaze steadily down on the other side, to Woolhampton.

Yet even here there was unhappiness. Riding down into the village he passed the dame's school he had attended as a very little boy, a school where he had first learnt to love, if little else: for at that time the dame had a niece to help her, a fresh girl quite pretty, though freckled as a thrush, and the infant Jack had lost his heart to her — followed her about like a puppy, brought her stolen fruit. And now here she was, her aunt's successor, surrounded by her pupils at the door, a simpering spinster, though freckled still; silly, withered on the branch, but resolutely juvenile, with ill-dyed hair and a skimpy frock. She asked after the General, and said that Captain Aubrey was a naughty boy not to have come and drunk tea with her — she vowed he was a monster, la — but she would forgive him this time — she would forgive our jolly tars anything.

It grieved his heart, and he turned his horse right-handed down an unfrequented lane at the side of Bulwer's rick-yard and so over fields and along bridle-paths for the rest of the way to Blandford, pure country, where he would see nothing but the unchanging crops, hares and partridges in the mown hayfields, the woods he had known as a boy. He was not an introspective man by any means, and his life had not left him much time for a great deal of self-examination; but long sad thoughts about age, death and decay, change, decrepitude, deterioration pursued him even into the chaise and followed him along the highroad. 'I must be growing old myself,' he reflected, settling his long legs diagonally in the carriage. 'It must be so, because I felt positively young with that girl in Halifax; and it is the exception that proves the rule.' He had not thought of her for a great while and for the moment he could not recall her name; but he did remember their reciprocal ardours, five times repeated, and although intellectually he disapproved his conduct — a damn fool thing to do, and probably immoral, with an unmarried woman — he went to sleep with a self-complacent smirk on his face that he would have found odious in any other man.

The smirk, even the remotest recollection of the smirk or of its occasion, had long since faded by the time he reached Ashgrove Cottage. A good many letters were waiting for him, and in duty bound he opened those from the Admiralty first. 'They mean well, I dare say, and they put it very civil,' he said to Sophie across the table, 'but it don't amount to much in fact. In view of my wound — which don't amount to much either, I may say: not now

— should I like *Orion* for the time being?'

'What is she?'

'An old seventy-four: receiving-ship in Plymouth. Stationary, of course. I could sleep ashore and take my ease; and naturally it would mean full pay.'

'What could be more perfect?' murmured Sophie; but her husband, deep in his thoughts, went on, 'I do not like to refuse employment in wartime — I never have done so — and I certainly should not now, was it an active command: I should leap at a heavy frigate on the North American station, for example. But this time I believe I shall beg to decline, with many, many thanks for their lordships' kind consideration and a strong proviso that I shall be perfectly well as soon as any fighting ship comes up: though it is almost certain to be a liner, you know. The *Orion* would not do: I should be perpetually to and fro between Plymouth and London, seeing Skinner about this legal business. No. Let us clear that out of the way, and then look about for a decent command: they can hardly refuse me one.' He paused, considered, and went on, 'I do not like to whine, Sophie, but I think they might have been a little more handsome: after all, it is not every day a man sinks a ship like the *Waakzaamheid* with a decrepit fourth rate. You will say it was only a chance shot, and the wicked sea did the rest, but even so —'

'I will say nothing of the sort,' cried Sophie. 'They should certainly have made you a baronet, if not a peer, and have given you the naval medal right away, like dear Sir Michael Seymour. But perhaps they will: they are always very slow.'

'Why, as for that, sweetheart, you know what I think of titles — a weight round a man's neck, as often as not, particularly hereditary ones. You have to be twice as tall as everybody else, and unless you are a Nelson or a Hood or a St Vincent or even a Keith you can't be twice as tall, not four and twenty hours a day, but only when your luck is in and everything is just so. However, I did think there was just a possibility they might give me the Marines: there was a vacancy.'

'Marines, Captain Aubrey?'

'It would have been *Colonel* Aubrey if they had. Have I never told you about the Marines, sweetheart? It is a plum they give you when you have done well. They cannot promote you — there is no such thing as promotion out of turn once you are a post-captain, and even the King could not make you an admiral over the heads of the captains above you on the list — if he did, half his senior officers would resign. So since they cannot promote you, and since you cannot eat a baronetcy or the naval medal, they make you a colonel of the Royal Marines instead, and you draw a colonel's pay, without doing anything for it.'

'But is that not corruption, Jack? You were always very much against corruption when you were young, I mean younger.'

'So I am still: corruption in others is anathema to me. But you would scarcely credit the depths of turpitude I should descend to myself for a thousand a year; and a colonel's pay is rather better than that. Let me see: eighty pound five and fourpence multiplied by thirteen; for they go by lunar months too, you know . . . one thousand and forty-three, three and fourpence, which is better than a shove in the eye with a dry stick. No, my dear, that ain't corruption; it is an understood thing, quite above-board, a reward of merit. But I don't suppose I am meritorious enough, nor senior enough — after all, I am not much more than half way up the captain's list yet.' Then, as he turned to the other letters, he said in a much more serious voice,

'No, but real corruption, corruption in the dockyards, the dirty jobs with contractors and private ship-builders, that is the real goddam bane of the Navy . . . This one is from Stephen's man, Mr Skinner.' He read, nodding with approval at each paragraph. 'I am very pleased with him. A capital man of business, clear-headed, and as brisk as a bee. He is carrying the war into their camp, the infernal dogs: that is what I like to see. Says a writ of duces tecum will compel them to show the paper I signed, and put an end to the uncertainty; and he has already sued one out. Duces tecum: that's the stuff.'

'What does it mean?' asked Sophie.

'I never was much of a fist at Latin,' said Jack. 'Not like Philip Broke. But I do remember dux, a leader, an admiral as you might say: and the plural is duces. So you could construe duces tecum as *the admirals are with thee;* and I don't ask better than that. Excellent Mr Skinner.' He passed over the sheets and turned to the remaining letters. 'This is from Grant,' he said, frowning.

'I hate him,' said Sophie. This was a rare, almost an unprecedented remark for her; but Mr Grant, an elderly, embittered lieutenant, had left Jack in the *Leopard* when that unfortunate ship struck an iceberg in the high southern latitudes and appeared to be sinking; he had reached Cape Town in the launch and England in a man-of-war; and he had written to Sophie to tell her, as he had already told his superiors, that there was no hope for Captain Aubrey — that his obstinancy in staying on board a sinking ship must have fatal consequences.

'The man has run mad,' said Jack. 'He says I have been spreading rumours that he behaved badly. And that is completely untrue, Sophie: I distinctly told Admiral Drury that Grant left with my permission, and that I was satisfied with his conduct up to that time. I went out of my way to do it. I never liked the fellow, though he was a good seaman, but I went out of my way to make the statement, because I thought it was due to him. Now he is unemployed — I don't wonder at it: the affair caused a good deal of comment in the service — and he says it is all my fault. He says that unless I immediately retract and do him justice, stating that I ordered him to leave — which is not the case: I only gave him permission — he will consider it his duty to his own character to lay the true facts of the case before the public and the Admiralty, including a number of circumstances such as my incapacity after the action and my keeping of false musters. Poor fellow: I am afraid his intellects are very much astray. I shall not answer; you cannot properly answer a letter of that sort. He would never have wrote it in his right mind: perhaps he was drunk at the time.' He laid it aside. 'Now here is one from Tom Pullings; I know his hand. Yes. He and Mowett and Babbington and young Henry James were all dining together in Plymouth, and they join in congratulations on my return and best wishes and everything that is kind. Beg to be remembered to you and Stephen, and have drunk to us in three times three. They wish us increase . . . They mean it kindly, I am sure, but three is quite enough, with wheat at a hundred and twenty-six shillings a quarter,' he said, turning the page. 'No. I am out — they wish us increase of health and wealth and happiness. That's more the mark. Honest fellows.' These young men had all been on Jack's quarterdeck as midshipmen and officers and they had followed him from ship to ship whenever it was possible: he was thinking of them with a smile on his face as he considered the next letter, turning it in his hand. He did not know the handwriting or the seal, and even when he had opened it some seconds passed before he realized that it was for him — that it was neither a joke nor a mistake. Miss Smith embraced this opportunity of a transport going home to write to her hero — a wounded officer of the 43rd Foot would put it in the post the moment he landed, for she was sure her hero would rejoice to learn that their love was to bear fruit ere long — if it was a girl she should call it Joanna — she was sure it would be a little girl. As soon as there was a place in a packet she should fly to his arms; but perhaps he might prefer her to come home in a man-of-war — a simple note to any of his friends on the North American station would surely be enough — she hoped Mrs A would prove more understanding than Lady Nelson — he was to tell her at once whether he preferred the packet or a man-of-war — she was sure he could not wait to fold her to his bosom — that should he be prevented from flying to meet her by the requirements of the service, she would quite understand — there would be no womanly reproaches: the service must come first, even before Love — and would her hero be so good as to place say five hundred pounds in Drummond's hands?

She could not move until she had paid her debts in Halifax — they had mounted surprisingly, perhaps because she had always scorned accounts — and she did not like to ask her brother. She did not in the least mind asking her hero, however; she felt no false shame, because it showed how entirely she was his — if the roles had been reversed, how delighted she would have been with this mark of confidence! He was to write immediately: she would sit on the quay every morning, scanning the horizon like Ariadne.

Stephen Maturin stood in the light of the declining sun, holding his face so that a horizontal ray impinged upon it as he shaved; the face itself was grave, and paler than usual: in an hour or so he was to address the Institut, and some of the keenest, most distinguished minds in Europe would be there. His black coat and his satin smallclothes, brushed and newly pressed, lay by his new and spotless shirt, his neckcloth and his silk stockings, below them his gleaming silver-buckled shoes: this was to be a full-dress evening affair, and although he had attended the Royal Society in pantaloons that would not do for a foreign guest in Paris on such an occasion.

'Come in,' he cried, in answer to a knock.

'Monsieur Fauvet asks if Dr Maturin can receive him,' said the servant.

'Dr Maturin infinitely regrets that he is unable to do so at the moment,' said Stephen, shaving on. 'But hopes to have the pleasure of seeing him at the reception.'

Fauvet was not the most outstanding of literary men in Paris, but he was one of the most fashionable and certainly the most persistent and indiscreet. This was the fourth time he had profited by Dupuytren's introduction to call on Stephen, asking him to take a letter back to England, a letter to the Comte de Blacas. Since Blacas was the exiled French king's chief adviser, it did not call for much penetration to be sure that the letter would contain protestations of unfailing loyalty to Louis XVIII, total devotion to the Bourbon cause, and utter rejection of the present tyranny: indeed, Fauvet had practically said as much at their second interview. And Fauvet was not the only one, by any means. During these last weeks he had been approached by several others who wished to ensure their position in the event of Napoleon's downfall and the return of the king. Most had been more cautious or more subtle than Fauvet, and some had sent their wives, as being more gifted for this kind of thing; but subtle or brutally direct, male or female, Stephen would have nothing to do with them. There was always the strong likelihood of an agent provocateur and in any case this was no part of his business in Paris: he had left intelligence, in the restricted meaning of the word, on the quay at Dover. He had listened politely, regretting his entire ignorance of political affairs and his total lack of acquaintance among the French émigrés in England, and pointing out the obligation under which he lay — the obligation of a guest to behave with perfect propriety. And he *had* behaved with perfect propriety: it is true that his mind sometimes wandered to Ponsich in the Baltic, and he read the *Moniteur* with particular eagerness, looking for news from those parts, but in all deliberate acts he remained the purely philosophical visitor. He had performed three dissections of the calcified palmar aponeurosis with Dupuytren; Corvisart had told him a great deal about his new method of auscultation; and he had attended three splendid concerts at the Hôtel de La Mothe. He had done what he intended to do. Yet from time to time, and as a matter of general rather than specific interest, he wondered how much these people represented. Perhaps not very much, although there were some exceptionally able, well-informed men among them. In spite of these gratifying signs of apprehension at the centre of things he had come to the conclusion that Blaine was in the right — that although the Empire had received some very heavy blows it was not crumbling yet — that one of Buonaparte's shattering victories or even dissensions among the allies could restore it to something like its full strength again — that in any case a great deal of hard fighting would be needed to bring it down — and that given the tyrant's skill in dividing his enemies, the least delay might be fatal: new armies were being raised with extraordinary speed. And as for those who suddenly found that they loved the Bourbons, it was surely natural that men who had lived through such remarkable changes of régime should provide themselves with life-lines at the least threat of still another upheaval. 'I shall know more this evening,' he reflected, folding his neckcloth with peculiar care. There had been rumours of a great engagement, of a three days' battle in Moravia, and the gathering was sure to be well attended: these functions were as much social as philosophic — perhaps even more so — and they brought together people of the political, artistic, and fashionable worlds as well as the learned: they were admirably designed for taking the pulse of the capital.

He put on his coat, felt in his pocket to make sure that his notes were there, thrust his green spectacles into their case, and walked to the door, endeavouring to quell an odd flutter of spirits. 'I must begin in a loud, determined, self-assured voice, so pitched as to carry to the farthest seats,' he reflected as he asked the porter to fetch him a hackney-coach. 'A hackney-coach, my friend,' he said again, seeing that the man looked at him in a questioning kind of way. 'And pray tell him to drive to the Hôtel de La Mothe.'

'At once, Monsieur,' said the porter, recovering his usual poise.

While the carriage was being brought Stephen studied the tall clock in the hall. It had an ornate pendulum, an ingenious affair of rods whose expansion compensated for the variations in temperature, guaranteeing a very close approximation to the right time. There was plenty to spare, but as he had never known Diana to be ready at the appointed hour he meant to be there early, so as to harry her with repeated messages from below.

Early he was, but to his astonishment he found her there in the drawing-room before him, an exquisite sight in filmy blue and a blaze of diamonds, those in her hair making her look taller and slimmer than he had ever known her — the new French fashion suited her extremely well. 'Upon my word, Villiers,' he cried, 'you look very fine.'

'So do you, my dear,' she replied, laughing with a whole-hearted merriment rare in her, a pure and kindly merriment that gave her face a far sweeter expression than it usually wore. 'So are you — a beautiful, beautiful coat, and such undeniable breeches. But Stephen,' she said, leading him to a mirror, 'pray look in the glass.'

He did so, and a grim reflection peered back at him, a small round close-cropped head, its sparse hair standing straight up like the bristles on an old worn-out scrubbing-brush. 'Jesus, Mary and Joseph,' he said in a low inward tone, 'I have forgot my wig. What shall I do?'

She said, 'Never mind, never mind. It will be here in a moment. Sit down: there is plenty of time.' She rang, and said to the footman, 'Run round to Beauvilliers' as fast as ever you can: the gentleman has forgotten his wig,' and then to Stephen, 'Never be so dismayed, love; it will be here with half an hour to spare. Sit down and praise my dress.' She kissed him as fondly as a sister: indeed, as he sat on the more or less Egyptian day-bed the same thought occurred to his agitated mind: 'My sister, my spouse. Oh Lord.'

'I was so afraid it would not be ready,' she went on, parading about and showing the dress from all sides, 'but it came not an hour ago. La Mothe likes it extremely, he has the purest taste in women's clothes. But he made me shorten the rivière so that the big stone came just here,' pointing to her almost naked bosom, where the Blue Peter shimmered among the gauze, a fountain of light in that dim drawing-room — 'so I put the other diamonds in my hair — they unscrew, you know — and he quite approved: I place the utmost reliance on La Mothe. I have never known anyone with a surer eye. And he was ravished with the dress.'

'So am I, Villiers. The general effect is quite superb — ethereal. A slim wisp of blue smoke rising.'

'I thought I should go the whole hog, le

porc inentamé, for your great day. And after all it is just about the last time I shall be able to look ethereal, or tolerably ethereal, for a long, long while.' Once more the thought was unwelcome and her face clouded, but as she stood there gazing down at the big stone it lightened again — a naive, unconscious delight that was singularly touching.

'You are much attached to those diamonds, Villiers,' he said kindly.

'Yes, I am. I truly love them,' she said. 'Above all the Blue Peter.' She detached the pendant stone and put it into his hand, where it lay, strangely heavy, sending out countless prismatic flashes at the slightest movement. 'I don't give a damn where they come from,' she went on, raising her chin. 'I love them passionately. I should not part with them for anything on earth and I shall certainly be buried in them. You will remember that, Stephen? If things do not go well this autumn, I am to be buried in them. I may rely on you?'

'Certainly you may.'

'I liked my pearls,' she went on, after a pause. 'You remember the pearls the Nawab gave me? But that was quite different: I let some of them go for the dressmaker without a qualm, almost. La Mothe took me to Charon's, and they gave me a very honest price. He is coming with the Clermonts, and then we are all to come back here for supper. Oh, and they valued those unmounted rubies I showed you, the ones I never really cared for, like great drops of blood: I was absolutely *amazed* . . .' Stephen's attention wandered; his anxious eyes were fixed on the clock, and he heard the footman's hurrying feet even before the wig appeared.

He clapped it on at once, fitted his spectacles under the side-curls, and said, 'We must be away.'

'There is plenty of time yet,' said Diana. 'This clock is half an hour fast. It would never do to be early. Sit down again, Stephen. Lord, my dear, how those blue spectacles do change your face! I should never have recognized you.'

'They are green.'

'Blue or green, pray take them off. They make me feel quite uneasy, as though you were a stranger.'

'Never,' said Stephen. 'Once I have them on, fairly fixed under my wig, I cannot take them off without disturbing its symmetry.'

'Why do you wear them? They make you look dreadfully old, and even, my dear, quite horribly plain. You can see perfectly well without.'

'Not always, when I have to read notes under a powerful reading-lamp. But the main reason I wear them is that I am nervous, and they give me countenance.'

'Nervous, Stephen?' cried she. 'I should never have thought it possible. Though now I come to think of it, you have been sitting on the edge of your chair this last age, glaring at the clock like a man due to be hanged. Pray do not be so absurd; you are a very distinguished creature. Everybody here says you have a most prodigious mind, and I have known it for ever. Come, drink a small glass of brandy; that will calm your spirits. Let us both drink a small glass of brandy.'

'You are very good, dear Diana: but the truth of the matter is, I am not at all used to addressing so large a gathering. And such a gathering! The Cuviers will be there, Argenson, Saint-Hilaire . . . or at least, I hope they will.'

'I am sure they will. I know the Cardinal is coming; La Mothe told me so.'

'Oh, him,' said Stephen.

'I thought you would be pleased. Surely a cardinal is next door to the Pope; and you are a Catholic, my dear.'

'There are cardinals and cardinals; and even some Popes have not always been exactly what one might wish. However, thank you for telling me, Villiers: I must begin with a Your Eminence. For although he is related to those vile Buonapartes I understand he is on bad terms with the chief malefactor; and in any case he is a prince of the Church. Come, Villiers, we must go.'

The great room was full, even fuller than he had expected: full of people and full of eager talk about the reported engagement in Moravia, or perhaps just in Bohemia — the Russian right wing had been entirely destroyed — the Prussians had fallen back on Polobsk — Vandamme's corps had suffered terribly — not at all, Vandamme was a day's march away, and the Prussians had held their ground — the Emperor had not been present — the Emperor had directed all. The noise died away as the Perpetual Secretary led him to the rostrum: here he laid his notes by the water-carafe, drew a deep breath, glared round the assembly in the expectant silence and began, 'Your Eminence,' in a voice so loud and aggressive that its returning echo shocked him extremely — shocked him almost fatally.

Most of the rest of his discourse was

delivered in a low mumble: those who were most deeply interested in Pezophaps solitarius craned forward, cupping their ears; the remaining five hundred or so gradually resumed their conversation, whispering at first, then more audibly by far. It was exceedingly painful for his friends; the beginning was bad, the continuation worse. It was clear that he neither saw nor heard his audience; from the inauspicious start he kept rigidly to his notes, his head bowed and his eyes fixed upon the paper. Occasionally he made a cataleptic gesture with his right hand and Diana was in an agony that he should dash the carafe to the ground. Once he turned over two pages, so that remarks on the dodo seemed to apply to the wombat of New Holland.

He was scarcely into the Ratitae when an officer came tiptoeing in to whisper into the ear of the minister of police: the minister left at once, also bowed and on tiptoe, and it was seen that he was grinning all over his false sly face. The talk redoubled. Stephen ground on, page after dogged, closely-reasoned page. He had dealt with the anastomosis of the carotid in Didus ineptus, and now he came to the loves of the solitaire. 'For the purpose of comparison, let us consider the intromittent organ of the raven,' he said, raising his spectacles and looking up for the first time. His eyes met those of Madame d'Uzès, sitting there in the front row: she leant forward and asked in her loud, deaf voice, 'What is an intromittent organ?'

Her neighbour told her. She said, 'Oh? Like a stallion? I had no idea. So much the better,' and laughed very cheerfully.

Stephen stared straight at her, repeating, 'Let us consider the intromittent organ of the raven.' She looked down, folding her hands in her lap, and returning to his notes he considered the organ at length, in a stronger, sterner voice than before, rhythmically waving a mummified example as he did so.

The minister's assistants, who had remained behind, leant over their chief's empty chair in quiet conversation. 'If that man has anything to do with intelligence, near or far,' said one, 'I am the Pope.'

'It was only a vague rumour,' said the other.

'The army sees spies everywhere. I checked, of course, but neither Fauvet nor Madame Dangeau could move him an inch: he was a mere natural philosopher, he said, knew nothing of politics, cared less, and must obey the rules. Madame Dangeau is sure he is a paederast, and I think she is right. He is a friend of La Mothe's.'

'What is his relationship with that woman sitting next to La Mothe, the woman with the amazing diamonds? They crossed together, but surely there could be no question of any liaison between such an individual and that magnificent creature?'

'He is her doctor. Her maid reports that he examines her — perfectly decent — quite unmoved. He must certainly be a paederast. Such a woman, and to be unmoved!'

'Poor brute: he is coming to an end at last.'

'A pitiful exhibition.'

Pitiful it might have been, but as far as foreign guests were concerned the standard of oratory was often in inverse proportion to the speaker's scientific worth; it was very usual for those who were not used to university chairs to blunder and mumble, and the Perpetual Secretary had seen far worse; so had the savants who had come to hear Dr Maturin rather than the gossip of the town. He had not flung his notes, exhibits and specimens to the ground; he had not come to an anguished halt in mid-career like the learned Schmidt of Gottingen, nor had he swooned away like Izibicki; and those in the front ranks had learnt a very great deal about the extinct avifauna of the Mascarenes. Their sincere congratulations, strong coffee, and the knowledge that the ordeal was over revived him. Diana and La Mothe and their friends assured him that he had done splendidly; they had heard every word; they even mentioned Pezophaps solitarius once or twice by name, and, more frequently, the dodo. 'It was very far from brilliant,' said he, smiling shyly. 'I am no Demosthenes. But I did what little my means allowed, and I flatter myself that we now have the solitaire's reproductive and digestive processes on a sounder basis than before.'

The fashionable people flocked out, leaving the place to the learned. Many of these came up to Stephen, making or renewing his acquaintance, and he conveyed kind remembrances from common friends in England: he also promised to take compliments back again, for here he had not the least scruple about acting as a messenger. Georges Cuvier gave him a copy of his *Ossements fossiles* for the worthy Sir Blaine, and Latreille the more appropriate gift of a bee in amber for the same gentleman. Larrey, the Emperor's surgeon, was particularly attentive. Gay-Lussac begged him to carry some curious pyrites to Sir Humphry Davy; another chemist gave him a phial whose exact nature escaped him; and presently his elegant pockets were bulging with presents for members of the Royal Society.

There were also many foreign savants present, and Stephen was gratified to see Benckendorff and Pobst and Cerutti; most were eminent in the physical sciences, but there were some mathematicians, historians and philologists too, and among them he perceived the long black beard of Schlendrian, that profound scholar, the foremost German authority on Romance languages. Schlendrian was standing somewhat apart, holding a glass of the Institut's lemonade, looking thoughtful and most uncharacteristically sad.

Their eyes met; they bowed; Stephen detached himself from a somewhat sterile conversation on chlorine, and they exchanged cordial greetings. But after the animation of the first compliments, congratulations and enquiries, Schlendrian's sadness returned; there was a silent pause in which he looked doubtfully at Stephen, and then he said, 'You have not heard the news, I presume?'

'Of the battle that is said to have been fought?'

'No. Of Ponsich.'

'What has happened to Ponsich?'

'I hardly like to tell you, on the day of your triumph.'

'Do not torment me, Schlendrian. You know how I love him.'

'So did I,' said Schlendrian, and there were tears in his eyes. 'He is dead.'

Stephen moved him away to an empty space by the door. 'How do you know? When did it happen?' he asked in a low voice.

'Graaf wrote to me from Leyden. It seems that Ponsich was in Sweden, or in the Baltic at all events, and that the ship he was travelling in met with a disaster. Many bodies were washed ashore in Pomerania, and he was recognized by a former student. Oh Maturin, what a loss for Catalan letters!'

'Listen, my dear,' said Stephen to Diana, drawing her from the concert-room in the Hôtel de La Mothe, 'I am about to take my leave. I am dropping with sleep I find, and tomorrow I must travel to Calais. I have made my excuses to Adhémar.'

'Already, Stephen?' she cried, her gaiety dropping at once. 'You are going back already? I thought you would stay at least till the end of the month.'

'No. I have done what I came to do, and I must be away. But before I go there are a few things I have to say.' She looked at him with concern; his face had a hard, contained expression, a strange contrast with the cheerfulness of the room they had just left. 'Listen,' he said again, 'I shall have news of you through my friends, and I may be over from time to time for meetings of this kind. And medically you are in the best possible hands; you must pay great attention to Baudelocque, my dear, and follow his instructions to the letter — a pregnancy can be a delicate affair. But should you have any uneasiness at all — it is in the last degree unlikely: your papers are perfectly in order and legally you belong to a friendly state — but if you should have any uneasiness either in Paris or Normandy, here is the direction of a sure friend of mine. Commit it to memory, Villiers, do you hear me now? Commit it to memory and burn the paper. And listen: should you ever be questioned about me you are to say that we are old acquaintances, no more; that I advise you as a medical man; and that there is nothing between us whatsoever, nothing between us at all.' He saw the flash of anger, the cruelly wounded pride on her face, took her hand, and said, 'You are to lie, my dear. You are to tell a black lie.'

Her eyes grew gentle again. 'I will *say* it, Stephen,' she said, with her best attempt at a smile, 'but I shall find it hard to be very convincing.'

He looked at her, standing there straight, her head held high, and his heart moved in him as it had not moved this great while: he said 'God bless, my dear. I am away.'

'God bless you too,' she replied, kissing him. 'Give my love to Jack and to Sophie; and pray, Stephen, pray take care of yourself.'

Chapter Six

For some time, for what seemed to him a very long time, Jack Aubrey had been fetching the post for Ashgrove Cottage himself. He dreaded discovery, and quite apart from the regular, the all too regular packets, a surprising stream of letters came from Halifax by the kind offices of returning men-of-war, transports, and merchant ships; and these letters, always speaking of an imminent return, kept him in a continual state of apprehension.

He was not, he never had been, a model of continence; but his affairs had always been of a warm and cheerful nature, with no vows or protestations; somewhat earthy affairs perhaps, of no real consequence; affairs with ladies of a like mind — no hint of seduction, still less of any high romantic frenzy. They were uncomplicated passing encounters, almost as evanescent as dreams and with as little tangible result; but this was entirely different.

The necessary subterfuge and concealment were extremely distasteful to him and the possible, the probable advent of a noisy, enthusiastic, hysterical Miss Smith was stark nightmare; but what grieved him most was the change in his relationship with Sophie. He could not talk to her with his usual complete openness; the deceit and the small ignoble lies set him apart; and he felt extremely lonely, sometimes quite desolate. In any case, he was no good at lying; he did it clumsily, and the doing filled him with anger.

More than once he thought of Stephen Maturin: he understood enough of his friend's occult activities to know that he must often lead a peculiarly solitary, cut-off life, perpetually watching himself, wholly free and candid with no one. He felt for him now: but, he reflected, Stephen's was at least an honourable secrecy, a long-drawn-out permissible ruse de guerre that could not damage him in his own opinion.

He was reading Miss Smith's latest effusions — three had arrived together — in one of the empty brick buildings by his abortive lead-mine deep in the deserted, desecrated wood when a shadow fell across the doorway. Darting the letter into his pocket, he whipped round with a very stern and forbidding expression on his face, an expression that instantly dissolved into one of lively pleasure. 'Why, there you are, Stephen,' he cried. 'I was thinking of you not five minutes past. How do you do? How come you here? We had not looked for you this fortnight and more.'

'Sophie told me I should find you here,' said Stephen. 'I called in on my way to London, and I have been sitting with her. She is worried about your health; and you are an ugly colour, sure. Will you show me your arm, now?'

'She knew I was here?' said Jack, his pleasure vanishing.

'Why, brother, one would think that you entertained the local nymphs in this forbidding bower,' said Stephen with a singularly ill-timed jocularity. 'Such guilty consternation I have rarely seen.'

'Not at all,' cried Jack. 'Oh, no,' and he asked after Stephen's voyage, after Diana, his reception in Paris, and the present state of France. Then, 'Will you walk up to the house? I was on my way there, with the post. You are staying with us, I trust? You will make the most welcome addition to our tête à tête, and we will have some music.'

'Alas, I am on the wing. My chaise is

waiting at the door, and I mean to be in town tonight. I have broken my journey to see you — indeed, I crossed to Portsmouth for the purpose — because I wished to know how you are situated.'

'I am situated in bilge-water up to the neck, Stephen. There is all this damned legal business — though your Mr Skinner is an immense comfort: I am very grateful for him — and then the Admiralty is being troublesome about payment for the *Waakzaamheid*; and there are some other things.'

'I am sorry for that. But what I really meant is how you were situated for a ship. Your plans were undetermined when last I saw you.'

'I have none. I refused the *Orion*, which they kindly offered me as a sort of half-leave on full pay; and having done that I cannot suddenly ask for another, though as things have turned out I should give my eye-teeth to be ordered on foreign service, to be right out of the country.'

'That is what I wanted to know: our purposes may suit. There is a possibility that I may have a mission in northern waters. It is no more than a possibility, but if I go, I had rather go with you than with any other. We are used to one another's ways; I do not have to play off any tedious mystifications with you; and I know you to be a rare hand at discretion. That is why I came: I wished to survey the ground and to know what I might suggest in London. May I take it that you would not be unwilling to accompany me, should the mission eventuate?'

'I should be very happy. Very happy indeed, Stephen.'

'I must warn you, that it is likely to be attended with a certain amount of risk, apart from the dangers of the elements. Have you heard of the fate of the *Daphne*?'

'Why, yes. It is common talk. It has not been in the newspapers that I know of, but everybody back from the Baltic speaks of it.'

'What do they say? I do not know the details.'

'The details vary, but all the accounts I have heard agree that she contrived to get too close to Groper Island —'

'Not Grimsholm?'

'It is all one. We call it Groper Island, just as we say Hogland, or the Belt, or the Sleeve; or Passages for that matter, or the Groyne. It seems that she got too close, probably in a flat calm, with the current setting in as it does in those waters, and that she was within gunshot before she was aware: otherwise, being a light thing, she would surely have towed into the offing, or even swept. However, what is certain is that they opened fire and sank her. They have forty-two pounders, perched high on the rock, with furnaces at hand — we used to see them glowing a great way off — and the likelihood is that they sent a red-hot shot into her magazine and blew her to pieces directly, for there were no survivors, and no trace of her that I can learn: only fishermen's tales.'

'Ay, that must have been the way of it. Well now, this same Grimsholm will probably be our destination.'

Jack whistled. 'A damned uncomfortable destination too,' he said. 'Shoal waters, ugly short seas, and then when you get there, such batteries! It is like a little Gibraltar, and not so little, neither: they have dug themselves in high up there, and they sweep a prodigious scope of sea. If those guns were well served, they could defy a fleet. Broadsides are not much use against well-placed, well-served artillery on a height, that can play on you with a plunging fire of red-hot shot. You know what the tower at Mortella did.'

'I do not.'

'Of course you do, Stephen. The Mortella tower in Corsica — the Martello, as some say, the round tower we have copied by the score all round the coast. It was ordered to be taken in ninety-three or ninety-four; and although it only had two eighteen-pounders and a six, with thirty-two men and a young ensign to serve them, Lord Hood sent both *Juno* and *Fortitude* in to batter it, while the army landed fourteen hundred men. Well, the ships battered away for two hours and more, and by the end of that time *Fortitude* had sixty-two men killed and wounded, three guns dismounted, her mainmast shot through and through, her other masts wounded, and the hot shot had set her on fire, so she had to haul off, damned lucky not to have run aground. So if one Martello tower can do that to two men-of-war, while at the same time it keeps off fourteen hundred soldiers, just think what Grimsholm, much higher, fifty times as strong, and with no soldiers to worry about, could do. It will be no picnic.'

'I do not suppose it is in contemplation to attempt the reduction of the place by brute force, but rather by subtler and I trust bloodless means,' said Stephen. 'At least they must be tried first. But now I come to think of it, you are a family man, a man with growing responsibilities, and this is more an employment for an unattached young bachelor: I perfectly understand your reluctance.'

'If you mean to insinuate that I am not game . . .' began Jack. 'But I dare say you mean it as a joke. Forgive me, Stephen; I usually see a joke as quick as the next man, but I am a little off colour these days.' They walked along in silence under the trees, and then he said, 'You are on your way to town. I have to be in Whitehall the day after tomorrow, about *Waakzaamheid*, so let me go up with you now. I should like to see something of you after all this while: we will go snacks for the chaise, and stay at the Grapes, and that will kill three birds at one blow.'

Stephen had been lucky in his carriage: it was unusually quiet and well sprung, and as it ran smoothly over the turnpike road in the darkness they could talk without the least constraint. The enclosed and as it were timeless space, moving through a largely unseen world and detached from it, was ideally suited for the free flow of confidence, and presently Jack said, 'I do so hope this scheme of yours comes off, Stephen. I have particular reasons for wishing to be abroad; or rather for wishing to be *ordered* abroad.'

Stephen considered this remark: in his younger, poorer days Jack had often longed to be out of the country to escape his creditors and imprisonment for debt; but this could hardly be the case now. Even if much of it was difficult to realize, he still possessed large remnants of his fortune; and although at the improbable worst his liabilities might prove greater still, only a court could decide upon that, at the end of long, long legal proceedings: and at present his interests were in the hands of a very able man of business who would never allow any sudden clapping of his client into a sponging-house. 'Yet I understood from Sophie that the first hearing, the mere preliminaries, was not to come up before the middle of next term,' he said.

'It is not that damned legal business,' said Jack. 'Indeed, sometimes I almost welcome all the endless paper-work; it acts as a kind of . . . No. The truth of the matter is — why, the truth of the matter is —.' He gave a short account of it, and ended, 'So, do you see, I hope that if I am ordered abroad, she will not come back here; or at least if she does that she will not settle just at hand. She spoke of Winchester, in her last. You need not tell me I am a scrub, Stephen; I know it very well.'

'I am not concerned with the moral issue,' said Stephen, 'but rather with what may usefully be done.' He was in fact surprised at such an abject degree of moral cowardice in a man whose physical courage could not be questioned: but, he reflected, he was not married; he did not know anything of domestic warfare at first hand, nor of the stakes involved, though he had some notion of the crushing nature of either defeat or victory and the extraordinarily powerful emotions that might come into play. He loved Sophie dearly, but he knew, and had long deplored, the jealous, possessive side of her character. The post-chaise bowled along: his mind drifted off to considerations on marriage, on the small number of successful unions he had known, and upon the probable balance of happiness and unhappiness, on the advantages and corresponding defects of other systems. 'Monogamy seems the only solution, alas,' he said to himself, 'although in a way it is as absurd as monarchy: Heaven forbid that we should fall into the errors of the Musulmans and Jews.'

'I will just say this,' said Jack, breaking in on his thoughts, 'though I know it don't amount to much. I have sent all I could: at least she is not short of money.' A pause, and he added, 'That is why the delay over the *Waakzaamheid* is so uncommon awkward, coming at this time, when most of what I have is tied up. It affects you too, Stephen: you share in head-money and gun-money; and seeing that you are pretty nearly the only surviving warrant officer, it should be a tidy sum.'

'I have a few observations to make,' said Stephen, brushing the *Waakzaamheid* aside. 'I offer them for what they are worth: they may be pertinent: they may be of some comfort to you. In the first place you must know that in women of an hysterical tendency, like the young person in question — for it would be idle, as well as uncandid, to feign that I do not know who she is —'

'I named no names,' cried Jack. 'God damn me, Stephen, if I so much as hinted at her name.'

'Ta, ta, ta,' said Stephen, waving his hand. 'In women of an hysterical tendency, I say, false pregnancies are by no means rare. All the gross symptoms of the nine-months disease are to be seen, the tumid belly, the suppression of the menses, even the production of milk; everything, except for the result. Secondly, I must tell you, as I told another friend not long ago, that even in the case of true pregnancy, rather better than twelve out of a hundred women miscarry. And thirdly, you are to consider the possibility of there being no pregnancy at all, true or hysterical. The lady may deceive herself; or she may deceive you. You would not be the first man to be cozened so. As I understand it, she has in fact made no very strenuous attempts to return, though several packets have gone to and fro. And it cannot be denied that a demand for money has a sadly untoward appearance.'

'Oh come, Stephen, what a blackguard thing to say. I know her. She may be rather — she may not be very wise — but she is incapable of doing that. Besides, I have begged her not to come — not yet. I tell you, Stephen, I *know* her.'

'Oh, as for knowing a woman . . . We read *enter in unto her and know her:* very well, and for the space of that coming together there is perhaps a true knowledge, a full communication; but after? It was a blackguard thing to say, I admit; but this is a blackguard world, in parts; and I should never have said it if I had not reasons to suppose that there might be some truth in it. I assert nothing, Jack, but the lady's reputation is very far from being perfect, as I know from another source, and I strongly advise you to take no decided step until you have some irrefragable independent evidence of her state — until you have really sifted the matter.'

'I know you mean it very kindly, Stephen,' said Jack, 'but I do beg you will not say things like that. It makes me feel more of a scrub than ever. I really cannot behave like a thief-taker towards a person who has . . . London Bridge already,' he cried, looking out of the window.

A few minutes later they were at the Grapes, where they had stayed together years ago, when Jack was evading his creditors; for the Grapes lay within the liberties of the Savoy, a refuge for flying debtors. Stephen was a poor man; that is to say, he usually lived like a poor man, and an abstemious poor man at that; but he did allow himself some indulgences, and one of these was the keeping of a room in this small quiet comfortable inn all the year round. The people were used to his ways, and he was welcome whenever he came; he had cured Mrs Broad, the landlady and an excellent plain cook, of the marthambles, and the boots of a less creditable disease; he could do much as he pleased at the Grapes and more than once he had brought back an orphan child — a dead orphan child — for dissection, keeping it in his cupboard without adverse comment. Nor was there any comment now, when towards the end of a very late supper of codlings and humble pie he made an unseasonable call for a coach.

'Do not stir, Jack. We will meet for breakfast, if God allow. Good night to you, so,' he said; and as he put on his greatcoat he observed with satisfaction that however Jack might protest Miss Smith's perfect innocence he had evidently digested at least some of his words as well as three quarters of the humble pie; he was now looking brighter by far, scarcely hangdog at all, and he was laying into the Stilton with a fine healthy appetite.

Once again it was Sir Joseph who opened the door. 'Here you are at last! Come in, come in,' he cried. 'You have heard the news of poor dear Ponsich?' he asked, showing him upstairs.

'That is why I came back,' said Stephen.

'So I hoped. So I have been hoping ever since the telegraph brought your signal.

Come, sit by the fire: I will move these papers — forgive the disorder — there is a mort of work in hand. The Americans are giving a great deal of trouble, in spite of your splendid work: half the Spaniards in Wellington's rear are Frenchmen at heart: things are not going well. And now there is this cruel news from the Baltic. If that Emperor of theirs is given a moment's respite he will bounce up like a jack-in-a-box, and all will be to do again. We have been longing for your return ever since the report came in.'

'Do you know what happened?'

'Yes. There was a lack of caution, I fear; and only too well do I remember Ponsich saying that he should take the bull by the horns. The sloop stood in, either underestimating the carry of those great guns or trusting too much in her Danish colours, and before she could even hoist out a boat with a flag of truce they opened a very accurate fire with red-hot shot: one struck her magazine, and she was utterly destroyed. We should have sent a more experienced commander.'

'He was a young man?'

'Yes. Just made commander into the *Daphne*, a very gallant officer, but scarcely twenty-two. Yet even before we had the first rumours and then the confirmation of the disaster we had grown exceedingly uneasy. From the moment Prussia declared the island became an object of great significance, but now, with the political situation changing so fast, it has grown even more important — it may be the price of Saxony's defection. If only we could win the King over on to our side, that would deal the French a very heavy blow, perhaps even a fatal blow; but one of his prime conditions is that we should be able to protect him and Prussia by landing on the Pomeranian coast, to cut off the French in Danzig and elsewhere and to harry their left wing from behind. This we cannot do without Grimsholm. Are you acquainted with the Baltic, Maturin?'

'Not at all,' said Stephen, 'though I have long wished to know it.'

'Then pray study this map. Endless dunes all along here, you see,' he said, pointing at the eastern shore. 'Shallow water, and with the prevailing westerlies, a bad lee shore: few good places for landing apart from the estuaries, and the best of those few commanded by this damned island. A meeting of admirals unanimously agreed that even without its protecting shoals, the bad holding-ground and the prevailing winds there was no possibility of taking Grimsholm from the west — from the side of the open sea. And although thet senior Marine officer advanced a plan for an assault from the east, his scheme called for a powerful squadron of ships of the line to provide a covering fire, to say nothing of innumerable transports and bombs. His estimate of the probable losses was shockingly high; but even if the losses had been acceptable and the chances of success far greater than he assumed the plan was obliged to be dismissed: we do not possess the men-of-war and transports to carry it out. We simply do not know where to turn for ships. This wretched American war drains our resources, and every day we have complaints from Lord Wellington that we do not cooperate with him on the north coast of Spain, that the Navy is scarcely to be seen, and that the French squadrons in the Bordeaux stream and farther north may attack his dangerously extended lines of communication at any moment. We are terribly short of ships, Maturin; and in this war everything depends on them.'

'Our new allies are little help, I collect?'

'Not at sea. The Swedes and the Russians may be very good soldiers, but it is the sea that decides the issue here. Besides, at this juncture you can scarcely call Bernadotte an ally at all. As you know, he is a slippery customer, a fellow that could give Judas a hint or two; and at present his chief aim is to take our subsidies in order to lay hold of the unoffending Norway. In any case the Swedes have little in the way of a working navy; nor have the Russians. That is to say, they possess some ships, but they do not know how to manage them. Ever since the English officers withdrew when those countries became our enemies, they have been quite incapable of handling them: and in addition to that, they are desperately slow and stupid. There was a Russian admiral at the meeting, and he suggested that we should starve them out. It was represented to him that they had six months' victuals in the place. Starve them out with a close blockade, says he again, in his execrable French. Starve them out with a six months' close blockade, when we did not possess the ships to do it and when every day is of prime importance! When a week might change the whole face of the northern war! However, not all foreigners are fools. We have a brilliant young Lithuanian, a cavalry officer seconded to us from the Swedish service, and he has provided us with a great deal of fresh intelligence that will I trust enable us to have another go, if you will allow me that low expression, another go with a clearer view of the situation.'

'Be so kind as to outline your clearer view.'

'It is very curious. In the last weeks there have been violent changes, caused by differences between the groups on the island. I believe the details are in that yellow folder beside you, if you will be so good. Yes,' he said, putting on his spectacles, 'here they are. I remember the last time you asked me about these groups, these organizations, I could not tell you; but there they are — now I have them. The Catalan force on the island was made up of three main bodies, the Lliga, the Confederació, and the Germandat.' Stephen nodded: he knew them well. 'The Lliga, the Confederació, and the Germandat — you will forgive my pronunciation, Maturin — each under its own leader, and they under the command of a French colonel of artillery. This colonel was called away to the siege of Riga, and in the confusion of events he was not immediately replaced: great dissensions broke out on the island, and the leader of the most powerful group took advantage of the colonel's absence to assume command and to send the officers who disagreed with him to the mainland, where they have been drafted into the Spanish Legion. He now refuses to place himself under the orders of the colonel's replacement, a Major Lesueur, on the grounds of Lesueur's inferior rank and of some alleged irregularity in his appointment by Macdonald. He has written to General Oudinot, stating that as a lieutenant-colonel — I fancy he promoted himself — he would rather die than submit to the affront: we have his letter.'

'Pray, Sir Joseph, what is the name of the now dominant group and of its commander?'

'The group is the Germandat,' said Sir Joseph, passing the letter, 'and you will make out his name better from the signature than from my attempt at pronouncing it; he writes like a cat, in any case.'

Ramon d'Ullastret i Casademon. In some degree Stephen had expected it: the word Germandat had already raised his heart, and perhaps a half-conscious sight of the handwriting had prepared him; but even so he stared at that familiar yet fantastic signature, his godfather's signature, for a long moment before it became real to him, before phantasm and reality could coincide.

'You know the gentleman?' asked Blaine.

It would have been strange if Stephen had not known him. The relationship was taken very seriously in the Catalonia of his childhood and he had spent many, many days in his godfather's house. En Ramon was a hero to him then: a most fervent patriot, one who traced his descent, in the female line, from Wilfred the Shaggy and who refused to speak Spanish unless he was, as he put it, abroad, that is to say in Aragon or Castile; a passionate hunter as much at home on the mountain or in the forest as any other predator, and one to whom the boy Stephen owed his first wolf, his first bear, his first imperial eagle's nest, to say nothing of the desman and the genet; an accomplished horseman; an untiring orator. The heroic light faded somewhat as Stephen advanced in years: En Ramon's pride was seen to contain a fair proportion of vanity; to a more objective eye his eager desire for pre-eminence, to lead rather than to be led, showed as something of a hindrance to the cause of Catalan autonomy; and a truer judgment detected more than a little headstrong foolishness in his godfather. But for all that Stephen retained a lively affection for him; his harmless delight in finery, his stickling for precedence, and even his more serious flaws did not amount to a great deal when they were compared with his courage, his delicate sense of honour, his generosity, and his unvarying kindness to his godson. Stephen could see him, pacing up and down the cold hall at Ullastret, his long knight of Malta's cloak sweeping from side to side as he declaimed a poem about the siege of Barcelona in his grandfather's time, when the Catalans and the English under Lord Peterborough routed the Spaniards, a poem which might have been more impressive, though it would certainly have been less touching, if the often-repeated Peterborough had not so consistently rhymed with mugger. 'I know him,' he said with a smile. 'How is his garrison usually supplied?'

'Sometimes from Danzig, more often from farther down, by Danish vessels. We took one of them very recently — the day the dispatches were sent — but its only cargo was wine and tobacco; I am afraid they are in no need of munitions or essential food. Their store-houses are crammed with biscuit and salt provisions, and they have all the fresh water they could want. At a pinch they could hold out well over six months.'

'Wine and tobacco may not be essential,' observed Stephen, 'but they are a wonderful comfort to the Mediterranean mind. Now this, I take it, is a plan of the fortification itself?'

'Just so. And these are the emplacements. We owe the maps to the young Lithuanian I mentioned just now, a very active fellow and one of the most remarkable linguists I have met. He speaks all the Baltic languages, and although he admits that his Esthonian and Finnish leave something to be desired, his English is well-nigh perfect, and so as far as I can judge is his French. He is an engaging creature and I am sure you would find him useful: that is to say, if you will consent to go, after this inauspicious beginning. It is true that the undertaking is by no means as straightforward as I had supposed.'

'Oh, clearly I must go,' said Stephen. 'There can be no question of that. Indeed, I have already taken the liberty of mentioning this possibility to my friend Aubrey: that is why I was so late — I stopped at his house for the purpose. I had much rather sail with him; I had much rather have him in the background than any stranger. He is a man of great experience, which as you so rightly observed is essential for an operation of this kind, a Ulysses by sea, whatever he may be by land; and he is at present both willing and able to go with me.'

'I am sure we are very much obliged to you, dear Maturin,' said Sir Joseph, shaking his hand. 'Very much obliged indeed. As for Aubrey, he would be ideal, always providing we can get round the difficulties of rank; sea-officers, you know, are wonderfully tenacious of their prerogatives, and the vessel we had in mind was only a sloop — but that is a mere detail. I am sure it can be dealt with.'

'Tell me,' said Stephen, after a silence, 'did Ponsich impose any conditions when he agreed to go to Grimsholm?'

'Yes, he did.'

'I wonder whether they were the same as mine. For I should require a clear understanding that in the event of my succeeding in the negotiation, the Catalan troops should not be regarded as prisoners of war, but that they should be carried to Spain as free men with their arms and baggage, and treated with proper regards. I should in any case need to be able to promise this, and I should be most unwilling to be disavowed: in fact, I should insist upon a categoric assurance.'

'I understand you perfectly. Of course, *I* cannot give the assurance: that must come from on high. But as Ponsich received an almost identical promise, I have no sort of doubt that it will be forthcoming.'

'Good. Very good. Have you any more documents that I should see?'

'Plans, plans and appreciations of the military position: nothing of real interest to you or me. Perhaps we might leave them until tomorrow, when the young man I have mentioned can explain his annotations: he has many talents, but writing a clear hand is not among them. In the meantime let us have a pot of coffee: I am longing to hear of Paris and your reception there.'

While he was away Stephen looked round the room. It had changed in some way, and after some moments he realized that the erotic bronzes and pictures had disappeared, and that vases of flowers stood here and there. 'Past three o'clock, and a dirty threatening night,' called the watchman in the street below, just as Blaine returned, 'looks mighty like a storm.'

They drank their pot; they drank the best part of a bottle of old pale brandy and talked of Paris. Stephen conveyed their friends' greetings and their presents. Sir Joseph asked civilly after the progress of Captain Aubrey's legal affairs, and rejoiced to hear that his suggestion had been of some use. And then, as Stephen was gathering himself to rise, he said, 'I wonder, Maturin, I wonder whether I might consult you as a physician?'

Stephen bowed, settled back in his chair, and said he should be happy.

'For some time past,' said Sir Joseph, fixing the coffee-pot with his gaze, 'for some time past, I have been contemplating marriage.'

'Marriage,' said Stephen in a neutral tone; for his patient seemed unable to get along — seemed almost to suppose that this was a sufficient description of his complaint.

'Yes,' said Blaine at last. 'Marriage. Liaisons are very well; indeed, very agreeable at times; but there is a certain shall I say restless sterility about them and in any case the lady in question is strictly virtuous. Yet perhaps I may have left it too late. Of recent months I have become most painfully aware of a certain — how shall I put it? Of a certain want of vigour, of a certain debility, as though I too should sing vixi puellis nuper idoneus. Is there nothing that physic can do in such a case, or is it inevitable at my age? I have passed Horace's lustra decem; yet I have heard tell of elixirs and drops.'

'It is not inevitable at all,' said Stephen. 'Consider Old Parr, the old, old, very old man. He married again, fruitfully, I believe, at a hundred and twenty-two; and if I do not mistake he was prosecuted for rape at an even later date. My colleague Beauprin, whom I had the pleasure of knowing in France, was only eighty when he married again, but his wife brought him sixteen children. Yet before I speak as a physician, may I ask you as a friend whether you have fully considered the wisdom of reviving these fires? When a man looks about him, surely he sees that in general the pain outweighs the pleasure? Your own Horace begged Venus to spare him — parce, precor, precor. Is not peace the greatest good? Calm rather than storms? I once sailed with a young man well versed in Chinese, and I remember his quoting a passage from the Analects of Confucius in which the sage congratulated himself on having reached the time of obedient ears, the time at which he could do whatever his heart moved him to do without the least transgression of the moral law. And Origen, as you recall, struck off the offending member, and returned to purer contemplations, undisturbed.'

'I quite take your point, and a very cogent point it is; but you forget that I am speaking not of a loose, irregular connexion — it is marriage that I have in mind. Yet even if that were not the case, I should still ask for your help. I do not think that I am a man of an unusually warm temperament, a particularly amorous man; when I take off my shoes and stockings I do not see a satyr's leg. But since this weakness came upon me I find that I must always have looked at the more personable members of the sex with a certain eye, an appreciative, even a remotely concupiscent, a faintly hopeful eye; and with that eye extinguished, it is as though the spring of life were gone. I had no conception of its importance. You are younger than I am, Maturin, and it may be that you do not know from experience that the absence of a torment may be a worse torment still: you may wish to throw a hair-shirt aside, not realizing that it is the hair-shirt alone that keeps you warm.'

'A Nessus' shirt might be more apt,' said Stephen, quite unheard.

'And I must remind you that Origen's rash gesture was condemned by the second Council of Constantinople, together with many of his pernicious doctrines; that although St Augustine prayed for the gift of chastity he added the rider *but not yet, oh Lord,* doubtless feeling that where there was no temptation there was no corresponding virtue; and that the peace of which you speak has a close resemblance to death. We are all Stoics in the grave.'

'It shall be as you wish,' said Stephen. 'Yet before the consultation proper begins, I beg leave to observe, that the spectacle of a swimmer who has reached the edge of the Maelstrom, who can leave the vexed waters, the whirling turbulence, and who voluntarily plunges back again, is one that would have made my philosopher cry out in wonder.'

'Even if we grant that your sage knew the Maelstrom, which is extremely unlikely, we cannot push credulity so far as to suppose that he ever met anyone like Miss Blenkinsop: otherwise we should never have heard so much about these ears of his.'

* * *

Jack and Stephen did not meet for breakfast. There was no sign of Dr Maturin at all, and when Jack had twice poked his head in at the door, each time hearing the rhythmical wheeze of a man at peace, he put on his best uniform and walked off to the Admiralty to see whether his appointment might be set forward a day. It might, he found; but the gentleman who received him was one of the civilian officials, and like most of his kind he treated sea-officers not indeed as enemies, but as creatures always eager to claim more than their due in employment, promotion, allowances, compensation, prize-money, head-money, gun-money: people to be treated with a distant reserve. Often their claims could be referred to the Navy Office, the Transport Board, or the Sick and Hurt people for comment or clarification, so that a man without interest might wait a very long time for a satisfactory response or even any interview at all, and many lieutenants and commanders did so; yet a fairly senior post-captain was used with more outward deference, and Mr Solmes not only rose to greet Jack Aubrey, but even placed him a chair.

After some civil preliminaries he drew

out a folder, opened it, and said, 'I am to advert to your action with the *Waakzaamheid*, and in the first place I am to ask you how you can be sure of her identity.'

'Why, Captain Fielding of the *Nymph* reported her off Cape Branco, so when we ran into a ship of the line under Dutch colours almost immediately after, we naturally assumed that she was the same.'

'But there being no prisoners and no documentary evidence of any kind, we have no absolute proof that the vessel in question was the *Waakzaamheid*, as you call her.'

Jack made no reply for some seconds: he was beginning to feel extremely angry. Then he said, 'The *Leopard* under my command sank a Dutch seventy-four in latitude forty-two south. The conditions in those waters, with a full gale and a heavy following sea, are sufficiently well known to require no explanation of the fact that no prisoners or documentary evidence can be produced. Why, sir, the moment her foremast came by the board she broached to and vanished directly. In seas of that kind there is no lying a-try, no looking for survivors or documents: a ship must scud or perish.'

'I am perfectly convinced of it, sir,' cried

Mr Solmes, who could not fail to notice the stern voice and the way Captain Aubrey seemed to swell in size. 'And you will appreciate that I act under direction in dwelling on this point. Departmental rules have to be obeyed; and this is an exceptional case.'

'I cannot see where the exception lies,' said Jack. 'Plenty of enemy ships have been destroyed without a scrap of material evidence to prove they ever swam. I could cite a dozen precedents. The log and the unanimous statement of the officers has always been accepted. It is the immemorial custom of the service.'

'I quite agree,' said Solmes. 'But — you will forgive me, Captain Aubrey — but in this case the statement of the officers is not quite unanimous: it is that which makes it so exceptional. We have received a communication from your former first lieutenant in which, among other things, he acquaints us with his impression that the vessel was a Dutch store-ship, armed en flute.'

'A store-ship?' cried Jack. 'The man is mad. I may not have seen the *Waakzaamheid*'s name on her stern, but by God I saw her broadside: and tasted it, too. A post-captain of my service and seniority not to know a ship of the line when he sees one — not to know a seventy-four when he engages her! By God, sir, it is monstrous! The man is mad.'

'No doubt, sir, no doubt. But until he is certified insane we are bound by the rules to take notice of what he says. May I suggest that you procure affidavits from your surviving commissioned officers and warrant officers of wardroom rank? I see that you had Lieutenant Babbington, Lieutenant Byron, and the surgeon Maturin. Come in.'

The messenger came in: Admiral Dommet had heard that Captain Aubrey was with Mr Solmes: would be happy to see him when he was at liberty.

'Aubrey,' cried the Admiral, 'I am very happy to see you. We were just about to send when we heard you were already here — here already, in Whitehall! That is what I call a coincidence. You think of a man one minute, and you see him the next! It almost makes you believe in crystal-gazers. Well now, the point is this: there is a delicate, pressing piece of work that calls for a cool, experienced hand. It was suggested that you might not like being offered a sloop, but I said "Pooh, pooh, Aubrey don't have to stand on his dignity —

Aubrey don't top it the Great Mogul — Aubrey would take a punt against the enemy, so long as there was a gun in it". Ain't I right, Aubrey?'

'Quite right, sir,' said Jack. 'And I am obliged for your good opinion of me.' He knew very well that this was the Admiral's idea of deep manipulation: in the circumstances he did not resent it at all. 'May I ask what sloop, sir?'

'*Ariel*,' said the Admiral. 'She is lying at the Nore. You can post down and catch the morning tide. God send the wind stays in the south-west.'

'May I not pick up my dunnage, sir, and have a word with my wife?'

'Heavens, no, Aubrey. This is an urgent business, as I said — I will telegraph Portsmouth and they will tell her to expect you back next month with a feather in your cap — but time and tide wait for no man, you know.'

'No, sir,' said Jack; and not to be outdone he added, 'And they say that a feather in the cap is worth two in the bush.'

'Ay, so they do. Well, come now: we must not lose a minute. The First Lord wishes to see you.'

In far graver, far more measured terms

the First Lord told Captain Aubrey all that he had already heard from Stephen and Admiral Dommet, congratulated him on his escape from America, on having been present at the noble victory, and on his readiness to set formality and his own convenience aside for the good of the service; stated that it was of course fully understood that the command of the *Ariel* in no way represented the Board's estimate of Captain Aubrey's merits; and finished by saying that although no promises could be made at this stage, there was a possibility of his being offered one of the new heavy frigates now preparing for the North American station on his return. Captain Aubrey's orders would be sent to him as soon as they were written out; and if he would like to save coach-hire, he might choose to travel down with the King's Messenger, who would be setting out shortly after dinner.

'I should have asked when King's Messengers were fed,' thought Jack, walking quickly along the Strand. 'Are they fashionable eight o'clock coves, or are they not?'

He was not himself a fashionable cove, nor was his stomach: years of life at sea had trained it to expect its due at the old-fashioned early naval hour and to cry out when that hour was past. It had been past for some time now, and on entering the Grapes he too cried out 'Mrs Broad, Mrs Broad, there. Please to put dinner in hand directly. I faint, ma'am, I fail. Where is the Doctor?'

'It is all laid in the snug, Capting, and only waits on the Doctor's pleasure. He is upstairs with a foreign young gentleman, talking foreign twenty to the dozen.'

'Such a sweet young gentleman,' observed Lucy through the hatch.

'If I have told him once,' said Mrs Broad, 'I have told him ten times. No joint, no, nor no fowl, will bear such treatment. I will call him again.'

'Let me go up, Aunt Broad,' cried Lucy, darting from behind the bar.

Jack walked into the snug, seized a piece of bread and ate it. A few moments later Stephen came in, followed by the sweet young gentleman, a slim officer in a mauve coat with silver lace; he had surprisingly golden hair, bright blue eyes, large and set wide-apart, and a complexion that any girl might have envied. His air was modest, but by no means unmanly: Lucy gazed steadily at him with her mouth open, standing ready to pull out his chair, while

Stephen said, 'Allow me to present Monsieur Jagiello, of the Swedish service: Captain Aubrey, of the Royal Navy.'

Jagiello bowed, blushed, and said that he was deeply honoured, most sensible of the occasion.

The meal began. Jack set the young man at his right hand and entertained him with small but civil talk, to which Jagiello responded in fluent, almost perfect English, with only the occasional confusion of v and w or j and y that made the native agreeably aware of his superiority. Stephen said nothing except during a silent pause: Jagiello was carving a fowl; Lucy and Deborah could be heard quarrelling about who should bring the next dish in; and in a quick aside Jack told him 'that they had their marching orders'. 'So I understand,' he replied. 'Monsieur Jagiello accompanies us.'

'I am heartily glad of it,' said Jack, who had taken a liking to the young man. 'I hope, sir, you are a good sailor?'

Before Jagiello could answer an Admiralty messenger came in, brought by both Deborah and Lucy, and delivered his official packet into Jack's own hands; the messenger had to find his own way out, however, since both girls stayed to stare at

Jagiello in a very simple, moon-struck fashion, until Mrs Broad's voice called them about their business. Even then they kept coming in and out on one pretext or another — more salt, more gravy, a little mustard, would the gentlemen like more bread? — but at the end of dinner they had a far more valid excuse, since Jack always liked to do foreigners honour in his own country, and his favourite way of doing so was to fill them with as much port wine as ever they could hold, so that while they waited for the King's Messenger the bottles came in, pint after pint, a most surprising number.

Jagiello held it very well, but in time his beautiful complexion became pinker, his blue eyes brighter still, and he himself grew musical: he had spoken of English popular songs with an appreciation not far from enthusiasm, and now, after a proper reluctance, he obliged the company with The Lady and Death in a pure, true-pitched tenor. Chevy Chase followed, and All in the Downs, with Jack's deep voice making the glasses rattle, while Stephen's harsh and disagreeable croak convulsed the maidens clinging to one another just outside the door.

To this nest of singing-birds there

entered a thin silent disapproving gentleman in a sad-coloured coat with stuff-covered buttons and starched white neckcloth who seemed to have dined on cold vinegar. He put out their gaiety at once, and they followed him into the coach looking as though they had been detected in a peculiarly shameful fault: Stephen, darting back for a forgotten handkerchief, observed Lucy setting her lips to the edge of the sweet young gentleman's empty glass.

The sweet young gentleman's rosy flush faded in the open air; for some time he looked but palely and it was touch and go whether the lurching and jerking of the coach might not overcome him; but once they were clear of Blackheath he revived and looked about, quite ready for conversation. He met with no encouragement, however: the King's Messenger had taken out a book, and screwing himself round in his corner so that the page caught the light he screened himself from his companions; Dr Maturin was deep in a brown study, staring at his toes; and Captain Aubrey was asleep, snoring in a strong, commanding bass. From time to time the Messenger made awkward jerking motions, trying to kick the Captain awake without seeming to do so on purpose; but without success. Otherwise there was no animation in the coach at all.

The tide flowed up the Thames, the coach ran down towards its mouth. The tide slackened in the Pool, and all the close-packed shipping there rode high; the ebb began, and imperceptibly the masts sank lower, while foul black mud appeared on either side, yet down at the Nore the tide still had the best part of an hour to run when Jack's boat pulled a zigzag course among the men-of-war towards the *Ariel* in the twilight: for the last mile over the water it had been apparent that her commander was entertaining: light streamed from her stern-windows, and the sound of a party, a musical party, streamed out with it, while ladies were to be seen dancing on the little quarterdeck, a sight that evidently drew all eyes aboard, since the boat was not hailed until it was within spitting distance, and Captain Aubrey's reception as he came up the side was a sadly bungled affair. He had not told the boat to lie off to give them time for the proper ceremony, partly because he was in a tearing hurry — he had lost valuable minutes snatching up the bare necessities in Chatham — and partly because to one whose head was still aching from the Grapes's port this slackness seemed inexcusable.

'I had not expected you until the morning, sir,' cried the unhappy Captain Draper. 'The Admiral spoke of the morning tide.'

'I am sorry for that, Captain Draper,' said Jack, 'but it is the present tide that I intend to take. Pray let the hands be called aft.'

The wail and twitter of the bosun's pipes, the order 'Off hats', and Jack stepped to the mainmast; while Draper held a lantern for him he read in a strong, hieratic voice 'By the Commissioners for executing the office of Lord High Admiral of Great Britain and Ireland etc. and of all His Majesty's plantations etc. To John Aubrey, esquire, hereby appointed captain of His Majesty's ship the *Ariel*. By virtue of the power and authority to us given, we do hereby constitute and appoint you captain of His Majesty's ship the *Ariel*, willing and requiring you forthwith to go on board and take upon you the charge and command of captain in her accordingly, strictly charging and commanding all the officers and company of the said ship to behave themselves, jointly and severally, in their respective employments with all due respect and obedience unto you their said captain and you likewise to observe and execute the General Printed Instructions and such orders and directions as you shall from time to time receive from us or any other of your superior officers, for His Majesty's service. Hereof nor you nor any of you may fail as you will answer the contrary at your peril. And for so doing this shall be your warrant . . .'

He had read himself in: the moment he finished the *Ariel* changed from a sloop to a post-ship, with J. Aubrey as her captain, whose lawful order it was death to disobey.

'I am truly sorry to bundle you and your guests over the side,' he said to poor Draper; and then in a very much louder voice, 'All hands to unmoor ship.'

'All hands to unmoor ship,' roared the bosun and his mates, sounding their calls, although the order had been heard from stem to stern and even as far as the *Indomitable*, two cables' lengths to windward.

'There is Jack Aubrey getting under way,' observed the *Indomitable*'s first lieutenant to her master. 'I will lay you a bottle of port we see some fireworks before he clears the Mouse.'

'Lucky Jack Aubrey,' said the master.

'He was always a great one for the guns.'

While the hands were running to their stations and the carpenters pinning and swifting the capstan-bars, Jack said to Draper, 'Please to introduce the officers.' They were all there, just at hand: Hyde, the first lieutenant, Fenton the second, Grimmond the master, and the rest. Draper hurriedly named them: he was on fire to get his cabin cleared and his mumchance guests away. Jack stated that he was very glad to see them, begged Draper to make his humblest excuses to the ladies, said 'Carry on, Mr Hyde,' and took up his station near the wheel. Throughout the bustle of getting the guests ready he stood there, watching attentively.

The hands were very conscious of his gaze, and they jumped to their duties as they rarely jumped for young Mr Draper. They had known he was coming ever since the flag-lieutenant had brought a Baltic pilot aboard, together with orders for Captain Draper — the news, coming by way of the Captain's steward, had spread through the sloop in rather less than two minutes — and although many of the Ariels were landsmen or boys there were quite enough man-of-war's men aboard to tell them of

Lucky Jack Aubrey's reputation as a fighting captain, while the three or four who had sailed with him magnified it extremely: he ate fire for breakfast, elevenses, dinner and supper; it was his custom to head up defaulters in a cask and toss them overboard; he could do so without let or hindrance because why? because he had made a hundred thousand pounds, two hundred thousand pounds, a million of money in prizes, and rode in a coach and six; and the poor unfortunate buggers he served in this way were those that took more than forty seconds to fire their broadsides, or missed their mark. All those who could possibly do so eyed him as they heaved round the capstan-bars to the brisk squeaking of a fife, eyed him apprehensively, for he was indeed a formidable figure, standing there silent, larger than life in the twilight, by the nervous Mr Hyde: a figure that did not seem in the best of tempers either, one that obviously had the habit of command, a figure that emanated authority.

The starboard cable glided in; the afterguard, the Marines, and most of the topmen heaved; the others veered out through the larboard hawse; the quartermasters and the forecastlemen coiled the cable won in tiers, stinking of Thames mud. The cat-fall was overhauled, the fish was clear.

'Up and down, sir,' called the second lieutenant from the forecastle.

'Thick and weigh for drying,' replied Mr Hyde in his agitation, and then with a nervous glance at Jack, 'I mean thick and dry for weighing.'

The *Ariel*'s best bower broke the surface; the cat was hooked to the ring; her people clapped on to the fall, ran it up to the cat-head and fished it in a most seamanlike manner; and with scarcely a pause the ship began to move over to her small bower, the capstan turning steadily.

'Up and down,' came the cry, and now for the first time the new captain intervened. 'Vast heaving,' he called in a voice calculated for a far larger ship. 'Back and pawl. Side-boys aft,' for he had seen that Draper was ready, and he wished him to go over the side in proper style, although it would cost minutes of this beautiful windward tide.

This Draper did, to the wail of pipes, with something like a tear in his eye, and his glum companions mute in the boat; and the moment it was decently clear and pulling for the shore Jack called 'Away aloft. Trice up and lay out.' The topmen raced up the shrouds, ran out along the yards, cast off the gaskets and stood poised there holding the sails. 'Let fall. Sheet home, sheet home. Man the halliards: haul, haul. Belay.' The yards rose, the sheets were tallied aft, the billowing sails stood taut, and the *Ariel*, surging ahead, plucked her anchor from the ground. The hands at the capstan ran the remaining fathoms of cable in as briskly as the tierers could handle it, and the small bower was catted and fished just as she shaved past the *Indomitable*, a biscuit's toss to windward, passed between her and her next ahead, and headed out to sea on the tail of the ebb.

'She cast pretty,' said the master of the *Indomitable*.

'It was damned impertinence to go to windward of us,' said the first lieutenant. 'She would have ruined my fresh paint, with the least hint of a check to the anchor.'

A few minutes later the *Ariel* dropped her topgallantsails and Jack said, 'Lay me for the Mouse, Mr Grimmond. There is always some garbage there, at slack water.'

Up until this time Stephen, Jagiello, and the King's Messenger had been standing meekly out of the way, like parcels, by the ensign-staff. Jack called the first lieutenant, introduced him, and said 'Mr Hyde, we must bestow these gentlemen as well as we can. Dr Maturin can share my cabin, but you will have to find room to swing two more cots somewhere below.'

Hyde looked more anxious still. With a deferential mirthless smile he said that he should do his best, but the *Ariel* was a flush-decked ship.

If Jack had not already noticed that she lacked anything but a theoretical quarter-deck and forecastle — that her deck ran without a break from stem to stern so that although beautiful she was decidedly cramped — he noticed it immediately afterwards, when he led his charges below. Long experience had taught him to bend between decks, and without taking thought he ducked as he entered the cabin. Jagiello was not so fortunate: he struck his head against a beam with such shocking force that although he protested that it was nothing — he felt nothing — his face turned deathly white, so that the blood running down it showed even more distinctly. They sat him down on a locker — even the Messenger displayed a glimmering of humanity — and while Stephen mopped him, Jack called for grog, told him that it might happen to anyone, and that he should always watch out for low beams in unrated ships, particularly in French unrated ships. Captain Aubrey did not sit with them long, however: as soon as it became apparent that Jagiello would survive he went on deck again.

The squadron at the Nore was already far astern, Sheerness no more than a looming blur. The *Ariel* was slipping easily through the calm slack water, making a good five knots with the gentle breeze, her wake as straight as a well-drawn furrow.

He took half a dozen turns on the little quarterdeck, looking aloft, looking over her side, getting the feel of her. It was much as he had expected, the feel of a well-built, well-rigged ship, fast, weatherly, and easy in hand. He knew her well, having chased her twice without success when she was still a French corvette and having seen her often after she was captured, one of the few French ship-rigged corvettes that the Admiralty had not ruined by adding a superstructure, though as usual they had over-gunned her, cutting an extra port a side, which probably dulled her fine point of sailing and certainly brought her a little by the stern. A trim little ship, a frigate in miniature, but with a purer unbroken line; a formidable little ship too, with her sixteen thirty-two pounder carronades and her two long nines — formidable, that is to say, at close range, a match for anything of her own class, so long as she could get near enough.

From the moment she had been mentioned in Whitehall he had been confident that the *Ariel*, well handled, would do anything he asked her, within sea-reason: what he did not know was the capacities of those who were to do the handling. There were obviously some prime seamen among them; they had unmoored creditably and everything on deck was shipshape and Bristol-fashion except for that stray slab-line forward; but the *Ariel* was obviously short-handed, perhaps twenty below her complement of a hundred and twelve, and there was an undue proportion of boys. Yet the main question was not so much whether they could sail the ship as whether they could fight her guns. He knew nothing of the young men who had had her during the last two years, nothing of their standards of gunnery; and since tomorrow might find him at grips with a Dutchman out of the Scheldt, to say nothing of possible French or American privateers farther ahead and very probable Danish gunboats in the Belt, he wanted to know what he should expect, and in view of that knowledge, what tactics he should adopt.

'Come up the sheets half a fathom, Mr Grimmond,' he said to the master, who had the watch. 'We do not want to get there too soon. And perhaps we might have that slab-line belayed.' Another couple of turns, and he felt the *Ariel* slacken her pace, like a soft-mouthed mare gently checked by her rider. The Mouse was still quite a fair distance ahead.

'Pass the word for the gunner,' he said. And to the bright-eyed, round-headed young gunner he said, 'Master gunner, tell me the state of your stores.'

The *Ariel* was not very rich, but she was not destitute either: he could afford two or three broadsides, using a couple of half-barrels of the inferior white-mark powder. This would exhaust his Admiralty practice-allowance for the next eight months, but as soon as he touched at Carlscrona, where he was to join the Commander-in-Chief, Baltic, he would fill her magazines and shot-lockers out of his own pocket, as did most captains who could afford it and who were deeply convinced that accurate, rapid gunfire was the best way of beating the enemy at sea.

'Very well,' he said, as three bells struck, three bells in the last dog-watch. 'Mr Hyde, we will beat to quarters, if you please.'

'Beat to quarters,' cried the first lieutenant. But there followed a most horrid pause. Nothing of the kind had been expected so late in the day; the drummer was in the head, his breeches down; the drum could not be found, still less made to roar. However, encouraged by the bosun and his mates, all hands ran to their action-stations, and some moments later Jack was gratified with the ludicrous spectacle of the drummer, his shirt-tail hanging out, thundering madly to a motionless ship's company.

'Vast drumming,' roared Mr Hyde, shaking his fist at the unhappy man; and then turning to Jack he said in a quiet, respectful tone, 'All present and sober, sir, if you please.'

'Thank you, Mr Hyde,' said Jack, and he stepped forward to the imaginary line that separated the imaginary quarterdeck from the imaginary waist. The Mouse bank was coming near, and though the light was nearly gone he could still make out the long line of floating rubbish that gathered there between tides.

'Silence fore and aft,' he cried. There was not the least need: the entire ship's company was perfectly mute and the only sound was that of the breeze sighing in the rigging, the creak of blocks and the lap of the water down her side. But this was understood by all to be the only right beginning to the martial litany that ran on 'Cast loose your gun — level your gun — out tompion — run out your gun.' No surprise at all in this: but amazement when the Captain broke the ritual sequence by saying to the master at the con, 'Lay me within half musket-shot of that cask to leeward, Mr Grimmond,' and then in a louder voice, 'Prime your gun. The crate on the starboard bow is your mark. From forward aft, fire as it bears.'

A breathless pause, and the flash from the bow nine-pounder lit the sky, almost instantly followed by the starboard carronades in a rippling broadside.

'What did I tell you?' said the first lieutenant of the *Indomitable* to the master.

They both stared out northwards: the deep angry roar reached them, and a moment later the low clouds of the northern sky glowed red again. 'He has put the ship about,' said the master. Again the distant thunder, and now a pause, while the master counted aloud. He reached seventy, and once more the long flash lit the sky.

'He will get in a fourth,' said the lieutenant. But this time he was wrong. Jack gave the order 'House your guns,' said 'A creditable exercise, Mr Hyde,' and went below smiling, his headache and ill-temper gone.

Chapter Seven

No Dutchman from the Texel or the Scheldt came out to meet the *Ariel*, nor did she encounter any privateers. But the Danes had never cordially loved the Royal Navy since the bombardments of their capital and the taking of their fleet; danger lay ahead, and the little ship proceeded on her way, daily more prepared to meet it.

To his satisfaction Jack found that he had inherited a better ship's company than he had expected. The gunner had served under Broke, learning his trade in the old *Druid*; two of his mates had belonged to the *Surprise* when Jack had her; and although Draper, his predecessor, had been unwilling or unable to spend much on powder and shot, he had at least fitted locks and sights to the nine-pounders, while his officers, a decent average set of young men, were perfectly willing to enter into their new captain's notion of the standard of gunnery proper to a King's ship.

The *Ariel* sailed north, therefore, in an

often-renewed cloud of her own smoke, thundering by day and night, odd, unexpected intervals being the best training for an emergency; and although Jack could not hope for the speed he had achieved in long commissions nor anything like the accuracy — apart from all other considerations his short carronades were incapable of throwing a ball with the precision of a long gun — he was pleased with the result so far, and confident that the *Ariel* would do herself credit if she were to meet with a fair match. Indeed he longed for such an action, not only because of his natural love of battle — of the immense exhilaration, the magnifying of life — but because the Ariels, though a fairly good crew, were made up of three recent drafts and they did not form a whole. All through his naval life he had observed the attachment, even the affection, that sprang up between men who had been through a serious sea-fight together, and the very valuable change in the relationship between the hands and the officers, a change that worked both ways. For example, there was a bond between him and Raikes and Harris, the gunner's mates, because they had all three been mauled by a French ship of the line in the Indian Ocean: naval custom ruled out much in the way of conversation between them, but the special relationship, the esteem, was most certainly there.

'This is more like a proper life for a man,' he observed to Stephen, after one of these exercises had caused the Heligoland Bight to ring again.

'Sure, even the complexity of a vessel with as many masts as this, with all their ropes and the nice adjustment of their dependent sails, is nothing to the difficulties of life ashore,' replied Stephen, pulling up his collar. He had always noticed that Jack was quite another man at sea, a bigger man, capable of dealing both with strange surprising situations and the common daily round, and usually a happier one; but he had rarely seen the change so strongly marked before. A bitter drizzle was sweeping down from the North Frisian islands; a short cross-sea kept sending irregular dashes of spray across the windward side of the quarterdeck; and Jack's face rose above his inadequate, hastily-purchased pea-jacket, streaming with wet but beaming like a somewhat battered rising sun. 'Perhaps to some degree it may lie in the altumal simplicity of our diet, a diet produced by no effort of our own, and served up at stated intervals; whereas on land food is a frequent subject of consideration, and the gastric juices are therefore perpetually solicited; but no doubt a more important factor on shore is the presence of an entirely different sex, of the excitation of other appetites, and of the appearance of a whole new set of social and even moral values.'

'Why, as to that,' said Jack: but he was peering and craning to see the foretopmast crosstrees, and for the moment his mind was elsewhere. 'Mr Rowbotham,' he called to a midshipman on the leeward side, 'jump up to the foretopmast crosstrees and tell Mr Jagiello, with my compliments, that I would like to speak to him, when he is at leisure. And harkee, Mr Rowbotham, he is to come down through the lubber's hole, d'ye hear me? There is to be no skylarking, no sliding down the backstays.'

'No, sir. Yes, sir,' said Rowbotham, and shot into the rigging with the speed if not the grace of his cousin the ring-tailed lemur.

'I beg your pardon,' said Jack, 'but I really cannot have him wandering aloft like that, above all with his wounded hand. He is an unlucky wight, and will certainly break his neck.' It was true. Jagiello had already taken advantage of a temporary gap in the hammock-netting to fall into the sea, from which he had been plucked, laughing heartily, by a well-aimed log-line; and of the only time a hatchway had ever been left uncovered to plunge into the hold, where nothing but a heap of empty sacks preserved him; and he had very, very nearly been destroyed when Awkward Moses dropped the mizen topgallantmast fid just between his feet from such a height that the massive piece of iron stuck in the deck like a bar-shot; while only yesterday the lock of a nine-pounder had slipped its sear when he was being shown the mechanism, almost severing one finger and pinching the rest most cruelly. He was a popular figure aboard: the hands liked him not only because he had begged Awkward Moses off his flogging but also because he was always cheerful, and apparently quite devoid of fear; the gunroom liked him because he was good company, attentive to their anecdotes and appreciative of their wit. The stupider officers, like Mr Hyde, still addressed him in a loud, slow, barbarous jargon calculated for half-witted children and foreigners, but Graham the surgeon, a reading man when he was sober, and Fenton, the second lieutenant, maintained that it was great nonsense to say

'I'm called dog's body. 'Tis pease-pudden really, but we say dog's body. You — like — 'im, dog's body?' to a man who could play such a hand at whist and beat all comers at the chess-board. And in both cases his absurd beauty and an indefinable sweetness of manner no doubt had their effect.

'Ah, Mr Jagiello,' said Jack, 'how kind of you to come. I wanted to ask you in the first place whether you would favour us with your company at dinner — I am also asking Mr Hyde — and in the second whether you have any military connexions in the town of Gothenburg. Our lower tier of powder proves sadly damp, and I should very much like to replace it.'

'I should be very happy, sir,' said Jagiello. 'Thank you very much. And as for Gothenburg, I know the commandant; I am sure he will be delighted to give you powder, all the more since his mother is a Scotch.'

Stephen had spoken of the simplicity of their diet, and the Captain's dinner was a fair example of it. Apart from the marine glue, flavoured with sherry and thickened with crushed biscuit, that began the feast, and a dwarfish fowl which Stephen carefully divided into four wizzened pieces that tasted of tar, and some of yesterday's dried peas, boiled in a cloth until they merged into a homogenous mass, it was exactly the same salt horse and biscuit that had nourished the gunroom, the midshipmen's berth, and the mess-deck a little earlier in the day; for the *Ariel*, hurried so untimely to sea, had not had the leisure to lay in private stores. What little she had left had been devoured before she reached 54°N., and now all hands would have to be content with what the Victualling Office allowed them, at least until they reached Swedish waters.

'Perhaps you would be so kind as to cut up Mr Jagiello's beef for him,' said Jack to Mr Hyde, nodding at his guest's bandaged hand.

'By all means, sir,' cried the lieutenant, and he set to his laborious task. The beef had been to the West Indies and back, and now, in its raw state, it could be carved and filed into durable ornaments; and even after some hours in the steep-tubs and the galley copper it still retained something of its heart of oak. Stephen noticed that Hyde was left-handed, which gave him an awkward air; but his left hand was obviously powerful, obviously used to salt horse; and using immense pressure he was dividing the lump into reasonable gobbets. As he did so he said to Jagiello in an undertone, 'I hope 'im no hurt too much?'

'You are very good, sir,' replied Jagiello. 'It is nothing at all. I must confess that this morning I found a little inconvenience in shaving and in putting on my pea-jacket, but Dr Maturin' — bowing to Stephen — 'and Dr Graham . . .'

Here the beef shot into Jack's bosom with surprising force. It was in vain that they laughed, it was in vain that Jack told Hyde he should certainly be hanged for directing a lethal weapon at a superior officer: the poor man could scarcely smile, and when, the meal having begun again, he passed the pease-pudding to Jagiello, saying 'A little god's body, sir — dog's body, I mean?' he did so in a low and melancholy voice.

This was not the first time that Stephen had noticed Hyde's tendency to displace letters, and he wondered whether it might be connected with his left-handedness — whether the confusion of right and left (and he had seen Hyde pass the port the wrong way round) might not be related to the inversion of sounds, particularly at a time when the mind itself was confused. He did not pursue the reflection however but said, 'A little while ago we were speaking of sex. But now I come to think of it, perhaps this is not a proper subject for the Captain's table, from which politics and religion are excluded — a subject laudable on the deck but forbidden below it?'

'I believe I have known it raised at table,' said Jack.

'It was the sense of freedom, and of simplification, that prompted my observation. In this ark, this floating community, we are all of the same sex: what would be the effect if our numbers were evenly divided between the two, as it is the case on land?' He addressed himself more particularly to Jagiello, who blushed, and said he could not tell. 'I know very little of women, sir,' he said. 'You cannot make friends with them: they are the Yews of the world.'

'Yews, Mr Jagiello?' cried Jack. And to himself, chuckling much, he added, 'It would be a damned odd thing if they proved rams, you know.'

'Jews, I mean,' said Jagiello. 'You cannot make friends with Jews. They have been beaten and spitted on so long they are the enemy, like the Laconical helots; and women have been domestical helots for oh so much longer. There is no friendship between enemies, even in a truce; they are always watching. And if you are not friends, where is the real knowledge?'

'Some speak of love,' suggested Stephen.

'Love?' cried the young man. 'But love is a creature of time, whereas friendship is not. Your own Shakespeare says . . .'

The sailors never learnt what their own Shakespeare said, because a midshipman, sent by the officer of the watch, came to say that the weather, lifting to leeward, had disclosed twenty-eight sail of merchantmen, together with a frigate and a brig, thought to be *Melampus* and *Dryad.*

'A Baltic convoy for sure,' said Jack. 'No one could mistake *Melampus.* But still I think we may as well have a look. Doctor, will you entertain Mr Jagiello with reasons until we come back? I have great hopes we may finish our dinner with something better than condemned Essex cheese.'

'Mr Jagiello,' said Stephen, when they had gone, 'I should like to ask you about the ancient gods of Lithuania, which, I understand, still lead a ghostly life among your boors, about the worship of oak-trees, the white-tailed eagle and the plica Polonica, the beaver, the mink, and the wisent or European bison; but first, before it should slip my mind, I must tell you I am charged with a message, to be delivered in a most tactful, diplomatic way, so that it does not in the least resemble an order — so improper to a guest — but so that it shall have an equivalent force and effect. Your agility in the upper rigging excites wonder and admiration, my dear sir; but at the same time it causes a very great uneasiness of mind, an uneasiness proportionable to the esteem in which you are held; and it would please the Captain if you would confine yourself to the lower platforms, technically known as tops.'

'Does he believe that I shall fall?'

'He believes that the laws of gravity bear more severely on soldiers than on seamen; and since you are a hussar, he is convinced that you will fall.'

'I shall do as he wishes, of course. But he is mistaken, you know: heroes never fall. At least, not fatally.'

'I was not aware that you were a hero, Mr Jagiello.'

The *Ariel* took on a surprising lean as she brought the stiff breeze abaft the beam, set her topgallants and weather studdingsails and dashed down on the *Melampus* at a good ten knots, her lee-rail buried in the foam. Jagiello had a good hold on the table, but a lee-lurch unseated him and he slid to the deck, where for a moment his spurs, caught in the matting, held him prisoner. 'Of course I am a hero,' he said, getting up and laughing very cheerfully. 'Every man is a hero of his own tale. Surely, Dr Maturin, every man must look on himself as wiser and more intelligent and more virtuous than the rest, so how could he see himself as the villain, or even as a minor character? And you must have noticed that heroes are never beaten. They may be undone for a while, but they always do themselves up again, and marry the virtuous young gentlewoman.'

'I have noticed it, indeed. There are some eminent exceptions, sure, but upon the whole I am convinced you are right. Perhaps it is that which makes your novel or tale a little tedious.'

'Ah, Dr Maturin,' cried Jagiello, 'if I could find an Amazon, one of a tribe of women that never have been oppressed, one that I could be friends with, equal friends, oh how I should love her!'

'Alas, my dear, men destroyed the last Amazon two thousand years ago; and I fear your heart must go virgin to the grave.'

'What is that noise, like bears on the roof?' asked Jagiello, breaking off.

'It is the launching of a boat. And from

the howling of the mariners I collect that it will be some time before we see our dessert. What say you to a game of chess while we are waiting? It may be no conclusive test of our relative wisdom, virtue, or intelligence, but I can think of no better.'

'With all my heart,' said Jagiello. 'But if I lose, you are not to suppose that it will make the least difference to my conviction.'

The game might not prove much about the intelligence of the players, but it provided certain evidence that Jagiello's virtue or at least his kindness was greater than Stephen's: Stephen, playing to win, had launched a powerful attack on the queen's side; he had launched it one move too early — a vile pawn still masked his heavy artillery — and now Jagiello was wondering how he could play to lose, how he could make a mistake that should not be woundingly obvious to his opponent. Jagiello's chess was far beyond Stephen's; his power of dissembling his emotions was not, and Stephen was watching his expression of ill-assumed stupidity with some amusement when the boat was heard to return.

A moment later Jack came in, followed by his steward bearing a plum-cake the size of a moderate cart-wheel and by two powerful hands with a hamper that clanked glassy as they set it down, while the pitter of hoofs overhead and a melancholy baa told of the presence of at least one devoted sheep. Jagiello, with a look of relief, instantly moved the board to make room for the cake, solving his problem by upsetting all the pieces.

'I am sorry to have been so tedious long,' said Jack. 'But I am sure you will find it worth the wait: *Melampus* has always done herself as proud as the Mansion House. Cut and come again, Mr Jagiello: this only has to last us until Gothenburg.'

Gothenburg, a melancholy town, most of it quite recently burnt, inhabited by tall spare melancholiacs dressed in grey wool, much given to drinking and self-murder (the river brought three suicides past the *Ariel* during her brief stay), but kind to strangers if not to themselves. The Commandant at once provided powder, best red-letter cylinder powder, together with a present of smoked reindeer's tongues and a barrel of salted honey-buzzards. These he gave to Stephen, saying, 'Pray accept this small keg of buzzards.'

'Buzzards, my dear sir?' cried Stephen,

startled from his usual calm.

'Oh, not common buzzards,' said the Commandant, 'nor rough-legged buzzards; you need not be afraid. They are all honey-buzzards, I do assure you.'

'I am fully persuaded of it, sir, and return my best thanks,' said Stephen. 'May I ask how they came there?' he added, looking attentively at the cask.

'I put them there myself,' said the Commandant with pride, 'I put them there with my own hands, choosing each one. Fine plump birds, though I should not say it.'

'Did you shoot them, sir?'

'Oh no,' said the Commandant, quite shocked. 'You must never shoot a honey-buzzard: it ruins the flavour. No: we strangle them.'

'Do they not resent this?'

'I think not,' said the Commandant. 'It happens at night. I have a small house at Falsterbo, a peninsula at the far end of the Sound with a few trees upon it; here the birds come in the autumn, myriads of birds flying south, and great numbers roost in the wood, so many you may scarcely see the trees. We choose the best, pluck them down, and so strangle them. It has been done for ever; all the best salted buzzards come from Falsterbo; and no doubt they are used to it.'

'Do eagles also appear, sir?' asked Stephen.

'Oh yes, oh yes indeed!'

'Do you salt them too?'

'Oh no,' said the Commandant, amused. 'A salted eagle would be a very whimsical dish. They are always pickled, you know; otherwise they would eat intolerably dry.'

While the powder was coming aboard, Stephen said, 'How I should like to see this Falsterbo.'

'Perhaps you will,' said Jack. 'The Commandant tells me the Danes are very thick on the ground in the Belt; *Melampus* said the same; and I have a great mind to run through the Sound. Let us have a word with the pilot. Mr Pellworm,' said he, when the Baltic pilot came in, an ancient man, Jack's old and highly respected acquaintance, 'Mr Pellworm, I have a great mind to run through the Sound. I know the Danes have shifted their buoys, but do you think you could take her through the narrows in the night, the tail-end of the night?'

'Man and boy,' said Mr Pellworm, 'man and boy I threaded the Sound till I know it like the back of my hand. Like the back of my hand, sir. I do not need their old sea-marks to take a ship of *Ariel*'s draught through the narrows in the night; or right down to Falsterbo for that matter, with the Swedish lights.'

'And what do you think of the wind, Mr Pellworm?'

'Why sir, at this time of year we always say "in by the Sound, out by the Belt", because the westerlies always hang a little north in the one and a little south in the other. Never you fear for the wind, sir; it will stand fair for the Sound these next three or four days, or I am a Dutchman.'

'Then let it be so, Mr Pellworm. We will weigh the moment the powder-hoy casts off, and that will get us through the narrows in the darkness.'

The pilot was no Dutchman as far as the wind's direction was concerned; to begin with it carried the *Ariel* down the Cattegat at a fine brisk pace. But he was mistaken as to its force: in the middle watch Jack stirred from his sleep, listened to the song of the water along the ship's side, put a jacket over his nightshirt and went on deck. Diffused moonlight, a quiet black sea, and the *Ariel* slipping along under all plain sail: perhaps five knots, certainly not more. Far out on the larboard bow a light on the Swedish shore: surely it could not be the Kullen? Surely the Kullen must be well astern by now? He stepped over to the binnacle, took the log-board with its chalked record of wind, course, and speed, and quickly worked out his position: yes, it was certainly the Kullen.

The pilot came over to him and coughed apologetically. 'May I have the watch below to make more sail, sir?' he asked.

'No,' said Jack. 'It is not worth it. Let us wait until eight bells.'

They were sadly behind their time, but it was not worth calling all hands now: even with royals, skyscrapers, and studdingsails aloft and alow they would still have to pass the narrows in the daylight.

'Mr — Mr Jevons, is it not?' he said to a muffled midshipman in the dimness. 'Pray go below and fetch my boat-cloak: it is hanging by the barometer. And take great care not to wake the Doctor.'

Wrapped in his cloak, he stood by the stern lantern, watching the sky and the ship and considering his course of action: upon the whole he thought he should carry on rather than go round by the Belt; the danger was not very great, and the saving of time outweighed it; what he really disliked about this late passage was that the Danish gunboats from Copenhagen and

Saltholm would be perfectly ready for him, the news having run ahead. And that, if it were to fall flat calm, might be unpleasant: they were an enterprising lot, and they had already captured a number of sloops and brigs of war. However, he thought he should carry on. And while he turned this over in his mind he also reflected upon some aspects of life at sea and the unvarying routine he had known in every ship he had sailed in: a harsh cold, uncomfortable, demanding routine often enough, but one that did at least bring order out of chaos. An acknowledged framework; commandments from on high, sometimes arbitrary, sometimes archaic, but generally workable and always more immediate, more obviously enforced than the Decalogue. An infinity of problems within that framework of course, but the order provided answers to most of them: or cut them short with sudden death.

Seven bells, and from all round the ship there came the cry 'All's well.'

Eight bells, and while the frowzy larbowlines were being mustered, warm, pink and unwashed from their hammocks, the mate of the watch heaved the log.

'Turn,' cried the mate. Twenty-eight seconds later 'Nip' cried the quartermaster.

'What have you?' called Jack.

'Four knots and three fathoms, sir, if you please,' replied Mr Fenton.

It was much as he had thought; a steady decline. Still, he could always creep along under the Swedish batteries; or even put into Helsingborg. While both watches were on deck he gave orders to make more sail and returned to his meditation.

The eastern sky was lightening, and already the ritual of washing the almost spotless deck was well in hand; the pumps were wheezing round, all was awash, and Jack went below to put on some clothes and get out of the maintopmen's way as they moved aft with buckets, sand, holystones and swabs.

The *Ariel* was a very little ship, but she did her commander proud: as well as his 'great' cabin he had two little booths opening off it, his sleeping and dining cabins; and seeing that neither was encumbered with guns, *Ariel* being flush-decked, there was just enough room in each to sling a cot. He had put Stephen into one, moving the dining-table aft; and at this table he now sat comfortably enough until the rhythmical beating of swabs told him that the deck, unnecessarily washed, had now been unnecessarily dried.

He returned to his place, there watching the steady progress of the ship's exactly-ordered life, the unfolding promise of the day, scanning the clouds for the probable behaviour of the wind, and watching the coast move slowly, very slowly by.

He was still there when Stephen appeared, unusually early for him, carrying a borrowed telescope. 'Good morning, Jack,' he said; and then, staring about him, 'Mother of God, it is narrower than I had supposed.'

Narrow it was: on the shore to larboard walked Swedes, clearly to be seen in the bright sunlight, and on that to starboard Danes: three miles of sea between them, and the *Ariel* in about the middle, rather nearer the Swedish side, creeping south with little more than steerage-way upon her.

'Have you seen them yet?' he asked.

'Have I seen what?'

'Why, the eider-ducks, of course. Do you not remember that Jagiello promised us eider-ducks in the Sound? I had thought that was what you were looking at so earnestly.'

'So he did: but I have not really been attending. Still, I believe I can show you something that will please you even more.

Do you see those green roofs and terraces? That is Elsinore.'

'Elsinore itself? The very Elsinore? God bless my soul: and yours too, joy. A noble pile. I view it with reverence. I had supposed it to be merely ideal — hush, do not move. They come, they come!'

A flight of duck wheeled overhead, large powerful heavy swift-flying duck in files, and pitched between the castle and the ship.

'Eiders without a doubt,' said Stephen, his telescope fixed upon them. 'They are mostly young: but there on the right is a drake in full dress. He dives: I see his black belly. This is a day to mark with a white stone.' A great jet of white water sprang from the surface of the sea. The eiders vanished. 'Good God!' he cried, staring in amazement, 'What was that?'

'They have opened on us with their mortars,' said Jack. 'That was what I was looking for.' A puff of smoke appeared on the nearer terrace, and half a minute later a second fountain rose, two hundred yards short of the *Ariel.*

'The Goths,' cried Stephen, glaring angrily at Elsinore. 'They might have hit the birds. These Danes have always been a very froward people. Do you know, Jack, what they did at Clonmacnois? They burnt it, the thieves, and their queen sat on the high altar mother-naked, uttering oracles in a heathen frenzy. Ota was the strumpet's name. It is all of a piece: look at Hamlet's mother. I only wonder her behaviour caused any comment.'

The next shot pitched well over the *Ariel*, sending up its plume a cable's length to larboard. Jack took the telescope and trained it on the battery. Five whiffs of smoke that drifted away down the Sound; five fountains in the sea, three beyond, two short; and the long sullen roar. 'Tolerably good practice,' he observed. 'They are increasing their charge.'

The pilot came aft and said, 'Shall I put her into Helsingborg, sir?'

'No,' said Jack, glancing at the Swedish port a little abaft the larboard beam. 'Carry on down the Sound, Mr Pellworm. You may shave the Swedish shore as close as you please, however.' And to Stephen he said, 'Tossing a two-hundred-pound bombshell at a moving object is a chancy business at this range, you know; a hit or miss affair; nothing like lobbing them into a fortification, or an anchored fleet. And they have just as much chance of hitting us if we put back as if we stand on — indeed, rather more, since we should be going from them in a right line. Mr Jagiello, good morning to you. The Danes are busy, as you see.'

'I wish they may burst,' said Jagiello. 'Good morning, sir. Doctor, your servant.'

A group of three shells, directly in the *Ariel*'s path, sent up three distinct columns, instantly shattered into a confused mass of flying water as the charges exploded under the surface.

'Down with your helm,' called Jack, and the *Ariel* began to perform a languid jig, swerving, letting fly her sheets or hauling aft, diminishing and increasing her gentle pace: never by very much, but at least enough to make sure that every fresh discharge would have to be the result of a separate calculation on the part of the Danes.

'Mr Hyde,' he said to the first lieutenant, pointing to a number of large fish that lay belly-up where the shells had exploded, 'let a net be put over the side. We may as well profit by the situation.'

Slowly, slowly, the nearer sea moved by; the shore seemed quite motionless. Sometimes the courses and the topsails flapped, with no thrust in them; and the hands on the forecastle could be heard whistling quietly for a breeze. They had not much time for brooding, however: at seven bells hammocks were piped up, at eight the men were piped to breakfast, and the pleasant smell of frying fish wafted about the deck.

'Were you ever in Elsinore, Mr Jagiello?' asked Jack.

'Oh, many a time, sir,' said Jagiello. 'I know it well. I believe I could show you Hamlet's grave from here.'

'I was really wondering whether they were ten or thirteen inch mortars on the upper terrace,' said Jack, 'but I should be very happy to see Hamlet's grave as well.'

'Both ten *and* thirteen, sir. And if you go a little to the right from the farthest turret, there are some trees: and among those trees there is the grave. You can just make out the rocks.'

'So there he lies,' said Jack, his telescope levelled. 'Well, well: we must all come to it. But it was a capital piece, capital. I never laughed so much in my life.'

'A capital piece indeed,' said Stephen, 'and I doubt I could have done much better myself. But, do you know, I have never in my own mind classed it among the comedies. Pray did you read it recently?'

'I never read it at all,' said Jack. 'That is to say, not right through. No: I did something better than that — I acted in it. There, the upper terrace fires. I was a midshipman at the time.'

'What part did you play?'

Jack did not answer at once: he was watching for the fall, counting the seconds. At the twenty-eighth it came, well pitched up but wide to starboard. 'Port your helm, there,' he called, and then went on, 'I was one of the sexton's mates. There were seventeen of us, and we had real earth to dig, brought from shore; it played Old Harry with the deck, but by God it was worth it. Lord, how we laughed! The carpenter was the sexton, and instead of going on in that tedious way about whose grave it was he made remarks about the ship's company. I was Ophelia too: that is to say, one of the Ophelias.'

Another salvo tore up the sea, true in line this time, but short: and as he watched Jack caught the flash of a single mortar. Again the line was true and he saw the shell soar to its height, soar until it was no more than a small black ball against the pale sky, then curve down, racing down, growing fast, to burst well astern. 'Judging from the height,' he said, 'I fancy they have reached their full elevation and their full charge.'

The next salvo confirmed his judgment; the last hundred yards had carried them beyond the battery's malice; and he suggested that they too should have breakfast. 'The smell of that fish is more than I can bear,' he said privately to Stephen.

At the breakfast-table, with a fine view of the narrows and the now silent Elsinore, Stephen said, 'So you were Ophelia in your youth, Captain Aubrey.'

'A part of Ophelia. But in this case the part was greater than the whole: I was called back three times, and the other fellows were not called back at all, even the one that was drowned in a green dress with sprigs. Three times, upon my honour!'

'How did the poor young lady come to be divided up?'

'Why, there was only one midshipman in the flagship pretty enough for a girl, but his voice was broke and he could not keep in tune neither; so for the part where she has to sing, I put on the dress and piped up with my back to the audience. But neither of us was going to be drowned and buried in real earth, Admiral or no Admiral, so that part fell to a youngster who could not defend himself; and that made three of us, do you see.' Jack smiled, his mind going back to the West Indies, where the performance had taken place; and after a while he sang:

'Young men will do't
An they come to't
By Cock they are to blame.

Yes, alas; and it all ended unhappy, as I recall.'

'So it did, too,' said Stephen, 'the pity of the world. I believe I shall go upstairs again, if there is no more coffee left. I should be sorry to miss any of the Baltic's wonders, they being, as you might say, some compensation for all the grief there is by land.'

More eiders he saw, and later in the day, off the island of Saltholm, some very curious sea-duck that he could not identify, that he had no time to identify, for the breeze had freshened steadily, and now the *Ariel* was running at eight knots. It was vexing, but on the other hand without this fine turn of speed she would never have reached Falsterbo with enough light for a perfect view of a white-tailed eagle, an enormous bird in full adult plumage that plucked a fish from the sea not twenty yards from the *Ariel*'s stern; and then again her pace meant that no flotilla of gunboats, grim but slow, would attempt her.

'I am glad to hear it,' he said, when Jack told him that the ship was now well out of their range; that she was now steering to run between Bornholm and the main; and that if this breeze freshened still further, which seemed likely, they should join the Admiral in excellent time. 'I am glad to hear it, because after today's excitement I should like a long quiet night to collect my ideas; for who knows what tomorrow may bring? Bearded swans, the phoenix himself, maybe. I shall turn in at once.'

No swans of any kind, no phoenix: a low sky, scudding cloud, a short choppy grey sea, and the *Ariel* tearing along under close-reefed topsails. As it increased in force the wind veered into the west and then north of west, cutting up a sea that gave her a strong corkscrewing motion, while at the same time she pitched violently at short, very short intervals, working so that she spewed her oakum from the knightheads to the bitts. Stephen's stomach had withstood the Atlantic, the Pacific, and the Indian oceans, but the Baltic very nearly overcame him. He was not actually sick, but he exhibited a cold, copious salivation, a dislike for jovial company, facetiousness or merriment, and an intolerance of the notion of food. It was probably that nasty fish of yesterday, he thought; bursten-bellied fish might very well convey all manner of noxious principles; only a fool would eat them. And only a fool would go to sea, exposing his frame to the falling damps. He kept the deck for the most part of the forenoon. There it was not so much a question of falling as of horizontal damps, for every time the *Ariel* plunged her head into a sea sheets of spray and even solid water swept aft, piercing his armour at every joint, so that in time he was wet as well as cold, wet through and through.

'Perhaps I shall go and see my colleague, and beg ten drops of the sulphureous ether; or failing that, a little acid of sulphur, dulcified,' he said to himself. 'The man is a very mere sot, but at least he has a medicine-chest,' and he turned to find a quarterdeck messenger to show him the way, a jolly pink child who wore a winged cap, such being the *Ariel*'s whim. As they went below he heard a cry of 'Sail ho! A cat two points on the starboard bow,' but he never paused. They had sighted another sail earlier in the day, a Dane for sure said the officers who had cruised the Baltic all last summer in the *Ariel*; but with infinite reluctance Jack had let her run; his business was far too urgent for him to be chasing prizes, and it would be the same with this one. In any case Stephen was not in the least interested in a prize; all he wanted was sulphureous ether.

Alas, he found the mere sot in much the same state as himself, only worse: speechless, careless of the world, pale green, unshaven, malodorous; and what was far more regrettable he had drunk up all the ship's sulphureous ether, and had spilt the sulphuric acid. It was now eating its way through his counterpane, but he did not mind: the sooner it ate its way through the bottom of the ship the better, he whispered.

Stephen left him in disgust, and turning on the boy who had shown him the way to Mr Graham's cabin he said 'See what comes of your heathenish superstitious custom of whistling: your own surgeon sick, for shame. Let the Captain be told that I am retiring to meditate, and that I beg to be excused from dining.'

He had not taken breakfast; he did not dine; he did not share the Captain's tea; and when at last the *Ariel* shot into the calm waters of Carlscrona and saluted the Admiral he felt cold, glum, and weak; so weak indeed that when *Ariel*'s gig was alongside the flagship and he himself clambering awkwardly aboard, the manrope slipped from his hand and he fell, dropping like a sack. But Jack had prepared for this: his old friend was no seaman, never had been and never would be a seaman; from the beginning of their acquaintance he had fallen from motionless ships and spars, motionless boats; and more than once he had even plunged between ship and boat when going up the side. Captain Aubrey had therefore given orders that the gig should hook on to the flagship as tight as a limpet and that two powerful seamen should stand at the foot of the accommodation-ladder 'in case anyone should take a tumble'. These men, who knew very well what o'clock it was, caught Dr Maturin's frail body as easily as a corded hammock — it weighed little more — and propelled him up the side again, urging him 'to clap on with both hands, sir — never say die — one more heave and we're home, safe and dry.'

The Captain of the Fleet received them: received them coldly, observing that the Admiral was not at leisure, and that if *Ariel* were to be attached to the Baltic squadron, he would thank Captain Aubrey to wear an ensign of the proper colour. Sir James had recently been promoted vice-admiral of the red, which any man might have discovered by taking a little trouble. The reception was roughly what Jack had expected ever since he heard that Manby was Captain of the Fleet: in the course of his career, and particularly during the fierier, more undisciplined early stages of it, he had made many solid, reliable friends and some solid, reliable enemies, Manby being one of them.

Yet this disagreeable impression did not last for long. A few minutes later a number of Swedish officers left the ship and the Admiral's secretary, a grave young parson, showed Jack and Stephen into the great cabin, a noble room, although at present it looked more like a busy office than part of a man-of-war — files everywhere, a desk covered with papers, and behind the desk a pale Admiral, himself more like a jaded, work-worn minister than a sea-officer.

He was obviously tired, but he greeted them cordially. 'It must be years since we met, Captain Aubrey,' he said, having congratulated Jack on his rapid passage.

'The last time was at Gibraltar, sir, just after your splendid victory in the Gut,' said Jack.

'Yes, yes,' said Sir James. 'The Lord was

good to us that day.'

Stephen had been a spectator of that bloody affair: he thought the violent death of two thousand Frenchmen and Spaniards an odd proof of the Lord's goodness, but he had known other able men with the Admiral's view of divine Providence. During the brief interval while Jack delivered his dispatches before introducing him, he studied Sir James's face: grave, heavy-lidded eyes, a distinguished, earnest face, not much given to merriment. He knew Sir James's reputation as a blue-light Admiral, a friend to tracts and psalms, but he had known men of the Book prove most effectual men of the sword as well and when the Admiral turned to him and he caught his intelligent, penetrating, politely attentive look he felt his heart rise: this man was no fool.

'Allow me to name Dr Maturin, sir, who also brings you a communication from the Admiralty,' said Jack. 'Sir James Saumarez.'

'I am very happy to meet Dr Maturin,' said the Admiral. 'I had been half expecting you, sir, and I believe I know what your letter contains. If you will forgive me, I will read it at once. Will you take a little refreshment? I always drink a glass or two of wine at this time, and take a biscuit. My brother Richard recommends it; I believe you know him, sir?' — this with a bow to Stephen.

He rang his bell; the wine appeared on the instant, and having served the others he retired to his desk with his glass, his dispatches and the letter. Dick Saumarez: yes, of course Stephen knew him, though he had not made the connexion, a surgeon, a tolerably good physiologist, though obstinate and wrong-headed about the ligature of the external iliac in the case of aneurism of the femoral: Stephen thoroughly approved of his recommendation, however. The wine was champagne, a fine fruity champagne, not too cold, and it went down very gratefully with a biscuit: he felt his weakness recede, his mind grow sharper, less gloomy, more decisive. He reflected upon the medicinal use of alcohol. He also reflected — for the dispatch was long — on Jack's expression: it was respectful, naturally enough, for not only was a vice-admiral a very much greater man than a post-captain, but Jack also entertained a sincere regard for Sir James as a man and as a most capable, resolute officer; it also had a slight resemblance to Captain Aubrey's church-going face, with just a touch of sanctimoniousness or rather of primness, a look that sat uneasily on that red, weather-beaten, open, candid, habitually cheerful face. It was as though he were himself determined to follow the advice he had given before they set out across the harbour: 'Do not get drunk or talk bawdy or blaspheme or even swear when you are aboard the flag, Stephen: the Admiral is very particular, and it will cost you a guinea every time you take the Lord's name in vain.'

Jack, for his part, reflected upon the Admiral. Lord, how the poor man had aged. It was not surprising. Even as a commodore of a small squadron Jack had been cruelly harassed by paperwork, by the responsibility for very important decisions whose execution lay in others' hands, by the problems of cooperation with the army and with civilian authorities, by a thousand questions that had nothing to do with the running or the fighting of his ship: for the Commander-in-Chief in the Baltic it must be very, very much worse.

'It is much as I had expected,' said the Admiral, laying the letter on the dispatch. 'So you are poor Mr Ponsich's successor, sir? How I pray you may be more successful. Is Captain Aubrey aware of the nature of your mission?'

'Yes, sir.'

'Then I have no doubt that you would both like to see Mr Thornton, my political adviser. As far as I know the situation on Grimsholm has not changed, but he has all the most recent information.'

Stephen knew Thornton well, a Foreign Office man with a flair for intelligence and a singular grasp of detail. They greeted one another with the odd ambiguous civility that had become second nature to both, betraying nothing but some degree of social acquaintance, even in spite of the present circumstances.

'Dr Maturin has come out to take Señor Ponsich's place,' said the Admiral, 'and I have just told him that I know of no change in the position on Grimsholm; but I speak without the book, and I am sure you can make a more authoritative statement.'

'On the island itself there has been no material change,' said Thornton. 'We have two recent reports of a certain amount of discontent, caused by a lack of wine and tobacco, but it seems that Colonel d'Ullastret has the situation well in hand: he is popular with the garrison, and he has strengthened his authority by sending three more officers away to Danzig. But on the mainland the French take the matter very seriously indeed: a most reliable source tells us that in spite of all his difficulties Oudinot means to replace the Catalans by a mixed brigade of Poles, Saxons and French; and while these are being assembled and hurried to the coast he is sending a General Mercier, together with the former commandant, Colonel Ligier, to take control. They are to bring d'Ullastret the Légion d'honneur and the offer of an independent command in Italy: on Tuesday they reached Hollenstein on their way to Gobau. It is not impossible that they have already taken ship. In the meantime all supplies for Grimsholm have been cut off, both from Pomerania and Denmark. Apart from these reports I have nothing new except for a more exactly detailed account of d'Ullastret's forces and the disposition of his guns. He has started to excavate a new battery to sweep the approaches from the mainland.'

He handed Stephen the list of units, territorial units whose names were as familiar to Stephen as his own: San Feliu, Lloret de Mar, Palafrugell, Tossa, San Pere Pescador for the sea, Empurdá for the plain, Vich, Mollo, Ripoll and many more for the mountain. There were the names of their officers too, many of them equally familiar. He mused for a time, while Jack and the Admiral studied the chart of the waters around Grimsholm, a chart with recent soundings taken from a Danish pilot, or talked to Thornton about numbers, provisions, sources of supply.

In an expectant pause he said, 'It appears to me that this is a situation where we must risk all at one throw, and do so at once. There is no time for deliberation. I suggest that I should be landed on the island as soon as possible; certainly before this General Mercier arrives, if he is not already there. If once I can get ashore, I feel reasonably confident of success. But I cannot think that a man-of-war is the best conveyance: many of the soldiers on the island are sea-Catalans, and they would recognize her at once, whatever her colours or disguise; above all since, as I understand, the *Ariel* has often appeared in the Baltic. They would blow her, or any boat belonging to her, out of the water. No: I should prefer to go in a Danzig or Danish vessel ostensibly bringing supplies — nay, bringing supplies in fact, for if it were loaded with the wine and tobacco that the garrison have lacked so long my task would be sensibly lighter. No doubt, sir, you have a suitable prize?'

'I doubt it,' said the Admiral. 'So many foreigners are allowed to carry trade or naval stores to England under licence that we take very few; and my impression is that the few we have taken this last month have already been sent in. But I will make certain.' He rang and called for an immediate report. While it was coming Thornton spoke quietly to Stephen about the papers that Ponsich had taken with him to prove his statements — the proclamations, edicts, copies of the *Moniteur*, Catalan and Spanish broadsheets, even neutral publications which made it clear that the whole of Buonaparte's conduct was in complete contradiction with his promises. The atmosphere in the great cabin had become extremely grave: in the last few minutes the attempt had taken on a living immediacy, moving from the area of general discussion and the weighing of possibilities to that of immediate action; and all those present knew that when Maturin said 'all must be risked at one throw' the 'all' included his own life; they looked at him with some of the respect due to a corpse or a man under the sentence of death, and Jack with the deepest concern.

'I have other examples of nearly all Ponsich's documents,' Stephen said. 'I also have an authenticated copy of the unpublished great excommunication pronounced against Buonaparte by the Holy Father. Three of the gentlemen on Grimsholm are knights of Malta, and I believe it will have a very powerful effect on them.'

The report arrived: there were no Danish or Danzig prizes within a week's reach. 'I was afraid that was the case,' said the Admiral. 'Had you rather wait, Dr Maturin?'

'Oh no,' said Stephen. 'At this stage a day is a year.'

'If I may say so, sir,' said Jack, 'I believe I see a way out of the difficulty. We sighted two Danes this morning: since I was aware that speed was of the first importance I did not chase; but I did notice that one of them, a cat, made no attempt to escape. She carried on under courses, steering for Riga, and I make no doubt she was sailing under your licence. Now, sir, the wind serves, and the weather is clearing fast; *Ariel*, as you know, sir, is a very fair sailer, and if I might have your permission to as it were suspend the cat's licence, I believe I could overhaul her. She was heavy, she was slow, and I believe she was short-handed.'

The Admiral considered, whistling silently. 'That is a possible solution,' he said. 'It is not particularly scrupulous; but necessity knows no law. On the other hand there is the possibility of missing her and of thereby losing two days. The alternative is to wait until one of my cruisers picks up a Dane, licensed or not. It is more certain; but they are scattered from the Alands down to Rugen. Orders would have to reach them, and we should be obliged to pay for the certainty with time. What says Dr Maturin?'

'I have every confidence in Captain Aubrey's ability to seize upon anything that swims,' said Maturin. 'And this is a situation in which I believe we must not lose a minute.' Ever since he had taken to the sea he had been harassed by the cry 'Lose not a minute' and it gave him a certain pleasure to use it himself at last. 'Lose not a minute,' he repeated, savouring the words, and went on, 'As for the moral issue, are we to weigh the hypothetical inconvenience suffered by the cat against the certain death of several thousand men? For I understand that if the island cannot be induced to submit, it must be stormed.' Now that the whole process was in train, now that the long fuse had been lit, he felt a curious levity mingling with his thoughts and he was tempted to repeat Jack Aubrey's joke about always choosing the lesser of two weevils. In most circumstances he would have done so; but there was something about Admiral Saumarez, an indefinable unaffected magnitude, that made him keep his amusement to himself.

Yet for all Sir James's real dignity Stephen did not hesitate to interrupt the technical discussion between the sailors some moments later. 'I should like to raise the point of wine and tobacco once more,' he said, emerging from his thoughts. 'Would it be possible, sir, to charge the *Ariel* with an adequate supply of these commodities, so that the eventual merchantman will in fact be found to be what she professes to be?'

'Tobacco, certainly,' said the Admiral. 'Wine may be more difficult, though I dare say the wardrooms of the squadron would yield a fair amount; and we could always fill up with rum, if you feel that would be suitable.'

'Rum would answer tolerably well,' said Stephen, 'although wine would be better. And now, sir, I have some more important observations. This is clearly an expedition that must end either in complete success or in complete failure: there is little point in discussing the failure, so, if you please, I will speak only of the happier event. As you are no doubt aware, I made it a condition of my stepping in that the Catalan troops on Grimsholm should not be treated as prisoners of war, and that they should be carried to Spain with arms and baggage at His Majesty's charges. It is a small price to pay for the bloodless delivery of such a fortress, I believe; and in any case I am intimately convinced that once they are in the Peninsula they will at once engage on Lord Wellington's side.'

'It would indeed be a trifling price,' said the Admiral, 'and fortunately I have the transports here, just at hand. Mr Ponsich made the same condition.'

'Very good, very good,' said Stephen. 'I now come to another point: the commanders of the transports should be strongly impressed with the necessity for according the Catalan officers all the usual compliments of salutes and guns and flags and so on, with all or even more than all the usual ceremony. Their position is irregular; their pride susceptible to the last degree. The least appearance of a slight might have the most unfortunate effects.' He paused. 'But I am running too far ahead. Ideally, sir, the operation would proceed on these lines: the emissary is landed from the merchantman while the *Ariel* and the transports remain out of sight; he carries his point; after a stated interval the *Ariel* comes nearer to see his signal; she in her turn calls the transports, which come in with a body of gunners sufficiently numerous to man the batteries, and the transfer takes place at once, while the prospect of the journey home still has its full exhilarating effect and the indignation against the French is at its height; for the sooner they are out and the sooner the possibility of jealousies or disagreement is done away with the better. All this may be too much to ask, but perhaps some part at least may be feasible.'

'As far as the transports are concerned,' said Admiral Saumarez, 'I see no difficulty, always providing the wind serves; for as you know, Dr Maturin, we are wholly tributary to the winds. If Captain Aubrey can do his part with the necessary Dane, I believe we can do ours with the troop-carriers and the gunners, and indeed with the wine and tobacco that you mentioned. I fully take your point about the necessity for a very rapid transfer; and I see, sir, that the Admiralty was not at all mistaken in advising me to rely upon Dr Maturin's sagacity.'

'The Admiralty was too kind entirely,' said Stephen, 'too indulgent by far. But to tell you the truth of it, sir, this is a conjuncture in which I had rather be granted a single small cup of luck than a whole tun of wisdom.'

Chapter Eight

It was a black night for the squadron when the *Ariel* slipped her moorings and stood out into the rain-swept midnight sea, for she carried with her most of the wardrooms, wine and an uneasy proportion of the fore-mast-jacks' rum and tobacco, as well as twenty prime hands chosen from among the many Dutchmen, Poles, Finns and Letts in the fleet. She left something near prostration behind her, with little to enliven or revive it: in all his experience of naval life Stephen Maturin had never seen anything to equal the speed with which the *Ariel* was equipped — boats crowded about her, stores flowing in under the immediate supervision of Sir James. The Admiral contributed three tierces of a noble claret to the cargo, observing that he should willingly drink green tea for the rest of the commission rather than jeopardize *Ariel*'s chances; and after that no wardroom could do less. She stood out, therefore, deeper in the water than she had stood in, more crowded than ever, with barrels still lashed provisionally here and there on deck, the purser and the mate of the hold out of their wits, and more than half of her crew suspiciously jolly if not downright drunk.

'There will be a long defaulters' list tomorrow,' said Jack, in a tone that sensibly reduced the merriment. He had just emerged from a long session with Mr Pellworm and the master, in which they had each independently laid down a course to intercept the licensed Dane they had passed not long before, the creeping, short-handed cat: three courses that coincided almost exactly, courses designed to find the cat in the first hours of full day. 'Mr Fenton, we must have very good men at the wheel, and they must steer north seventeen east exactly. Wittgenstein, the quartermaster from the flagship, will do for one: an excellent seaman — I have sailed with him before. You will heave the log at every glass, keeping as near as possible to six knots, making or reducing sail accordingly; above all, do not exceed — we must not pass in the darkness. And although I do not expect to see her before dawn, you will keep sharp, sober men at the masthead, changing them every glass. The lookout that first sights the cat shall have ten guineas and remission of sins, short of mutiny, sodomy, or damaging the paintwork. I am to be called should anything occur, or should there be any change of wind.' In his earlier ships he would have gone on to say that he was about to sup with the Doctor on a very strange dish, a salted buzzard produced by the Commandant at Gothenburg, and they would probably have talked about tomorrow's prospects for a while: but this was a temporary command; he hardly knew his officers, and in any case they seemed so young as almost to belong to another species. Their deference was burdensome, and it would require a real effort on his part, even at a social gathering, to cross the gap, as far as it could be crossed at all. But the god-like remoteness of command came naturally to him now, and having desired Fenton to repeat his orders and to place the written copy in the binnacle drawer he went directly below.

He found the buzzard already in pieces, carved not with the Christian carving-knife and fork the steward had laid out but with an instrument that Stephen hid under his napkin as he said 'Forgive me, Jack. I have not actually begun, but I could not wait to see the creature's sternum. I learnt a great deal about sternums in Paris.'

'I am glad of that,' said Jack, 'and I am glad to see you are recovered.'

'It was only a passing indisposition, caused perhaps by over-indulgence in fish; in any event, the emotion of setting all in train has quite done away with it.' Jack had a notion that the easier motion of the ship might also have helped — the gale had blown itself out and she was now slipping along with a quartering breeze, little roll and an even pitch — but he kept it to himself. 'Will you look at this breast-bone, now, and at these sutures upon it?' said Stephen, holding up the buzzard's keel. 'You would say they were attachments for the sternal muscles, would you not?'

'I should have taken my oath upon it, I do assure you.'

'So should I, until a few days ago. But in fact it appears that they are the points of union of the bones that make up the sternum in the fowl's earliest youth. It was an eminent Academician who told me this, a man whose acquaintance I prize extremely. He envisages a whole new classification . . .' Jack's attention wandered to the *Ariel*'s topgallantmasts, struck down on deck in the recent blow, until Stephen said with unusual emphasis '. . . and those that put too much trust in a bird's toes as a generical symptom may find themselves compelled to call the nightjar and the osprey cousins.'

'That would never do, I am sure,' said Jack. 'It eats rather like pig, don't it?'

'Very like pig. But when you consider that the honey-buzzard's diet consists mainly in wasps and their brood, it is scarcely surprising. Allow me.' He took the bones from Jack's plate and wrapped them in his handkerchief. 'I was much impressed by your Admiral,' he said. 'Admirable Admiral, admirable force of decision: I had been so afraid of interminable shilly-shally, and reluctance to come to the hard point of assuming responsibility.'

'There is nothing like that about Sir James,' said Jack. 'You remember him at Gibraltar, tearing out after the combined squadron? No shilly-shally there, I believe. But Stephen, did you not remark how terribly he has aged? He cannot be sixty yet, but he looks an old, old man.'

'The appreciation of age is so relative: I dare say you look like a patriarch to the young men in the gunroom. I know that one of the midshipmen helped me across the street in Gothenburg as though I were his grandsire.'

'I dare say I do,' said Jack, laughing. 'I am quite certain they look terribly young, pitifully young to me. I hope to God they have had time to learn their profession. Are you away, Stephen?'

'I am. I mean to turn in, digest my buzzard in my cot, and sleep upon both ears for what is left of our time. Good night to you, now.'

Stephen was perfectly calm, in rather higher spirits than usual, and Jack had no doubt that he would sleep until the morning. He envied him. Although long training usually allowed him to drop off at any moment, Jack knew that tonight he would have little rest; he was extremely anxious, both reasonably and unreasonably anxious. He called for a pot of coffee, and as he drank it he checked his course again. The answer came out the same as before: but there were so many, many things that could go wrong, so many variables.

One of the variables would have been absent if he had had time to pick his own officers, men like Pullings and Babbington and Mowett who had sailed with him for years and whom he knew through and through; or any of the better midshipmen he had formed and who were now lieutenants. But of course these young fellows in the *Ariel*'s gunroom must know their profession: young though they might be, they had all served afloat since their childhood, and the ship was in excellent order. Sir James had remarked upon it: 'he had rarely seen a sloop of war in such good order.' Hyde might be no nine-days' wonder, no great seaman, but he was an adequate first lieutenant, a good disciplinarian, firm, but no bully; while the master was an excellent navigator, without any kind of doubt; and Fenton seemed above the average run of amiable, competent lieutenants — a man who might do very well if ever he had the good luck to be promoted. He dismissed that part of his anxiety as nonsense; and ten minutes later he was on deck to see whether they knew what they were about.

The rain had stopped, the sky was clearing: no moon: pitch dark. The ship was steering true, and a glance at the log-board showed that she had kept to a steady six knots; she was under topsails with a single reef and an easy sheet. Fenton certainly knew how to sail her. Although it was close on three bells in the graveyard watch and although there was no duty in hand the deck was unusually alive; the odd sheltered places forward or under the lee of the boats sheltered no sleeping figures, their heads wrapped in their jackets; all hands who were not high aloft were at the rails, staring out into the night. One of these was Wittgenstein, a Heligolander brought up in the Leith coal-trade: as a midshipman Jack had pressed him out of his collier, and they had sailed together in three or four commissions to their mutual liking. In the second of these, when Jack's navigation was still not all that it should have been, Wittgenstein was one of the prize-crew with which Jack had to take a valuable merchantman into Port-of-Spain; and thanks to Wittgenstein alone they had not only survived two very nasty blows that carried them a great way out of their course, but found their way, three weeks overdue, to Trinidad. He came aft to trim a stern-lantern, and Jack said, 'Well, Wittgenstein, I am glad to see you again. It must be seven or eight years since we were shipmates. How do you come along?'

'Pretty spry, sir, thank God, though we are none of us as young as we was; and I see you are pretty spry too, sir,' said Wittgenstein looking at him keenly in the yellow glow. 'Well, fairly spry, all things considered.'

Jack stayed on deck for a couple of glasses, and after that he appeared again from time to time to watch the steady working of the ship and gaze at the star-sprinkled sky. Mars was setting, tangled in Virgo, somewhere over Lithuania: Jupiter shone glorious astern. The night seemed never-ending, a continual easy glide through darkness.

Yet he was asleep, sitting in the ingenious swinging chair that Draper had slung in the great cabin, when a midshipman came to tell him that a sail had been sighted. He had slept through the changing of the watch, and now as he came on deck the first streaks of dawn were showing: the binnacle lights still gleamed, and at first he could make out nothing but the line of the horizon.

'Just forward of the shifting backstay, sir,' said the master, who had the morning watch.

He caught the lifting fleck of white, trained his night-glass on it, and stared long and hard. No: it would not do. This was not his cat. It was too early for his cat, and in any case the sail to leeward was steering south. Yet on the other hand . . . a train of possibilities raced through his mind as he automatically slung his glass and climbed into the maintop, a serious and rather stern expression on his face. He knew from the Admiral that there were no British cruisers on this station apart from the brig *Rattler*, and this was a three masted vessel: then again it was unlikely that any English merchantman should be sailing alone; they nearly all waited for convoy to protect them from the Danish privateers. The master followed him.

The light was growing fast: the distant ship — for a ship she was, though small — hung there, an inverted image in his night-glass, somewhat dreamlike. 'She is no cat, neither,' he observed, passing the telescope. 'What do you make of her, Mr Grimmond?'

'No cat, sir, I agree,' said Grimmond, after a long searching pause. 'I can see her topgallantyards as plain as plain. I should not like to take my oath on it, but she looks rather like the *Minnie*, a Dane out of Aarhus. We saw her often last year, and chased her twice. She has a fine turn of speed on a bowline, and she lies very close indeed.'

'Let us go up to the masthead, Mr Grimmond,' said Jack, calling to the lookout to slide down the stay. There was barely room at the main crosstrees of so small a ship as the *Ariel* for a sixteen-stone post-captain and a stoutly-built master, and the frail spars creaked ominously. Grimmond was horribly embarrassed as well as frightened: ordinarily two such figures would have clung close together, but he could not bring himself to such familiarity with the person of Captain Aubrey, and he was obliged to adopt an odd, crucified posture between a shroud and a backstay.

The first thing that Jack did was to search for his quarry, the cat heading for Riga. At this height he commanded a disk of sea twenty-five miles in diameter: there was no cat in it. Nor should there have been any cat. By all his calculations she should still be over the south-eastern horizon, crawling towards a point in the sea where the *Ariel* should cut her course at about the beginning of the forenoon watch.

'Yes, sir,' said the master. 'I am almost sure she is the *Minnie* now. Her topsides are all black, and she carries a boat on stern-davits.'

'And what may she be?'

'Why, sir, sometimes she is a trader, sailing under our licence or dealing with the French on her own account, and sometimes she is most likely a privateer: maybe both together, when the opportunity offers. She certainly had no licence when she ran from us, beating into Danzig.'

'She is fast, you say?'

'Very fast on a wind, sir; but going large the *Ariel* has the legs of her. We should have caught her the second time, but that she ducked in under the guns of Bornholm. We were coming up hand over fist.'

'What does she carry?'

'Fourteen Danish six-pounders, sir.'

A considerable armament for a merchantman, but even so no match for the *Ariel*. Jack considered, hanging there between the clear sky and the deck. The cat was hypothetical: likely, but still hypothetical. She was desperately slow, and sailing or towing her down the Baltic would eat up a great deal of time. The *Minnie* was no sort of a hypothesis: she was there, plainly to be seen; she was fast, she was heading in the right direction — a chase would take him on his way — and she was under his lee.

'Very well, Mr Grimmond,' he said, 'we will see if we can catch her this time,' and reaching out for a backstay he slid down on deck in one long smooth sweep.

Apart from the very beginning, when he was fairly sure he could rely on the *Minnie*'s lookout to ignore the *Ariel* for a while in the usual merchantman fashion and then upon a demi-privateer's curiosity and eagerness for prey, he knew that there would be little room for guile in this pursuit. It would be a straightforward race, a match of speed, perhaps of seamanship; and there was all day to run it in, a fair wind, and an open sea. He bitterly regretted his topgallantmasts, struck down on deck during yesterday's hard blow and never swayed up since — he had meant to leave it until both watches should be on deck.

There would be no room for guile in the long run, but still it would be foolish not to take whatever advantage there was to be gained; they were nearly five miles apart, scarcely hull-up from the deck, and it would take a long while to make up that distance, particularly as the *Minnie* already had her topgallantyards crossed and the *Ariel* was rather deep-laden. He sent her slanting casually across the sea to cross the *Minnie*'s wake, still under topsails, suspended the ritual of washing the deck, stated that hammocks would not be piped up until further notice, ordered hammock-cloths to be draped over the gunports, and topgallantmasts and yards laid along, ready to be swayed up and crossed at a moment's notice, with royals to follow them, and desired the officers to follow his example in changing their fine blue coats for pea-jackets. He had gone to sea with only one uniform, his best; and the *Ariel*'s gun-room, supposing this to be his own choice, his normal standard of dress, had hitherto presented an appearance that would have done credit to a flagship, with blazing buttons, epaulettes, and eminent hats, visible a great way off — certain marks of a King's ship. He also sent most of the hands below, keeping only about a dozen in view.

The *Minnie* sighted them earlier than Jack had expected. From the maintop he saw her people running about, a surprisingly heavy crew and an almost conclusive proof of her being a privateer — quite enough men to serve her seven guns of a side, or to board and carry any ordinary Baltic merchantman. She rounded-to for a closer look, and Jack called 'Danish colours, Mr Grimmond.'

The *Minnie* seemed pleased, and answered with the same, coming a little nearer.

'Steer to close her, Mr Grimmond,' said Jack in the waiting silence: but even as he spoke the *Minnie* smelt a rat, turned on her heel, dropped her topgallantsails and fled south-east.

Before the *Ariel* had loosed hers the chase already had her royals abroad, and the distance was growing rapidly. The delay irked Jack extremely — he could blame nobody but himself, and he urged the royal masts and yards aloft with a grim urgency that filled all hands with concern.

Yet in time masts, yards and a spider's web of stays were where they should be; all sail the ship could bear was set and drawing drum-tight; all falls were coiled down and cleared away; and the *Ariel*, under her own colours and with her pennant streaming forward high over all, bore away in the *Minnie*'s wake, gradually reaching the utmost speed that the fair breeze on her starboard quarter would allow. It was too soon to tell which was the happier on this point of sailing, but Jack was reasonably certain that he should overhaul the chase before the end of the day: there were few faster sloops in the service than *Ariel*, and he knew her pretty well by now.

'Very well, Mr Hyde,' he said, 'I believe we may remove the hammock-cloths and carry on with cleaning the decks.' The interrupted ship's day resumed its natural course: sand and holystone scoured the worn white wood, hammocks were piped up and stowed, the galley chimney started to smoke, hands were piped to breakfast; and all this time the two ships raced over the morning sea.

When Stephen came on deck, eager for his coffee, surprised and somewhat aggrieved at not even having smelt it yet, he was led by a gentle midshipman to the bows, where the Captain and the master were training their sextants on the chase.

'Good morning to you, Doctor,' said Jack. 'I hope you slept well?'

'Admirably well, I thank you; and am as a giant refreshed. My eyes are keen, my appetite and all my senses remarkably acute. Indeed, I perceive a sail a great way off — there, directly beyond the prow. But perhaps you have noticed it.'

'Mr Grimmond was good enough to point it out in the morning watch. She is your merchantman, though rather a queer one; and I am happy to tell you we are gaining on her at last. She went away very quick, to begin with.'

'So that is why you are sailing so fast, with such a quantity of sails.'

'Many a stitch saves time,' said Jack. 'But I doubt we hold on to our royals much longer.'

'The speed is quite exhilarating,' said Stephen. 'Do not you find the speed lift your heart, Mr Grimmond? See how the grey billow rises — we part it — white foam flies down our side! The brave boat, she would cut a slender oat straw with the excellence of her going. I could watch it for ever, although breakfast is going cold in the cabin. I say, although my coffee grows chill, Captain Aubrey.'

'I am with you this minute,' cried Jack: and so he was, for the space of a dish of burgoo and half a dozen fried eggs with a due proportion of bacon, toast and marmalade, Gothenburg and Carlscrona having done them so proud. But he carried his last cup of coffee on deck.

He had chased for a fortune before now, but he had not chased with so great an urgency in his heart: from a merely personal point of view, he had undertaken to do a very difficult thing and he must bring it off; but very much more than that, he fully understood the importance of the task in hand, the capital importance of Grimsholm. Nothing would prevent Stephen from making the attempt: nor should it. Jack had the greatest confidence in his powers; yet Stephen's danger must be far less if he were set down on the island before the French officers arrived, perhaps to reverse the whole situation. The Frenchmen had reached Hollenstein on Tuesday, and if they took passage in such a flier as the *Minnie* they might be in Grimsholm very, very soon indeed. It was in fact by no means impossible that they were aboard her this minute: her course would agree perfectly with such a voyage.

His officers, or most of them, were competent; but they had nothing like his experience in driving a ship, in getting the last ounce of thrust out of the breeze. And as the morning wore on this proved a tricky breeze into the bargain, sometimes coming in gusts strong enough to endanger her topgallants if not the upper masts themselves. A tricky opponent, too; the *Minnie*, put to her shifts, tried every change of helm to probe the *Ariel*'s best point of sailing, every combination of sails; Jack responded to all of these, and to every variation in the wind — studdingsails flashed out aboard the sloop, studdingsails aloft and alow on either side as occasion served, bonnets, drabblers; and just before they parted so they were taken in. There was an atmosphere of pleasurable tension and excitement in the *Ariel*; the hands jumped to their work; they plied the hoses in the tops, wetting the sails for a slightly greater thrust with a jet that reached the yard, and they whipped buckets up to the crosstrees to soak the topgallants with a splendid zeal; and as often as not they were ready at the sheets or halliards with an intelligent anticipation before the order was given. The gain was slight, sometimes no more than a cable's length in an hour, but it was certain. The chase had been hull-up since the middle of the forenoon watch.

By the time of the noon-day observation the *Minnie* had proved to her own satisfaction that she lost least by putting directly before the wind: and so she sailed, under a noble pyramid of canvas, starting her water over the side and tossing her guns after it, fourteen splashes that lightened her by as many tons.

'Shall you come to dinner?' asked Stephen, two hours later. 'The steward is in a great taking, and declares the sucking-pig will be spoilt.'

'No,' said Jack. 'Do you see his save-alls? The damned thing about chasing in the Baltic is that they nearly always have better gear — best Riga sailcloth, and such hemp for their cordage — and they can crack on when we dare not. That Dane needs watching. I shall take a bite on deck. A damned good seaman.'

'Will he succeed in running clear, do you suppose?'

'I hope not, I am sure. At the present rate of sailing, and if nothing carries away, we should be up with her a little after sunset; but this is a cross-grained breeze, and the more it slackens the less we gain. The *Minnie* is going very well, and I believe she would be happiest in very light airs; she swims high, as you see, and I am pretty sure she has been new-coppered: all the officers agree that she has never shown such a turn of speed. She would be the very thing for the Admiral. He is in great need of avisoes.'

'You are confident of taking her, I find.'

'Oh, I should never say anything as unlucky as that. I should never count the bear's skin before it is hatched: oh no. I only mean that were she taken she might be bought into the service. There is a fair chance, a very fair chance; but above all I hope to come up with her before night sets in: this is the dark of the moon, and there will be precious little starshine.'

The long, long afternoon, and still they ran. In spite of their increased numbers the *Ariel*'s crew were growing jaded with the incessant shifting of the upper sails and the pumping: but it was just as bad or even worse aboard the chase, reflected Jack; and in any case he had now settled upon the best trim — naked mizen, both mainsheets aft, foretopmast scandalized, forecourse in the brails, all the fore studdingsails setting beautifully and the bowsprit fully clothed — and now the hands should have a rest. What he really feared was the rising glass and the falling of the wind, which would certainly favour the lighter *Minnie*; not that in his deepest, least-avowed conviction he had any doubt of overhauling her sooner or later, even after a gust had blown the main-royal out of its bolt-rope. But *sooner* was so infinitely important, he reflected, looking angrily at the *Minnie*'s unyielding canvas as his own flimsy, worn-out Admiralty number eight raced aloft to replace the streaming sail.

The true cold fear, the doubt of total failure, did not come to him until much later, when the setting sun began to swallow the breeze and the *Minnie* drew perceptibly ahead. She had been within very long gunshot this last hour and he had cleared away the bow-chasers long since; but at no time had he been willing to maul a ship that he would have to use, and now there was a likelihood that gunfire would stun the remaining wind. Yet it might be the right solution; for if the *Minnie* gained like this, and if the breeze kept light and true, she might waft into Grimsholm before him — the island was directly in her path, and by now it was no great way off: a night's sail, perhaps.

Having ordered the perilous expedient of a skysail on the main — perilous, because the *Ariel*'s royal-mast had been sprung when the sail blew out — he turned the question over in his mind. The little quarterdeck was crowded, all the officers and young gentlemen having been there with scarcely a break since the beginning of the chase, but if they spoke at all it was in low voices: now they were all silent, waiting for what would happen when the skysail was sheeted home. The only sound that reached Jack in his holy area of deck by the starboard rail was the conversation between Dr Maturin and Jagiello: the significance of the skysail escaped them entirely, and they talked away with the freedom of perfect ignorance.

'Pray, Mr Jagiello,' said Stephen, 'what is the coast we see? Would it be part of Courland, or perhaps of Pomerania, or am I much astray?'

'I am totally in the sea,' said Jagiello cheerfully. 'It might be anywhere. All this part of the Baltic coast is much the same — flat, with immense sand-dunes for miles and miles, and shallow water. It is sterile, barren, no good to anybody, but Poles and Swedes and Russians and Germans have fought for it for hundreds of years. I can see a ruined castle with the telescope: but I cannot tell what it is.' He passed the glass, adding, 'The only thing it does produce is amber.'

'Amber?' cried Stephen: and at the same time a collective sigh rose from the professional part of the quarterdeck; the skysail held, and the scrap of canvas — for it was no more — gave the *Ariel* a slightly greater thrust, just enough to prevent the chase from gaining. This did not resolve Jack's problem, however, and he found himself wishing, with uncommon vehemence and a vexation of spirit rare in him, that the talk about amber, its origin, its electrical properties, its uses in classical antiquity, Thales of Miletus on amber, might stop.

'Mr Hyde, let the water be . . .' he began, his eyes fixed on the *Minnie*: but to his astonishment he saw her shift her helm, altering course to larboard until she had the breeze three points abaft the beam. He cut his sentence short and gave out a volley of orders — driver, mizen topsail, topgallant and royal, forecourse, foretopsail, together with the crowd of studdingsails and staysails that had been useless with the wind dead aft. And now the *Ariel*'s strong crew of man-of-war's men showed to full advantage: this cloud of canvas broke out with astonishing rapidity — sheets were tallied aft and belayed before the *Minnie* had spread more than half of hers.

But even before this was done, even before Stephen and Jagiello had been tumbled about more than twice by racing groups of men, Jack had sent a midshipman to the masthead. The *Minnie*'s change of course seemed mere suicide; not only had she proved that the *Ariel* outpaced her sailing large like this — proved it much earlier in the day — but now she had lost a cable's length in the last few minutes. On such a course she must lose close on a mile in an hour even with all the sail she possessed abroad; and the sun was still a handsbreadth from the horizon. The only explanation he could think of was that she had seen an ally inshore or an enemy in the offing.

'On deck, there,' hailed the midshipman.

'A sail, sir, a sail two points on the starboard bow.'

'Do you make out a pennant?' he called. It was an idle question: if the *Minnie* had not seen the pennant, the mark of a man-of-war, she would never have sheered off. But he wanted confirmation of his joy.

'Oh yes, sir. And I believe I know her. Hermaphrodite on the starboard tack — she's coming about — yes, sir, I recognize her for sure.'

'What is she?'

'*Humbug*, sir,' said the midshipman, in a rather hesitant roar.

Jack could not believe he had heard aright. 'What did you say?' he cried.

'*Humbug*, sir.' And from the bows came a peal of honest mirth, while within arm's reach of the Captain three young gentlemen writhed in an effort to contain themselves, and all the officers were on the grin. It was a current Baltic joke, but one that newcomers could not know: just before the Russians joined the Allies a facetious captain of the Royal Navy had captured one of their vessels, a very distinctive Tyne-built hermaphrodite, a fine sailer on a bowline, and he had changed her impossible Russian name to this, the only *Humbug* ever known or likely to be known in the Navy list.

Humbug, by God. The word had been used to him, publicly, on his own quarter-deck: the boy must be drunk. For a moment Jack's face took on a most forbidding look, and the grins died away. But then his pomp, his righteous indignation dissolved and he said 'Very well, Mr Jevons. You will stay there till I call you.' He gazed at the *Minnie*: she was jammed in a clinch like Jackson. 'Let us take in the skysail, Mr Hyde,' he said. 'There is no point in endangering the mast.' He was convinced that he could give the *Minnie* royals on this tack and even the foretopgallant, and still lay her aboard within the hour. He would not have to use his bowchasers.

'Yes, sir,' said Mr Hyde. 'No, sir: no point at all. And by the way, sir, the hermaphrodite really is called *Humbug*. Jevons meant no disrespect.'

'Is that so? Well, well. Then he may come down again. Where is the signal midshipman? To *Humbug*, since that is her name, *Enemy in sight. Chase to east-south-east*, and give her a gun. Mr Jagiello, I am sorry they knocked you down. You are all right now, are you not?'

'Oh, perfectly well, sir,' said Jagiello,

laughing, 'it was nothing at all. My spurs caught in the rope. I believe I shall take them off.'

'I beg your pardon, sir,' said Mr Pellworm, 'but she is heading for the Forten bank. Indeed, she is almost on the tail of the Kraken already, if I do not mistake.'

'Is she, though?' cried Jack. The Forten was a series of shoals a few miles off the flat sandy shore, and its winding channel was very little frequented. The *Minnie*, riding light, would draw two feet less water than the *Ariel*: her hope, her last hope, was to lead her pursuer over a bank — a bank where the *Minnie* would pass and the *Ariel* stick tight. That was one of the reasons for her sudden turn. 'The fox. Light along the lead, there. Mr Pellworm, can you carry us through?'

'I believe so, sir,' said Pellworm, glancing significantly at the vast spread of canvas overhead.

'Then she is yours. Reduce sail as soon as you please.'

The sun dipped. The pink sails came in one by one; the *Ariel* fetched the *Minnie*'s wake and glided along, no longer gaining, with the lead going on either side and the pilot, grave and concentrated, at the con, now fixing his seamarks, a tower on the shore and a distant spire, with his azimuth compass, now staring at the ship ahead to catch the least motion of her helm.

It moved often as she pursued her dog-legged course, apparently quite at home; with a fifteen-minute interval the *Ariel*'s rudder made the same motion as she glided over the seemingly innocent sea in the twilight. It was a strange procession: all the flying speed and excitement was gone, replaced by quite a different tension. Her bower anchors were ready, a-cockbill at the catheads, with a kedge at the stern- davits and hands stationed to let them go at the word: there was silence fore and aft, not a sound but the pilot's orders and the leadsman's chant: 'By the deep six, by the deep six: by the mark five; and a half five . . .' and so it went, until the leadsman's voice rose in a sharp emphasis 'And a half three, and a half three!' To a man the Ariels pursed their lips: precious little water under them now.

'Back the foretopsail,' called the pilot, taking the wheel.

'And a half three. By the mark three. A quarter less five. By the deep six; and a half six.' They were in the deep channel once more.

Jack breathed out at last. Water under his keel, thank God. But the *Minnie* was turning again, turning three points to starboard: there was ugly stuff coming, for sure. He must not worry the pilot, but Lord how he longed . . .

'She's struck,' came a bellowing mooncalf roar from the bows. 'She's grounded herself, the bloody old fatherlasher, hor, hor!' A quartermaster choked him short, a midshipman beat him with a speaking-trumpet; but what he said was true. The *Minnie* came gently to a halt in the sea: all her masts gave an easy lean forwards, and then a most furious lean as her captain dropped and sheeted home all his clewed-up sails in an attempt at driving her over the bank. A vain attempt: nor could he back her off. She was held fast, lying there on an even keel, as motionless as though she were moored head and stern: more so, since she did not even rock.

'Briskly with the lead, there,' cried Jack. 'Can you lay her alongside, Mr Pellworm?'

'Close on, sir,' said the pilot, chuckling.

'By the mark seven,' chanted the leadsman. 'And a half seven.'

'This is the Kraken channel,' observed Mr Pellworm. 'Stand by the kedge.'

The *Minnie* was coming nearer: nearer and nearer. Her people's faces could be seen, white blobs in the twilight, their voices heard. They were launching a boat over the stern, a little gig: Jack saw uniformed figures on her deck, French officers without a doubt. 'That will do, Mr Pellworm,' he said within a cable's length of the immobile chase: he did not wish the boat to be masked by the ship for any length of time: he did not wish to come too close, spoiling his line of fire. 'Let go the kedge. Let go the best bower. Brail up, clew up.' He took a speaking-trumpet and hailed '*Minnie*, hoist in that boat or I shall blow you out of the water.'

No response, but a furious altercation and a pistol-shot aboard the chase.

'Mr Jagiello,' he called, 'pray hail them in Danish and repeat what I said. Mr Hyde, a spring to the cable.'

Jagiello shouted the message high and clear over the two hundred yards of sea, shouted it in different languages. The boat splashed down into the calm water: the French officers jumped into it and at the same moment, as though by an afterthought, the *Minnie* struck her colours. The boat vanished along her starboard side.

'Quarters,' said Jack, and in a moment the gun-crews were at their stations: the guns themselves had been run out long ago. 'Mr Hyde, three quarters on, then full.'

The *Ariel* turned on her spring, then steadied, almost as firm as the *Minnie*. When the boat reappeared, crossing the *Minnie*'s stem and pulling inexpertly for the land, it was directly in the starboard bow-chaser's line of fire: another turn of the capstan would bring the whole broadside to bear, and at point-blank range. From a steady platform, an unmoving ship, a crew far less skilled than the *Ariel*'s could scarcely miss.

'Mr Nuttall,' he said to the gunner, 'single round-shot, and pitch it beyond them.'

The gunner laid his piece: fired: the ball struck fifty yards beyond the boat, in a true line, and went skipping across the sea in a series of enormous bounds. The boat rowed on.

'Again,' said Jack.

This time the smoke obscured the fall of the shot, but as it cleared there was the boat, still heading for the shore. 'Full on, Mr Hyde,' said Jack in a harsh voice: it was a sickening business but his carronades would not reach much farther and no single gun could be perfectly relied upon. He must get it over at once. The ship was broadside on, the gun-crews poised about their carronades. 'From forward aft,' he said, 'deliberate fire; wait for the smoke to clear. Fire one.' The first shot pitched a little wide; the second rocked the boat, and in the eddying smoke he saw a man stand up. Was he waving a handkerchief? In the split second of his thought the third gun fired, striking the boat fair and square. Planks flew up, and something like an arm. A savage cheer all along the deck, and the gun-crews turned their beaming faces, clapping one another on the back.

'House your guns,' said Jack. 'Cutters away. Mr Fenton, see if there are any survivors. Mr Hyde, take possession of the prize, and make the master lighten her at once. Anderson will interpret for you. Mr Grimmond, a light in the maintop to guide the *Humbug*, and rouse out an eight-inch hawser. We must heave her off at once; there is not a minute to be lost.'

Every minute was indeed irreplaceable, yet they flowed away by the score and by the hundred. The *Minnie* would not move. The channels were so narrow, the navigation so intricate, that a vessel of *Ariel*'s draught could not move with any freedom, could not take up a proper station; with infinite labour they laid out anchors by means of the launch, dragging the heavy cables behind them, and every time the capstan turned, taking the full strain and transmitting it to the *Minnie*, the anchors came home again.

The situation was already difficult by the time Fenton returned with the one survivor, a youth of about seventeen, wounded in the leg and head, unconscious. It was far more complicated some time later, when Stephen came up from the sick-bay; there were ropes leading in every direction, stretching out into the darkness; in the glow of the lantern the faces of the men at the capstan-bars looked worn and jaded, all excitement gone. Jack had just finished a roared series of instructions to some distant boat when Stephen appeared. 'How does he come along?' he asked in a hoarse voice.

'I believe we may save him,' said Stephen. 'The ligature seems to hold, and the young are wonderfully resilient. You seem in a sad way, brother?'

'Tolerably so, tolerably so. Her after-bitts gave way, and we have lost our small bower, parted at the ring; but it could be worse, and I dare say *Humbug* will be here presently. She don't draw more than a few feet.' He sounded cheerful, and in fact the incessant activity kept the surface of his mind from brooding on the prospect of the hours ahead; but at no great depth he was aware that dirty weather was brewing in the north, that the *Humbug*, creeping over the shoals from the other side, creeping over the far extremity five miles away, had missed the channel and had already grounded twice; and that if anything of a sea got up he should be obliged to slip his cables and run, abandoning the *Minnie* and perhaps the whole enterprise, so promising not long ago. 'Were you able to get anything out of him?'

'I was not,' said Stephen. 'He is in a deep coma. But I am afraid his uniform has nothing of the aide-de-camp's glory about it at all; and his letters are those of an ordinary subaltern. Besides, such a wild dash was surely the act of boys rather than of sober, reflecting senior officers.'

'I don't know,' said Jack. 'If I had command of a place like Grimsholm, I think I might have tried it; I think I might have tried for a horse on shore — it is not many hours ride. But I am very certain that I should have pulled away on the blind side for a mile or two. What is it, Mr Rowbotham?'

'If you please, sir, the spare anchor is

new-puddened.'

'Very good, very good: then bend the bitter-end to it. The bitter-end, Mr Rowbotham.'

'Oh yes, sir: the bitter-end it is.'

The second lieutenant came for fresh instructions, and while the urgent technical talk flowed past his ears Stephen watched the lights far over the bank, the lights of all *Ariel*'s and *Minnie*'s boats busy about the radiating arms of rope that were to pull her off: of all the boats except the gig, which was carrying Pellworm away to the distant *Humbug*, to bring her in through the devious channels.

A small dismal rain began to fall, veiling the lights. Fenton ran aft, and Stephen said, 'But if I may have a word with the *Minnie*'s captain, we may learn all there is to be learnt. I must speak to him in any event, to hear what he has to say about Grimsholm. I understand that the *Minnie* goes there from time to time.'

'As soon as we have a boat free I will send for him,' said Jack, and raising his voice he called, 'Mr Hyde, tell the *Minnie*'s master to stand by to come across in the next boat. He is to bring the ship's papers, too.'

'Sir,' came Hyde's reply out of the wet

darkness, 'the Frenchmen pistolled him. Shall I send his mate?'

Two dim wet figures came to report; an unseen boat hailed to say that the warp was entangled in a sunken wreck.

'Never fret your spirit now, my dear,' said Stephen. 'It would advance us nothing at this stage to know whether General Mercier is living or dead; tomorrow morning would answer very well, so it would.'

A violent rending sound, a confusion of voices in the darkness, and Jack disappeared. Stephen waited, and then, the rain increasing, he went down to his cot, where he lay staring at the candle-flame in his lantern, his hands behind his head. Physically he was tired and his body relaxed throughout its entire length: his mind was in much the same state, floating free, detached, as though he had taken his old favourite, the tincture of laudanum. He felt no particular anxiety. The attempt must either succeed or fail: he hoped with all his heart for success, but 'all his heart' did not amount to a great deal now that some essential part of its core seemed to have died. Yet on the other hand he felt more able to command success in that it meant no less to him — to command it with a strength that arose not indeed from a fundamental indifference to his own fate but from something resembling it that he could not define; it had a resemblance to despair, but a despair long past, with the horror taken out of it.

The *Humbug* came through the fairway late in the middle watch, having had to fetch a long cast to windward, beating up tack upon tack; she brought the growing breeze with her and the threat of a dirty end to the night. The lantern swung wider in the small silent cabin: Stephen slept on.

For the next hour and more the hermaphrodite laid out anchors and buoys; the ablest seamen in all three vessels spliced cables end to end. The cables ran through the hawse-holes until there were none left in the tiers; and gradually the whole series of purchases designed either to pluck the *Minnie* from her bed or to tear her guts out took form.

Stephen woke to the sound of a familiar voice raised high, so high that it pierced the deck, for now the whole system was to be put to the test, and now the strain was on — a strain divided between four anchors, nearly a mile of cables and hawsers, and all concentrated on the *Ariel*'s capstan. 'Stamp and go,' cried Jack to the hands at the bars, 'stamp and go. Heave,

heave her round. Heave hearty there.' By now most of the men were Minnies, pressed into the present service; though they might not understand the actual words the gist was plain enough. They could scarcely gain an inch as they heaved and the brisk clicking of the pawls faded steadily to no more than a click a minute; and then to none. Now the full force was on; the cable between the two ships showed never a curve as it vanished into the faint but growing light. 'Heave and rally. Heave, heave and rally. Bosun, start that man. Heave and pawl. Well fare ye, my lads. Now heave with a will.'

A distant cry: 'She stirs.'

The bars moved, the gasping men advanced half a step, the capstan turned, turned faster. 'Well fare ye — heave and aweigh,' cried Jack: the *Minnie* slid stern-first from her bank, gliding into deep water, where she lay rocking easy, and half a dozen hands collapsed at the bars. Stephen dozed off for a time, while innumerable ropes of all sizes were recovered and stowed away. He heard a last cry of 'Splice the mainbrace' and sank far down into sleep.

It was full day when he woke. The rain had stopped and the *Minnie* was alongside, receiving the Ariel's wine and tobacco: far, far astern the *Humbug* could be seen sweeping for the lost small bower. All hands apart from the spry and cheerful Jagiello looked somewhat bleary, but none so bleary as a glum middle-aged man in a sheepskin cap with books under his arm, who was pointed out to Stephen as the *Minnie*'s first mate.

'Mr Jagiello,' said Stephen, 'I am just about to visit my patient: when I come back — and I do not expect to be long — may I ask you to be so kind as to desire that man to come downstairs, to your cabin if you please? With your help, I should like to ask him some questions.'

The visit was indeed quite brief. The young man was still in his coma, looking little more than a child, in spite of his carefully-trained nascent moustache; he was breathing easily, deeply, and the surgery seemed successful so far — at least the delicate ligature had held, and would hold now — but Stephen had a keen sense of approaching death and he believed he felt it now. There was nothing he could do at present and he walked back to Jagiello and the mate.

The questions were asked. Who were the French officers in the boat? What were the signals used for approaching Grimsholm? What were the formalities of landing?

But little response did they obtain: the mate took refuge in ignorance and forgetfulness — this was his first voyage in the *Minnie*; he knew nothing of Grimsholm; he had never seen the Frenchmen; he did not remember anything about them.

'I think I shall leave this sullen fellow for a while,' said Stephen, looking at the *Minnie*'s muster-roll. 'A period of recollection may make him more amenable: at present he is lying, mechanically and doggedly lying — the roll shows that he has been in the vessel for a year and four months. And in any case I yearn for the coffee I smell at no great distance. Will you accompany me?'

'Thank you,' said Jagiello, 'but I have already had my morning draught in the gunroom.'

To his surprise Stephen found Jack already at table, shaved, pink, and eating voraciously. 'Are you not abed yet, for all love?' he cried.

'Oh, I took a cat-nap in Draper's chair,' said Jack. 'It sets you up amazingly. Have a beef-steak.'

'I thank you, Jack, but a cup of coffee and a piece of toast would answer very well for the moment. I mean to go back to the prisoner very soon; I have thought of a means of confounding the stupid creature. But first let me congratulate you on having refloated the *Minnie*: a noble feat, upon my word.'

'It was the tide that turned the day,' said Jack. 'You would hardly credit that a few miserable inches — and it is no more in the Baltic, you know — could have such an effect. But it gave just that trifle of lift at the very moment we needed it: another half hour and I should have had to slip and run. It was nip and tuck, I do assure you. But tell me, what news of the French officers? And what news of the young fellow? How does he do?'

Stephen shook his head. 'He is still in his deep coma,' he said, 'and I fear I may have been too sanguine last night. The mechanical processes function well enough, and the ligature has held; but the spirit is on the wing, perhaps. However, I hope to learn something about his companions directly.'

He carried his coffee back to Jagiello and once again there was a surprise for him. Something had happened during his absence: the young man had the pleased, slightly mad look of an Apollo — a primitive Apollo — who has just made a neat job of Marsyas; whereas the captive was so pale that his lips showed yellow.

'He has told me quite a lot,' said Jagiello, as he set a chair for Stephen and put a cushion in it, 'and now he is speaking the truth. He really does not know who the French officers were, because they stayed in the cabin all the time; in principle the ship was bound for Bornholm, but they could easily have put into Grimsholm on the same voyage. Only the *Minnie*'s captain would have known just where he meant to touch. He did see them when they were launching the boat and he says they were not old; but that proves nothing — a French colonel or even a general might be quite young. As for Grimsholm, he knows there is a private signal, and the last time the *Minnie* was there it was a Hamburg jack upside down on the front mast, but it might have changed since then. Only the captain would know. And then he says no one is ever allowed to land: they must stop at a little island near the shore, present their papers at the wharf, and unload by boats. They talk only to the French, who receive their papers. The little island is at the bottom of the bay, and it has a landing-place, a wharf: it is the third of such islands. Draw, incest,' he said to the Dane.

Stephen took the drawing and considered it. 'Come,' he said, 'let us check these statements with the more prudent, responsible members of the *Minnie*'s crew: and allow me to observe, Mr Jagiello, that a gold piece, decently proffered, will often obtain the best intelligence; and that the prospect of more in the event of success may elicit a flood of information untainted by concealed malignity. What we have here is very well, very specious; but believe me, I should not move an inch upon it without confirmation.'

Jack was still eating, but slowly now, when Stephen returned to the cabin: he had appeared briefly on deck when the loading of the prize was completed; had observed that the wind was steady in the west-north-west; and had given orders that her own people, with a competent guard of marines, should sail the *Minnie* under the lee of the *Ariel* and her guns, to give his own men a rest. He had also fixed the *Ariel*'s position: if the transports were true to their rendezvous they should show to the north-west in about an hour; and two hours after that Grimsholm should rise in the south-east.

'I have ascertained these facts,' said Stephen, rehearsing them and showing the drawing. 'They are corroborated by the *Minnie*'s carpenter and bosun, questioned separately; I do not count her second mate, for he has found means to be drunk, weeping drunk.'

'It is very good as far as it goes,' said Jack. 'But I am not happy about the private signal. The *Minnie* has not been here for months, and it is very likely to have been changed.'

'I abound in your sense, brother,' said Stephen. 'And I have been thinking. I have been thinking about Artemisia.'

'Indeed?' said Jack.

'Do not suppose I refer to Mausolus' wife . . .' said Stephen, raising one finger.

'If you mean the frigate, she is in the West Indies.'

'. . . for it is Lygdamus' daughter that I have in mind, the Queen of Cos. As you will recall, she accompanied Xerxes, with five ships, and she took part in the battle of Salamis. Perceiving that the day was lost, and that several Athenians were in pursuit of her, she at once attacked a Persian ship. The Athenians assumed that she was an ally, gave over their pursuit, and so allowed her to escape. Now it occurs to me that there is a certain analogy here: suppose the

Minnie were to fly into Grimsholm, all sails abroad, pursued by the *Ariel*, firing guns, do you not think it would take? Do not you think that any error in the private signal would be overlooked in such a case, particularly as the Hamburg jack was valid at the time of the *Minnie*'s last visit?'

Jack thought for a while. 'Yes, I think it would,' he said. 'But it would have to be convincing. You tell me that a good many of the people on the island are seamen: it would have to be damned well done to convince a seaman. Still, I think it could be managed: yes, I certainly think it could be managed. I like your scheme, Stephen.'

'I am heartily glad you approve it. And since you do, I shall offer some further observations. It would be the pity of the world if the Dutch and Baltic hands Sir James was so kind as to give us were to betray the stratagem by the propriety of their conduct or the uniformity of their dress: they are neat, well-behaved men, accustomed to the discipline of the Royal Navy, and I see that they all wear much the same kind of purser's slops. I suggest they should exchange clothes as well as places with the Minnies; for what could be more authentic than the Danish garb itself, taken from a Danish back? And then, so that there should be at least some familiar faces aboard, I suggest that her cook and carpenter should remain; they have both accepted a douceur in exchange for information, and they both stand to gain a considerable sum if all goes well.'

'It shall be as you say,' said Jack, draining the coffee-pot. 'I will put it in hand at once.'

He went on deck, and shortly afterward the Minnies began to come aboard in batches. When first they were told to strip they looked very blank and apprehensive, and even when they were made to understand that this was an exchange, even when they were dressed again, in the *Ariel*'s slops, they remained exceedingly suspicious.

Back in his cabin, with the ship's books before him, Jack was studying the record of his new hands when Hyde came in. 'I beg your pardon, sir,' said he, 'but the men say the Danes are lousy, and beg to be excused from putting on their clothes.'

'They will be complaining of the weevils next,' said Jack.

'I made that point, sir; but Wittgenstein, who speaks for them, said weevils were natural, whereas lice were not, being one of the plagues of Egypt, and therefore irreligious. They are afraid for their slops and hammocks, but very much more for their hair. They are extremely unwilling to have to cut off their pigtails, sir, and although they spoke respectfully, I believe they take it very much to heart.'

'Let them be called aft, Mr Hyde,' said Jack; and Stephen observed, 'They do not distinguish between Pediculus vestimenti, the body-louse, and Pediculus capitis, which infests the hair; their pigtails are in no danger at this stage, if they do not put on Danish hats.'

The hands came aft, the men condemned to wear the lousy clothes looking grim and deeply displeased, the others amused and facetious: Jack took their mood at once, and said, 'Men, I understand you don't like lice. Well, I don't like 'em neither. But this is an urgent business we have in hand: there is no time to ship wash-tubs and boil everything, and to get into Grimsholm you have to look like sloppy-joes, not like man-of-war's men. I am sorry for it, but there is nothing I can do: it is all in the line of duty. And you need not fear for your hair, so long as you do not put on their hats. A very learned gentleman has told me that these are innocent lice: they only go for your body, never for your pigtails. There is Pediculo vestimento, and there is Pediculo capito, two quite different kettles of fish — vestments and caps. It is all in the line of duty, as I say; but it comes under the article of hard-lying, and each man shall have one and fourpence a day extra. What is more, the prisoners have been given new slops, and they will not lie in your hammocks but berth in the hold, on straw. You cannot ask fairer than that.' He knew he had satisfied them; Pediculo capito had turned the scale before ever he came to the hard-lying money. 'Dismiss the hands, Mr Hyde,' he said, 'and let us carry on.' In the cabin once more he said, 'I intend putting Wittgenstein in charge of the *Minnie* to take her in, together with Klopstock and Haase as his mates. I do not contemplate sending any officers.'

'Oh sir,' said Hyde in a tone of deep distress, 'I had hoped . . .'

'I know,' said Jack, who understood his feelings perfectly, 'but this is a special case. Her crew must look like common Baltic sailors, and our hands can wear what they please without infringing the rules of war. If they are taken, they are ordinary prisoners. If an officer is taken, disguised, he is shot as a spy.'

'Yes, sir. But I could be in my shirt-sleeves, with my uniform coat stowed away, and my commission in its pocket. Sir, you know how hard promotion is to come by nowadays: a man has to jump into the mouth of a cannon and crawl out by the touch-hole, as they say. And even then he is not always noticed.'

Jack hesitated. What Hyde said was perfectly true; and there was a moral obligation on a captain to give his officers their chance, usually in order of seniority. But in addition to the perfectly valid point about uniform there was another he did not choose to mention. Hyde was a decent, conscientious young fellow and very good at the shipkeeping side of his task; but he was no great seaman. His one idea of increasing speed was to pack on more sail, whether it pressed the ship down or not; he put her about in a poking, hesitant fashion; and once his unfortunate confusion of right and left had caused the *Ariel* to miss stays. If he had been sending an officer at all, Jack would have been far happier with Fenton, a natural-born sailor; but that would be seen as a direct slight. His hesitation did not last long: the issue was clear — no fine feelings must put the enterprise and Stephen's life in hazard. 'I am sorry, Hyde,' he said, 'but you must look upon this as being in the line of duty, like the lice. I am sure you will have some other chance of distinguishing yourself presently.' He was not sure of it at all; he felt that his words carried neither conviction nor comfort; and he was glad when four sail of ships were reported on the starboard beam.

They were far away, just topsails up, but their course was converging with the *Ariel*'s; and until they could be certainly identified he called Wittgenstein and his mates below, solid, middle-aged men with close on a hundred years of service between them. He explained that they were to take the *Minnie* into Grimsholm, making all possible sail from the pursuing *Ariel*; they were to wear a Hamburg jack and Danish colours; they were to anchor off this island — showing them the drawing — and then put Dr Maturin ashore. Dr Maturin was to do all the talking, and they were to obey his orders to the letter. They were to speak no English in hearing of the island. They listened attentively, and he was particularly pleased to see how quickly and intelligently they took the point about sailing and behaving like merchant seamen.

He was about to go over all these points

a third time when Wittgenstein said a little testily, 'Yes, sir. I understand: I ain't no lubber. And by your good leave I think we ought to go aboard now, promiscuous, to see how she handles.'

Jack saw them pull across with their chosen band in their lousy coats, and he saw how quickly they threw off years of discipline, lounging about the deck, talking, leaning on the rail, chewing their quids and spitting, scratching themselves, hanging up their clothes here and there. The *Minnie* had never been what the Navy would have called a neat ship; now she looked thoroughly low.

By this time the *Ariel* and the four ships in the northwest had exchanged numbers; as Jack had supposed, they were the transports, escorted by *Aeolus*. 'It is damnably like counting your chickens,' he thought, looking at the troop-carriers far over the water and then southward towards the point where Grimsholm should heave up in time. 'I hope to God it may not bring ill-luck.'

Seven bells in the forenoon watch had struck some while ago, and the sand in the half-hour glass had nearly run its course. In spite of the general sense of impending crisis — for all hands knew very well what the *Ariel* was about — the ship was filled with the liveliest anticipation of dinner; yet their usual cheerfulness at this hour was somewhat dampened by the knowledge that they were carrying a corpse, that unlucky thing. The young Frenchman had lost the number of his mess, and the sailmaker had been sent for to sew him into a hammock, with two round-shot at his feet.

The officers took their noonday observation with particular care, a good observation that showed Grimsholm somewhat nearer than dead-reckoning would have it. The glass was turned, the bell struck, and the hands were piped to their longed-for meal: by the time it was finished the island would have nicked the clear sky; shortly after that Stephen would go aboard the *Minnie*, and the apparent chase would begin.

'Would it be improper to suggest our dining now?' he asked.

'Not at all,' said Jack. 'I will give the word at once.' He bent to the cabin skylight and hailed the astonished steward: 'Dinner on the table in seven minutes. Caviare and the Swedish bread, omelettes, beef-steaks, the ham, what is left of the cold goose-pie, and rouse out a bottle of champagne and two of the burgundy with the yellow seal.'

In seven minutes they sat down, Jack having given orders that he should be told as soon as Grimsholm came in sight. 'I have never eaten enough caviare,' said Stephen, helping himself again. 'Where did it come from?'

'The Czar sent it to Sir James, and he passed a barrel on to us. Rum stuff. I dare say it was caviare to the Admiral too.' This was his only small attempt at wit throughout the meal: and a little caviare was almost all he ate. His stomach was closed, and he could not even drink with relish.

Stephen on the other hand downed his omelette and a pound of steak, finished the cold goose-pie and cut a slice of ham in what would ordinarily have been a very festive way for him. But the feast was no feast. The atmosphere was entirely wrong. They were polite to one another, and there was almost no real contact; it was as though Stephen were already gone, removed to another plane.

It was only when they were drinking their port and Stephen said how he wished they might have some music — in former voyages together they had played innumerable 'cello and violin duets, often in trying circumstances — that their old relationship came back to life. 'We might try a glee,' said Jack with a poor smile, but at that point a midshipman came to say, with the master's duty, that Grimsholm was sighted from the masthead.

'It is nearly time,' said Jack. 'We must be chasing long before they see us.' He reached for the decanter, filled their glasses, and raised his, saying 'Here's my dear love to you, Stephen, and —' the glass dropped from his hand and broke. 'Jesus,' he said in a low voice, appalled.

'Never mind it, never mind it,' said Stephen, mopping his breeches. 'Now listen, Jack, will you? There are just three things I must say before I go aboard the *Minnie*. If I succeed I shall hoist the Catalan flag. You know the Catalan flag, I am sure.'

'I am ashamed to say I do not.'

'It is yellow, with four bloody stripes down it. And if you see it — when you see it — you must send to the transports, which will obviously be out of sight of the island, to tell them to come in, and you must come in yourself at once, flying the same flag in some place of honourable distinction. I suppose we have one?'

'Oh, the sailmaker will run up half a

dozen — yellow jack with strips of the spare pennant.'

'Just so. And I beg, Jack, that you will salute the fortress with all the guns proper for such a place, or even more; and that you will receive the commanding officer with the ceremony due to a nobleman.'

'If he comes with you, Stephen, he shall have a royal salute.'

Stephen crossed the lane of water and they saw him hauled aboard the *Minnie*. The *Ariel* signalled to the remote *Aeolus* to haul her wind, backed her topsails to give the *Minnie* two miles start, and at last the long hours of chase began.

Stephen sat on an old kitchen chair by the mizenmast, out of the way; he had a satchel of papers on his lap, and he looked steadily forward at Grimsholm, fine on the larboard bow and growing larger. There was no point in preparing a careful, ordered statement; everything would depend on the first moments, on the presence or absence of French officers, on his reception; and from that point on it would be an improvisation, a cadenza. He whistled the Montserrat Salve Regina, embroidering the theme.

From the *Ariel*'s bows Jack could see him

plainly over the clear grey sea, even without his glass, a black figure sitting there. All too plainly: with this fine breeze well abaft the beam the *Ariel* had been overhauling the *Minnie* faster than was right this last half hour. 'Let her go and veer away,' he said, and the spritsail course, its clews stopped, dropped into the sea over her blind quarter, acting as a drogue. It checked her speed, but not too obviously; she still gained a little, and ten minutes later he said to the gunner, 'Very well, Mr Nuttall, I think we may open fire. You know what to do. Take great care, Mr Nuttall.'

'Never you fear, sir,' said the gunner. 'I filled all our rotten old white grain: she's in no danger.'

He fired. The ball pitched two hundred yards short and fifty yards wide. The *Minnie* responded with a foretopgallant weather-studdingsail.

'It must look right, though,' said Jack.

'Never you fear, sir,' said the gunner again. 'Just you wait till the gun warms up.'

The gun warmed up, the guns indeed, for the Ariel kept giving a slight yaw to bring first one chaser then the other into action, increasing her rate of fire but diminishing her speed; the carefully-chosen round-shot cut up the water so close to the *Minnie* that once or twice the spray came aboard her. It was pretty practice, but it did not give the more experienced seamen in the *Ariel* as much satisfaction as the sailing of the ship — the perpetual slight rising of sheets, the over-press of somewhat unbalanced sails, all the hundred capers her captain had learnt in the oceans of the world, everything to give the impression of great eagerness and of the utmost haste, without in fact gaining very much. The stroke that gave most pleasure was his order to set the main-royal, a risky sail in such a breeze even with sound spars.

'You are forgetting, sir,' said Mr Hyde. 'The mast is sprung.'

'I have that in mind, Mr Hyde,' said Jack. 'Away aloft.'

Mast, sail and yard carried away after the first minute, a most spectacular sight from the land. And all the while Grimsholm came nearer, with the whole broad range of mainland shore that it guarded, miles of shoal-free coast with perfect landing-places for an army, quite apart from the river-port of Schweinau: for some time now the higher batteries had been in view, with the smoke wafting from their hot-shot furnaces, and in the transparent evening air good eyes could make out the red of the tricolour at the flagstaff.

Nearer still lay the ill-defined limit of the battery's range of accurate fire. Wittgenstein evidently thought he was close to it, for he had already broken out the Hamburg jack.

If the ruse had taken, if the watchers on that hill had been deceived, the *Minnie* would pass the invisible frontier unharmed: if not she would probably be damaged, possibly sunk. In his telescope Jack could see the artillery-men busy about their batteries, and the smoke from the furnaces had increased.

'Surely to God they can reach this far?' he said to himself, standing there on the forecastle with his hands clasped behind his back. 'Forty-two pounders, and with all that height . . .'

Closer, closer still. And at last the long-expected flashes, the jetting smoke, and then the roar, deeper than the guns of any ship. 'Cast off the drag-sail. Stand by the starboard guns,' he cried; and as he spoke the shot pitched, well-grouped and in a deadly true line, a cable's length beyond the *Ariel*. Beyond the *Ariel*, by God. 'Hard a-weather,' he cried. 'Fire as they bear.'

The *Ariel* turned on her heel so fast that the broadside went off as one gun: it should have been a harmless discharge for carronades at this range, but one freakish ricochet went home, piercing the *Minnie*'s mizen topsail. Jack had not time to notice that, however; he was wholly taken up with manoeuvring his ship out of the shocking fire that opened upon her. They had lured him in, well within the limit, and now the sea spurted white on either hand. Had he not had a fine brisk breeze and a handy crew he must have been severely mauled, if not sunk, by the tons of red-hot iron they flung at him with such appalling accuracy. As it was his sails were much tattered, a fire had started in the starboard head, one cutter had been destroyed and the foretopgallantmast wounded before he ran out of range. When he was quite sure that the upper batteries were not playing fox, but were in fact unable to reach him, he brought the *Ariel* to the wind, told Hyde to set about knotting and splicing and bending new sails, and ran up to the maintop.

From here he could see the whole bay perfectly well, the small islands at the bottom of it, the officers' houses and the barracks beyond, and half way down the bay, between the two flanking batteries, the *Minnie*, slowly taking in her topgallants as she glided towards the landing-place. A long, long pause while the work of the ship went on all round him and the *Minnie* crept on. At last she rounded-to and dropped her anchor some way from the shore. They seemed to be hoisting out a boat, but the declining sun sent such long shadows that he could scarcely make it out.

'On deck, there,' he called. 'Send up a telescope.'

Hyde brought it up himself. 'I can see them, sir,' he said. 'Just to the right — I mean to the left — of the large red house on shore.'

Jack made no reply: he was hardly aware of the man's presence. There was Stephen, sharply focused in his glass, looking pale, but no paler than usual, sitting in the sternsheets while Wittgenstein pulled him towards a low jetty full of men drawn up in formal ranks that dissolved as Jack watched, leaving him in a state of the utmost doubt: he could not tell what it signified.

In the boat itself Stephen sat quiet. The first signs had been favourable: the *Minnie* had not been fired upon; a voice from one of the flanking batteries as they sailed close in had called out to know whether they had brought any tobacco and the Danish cook's reply had brought a roar of satisfaction: but these were only preliminaries. The real test lay a hundred yards ahead, where those soldiers were waiting under arms. He had been weak enough to let himself be influenced by Jack's dismay at the childish omen, and by the young man's death; and although this was in some ways the easiest of his important missions he had a premonition of disaster. He wondered at it, and at his own attachment to life. There were so many exquisite things in it — the smell of the clean sea, the golden light of the westering sun, to say nothing of an eagle soaring on the wind. His strength was not as great as he had supposed.

These contradictions, this conflict between theory and practice, were turning in his mind when his whole spirit was jerked into the immediate present by the sight of the ordered ranks on the jetty dissolving into an ordinary crowd, no more. It had been a guard of honour. At the sight of a mere black coat coming ashore it had been dismissed: its function was to honour superior officers, not civilians.

Wittgenstein spun the little boat about and made a stern-board so that it bumped against the jetty. Stephen stood up, hesitated, leapt for a bollard with a sergeant standing by it, and missed his hold. He fell between the jetty and the boat, and coming to the surface called out in Catalan, 'Pull me out. Hell and death.'

'Art a Catalan?' cried the sergeant, amazed.

'Mother of God, of course I am,' said Stephen. 'Pull me out.'

'I am amazed,' said the sergeant, staring; but two corporals next to him flung down their muskets, leaned over, took Stephen's hands, and drew him up.

'Thank you, friends,' said he above a whole crowd of voices that wanted to know where he came from, what he was doing here, what news of Barcelona, Lleida, Palamos, Ripoll, what the ship had brought, and was there any wine. 'Now tell me, where is Colonel d'Ullastret?'

'He wants the Colonel,' said some; others said 'Can't he see him?' and the crowd parted, pointing. Stephen saw a small, upright, familiar figure. 'Padri!' he cried.

'Esteve!' cried his godfather, raising his arms, and they ran together and embraced, patting one another on the back in the Catalan manner.

This Jack saw among the lengthening shadows as the sun dipped over Sweden, but he could not make it out clearly for the crowd. Was it a greeting? Was it an arrest? A savage conflict? Nor could he tell what it meant when the whole group moved off to the large house painted red, though he stared until the red faded and the whole bay was filled with darkness, pricked with lights here and there and the old glow of the furnaces.

The *Ariel* stood on and off all night. He slept, or at least he lay down, until the middle watch, the dead hours of the night, when he climbed slowly into the dew-soaked top and sat there wrapped in his cloak, watching the stars and the lights of *Aeolus* and her transports, that had orders to close within signalling distance after sunset.

He was there still at the changing of the watch, when the master came on deck and Fenton said 'There you have her. Topsails and jib, course north-east by east a half east one glass, south-west by west a half west the other glass, Captain to be called if anything happens — any lights or activity on shore.' Then, in a lower voice,

'He's in the maintop.'

He was still there at the break of dawn, and as the light slowly mounted in the sky he wiped the dew from his objective-glass. He trained it first on the empty flagstaff and then at the end of the bay. They had already cleared all the deck cargo off the *Minnie*: but that proved nothing. Soldiers were already moving about, and he heard a trumpet high and clear, sounding a call he did not know. Gradually the red house resumed its colour; and presently he saw movement there, but too dim and far for any real distinction.

Two bells, and they began to clean the decks below him: up to the flagstaff again, for the twentieth time, and this time there was a group of men at its foot. He saw the rolled colours run up, a small black ball, hesitate at the top, and break out, streaming bravely southwards: yellow with four red strips. Joy filled his thumping heart and he fixed it while he might have counted ten, to make certainty doubly sure; and as he looked he saw the little group of men throw up their hats, join hands, and dance in a ring: he thought he made out cheering from the shore. Then leaning over the rim he called 'Mr Grimmond, take her into the bay.'

He was so stiff that he went down through the lubber's hole, chuckling to himself as he did so — 'Lord, what a fat-arse I have become.' On the quarter-deck he gave orders for the signal that should bring the transports in, for the Catalan flags that should adorn the *Ariel*'s mastheads, and for the coffee and Swedish bread that should still the grinding of his famished stomach. 'Mr Hyde,' he said, 'I should like the ship to look particularly well today, if you please: fit to receive a nobleman.'

He stood there, eating and drinking on a cleaned, dried patch of deck, as the *Ariel* repassed the dreaded limit of the great guns' reach, and he noticed that the officers looked uncommonly alert and grave, staring up at the great batteries.

'Pass the word for the gunner,' he said after a while. 'Mr Nuttall, we will salute the fortress with twenty-one guns, when I give the word.' He waited, waited until the *Ariel* was right between the two deadly flanking-batteries far within the bay and then said 'Carry on with the salute.'

Crisp and clear, at precise intervals it came, and the moment the twenty-first gun had spoken, the rocks on either hand, all the great casemates rising one above another overhead, vanished in a swirling cloud of smoke that dimmed the sky and an enormity of sound, a universal roar. A cloud perpetually renewed, perpetually stabbed with flashes from every gun in Grimsholm, so that to the watching transports the whole island seemed to be in eruption; and this in a volume of sound so prodigiously great that the air, the sea, and the *Ariel* trembled and all her people stood motionless, stunned, amazed, deafened, until the last echoes rolled away and they slowly realized that this was the returning of their salute, their peaceful welcome.

Chapter Nine

They had set out from Carlscrona on a dirty night, taking anxiety with them and leaving anxiety behind, an anxiety perhaps harder to bear, since the Admiral and his political colleague could do nothing but wait for the event of the exceedingly important transactions taking place on the far side of the Baltic.

They returned in the early afternoon of a charming day, transports, prize, *Humbug* and all ghosting over a light-green sea with barely a ripple on it, the warm southern air just far enough abaft the beam to allow all studdingsails to stand, so that even the overcrowded, slab-sided troop-carriers were a noble sight as they stood in, led by the *Ariel*, in a perfect line astern, each ship a cable's length from her neighbour, with the *Minnie* bringing up the rear. And they found a different Admiral, a younger, jolly man, no longer mordant or severe; the *Ariel* had telegraphed her news from as far as signals could be made out; the flagship had been in a state of cheerful activity ever since, preparing for her guests, and the galley had been entirely taken over by the great man's cook and his mates.

'I knew it, I knew it,' he said to Mr Thornton as they watched the *Ariel*'s boat come across. 'I knew the man — I knew what he could do. It is the finest thing — I knew it would be so.'

In the boat itself there was a grave silence: Jack was exhausted, not only by his exertions when the *Minnie* was aground, by the sleepless nights, by the general wear of spirit during the transfer, and by the writing of his official report, but even more by Colonel d'Ullastret's extraordinary loquacity. The Colonel spoke no English, but he was fluent, dreadfully fluent, in French, a language in which Jack could at least listen and in which, mindful of Stephen's warning that their guest must be handled with the greatest care, he had listened for hours and hours, doing his best to follow and in the rare pauses contributing remarks that might perhaps be appropriate and which he knew to be French, such as holy name of a dog, look me that, and blue belly — hours in which Stephen had deserted him to swim in the newly-recovered Catalanity of the transports. Now however the Colonel had fallen mute. Not only was he a dressy man even in time of peace, but like many soldiers he believed that there was a direct relation between military worth and perfection of uniform: his own had suffered grievously from the Baltic damp; its amaranth facings were now the colour of the mud at the bottom of a wine-barrel, the lace was tarnished, the tassel of one of his boots was gone, and perhaps worst of all his coat did not bear the marks of his present rank. The telescope had shown him the glittering array aboard the flagship, the scarlet and pipeclayed marines, the officers in their number-one cocked hats, the Admiral glorious in blue and gold; and Stephen could see that he was uneasy in his mind, discontented, ready to take offence and to detect a slight. The brooding expression softened a little as the flagship began the salute, the purely personal salute this time, and Stephen saw his godfather counting the guns one after another: thirteen, and he looked quite pleased; fourteen, then the fifteenth due to a grandee or a full admiral, and the Colonel nodded gravely. But his expression was still tense, and Stephen knew that it would not relax entirely until he had been welcomed aboard in a manner he thought appropriate and until he had a good dinner with at least a pint of wine under his shabby sword-belt.

'Should I embrace the Admiral?' he whispered.

'I doubt it,' said Stephen.

'Lord Peterbuggah embraced my grandfather,' said the Colonel, with a dogged look.

The boat hooked on: a moment's hesitation at the entering ladder, and they were in the midst of high naval ceremony, the wailing of bosun's calls, the grind, stamp and clash of Marines presenting arms, and here was the Admiral, stepping forward with his hand outstretched to greet Captain Aubrey. 'I knew it,' he said, 'I knew it would be so — I knew what you could do!'

'You are very good, sir,' said Jack, 'but I did little more than stand off and on. The credit,' he added in a lower tone and with a significant look, 'lies in quite another place. Now, sir, permettez-moi de — how shall I put it?'

'Présenter?' suggested the Admiral.

'Thank you, sir: présenter Don d'Ullastret — l'Amiral Saumarez.'

The Admiral swept off his hat: the Colonel spread his arms. After the very slightest pause, and to the unspeakable gratification of the quarterdeck, the Admiral embraced him on both cheeks, assured him with great truth and sincerity that he was very happy to see him aboard, and invited him to dinner, all this in a French somewhat more current than Jack's and certainly less hideous than the Colonel's; for the Admiral was a Guernsey man.

Yet although his tongue was French his stomach was English, and the Colonel was faced with a dinner that would scarcely have been out of place at the Mansion House: much of it was very strange to him and much more was inedible for a Papist, this being Friday; but he was at the Admiral's right hand; he had precedence over a visiting Swedish officer of equal rank; and he steered his way between damnation and ill-manners with great good humour, eating the root-vegetables and greenstuff untainted by flesh, concealing as much meat as possible, and staying himself with bread and wine, drinking glass for glass with the Admiral, although the Admiral was twice his weight.

At the other end of the table Mr Thornton was telling Stephen of their anguish of spirit during the *Ariel*'s absence, an anguish made all the more poignant by the arrival of a cutter at dawn with the intelligence that General Mercier had embarked in the *Minnie*.

'You talk of anxiety,' said Jack, catching the word during a pause in the happy laughter either side of him, 'but how would you like to be answerable day and night for a fragile, costly affair, the property of the King, perpetually at risk, in season and out? There is anxiety for you, I believe. We sea-officers are much to be pitied.'

'Hear him, hear him,' said his neighbours.

'You young fellows may prate about your cares,' said the Admiral, 'but what would you say if you had a squadron on your hands? You cannot conceive — but I was forgetting: Aubrey, you had the Mauritius command, so you know what it is. Yet even so, you can have no conception of the jading worry of settling a Baltic convoy, five or six hundred sail of merchantmen, even a thousand just before the ice stops navigation, and almost nothing to convoy them with. No, no; you are very well as you are, going quietly about your concerns, gathering all the glory and most of the prize-money.'

Their respect for the Admiral was such

that at any other time this might have passed, but now there was a general atmosphere of holiday and relaxation and cheerfulness, and the Admiral's good wine had been going round and round; passionate dissent broke out — there was no prize-money in the Baltic, and by the infamous new regulation that nothing was most scandalously divided — the captains had lost a whole eighth — and that eighth was most absurdly minced up and given to people who only played ducks and drakes with it, their share being so small, while the captains were reduced to abject poverty.

'Never mind, gentlemen,' said the Admiral, 'there is still glory to be picked up in the Baltic — look at Aubrey here, as far as you can see him for his fresh laurels — and in any case who cares about filthy lucre?'

Some of the captains looked as though they cared very much indeed, and one even observed 'Non olet' in an undertone; but when the Admiral called down the table to his flag-lieutenant, desiring him to 'tip us Heart of Oak', they listened to the young man's pure tenor with great approval as he sang 'Come cheer up my lads, 'tis to glory we steer,' and they joined in the chorus:

Heart of oak are our ships,
Heart of oak are our men,
We always are ready,
Steady, boys, steady . . .

with a fine growling roar, the last deep *steady* making the wine ripple in the decanters.

'We are singing about glory, sir,' said the Admiral to Colonel d'Ullastret.

'There is no better subject for a song,' said the Colonel. 'Far more suitable than whining about some woman. I am a great friend to glory; and to song. With your permission, I will sing you one about Lord Peterbuggah and my grandfather, when they took Barcelona together — the most glorious feat of united British and Catalan arms.'

The song was quite remarkably well received: indeed the whole afternoon passed off very pleasantly, not only in the flagship but aboard the transports too, where ring within ring of Catalans danced the sardana on the forecastle to the sound of oboes and a little drum, while during the intervals the foremasthands showed them the finer points of the hornpipe.

'Lord, Stephen,' said Jack, when they had returned to the *Ariel*, 'I do not know that I have ever been so sleepy: I shall turn in as soon as we have unmoored.'

'Surely we are not to set off again without a pause, for all love?'

'Eh?'

'Are we to set off at once? And on a Friday too?'

'Yes, of course we are. You said yourself that the sooner they were repatriated the better; the Admiral and the politico quite agreed; so here it is in my orders. You had better look at them: they speak of you. And as for its being Friday, I don't believe in omens any more, not after this last caper.'

'We really might be a parcel of Wandering Jews,' said Stephen in a discontented voice. He took the orders and observed, 'There seems to be a somewhat petulant insistence upon command and authority here. After so agreeable and shall I say *matey* afternoon I should have looked for *My dear Aubrey* rather than this cold and peremptory *Sir;* and surely the whole tenor is arrogant, devoid of common amenity, calculated to arouse a spirit of indignant revolt. *Sir, You are hereby required and directed to proceed without a moment's loss of time, in His Majesty's ship under your command, together with the ships and vessels named in the margin, to Hano Bay, where you will find a convoy under the protection of His Majesty's ships* . . . I wish *Humbug* had been among them: such pompous hectoring tautologous semi-literate stuff . . . *you will leave the convoy when you reach the Broad Fourteens and make your way with the utmost diligence to the Bordeaux stream, where you may expect to find His Majesty's ship Eurydice for intelligence of the situation in the Bight of Biscay; failing her you will proceed to Santandero or Passages for the same purpose . . . and in all matters having to do with the landing of the Spanish troops you will follow the advice of Dr S. Maturin, who alone is to determine . . . seek his guidance on the opportunity of . . . Marquess of Wellington . . . submit to his judgment* . . . A man of any spirit would be more inclined to toss S. Maturin into the sea than to ask his advice after this . . . *Spanish troops,* forsooth.' He had been aware for some time that Jack was asleep, but he maundered on until Hyde came in with the news that the *Ariel*'s signal to proceed to sea was flying aboard the flagship.

Light airs all night, wafting the *Ariel* and her charges south and westward through a gathering haze, her captain as it were stunned in the ultimate depth of sleep. Towards five o'clock he began to snore, a profound, deliberate, rhythmic sound that filled the cabin. 'Ah, your soul to the devil, Jack,' said Stephen, making an ineffectual lunge towards his cot. The snoring continued: Stephen thrust the wax balls deeper into his ears; but no bee had yet made the wax that would keep Captain Aubrey out and presently Stephen left his bed in despair.

A little after the changing of the watch the noise stopped and Jack sat up, wholly alive and conscious. It was not the noise of the ship's bell that woke him, for it had been tolling all night, ever since they entered the fog, with a musket-shot every two minutes, nor the sound of the swabs and the holystones, which were something of a lullaby to him, nor yet the light of day, there being so very little of it, but rather the working of some calculating-machine within that had sensed the shifting of the wind both in force and direction, and plotting these against the variations in the ship's course, with allowance for leeway and indraught, now informed him that they had opened Hano Bay.

He sat up, saw that Stephen's cot was empty, opened the slide of the dark-lantern, looked at the tell-tale compass overhead, looked at the barometer — still sinking steadily — silently drew on his clothes and crept out, moving with great caution in case he should wake Colonel d'Ullastret, who, the little ship being so crowded, slept in the dining-cabin, an ever-present menace.

On deck he could scarcely see beyond the bowsprit, but he heard the convoy at once, a remote braying of conchs, the sound of bells, the occasional musket, and far off the thump of the escort's signal-gun: the senior captain keeping his flock together. He exchanged good mornings with the pilot and the officer of the watch, noticed that although the courses and topsails hung slack from their yards the invisible topgallants must be drawing, since the ship made more than steerage-way, and looked at the log-board, saying, 'Well, Mr Pellworm, how long do you think it will last?'

'Well, sir,' said the pilot, 'I reckon it will burn off with the sun: but I don't quite like the way the glass keeps dropping. I dare say it will start to blow from the north presently, and then back into the west; and with all this here convoy, the Langelands Belt is none too wide.'

Some freak of the air brought a passionate skipper's cry, 'If you foul my hawse

I'll cut your cable, you hulking Dutch-built bugger,' as clear as if he had been only a hundred yards off, instead of far along the bay; and immediately afterwards Stephen's voice floated down from the upper regions to say that if Captain Aubrey chose to come up he would see a most remarkable sight; he might make the ascent quite easily and safely by the ropes on the left, on the larboard side looking forward.

'What the devil did you let him get up there for?' said Jack, frowning upon Mr Fenton. 'He must be at the crosstrees.' And pitching his voice aloft, 'Hold fast. Do not move. I am with you this minute.'

'I am very sorry, sir,' said Fenton. 'They said they were just going into the top: Mr Jagiello is with him.'

'You might perhaps term it a hapax phenomenon,' said Stephen.

'Hapax phenomenon,' muttered Jack, climbing fast. They were not at the crosstrees: by some miracle they had managed to reach the topgallantyard and to crawl out on it. There they stood, their feet upon the horses, their hands grasping various ropes, leaning over the yard, very much at their ease. Physically very much at their ease, with Stephen positively gay:

Jagiello, however, was far less cheerful than usual. 'There,' cried Stephen when Jack appeared in the frail topgallant-shrouds, 'are you not amazed?' He pointed cautiously with one finger and Jack looked out to the south-west. At this height they were above the low blanket of fog that covered the sea: clear sky above, no water below; no deck even, but a smooth layer of white mist, sharply cut off from the clean air; and ahead, on the starboard bow and on the starboard beam the surface of the soft, opaque whiteness was pierced by an infinity of masts, all striking up from this unearthly ground into a sky without a cloud, a sky that might have belonged to an entirely different world. 'Are you not amazed?' he said again.

Jack was ordinarily a good-natured man, but today he had not breakfasted and in any case the sight of his friend trusting his life to an unstoppered signal-halliard was more than he could bear. He roared, 'On deck. Belay the signal-halliard. Belay everything that belongs to the maintop-gallant,' and said, 'Amazed and gratified. Stephen, leave go that rope, clap on to the yard and come in towards the tye. I will guide your feet.'

'Oh,' said Stephen, giving a galvanic leap

and throwing his arms about, 'I am not at all nervous. Now that I cannot see the deck, it is as though the height were abolished. I am not at all nervous, I assure you. But tell me, have you ever beheld such a sight?'

'Not above a few hundred times,' said Jack. 'We call it the day-blink: it often happens when the breeze lies just so, or dies away — it will clear as soon as the sun is well up. But I am very grateful for having been called aloft before breakfast to see it again. Put your foot here, round the stirrup — you have fouled the stirrup. Your shoe is foul of the mouse. Mr Jagiello, leave that becket alone. Stephen, give me your hand: handsomely, now; handsomely does it.' At this point Stephen dropped abruptly from the yard; not perpendicularly, however, for Jack's powerful arm swung him inwards to the cap, while the shoe continued its free fall to the deck. 'Thank you, Jack,' he said, gasping, as he was settled on the crosstrees with a turn about his middle. 'I am obliged to you. I must have made a false movement.'

'Perhaps you did,' said Jack. 'But what in God's name are you doing up here anyway? Jagiello, leave that becket alone. You know I have begged you both not to go above the top.'

'The fact of the matter is that Mr Jagiello is in an embarrassing position.'

'He will be in kingdom come if he don't leave go that becket. Mr Jagiello, leave go that becket: clap on to the robbens with both hands and come in to the big block in the middle.'

'We could not discuss it on the deck, since the people kept desiring us to move out of the swabbers' way, so we went up to the top; but there again buckets of water were flinging about, so we climbed still higher. He has found a woman in his bed.'

'Just so, just so,' said Jack. 'Mr Fenton, secure the Doctor's shoe.'

'Yes, sir,' said Jagiello, who had worked his way to the backbrace and whose blushing face now peered down at them. 'I found her there when I went to my cabin just now.'

'What had you been doing all night?'

'I had been playing cards in the gun-room with the Catalan officers.'

'And I collect that she is not wanted on the voyage?'

'Oh no, sir: not at all.'

It occurred to Jack that this was a very ridiculous place for a conference of such a nature, with the two landsmen poised in awkward postures between heaven and earth and himself deprived of his breakfast. He called down, 'Mr Fenton, send me up a couple of prime upperyardmen with a snatch-block and line for a whip.'

While they were coming Stephen said in a low voice, 'There: it is almost gone. And yet in its prosaic way this is almost as striking.' The mist, lifting and dissolving with the first rays of the sun, showed 783 vessels all merchantmen except for one frigate, the old *Juno*, three sloops-of-war and a cutter. 'Never have I had so strong an impression of the vast magnitude of sea-borne trade, of mercantile enterprise, of the interdependence of nations.'

'There is Ahus,' said Jack, nodding towards a town, now clear on the shore of the bay. 'The lady will take her breakfast on dry land. Mr Fenton, lower down the gig.'

The topmen came running up, one of them bearing Stephen's shoe: Jack cast a loop round his waist, made all fast, bade him hold on to the knot, called 'Lower handsomely,' and Stephen made his ignominious descent, as he had often done before.

Jagiello followed him, and then Jack: broad grins on the quarterdeck, and a lively air of expectation. 'Now, Mr Jagiello,' said Jack, 'you must signify to the lady that she is to be over the side in two minutes. There is not a moment to be lost.'

'If you please, sir,' said Jagiello, blushing to the eyes, 'I had rather not. It would seem so unkind; and it would take so very long — tears, you know, and reclamations. Perhaps Mr Pellworm would be so infinitely obliging; he knows her, and he speaks the Swedish. Mr Pellworm is a married man.'

'You are acquainted with the lady, Mr Pellworm?'

'From afar, sir, from afar. I have seen the young person from afar. Who has not, that has ever put into Carlscrona and attended the theatre? I may have spoken to her once or twice, just to pass the time of day, as I did when she came aboard, but only when I was with officers, the young person being known to one and all, to all and sundry, sir, as the Gentlemen's Relish; and I hope I know my station. Besides, I am told she is now the Governor's private piece . . . a singing harlot of enormous price, in the words of the poet. But if you wish me to turn her ashore, sir, I will speak to her now — speak to her like a Dutch uncle.'

'Ay, pray do, Mr Pellworm,' said Jack. 'A man-of-war is no place for women.'

Pellworm nodded, and he walked off with a heavy tread, composing his face into a severe, determined, and even brutal expression.

A singing harlot she might be, but it was in a singularly harsh and unmusical voice that she addressed the *Ariel* from over the water as the stolid, reliable, middle-aged forecastle hands rowed her ashore.

'What does she say?' asked Stephen.

'Loins as hot as a goat, Heart as cold as a stone,' said Pellworm. 'That is poetry too.'

'It is not true. She knows nothing whatever about my loins: has never seen them,' cried Jagiello from his lurking-place on the far side of the mizen-mast. He added, 'I never invited her, and I begged her to go away.'

'If only all these problems could be resolved so easily,' murmured Jack as he watched the Gentlemen's Relish growing smaller and smaller. 'Mr Fenton, we may edge down on the *Juno* and pick up the gig on the way.'

Stephen glanced at him and at Jagiello. 'Poltroons,' he said to himself, 'Scrubs.' And looking along the deck he noticed that apart from a few grinning ill-conditioned men and boys most of the hands looked ashamed and concerned.

'It is a very curious thing,' said Jack to Stephen over breakfast, 'but I learn that Jagiello went ashore while we were aboard the flag, and he had not been back above half an hour before three young women put off to the ship. Two were the Swedish admiral's daughters — amazingly pretty, says Hyde — and the third was the Relish, who kills at a mile. But what I cannot for the life of me understand is what they see in him. He is a good fellow, to be sure, but he is only a boy; I doubt he shaves once a week, if that. And indeed he is rather more like a girl than anything else.'

'So it seems was Orpheus; but that did not prevent women from tearing him limb from limb. His head, his beardless head, floated down the swift Hebrus, together with his broken lyre, alas.'

'Oh my God, here is the Colonel,' said Jack, grasping his cup and a piece of toast and hurrying on deck.

It was here that he spent most of the day, for a thin drizzle succeeded the mist, keeping the Colonel below. And although the convoy was not due to sail until the evening the *Juno* asked Jack to take up a station ahead of the main body, and moving the *Ariel* and her transports through this vast crowd of shipping with light and variable airs took a very long time, the more so as many of the merchantmen lay in a curiously haphazard and whimsical fashion, as though their masters could not tell starboard from larboard, hay from straw. The Captain and the Colonel met for dinner, however, when the gunroom invited them to a noble spread and when Jack endured the purgatory of an hour or so of French, mostly, as far as he could tell, about the fine women who had pursued d'Ullastret, regiments of women it seemed, married and unmarried, with some very pathetic cases among them.

The last arrivals joined the convoy from Riga, bringing up a fine breeze from the north-east: the *Juno* anxiously counted her charges, signalling with scarcely a pause, receiving meaningless or contradictory replies, emphasizing her orders with guns, sending her boats hither and thither to convey her captain's wishes by roaring word of mouth: yet the regulation of even so vast a convoy had an end at last, and eventually the *Juno* gave the word to weigh. Thousands and thousands of sails appeared, lightening the grey air over the whole spacious bay, and they moved off in three amorphous divisions, gliding gently into the night at the speed of the slowest, an ill-conceived, undermanned, over-insured pink from Cork.

The divisions were sadly scattered by dawn, in spite of the lights they all carried in their tops, but the good north-easter enabled them to gather in some semblance of order and carried them briskly through the difficult Fehmarn channel by sunset, when it abruptly chopped into the south and became a perfect leading-wind for the still more difficult Langelands Belt. They threaded the long channel in the night, scarcely touching a sheet or brace; and from the shore they looked like some prodigious constellation, enormously rich in stars, that had strayed to the surface of the sea. They sailed with a wind that kept the hostile gunboats in port, and the only untoward event was a Dane's diabolical attempt at insinuating himself into the procession in the hope of carrying a straggler by surprise and darting into Spodsbjerg with her; but he was detected; the signal for a stranger in the fleet brought the hindmost sloop-of-war tearing up from the rear; and although the Dane did indeed dart into Spodsbjerg he darted alone, with tattered sails and five gaping holes between wind and water, leaving no more damage behind him than three merchantmen that had fallen aboard one another in their alarm and that had to be taken in tow.

But this happened at midnight, and so far back in the immensely long convoy that the *Ariel* was hardly aware of it. When the grey weeping dawn began to light the greyer sea the van was already far out into the Great Belt itself, with Zealand faintly looming on the starboard beam and Funen lost in the distant rain to port.

'Well, Mr Pellworm,' said Jack, shaking the wet from his pea-jacket and looking up at the cloud racing up from the south with strong approval, 'I am afraid you are disappointed of your wind out of the north.'

'I am not complaining, sir,' said Pellworm. 'As pretty a breeze, as pretty a passage as you could wish — the answer to a maiden's prayer, as the poet says — and I dare say it will carry us right up the Cattegat; but mark my words, sir, mark my words, we shall have our blow yet, and I only hope we may have weathered the Skaw before it starts. You cannot set sail of a Friday, the thirteenth of the month, with a woman on board into the bargain, without you have a blow. I am not in the least superstitious — I leave crows and pies crossing my path and cards and tea-leaves and such to Mrs Pellworm — but it stands to reason that what seamen have found to be the case ever since the memory of man saith not to the contrary must have something in it. There is no smoke without a fire. Besides, the glass is dropping yet; and even if it were not, a Friday is always a Friday.'

'Maybe, maybe; but a good many of these omens are all cry and no wolf.'

'Is it not wool, sir?'

'Come, come, Mr Pellworm,' said Jack, laughing aloud. 'Who would cry wool too often? What would be the point of crying wool? There is no danger in wool, you know; indeed, London Bridge is founded on it, and you cannot say fairer than that, I believe. No, no: your omens keep threatening disaster — they did so before Grimsholm, and you see what happened: all cry with no wolf at the end of it. I have done with omens,' he said, grasping a belaying-pin. 'But your falling glass is another kettle of fish: your glass is scientific.'

Pellworm's face took on a dogged expression and he said, 'As you please, sir; but there are more things in heaven and earth, Captain Aubrey, than you philosophers dream of.'

'Philosophers, Mr Pellworm?'

'Oh, sir, that was only poetry. I meant no disrespect.'

'Philosophers, Mr Pellworm,' began Jack, but he broke off at the sight of the *Ariel*'s master, who was approaching the first lieutenant on the leeward side of the quarterdeck with small, constrained steps, consternation all over his face, and his hands clasped in front of him. 'What's amiss, Mr Grimmond?' he cried.

'Sir,' said Grimmond in an unnatural voice, 'I am very sorry to have to report that the timepiece is broke. I dropped it on the deck.' He opened his hands, and there nestling in his handkerchief lay the wreck of the *Ariel*'s chronometer: it had had the unluckiest fall, striking its most vulnerable joint on a ring-bolt, and now its works lay all abroad.

There was little point in asking the master why he was looking at the chronometer at this time of day, far from the regulation time for winding it, or how he came to drop it; and although these questions at once presented themselves, together with the observation that one should always take very great care when handling anything so delicate, Jack only said, 'Well, well: my hack-watch is fairly accurate. Though now I come to think on it, the Doctor's is a great deal better.'

To the Doctor he said, 'Stephen, a damned thing has happened: the timepiece is broke. Will you lend me your watch?'

'You are welcome to it, sure,' said Stephen, producing his severely beautiful Bréguet. 'But what is wrong with the other chronometers?'

'There ain't any other chronometers.'

'Come, brother, I remember to have seen a whole array in our various ships, and distracted young gentlemen trying to find the mean of them all while you bullied them, holding your hack-watch in one hand and peering at the celestial bodies with the other.'

'Yes, but that was because I have always had my own, ever since I could afford it; and if a captain buys one, the Admiralty lets him have two more. Otherwise he carries just the single timekeeper, and then only if he is going foreign, in most cases.'

'The machine is used for finding out the latitude, I believe?'

'To tell you the truth, Stephen, most people rely on the sextant for their latitude: the timekeeper is more for the other thing — east and west, you know.'

'East and west of what, for all love?'

'Why, of Greenwich, naturally.'

'I am no great navigator —' said Stephen.

'You are far too modest,' said Jack.

'— though I have often wondered how you mariners find your way about the dank wastes of ocean. But from what you tell me I see that for your countrymen Greenwich rather than Jerusalem is the navel of the universe — lo, Greenwich, where many a shrew is in, ha, ha — and secondly that whereas a poor man can fix his position only with regard to north and south, to up and down, his wealthy brother is secure to right and left as well. There is no doubt a logic in this, although it escapes me, just as the use of the timepiece escapes me, with its peevish insistence upon accuracy in the measurement of what is after all a most debatable concept, quite unknown, we are told, in Heaven. Tell me, is it really capable of telling you where you are, or is this just another of your naval — I must not say superstitions — like saluting the purely hypothetical crucifix on the quarterdeck?'

'If you have exact Greenwich time aboard — if you carry it with you — you can fix your longitude exactly by accurate observation of local noon, to say nothing of occultations and the finer points. I have a pair of Arnolds at home — how I wish I had brought 'em — that only gained twenty seconds from Plymouth to Bermuda. In these waters that would tell you where you were, east or west, to within three miles or so. Oh, the lunarians may say what they please, but a well-tempered chronometer is the sweetest thing! Suppose you were riding along, with your watch set to Greenwich time in your pocket, and suppose you happened to take a noon observation and found that the sun southed at five minutes after twelve, you would know that you were almost exactly on the meridian of Winchester, without having to search for a finger-post. And the same applies to the sea, where finger-posts are tolerably uncommon.'

'Heavens, Jack, what things you tell me. And I dare say this would answer for let us say Dublin and Galway?'

'I should not care to affirm anything about Ireland, where people have the strangest notion of time; but at sea, I do assure you, it answers very well. That is why I should like to borrow your watch.'

'Alas, my poor friend, not only is it set to Carlscrona time, but it loses a minute or so a day; and from what you tell me, that would represent a span of some twenty miles. I am afraid we must imitate the ancients and hug the shore, creeping from promontory to promontory.'

'I very much doubt the ancients did anything of the kind. Can you imagine anyone in his wits coming within sight of a lee-shore? No, no: blue-water sailing for me; and after all, the old 'uns found their way to the New World and back again with no more than lead, latitude and lookout. Even so, a watch true to a minute would be useful in case of dirty weather; I shall signal *Juno* and set it by their reckoning.' He cocked his ear to the sound of Colonel d'Ullastret singing 'Bon cop de falç' as he shaved in preparation for his first appearance, a harsh, disagreeable voice, not unlike Stephen's, and went on. 'Though now I come to think on it, I believe I shall go across. Maudsley owes me a mutton-chop.'

'The Colonel would be disappointed not to see you at dinner. Besides, the sea is rough, the day inclement.'

'Nelson once said that love of his country served him for a greatcoat. It is my clear duty to pull across whatever the weather and take an accurate reading. You will make my excuses: as an officer, the Colonel will certainly understand. Besides, you can invite Jagiello — Jagiello will entertain him. He speaks French quite as well as I do. Yes, that is the very thing: you must ask Jagiello to dinner.'

Captain Aubrey had a rough trip of it on his way to the *Juno*: he had an even rougher, wetter, return, and although he was buoyed up with Maudsley's capital dinner there were times when he and the coxswain and every man in the boat thought he had misjudged it — that the ugly short cross-seas cut up by the strengthening wind as it backed must swamp them. As it was the launch was very near stove alongside, and when Jack came aboard in his dripping borrowed boat-cloak he caught the pilot's eye fixed upon him with a look of triumph.

'Well, Mr Pellworm,' he said, 'here is your blow at last; but at least I hope it is come late enough to let us weather the Skaw.'

'I hope so too, sir, I am sure,' said Pellworm, obviously convinced that they should do nothing of the kind. 'But it is backing uncommon fast, and once it comes full north, farewell, adieu.'

'That bloody-minded old Pellworm,' said Jack, as he changed into what few dry garments he possessed. 'He would rather we beat to and fro for a week trying to get out of the Sleeve, and then after all having to stretch away to lie in Kungsbacka to wait for a fair wind, rather than have his prediction fail. He will bring us bad luck. Mingus,' he called to the steward, 'take these along to the galley to dry, and take care of the lace as you value your hide. Stephen, I am going to sleep until the setting of the watch: we have a heavy night ahead of us. Where is the Colonel?'

'He is already gone to bed. He finds himself incommoded by the motion: leaves his compliments and excuses, however.'

A heavy night they had, but Stephen and Jagiello knew little of it, apart from thumps, hoarse nautical cries, pipings, the muted thunder of feet as the watch below was turned up to make sail or take it in, and the wild swinging of the lantern that lit their little green-topped card-table. They had tacitly abandoned chess and taken to piquet: Stephen had always been lucky at cards; Jagiello was quite disastrously and uniformly unfortunate. By three bells in the middle watch he had lost all his money, and since they had agreed to play only for visible coin the game necessarily came to an end. He looked wistfully at his entire fortune lying there on Stephen's side —

seventeen shillings and fourpence, mostly in very small change — but after a moment his native cheerfulness returned and he declared that the moment they set foot on land he should cash one of his letters of credit and beg for his revenge. 'That will be next week, I suppose?' he said.

'Perhaps you may be too sanguine,' said Stephen, cutting the ace of spades and then immediately after the ace of hearts. 'From what I am told by Mr Pellworm, an old experienced Baltic pilot, it is more likely to be next year.'

'But I have heard of the passage made in four days — we came very quickly — and the wind is now blowing towards England. Mr Pellworm is trying to make our meat creep: he told me the same thing.'

'Certainly there is a very vicious tendency in Mr Pellworm and in many other mariners to terrify the landsman; and to be sure the wind blows from the north-east. But you are to consider that we are not yet out of the Sleeve; we have yet to weather the Skaw, and the wind is coming more northward still.'

'Oh, indeed,' said Jagiello, looking perfectly blank.

'As a cavalry officer,' said Stephen, 'you have perhaps not fully appreciated the importance, the primordial importance of the breeze in maritime affairs. Even I was not wholly imbued with it until I had been many years at sea. Let us suppose that this three-shilling piece represents the Skaw, that notorious headland, innocent in appearance but death to ships,' he said, placing a coin on the left-hand side of the table. 'And this,' placing another on the right, 'Gothenburg, on the Swedish main, with some ten leagues between them. And here, with the island of Lesso somewhat behind us, or *abaft,* as we say, is the convoy, represented by these pennies and ha'pence. Now you must know that a ship's head can be usefully pointed no nearer the wind than six points of the compass, or sixty-seven and a half degrees; and although she may appear to be travelling that close to the origin of the breeze, in fact her true course is by no means the same, for there is also a lateral motion, execrated by the seamen, known as leeway. This depends on the impetuosity of the billows and a host of other factors, but I believe I may say that in the present conditions it must amount to two points. That is to say, we are really moving at right angles to the wind.'

'Then all is well,' cried Jagiello, 'because

the wind being in the north-east we clear the Skaw.'

'With all my heart,' said Stephen, 'but if it moves to the north, if it moves the four points between north-east and north, then the other arm of the angle inevitably moves a corresponding distance south; and you will readily perceive that the arm strikes the headland as soon as it has passed through fifteen degrees, or considerably less than the four points of which I speak. Furthermore, Mr Jagiello, furthermore, even if we do creep round the Skaw, Mr Pellworm promises us the wind is likely to shift even west of north, perhaps even into the dreaded west itself, growing more violent as it does so; and once the breeze rises to a gale, the leeway to which I referred increases, so that when topsails are obliged to be taken in, or *handed,* we reckon at least four points. So that once we are round the Skaw we have Jammer Bay under our lee, with the wind blowing directly upon it: we no longer travel at right angles to the wind but at some hundred and twenty degrees from it, gradually slanting towards the hostile coast and its mortal breakers. We may throw out anchors; but there is little confidence to be placed in anchors during a gale of wind.

They drag; the ship drives; and in the hours that follow we have ample time to deplore our ineluctable fate, regretting, no doubt, lost opportunities of pleasure, even of reform. Such, Mr Jagiello, are what a former shipmate of mine called the impervious horrors of a leeward shore. Small wonder that Captain Aubrey regards the coast as being far too near at twenty miles away; small wonder that Mr Pellworm, who has seen the ships of a numerous convoy together with two great men-of-war miserably shattered along the reefs of Jammer Bay, should wish to bear up, or down, or away, and run for Kungsbacka.'

Twice in what was left of the night he heard Jack come below and move quietly about, drinking from the jug of negus or groping for a piece of Swedish bun; but having fallen into a deep sleep a little after dawn he did not see him until breakfast.

Captain Aubrey's face, though pink and freshly shaved, showed marks of a long active anxious night; it was comparatively thin, and he was setting about his meal with a wolfish appetite. 'There you are, Stephen,' he cried. 'Good morning to you. I did not look to see you yet awhile, and I am sorry to say I have ate the last of the bacon. The dish was empty before I was aware.'

'It is always the same old squalid tale,' said Stephen. 'May I at least hope there is a tint of coffee left?'

'Had you shown a leg sooner, you would have saved your bacon,' said Jack. 'Ha, ha, ha, Stephen: did you hear that? Saved your bacon: it came to me in a flash.'

'Sure there is nothing like spontaneous wit,' said Stephen: and after a pause, 'Tell me, what of the night? And how do we stand?'

'It was tolerably rough, but consummate seamanship brought us through, and we just weathered the Skaw in the middle watch, though with precious little to spare — five miles at the most.'

'So we are round?' said Stephen, rasping his three days' beard. He was still stupid from his heavy sleep; the memory of an erotic dream (the first since his renewed acquaintance with Diana) was still strong in his mind. He was a frowzy, unwashed object, his wits not yet gathered into an orderly troop, whereas Jack was in the full tide of daily life.

'Yes and we are bowling along under all plain sail at a good seven knots, the breeze at north by east. When you come on deck you will see the Holmes six or seven leagues on the larboard beam. But poor Maudsley had to bear up, with his merchantmen sagging to leeward so. The convoy has run for Kungsbacka.'

'Do not tell me the transports have turned back, God forbid — oh surely the transports are round?'

'Of course they are. What a fellow you are, Stephen: how could I have possibly left them in the Sleeve? They may not be much to look at, but they are good weatherly ships and they came round as well as the *Ariel.* Good officerlike captains, too: I shall invite them to dinner, as soon as the weather moderates.'

'So Pellworm's west wind did not eventuate, at all?'

'Not so far, at any rate.'

'And there was I, telling Jagiello of the perils of a leeward shore with a wealth of technical detail that would have amazed you.' Jack smiled. 'I say the accuracy of my account would have amazed you,' said Stephen. 'And I flatter myself that even you would have found no fault in my description of the long-drawn-out horror of a vessel so situated, or entrapped.'

'I am sure I should not,' said Jack

gravely. 'You could not exaggerate it if you tried.'

'Why I did so I cannot tell,' observed Stephen, more human now that he had absorbed his morning draught. 'Perhaps it was some obscure derangement of my humours. My intention was certainly malignant: I wished to make him uneasy, to take away from his superabundant cheerfulness. I believe I succeeded: I certainly brought truth and deep conviction to the task. I regret it now.'

'Never be so concerned. If you frightened him, the effect wore off in the night; I saw him running about on deck before I came below, laughing like a holiday.'

'What a daedal maze,' said Stephen, referring to the workings of his mind and holding up a piece of toast as he did so. 'Although I like Jagiello and esteem his parts, there are times when his youth and energy and high spirits and beauty arouse ill feelings in my bosom. It is envy, no doubt, mere base ignoble grovelling envy. No Gentleman's Relish ever pursued me in my youth, nor at any other time.'

'He is an engaging young fellow, to be sure; but upon my sacred honour I cannot tell what women see in him.'

'This is the last of the toast, I presume?'

'I am afraid it is,' said Jack, 'and I am afraid there will be no more soft tack to make it with until we are in the Downs.'

'When will that be, do you suppose?'

'If only this breeze holds, in a couple of days now that we are no longer tied to the slugs of the convoy. But I should not like to answer for the wind: the weather is all ahoo — the glass skips up and down — and we may have Pellworm's blow upon us yet. Still, if it does not come much south of west, we might strike the Broad Fourteens on Thursday, and so tide it down the Channel.'

The weather was indeed all ahoo, upset, chaotic, unpredictable; and there was a very great deal of it, almost always thick, with winds from north-east and north-west varying from light airs to close-reefed topsail gales, often accompanied by rain and heavy seas. These at least kept the Colonel below, but otherwise Jack had a somewhat disagreeable time of it. For one thing, he was frustrated in his wish to invite the captains of the troop-carriers, all elderly lieutenants who lacked the influence or the luck of successful action needed for promotion, but all excellent seamen who brought their ships along in a manner he whole-heartedly admired, hardly keeping the *Ariel* back at all. And then in his reckoning he had to allow for the curious North Sea indraught, irregular variation of the compass, the lack of observations, and the absence of a chronometer, so that what was ordinarily a simple routine passage became a long-lasting anxious test of navigation by instinct, with the devil to pay if his guess proved wrong. Yet not by instinct alone, for although the sky remained impenetrable for most of the time, and the grey waves told him little, the bottom of that shallow sea was a vast mosaic of different colours and he kept the lead going continually — wet, miserable hands in the windward mainchains uttering their dismal chant by day and night — and together with Pellworm and the master he continually examined the samples that the tallow on the lead brought up; grey sand, fine yellow sand with shells, sludge, coarse ground with small black stones, shingle. But the tesserae of this mosaic were often many miles across; the appreciation of their nature varied from man to man, so that the master and the pilot were sometimes in strong disagreement; and there were occasions when Jack was tempted to ask his way of the many fishermen, English and Dutch, who haunted those perilous banks in their shallow-draught doggers, schuyts, busses, howkers, and even bugalets, and who made his progress all the more uneasy by lying across his hawse until the last possible minute or suddenly looming out of the darkness without a single light so that he had to throw all aback. Like most English commanders, Jack never interfered with fishermen, whatever their nationality; and twice he was rewarded by strong Dutch voices out of the gloom cursing him for a Goddam boggart for having fouled their hand-lines. As for Stephen's watch, it was an elegant machine and admirably calculated for taking a pulse, but it asserted that the ship was ten miles clear of the Galloper at a time when they could actually see the light-ship guarding the shoal hoist its lanterns in the western murk.

'God send we may not run plump on to the Goodwin,' said Jack to the master as the *Ariel* and her charges hauled their wind and fled to the deep-water channel.

'Oh sir,' said Grimmond, who never expected facetiousness from so imposing a figure, 'Surely that is well to the south.'

They were spared the Goodwin, as they had been spared the Haddock Bank, the Leman, the Ower, and the Outer Dowsing:

indeed they ran into the Downs on the one clear morning of the week, and it was just as well that they did so, for the roadstead was crowded with shipping, great convoys for the Indies, East and West, the Mediterranean, and the Guinea Coast, and if the weather had been as dirty as they had found it these last few days it would have been difficult to thread through the various fleets. There were few merchantmen setting off on their own, however, in spite of the favourable wind: the French had been unusually busy in the chops of the Channel, and it was rumoured that two American frigates were lying off the Land's End.

The *Ariel* only paused long enough to hail a Deal pilot-boat, to set Mr Pellworm ashore: as he went over the side he said, 'Mark my words, sir, mark my words: it will come into the west yet, whatever Mr Grimmond may say; and when it does come, it will blow all the harder for the waiting.' He moved three steps down the ladder and paused, his eyes just over the rail. '*Sick Earth convulsive groans from shore to shore. And Nature shuddering feels the horrid roar*,' he said: his eyes took on a particularly knowing and significant look for a moment, and then vanished.

The quarterdeck frowned: Pellworm might be an old respected pilot, but this was coming it too high by half; this was taking a liberty with their Captain.

'Fill the maintopsail,' said Jack in a strong, displeased voice; and more privately to Stephen, 'I am glad we are shot of Mr Pellworm. He is an excellent pilot, but he prates too much. Poetry is not at all suitable on the quarterdeck of a man-of-war, particularly on such a subject: it might make the hands uneasy.'

It might also be right. There was perhaps something unpleasant in the smiling sky; and although the breeze seemed firmly settled in the north-east Jack was determined not to lose a minute of it but to run down-Channel with a press of sail until he could round Ushant with plenty of sea-room. He would not even stop long enough to take in fresh supplies from the bum-boats that came round the ship, observing in his decided manner 'that they were not here to blow out their kites with lobscouse, nor to choke their luffs with figgy-dowdy, but to convey the Catalan troops to Santandero without a moment's loss of time — dried peas would answer very well until they should reach Santandero,' and with a fresh breeze, a following tide, and a fine sense of urgency they stood south-west.

A fair wind right down the Channel was rare enough: often and often he had had to anchor for the tide, beat up tack upon tack in the narrow seas, winning a few miles only to be driven back again — weeks sometimes before he could get clear into the Atlantic; but now the familiar landmarks filed by in fine brisk succession: the South Foreland, Dungeness, Fairly, and Beachy gleaming through a wall of rain with solid blue-black cloud behind it; and then late in the evening there was the Wight clear on the starboard bow. Jack climbed into the mizentop with a telescope and before the green light vanished in the west he thought he caught the glint of his observatory dome at Ashgrove Cottage. He stared at it in a strange confusion of spirits, as though at another world, farther from him now than when he had been in the Antipodes.

The wind increased with the setting of the sun, and seeing that it would certainly come on to blow they struck topgallantmasts, reefed topsails and made all snug, even to the extent of rolling-tackles and puddening — storm-canvas had been the order of the day since Jutland — and they passed the Start as though they meant to fly out of the Channel without once changing course and reach the Spanish coast before the end of the week, a fitting crown to a most uncommon expedition.

Once again the dawn broke fair enough after a rainy night, though a heavy swell was setting from the southwest against the wind and tide, sending green water over the *Ariel*'s bows, and they ran past the Eddystone, with Rame Head and the homelike entrance to Plymouth plain beyond it, past the Dodman; and between the Dodman and the Lizard their luck failed them. Without any warning but three black squalls in quick succession the wind chopped about into the west, blowing right into their teeth and bringing very heavy rain. 'We were so nearly clear,' said Jack. 'Another hour and I should have stood south: such a run it would have been! However, whining will do no good, and at least we have a couple of hundred miles under our lee.' He tied his sou'wester firmly under his chin, advised Stephen to make all fast, and returned to the streaming deck.

'What is amiss?' asked Jagiello.

'It is another of these vile headlands,' said Stephen. 'This one is called Ushant, and we must get round it, we must *weather* it, to clear the Channel and reach the Biscay shore.'

'There are too many of these headlands at sea,' said Jagiello. 'Give me a horse, any day.'

Jack knew the *Ariel* by now, he knew her well, a fine, living, responsive little creature; and this was the kind of sailing he liked, driving a stout, well-found ship in a hearty blow, taking advantage of every lull, every kind run of the sea or tide to cling to his windward gain or increase it: he had capable officers, an adequate crew, a well-tempered instrument; and in any case he was glad to have no room for any other kind of thought at this juncture. The sight of home had troubled his mind extremely — recollections of Amanda Smith, legal complications, self-reproach, the potential ruin of his heart, the probable shipwreck of his fortune, all these things pell-mell in a confusion of distress. He kept the *Ariel* under close-reefed topsails, not to outrun the poor transports, with their load of misery — their hundreds of seasick soldiers below — and their ungainly build, but he could have carried more. Although the little black stormy petrels fluttered on either hand, the breeze was still something short of a fresh gale, and in spite of the heavy seas on the larboard bow he was convinced that he was gaining half a point. The only trouble was the impenetrable thickness of the weather: there would not be the least possibility of an observation today or tonight, nor in all likelihood for some time to come.

Before darkness they passed a ship of the line and two frigates on the opposite tack, on their way to the Brest blockade: *Achilles*, *Euterpe*, *Boadicea*. They exchanged numbers, private signals, and greetings, and Jack looked long and intently after them, particularly the *Boadicea*; he had commanded her in the Indian Ocean and he retained a strong affection for the broad-beamed, comfortable ship, slow perhaps, but so reliable once one knew her ways. Standing on a carronade-slide, his arms round a stay, the heavy rain and the flying water beating on his back, he watched her tearing along, all possible canvas abroad to keep up with the swift-sailing *Achilles*. Mitchell had her now: he had added iron stern davits and a quarterdeck carronade on each side, but he had hardly altered her paintwork at all, the true Nelson chequer; and she still had that odd, fetching, slightly hesitant second lift before she shouldered a heavy sea down her side. 'I shall not crack on like that, however,' he reflected. 'Festino lento does it, as Stephen would say.' And 'God help the inshore squadron on a night like this,' he added, remembering his own time off the Black Rocks and Camaret, the iron-bound coast of Brittany.

They were blotted out by another squall, coming more from the south this time; and then it was night, a black night full of rain and shattered salt-water that showed bright as it swept over the binnacle lights and the stern-lanterns, the only light in the darkness, a darkness that enveloped the whole ship as she stretched close-hauled for the Lizard over a sea visible only as it broke white over the bows.

The routine of the ship carried on, of course: dim figures relieved the watch, relieved the wheel, relieved the lookouts, made their way groping along the manlines to strike the bell, heaved the log and recorded the result, huddled carefully over the folding boards in the companion-way. After an hour, when he judged he might have the Lizard fine on the starboard bow five miles away, he made the night-signal that told the transports to wear in succession, put the ship about, and hauled his wind on the other tack. When he had seen them all round in good order, the string of lights heading southward on the long leg that might with luck carry them round Ushant into the Bight of Biscay, he went below. Young Fenton had the deck, no phoenix perhaps, but a steady, reliable officer; and in any case the situation called for no extraordinary exertions, no extraordinary talents; there was nothing unusual about a westerly gale in the mouth of the Channel, however wet.

'What of the night?' asked Stephen again.

'Oh,' said Jack, shedding water in every direction, 'it is rather moist. But if this is all the blow Pellworm prated about, it don't amount to much: we could carry whole topsails if we chose, and earth don't groan from shore to shore, not with whole topsails, you know. We wore ship not long ago, and are close-hauled on the starboard tack.'

'Will that bring us clear of Ushant, do you suppose?'

'It might, if only the breeze would keep due west; but I am afraid it will back a point or two. We may have to run up to the Scillies to make our westing: still, we shall see in the morning,' said Jack, throwing off his outer clothes and settling in the swinging chair.

'If we are spared,' said Stephen. 'There is a horrid roar outside, and wet is creeping in.'

'That is only the ship hauling under the chains with the swell. I dare say it is blowing great guns off the Azores, but here it does little more than make the passengers a trifle queasy and increase our leeway by perhaps a point.' He yawned, stated that the glass was rising, repeated that they should see tomorrow, and went fast to sleep.

For once Captain Aubrey spoke too soon. They did not see tomorrow: tomorrow there was nothing to be seen but even heavier rain, even more spray and spindrift, a narrow horizon of high spiky waves, and dimly the transports, still in accurate line astern: no sun, no hint of the sun at all, and the dead-reckoning of the ships differed by forty miles.

Once again they wore and once again they ran north through the obscure confusion of elements: the day, such as it was, and the night were repetitions of those that had gone before. To those used to the sea it was not particularly dramatic, little more than thick and dirty weather in the western approaches, but for the landsmen it was an unending present filled with meaningless noise and motion, and for many with seasickness as well. From Ushant to Scilly 'tis thirty-five leagues they were told, and it seemed to them that they must have traversed each one of those leagues many many times, with short intervals for brief, ill-dressed meals: and in the end boredom overcame terror except now and then, when a more than usually heavy lee-lurch sent them flying about the deck. Even Jagiello sank into a kind of dismal torpor. The fore and main hatches had been laid long since, and although a good deal of water came in through the *Ariel*'s sides because of her working, very little fresh air joined it: it was long since hammocks had been piped up, and as the hard-working hands were not washed by anything but the rain — since they had no means of washing apart from tubs on the now impracticable deck and then only for their hands and faces — they and their damp, close-packed beds filled the unventilated 'tween-decks with a strong, all-pervading smell of frowsty carnivores, far worse than the collection of vegetarian marsupials Stephen had carried from New Holland in an earlier voyage. He was used to it however; human filth in foul weather had been with him from his first days in the Navy.

He saw little of Jack Aubrey, but that little was always cheerful and generally hungry. Once he reported that a favourable shift of the wind had brought them well to the west of the Scillies, and once he said that a fleeting glimpse of some star had confirmed him in his persuasion that the next leg would do it; but most of his time below was spent in sleep.

From this sleep he was aroused after a very late and scrappy dinner by the signal midshipman, a tall thin dark conscientious youth who instantly said in a voice trembling with excitement, 'Mr Grimmond's duty sir and two sail to windward one is *Jason* and t'other a French two-decker.'

'Very good, Mr Meares. I shall be on deck directly: in the meantime make the private signal and our number. But first pray pass me my sou'wester.'

On deck all eyes were fixed to windward, staring into a particularly heavy downpour. For a moment Jack saw nothing, but then the rain swept over them and beyond, the veil lifted, and there on the larboard quarter lay the two ships, steering south-east with the wind at west, racing along in a white turmoil of their own making.

The position was clear: the French ship

was certainly running for Brest and the *Jason* was certainly in chase. Whether the *Jason* would ever come up with her was another matter: they were at least two miles apart, much too far for the *Jason*'s bow-chasers to reduce the Frenchman's speed by knocking away a spar; and the *Jason*, right in the Frenchman's wake, had already spread all the canvas she could possibly bear with safety, probably even more, whereas the chase still had a reef on her topsails. The *Jason*'s only hope was chancing upon an English cruiser, or the blockading squadron in with the land. The *Ariel* was not cruising; nor was she a cruiser at all where an enemy line-of-battle ship was concerned; but by instantly putting her head south-eastwards and by carrying a press of sail she might cut the line between the chase and Brest at some time in the late afternoon; she might possibly delay her long enough for the *Jason* to come up. On the other hand, there were his transports: there were his direct orders . . .

'*Jason* signalling, sir,' said Meares, his telescope to his eye. '*Enemy in sight* and she gives the bearing.' Jack smiled: he had seen some foolish signals in his time, but few as inept as this. 'Again, sir: *haul your wind on the starboard tack.* And now *chase to the south-east.*'

'Acknowledge,' said Jack.

'Again, sir: *make more sail.*' And five miles away a puff of smoke appeared momentarily on the *Jason*'s leeward quarter as she emphasized the order with a gun.

Jack smiled once more: Middleton — and Middleton had the *Jason* now — had always been very talkative. Yet Middleton was junior to him. Middleton could not know it — he could not know that for the moment the *Anel*, a sloop, was commanded by a post-captain — but in fact Jo Middleton had no right to be giving orders. This was no time for formalizing, however; it was a time for decision, instant decision: if he were to act at all it must be now. In this heavy sea the *Ariel* could not sail as fast as a two-decker. In order to cross the enemy's line or even to reach a point within the short range of the *Ariel*'s carronades before nightfall he would have to take advantage of every cable's length of advance he possessed. Even at this point, even at the point the Frenchman had already reached, the angle was critically fine.

These thoughts passed through his mind

with great rapidity as he stood mechanically assessing the speed and course of the ships far to windward, the strength of the south-west wind, the scend of the sea, the possibility of useful intervention: before the remote thump of the *Jason*'s gun reached them his decision was clear in his mind. He was only sorry he had no time to send Stephen and Colonel d'Ullastret aboard the transports. He said, 'All hands to wear ship,' and he noticed a general look of pleasure on the quarterdeck, nods and grins exchanged. Fulfilling these young men's expectation of him had formed no part of his calculations; but he was glad they were pleased. He reached for the azimuth compass, carefully took the bearings of both ships, and said, 'Mr Meares: to *Jason*, *steer south twenty-seven east*. Then alphabetical, *Aubrey*. Another hoist, and keep it flying: *Enemy in sight, chase to south-west*.' That should cut Middleton's cackle; but infinitely more important than that, it might win him half a mile or so. There was a strong likelihood that the Frenchman could read the signal, and in any case the sight of the *Ariel* wearing out of the line would almost certainly make him head farther south for a while. At this distance and in this visibility the *Ariel*, though clearly a single-decked ship, might be a frigate, even a heavy frigate with a bite worse than her bark; furthermore, her signal to friends beyond the Frenchman's horizon might be true — it might bring half the off-shore squadron pelting down.

'Mr Grimmond,' he said, 'lay me under the *Mirza*'s lee,' the *Mirza* being the senior troop-carrier. Then, with the *Ariel*'s maintopsail backed, he took a speaking-trumpet and roared through the wind, 'Mr Smithson, rendezvous in the Bordeaux stream — if I am not there report to the senior officer Santandero — go easy — carry nothing away — no royals, no kites.'

'Never you fear for us, sir,' called Smithson, waving his capable right hand. 'Good luck to you.'

The transports knew perfectly well what was afoot, and they gave the *Ariel* a hearty cheer as she filled and passed down the line.

'Course south-east by east a half east,' said Jack with the French ship firm in his glass. 'Shake out the foretopsail reef.' Through the murk and the flying spray he caught the movement as the chase braced up, bringing the wind before the beam as he had expected, veering southward from the danger, perhaps the very serious danger, in the north-east. But even so, it would be a near-run thing, he reflected as he stared at the white sails under the low grey sky: the chase must be making nine or even ten knots, and if he failed to cross her forefoot — if he merely fetched her wake — his intervention, brief as it must necessarily be, would prove of little use. Little use, but quite as dangerous.

'Mr Meares,' he said, 'pray be so good as to ask *Jason* for her position, and repeat it to the transports.'

A long pause, caused partly by the difficulty of seeing flags through five miles of haze and rain in a thin grey light and partly by hesitancy aboard the *Jason*.

'No observation three days,' said Meares at last. *'Estimate 49°27′N. 7°10′W. Chronometer five hours twenty-eight minutes past noon.'*

As he checked the difference between Stephen's watch and the *Jason*'s — a pretty wide variation — Jack smiled again: Middleton was no scientific sailor — board 'em in the smoke was more his line — but he or his master could not be very far out in the longitude, and that meant the Frenchman had no possibility of fetching La Rochelle with this wind. It was Brest or Lorient for him, unless he chose to run for

Cherbourg, through a Channel filled with English squadrons.

A fine ship, he thought, gazing over the ocean; she was as close-hauled as she could be, yet she was throwing an enormous bow-wave half down her side. The *Ariel* would have to spread more canvas if she were to come up with any time and space for manoeuvre; and a ship of the *Ariel*'s size needed plenty of both if she were to do anything at all to a seventy-four. 'Pass the word for the bosun,' he said; and when the dripping bosun came plunging aft from the forecastle, 'Mr Graves, let us get light hawsers to the mastheads as briskly as we can.'

'Hawsers to the mastheads, sir?' cried the bosun, amazed.

'Yes, Mr Graves,' said Jack pleasantly, ducking under the perfect deluge of sea-water that came over the weather-rail. 'I should like to see them all set up before the last dog-watch. I doubt we shall beat to divisions today.'

The bosun smiled, as in duty bound. He said, 'Aye aye, sir. Light hawsers to the mastheads it is,' in a low, wondering tone, and padded off. 'Mr Graves,' called Jack after him, 'be sure to let them take the wet before you set them up taut: we must not wring the masts.'

It was an operation he had used with much success: the great extra strength of the hawsers would allow him to set topgallantsails without the masts complaining or infinitely worse carrying away; and although it could not be done in a crank ship because of the increased top-hamper, the *Ariel* was by no means crank, but admirably stiff. The greater thrust, the greater speed had kept him alive before this, particularly when he was flying before a wicked Dutchman in the high southern latitudes, and obviously it would answer the other way about: he wondered the practice was not more generally known.

The hawsers were not to the mastheads before the last dog-watch, nor anything like it. Squall after squall of very heavy rain swept down on the sloop, rain so thick that fresh water gushed from the lee scuppers and the hands could hardly tell what they were at, while at the same time the turning gusts within the squalls knocked her about most brutally, taking her aback three times, and making it impossible to keep her steady on her course. The French ship and the *Jason* vanished entirely for the best part of an hour.

'Should I feel better if I were to vomit?'

asked Jagiello.

'I doubt it,' said Stephen. 'It has done nothing for the Colonel.'

The pursued and the pursuer were still there, in their expected positions, when the last squall passed away into the dark north-east, blotting out the horizon to leeward but leaving the sea clear to starboard. The Frenchman was still reaching as far south as ever he could, veering from the imaginary danger — he had not yet discovered the cheat — but he had set a forestaysail, he had let out his remaining reefs, and he had gained perceptibly on the *Jason*. On the other hand his course and the *Ariel*'s were converging, although the sloop kept the wind a whole point free for greater speed; the chase was nearer by half a mile, and clearer by far.

'She is the *Méduse*,' said Hyde.

'Then let us hope we may trim her locks, with *Jason*'s help,' said Jack at once, and he laughed aloud. His spirits were at a fine tearing pitch; he felt extremely well; even if it had been remembered, nothing on land had the least importance: yet beneath the glow of well-being his mind continually worked upon the changing factors, upon the three visible moving points of the triangle and the unseen variables that would affect them. And beneath the eagerness there was a clear-headed realization of the danger of his present course: although he intended no more than a hit-and-run delaying action, it meant bringing his stumpy carronades well within the reach of the Frenchman's far-reaching long guns, with a broadside of at least 840 pounds as opposed to his 265. In moderate weather, with her lower tier of gunports open, the *Méduse* would certainly sink the *Ariel* at a mile, destroying her before she could open an effectual fire: even in these circumstances there was a fair possibility that none of these cheerful young men around him would live until tomorrow. Everything depended upon speed.

'Hawsers to the mastheads, sir,' said the bosun.

'Very good, Mr Graves,' said Jack. 'You have done very well.' A rapid survey, and back to the quarterdeck. 'Hands to make sail,' he called. 'Away aloft. Lay out: let fall.' And raising his voice to carry half a mile, wind or no wind, 'Foretopgallant halliards, there. Handsomely now, handsomely. A fathom. And a fathom. Up she rises: tally and belay.'

One after another the sails rose slowly up on their yards, each ballooning wildly to leeward at first and each gradually brought to a fine taut curve; smoothly and evenly the full strain of the far greater thrust came to the powerful hawsers; and as each sail filled the *Ariel* took on a greater heel, so that with the third her deck was at the slope of a moderately high-pitched roof, while her larboard cathead and much of her lee rail vanished under a smother of white foam.

Jack hooked himself on to a weather backstay and reached aft for the hawser that trebled its power — taut, but not iron taut: nowhere near its breaking-strain. 'Mr Hyde,' he said, smiling at his lieutenant's anxious face, 'Let us try the log: we may be making close on eleven knots.'

'Eleven knots and two fathoms, sir,' came the reply, delivered by a delighted midshipman, his red face shining as he scrambled up the slope from the leeward side.

Eleven knots was very well, but the *Méduse* was a new ship, a beautiful sailer like so many of the Frenchmen, and well handled; and once she brought the wind a point free she would move even faster. He would probably cross her path by sunset at the present rate, but he would be far happier with something more, with the time in hand to lie on her bow, cross her stem and wear, hitting her twice before he ran. 'I believe we may venture upon a maintop-mast staysail,' he said.

The staysail was sheeted home — it took thirty men to bring the sheet right aft — and the *Ariel* heeled another seven degrees.

'How strangely the floor is sloping,' said Jagiello. 'I can hardly sit in my chair. What do you suppose they are doing?'

'I cannot tell,' said Stephen. 'It is a melancholy reflection, that the passenger is a mere helpless, unhelpful parcel when the tempest roars.'

'Does not the Captain seek your advice, sir?'

'Not always,' said Stephen.

The rain had stopped. The Captain and the gunner had made a tour of the sloop's armament. Returning to the quarterdeck Jack said, 'The rain has stopped for the moment. Perhaps the Doctor would like to see how the sloop is coming along. Mr Rowbotham, pray jump below and tell him, with my compliments, that we are making twelve knots, and that if he would like to see, now is the time. It may come on to blow presently.'

'The Captain's compliments, sir,' said Rowbotham, 'and we are making twelve knots. Twelve knots, sir!'

'Why?' asked Stephen.

'To catch the *Méduse*, sir. She is on our starboard beam,' said Rowbotham. 'A French seventy-four, sir,' he added, seeing incomprehension before him, 'and we hope to trim her locks directly, with *Jason*'s help. *Jason* is only two miles astern, and coming down like thunder.'

'Dear me, is there to be a battle?' cried Stephen. 'I had no idea at all.'

'A battle?' cried Jagiello, his torpor vanishing. 'May I come too?'

After a first wild flurry that would have flung them into the leescuppers, if not into the Atlantic, but for the powerful arm of the quartermaster at the con, they were made fast to stanchions on the weather quarter, well out of the way.

'I thought you would like to see the position,' said Jack, and he outlined it in a mild roar. 'And I thought you would like to see what the ship can do when she is put to her shifts.'

'Sure this is speed itself,' cried Stephen, the foam flying past his face, 'the racing exhilaration of —' He had been going to say 'of Icarus before his fall', but he checked himself, preferring 'a swooping elegance — an appearance of extreme danger just averted — a falcon's flight, so it is.'

'She is a sweet creature,' said Jack. 'I am glad you have seen her at her best. Now is the time, because we shall be busy in half an hour; and,' — nodding into the black, tormented west, a darkness shot through and through with hidden lightning — 'it will come on to blow tonight: Pellworm's blow, I dare say. We are forereaching on her, as you see, and we mean to haul our wind, shoot up, cross her stem, rake her, wear and rake her again, and fly for our lives before she can yaw: we are twice as nimble, you know, and with our carronades we can fire twice as fast.' He moved off to measure the angles with his sextant, and Jagiello said into Stephen's ear, 'That ship looks three times as large as the *Ariel*.'

'It is as I understand four times the size,' said Stephen. 'But the disproportion is not as great as you might suppose, since as you perceive their lower range of guns on this side are buried beneath the waves, because of her lean, or *list;* whereas ours are all raised well above the surface. I have known Captain Aubrey attack at even greater odds and succeed.'

'When will the battle begin?'

'In about half an hour, I am told.'

'I shall fetch my sword and my pistols.'

In fact it began far sooner. The *Méduse* suddenly bore up, as though to pass under the *Ariel*'s stern and destroy her. Jack at once hauled his wind and the ships converged at a shocking speed under the low grey racing sky. He would still have just time to cross the Frenchman's stem if he were not knocked out first. Nearer, nearer, fine on the *Méduse*'s larboard bow: nearer still, almost within reach of the carronades.

'Fire at the word. Fire high. Aim at her tops,' he called again down the tense line of waiting gun-crews.

The *Méduse* yawed to port at last and let fly with her upper-deck guns, a well-grouped broadside but a trifle high — they heard the scream of iron overhead, shriller than the wind, and then the huge thunder.

Nearer still. 'Fire,' said Jack and the *Ariel*'s starboard carronades replied at the limit of their range: a staysail ripped loose aboard the Frenchman and tore to pieces, flapping down the wind: the Ariels cheered as they reloaded with furious speed. But now the *Méduse*'s lower ports were opening and the great guns running out, free of the water on the upward roll as she came tearing down on the *Ariel*'s beam.

'Fire,' cried Jack again. The two broadsides bawled out at the same moment and the *Ariel*'s foretopmast went by the board, cut clean away. Her foreyard parted at the slings and she shot up into the wind, spinning fast on her heel.

'Larboard guns,' roared Jack, ignoring the chaos, the wild confusion of sailcloth and rigging and spars, and leaping for the nearest carronade himself: the quicker-witted men were with him and as the *Méduse* swept past they shattered her spanker-boom and blasted five cloths from her maincourse. Two minutes later and close on a mile away she answered with a careful, studied discharge from her after guns that sent solid water over the *Ariel*'s deck and shattered the boats on the beams; then she was out of her range, still running fast, but by no means as fast as before.

They had only just managed to clear away the chief of the wreckage and get her head before the wind when the *Jason* came hurtling down in the *Méduse*'s wake; she was already trying long shots with her bow-chasers, and she flew the signal *Do you require assistance?*

'Negative,' said Jack, and they cheered one another as she went by.

There followed a period of the most intense and strenuous work before the *Ariel* could haul to the wind again and stand on after the ships of the line, still visible in the south-east, and now steadily engaging at the extremity of their range. She had a spare maintopgallant mast at the fore, swayed up by main force and the grace of God in an impossible sea, a crossjack yard for her forecourse, and her knotted rigging was an ugly sight; her speed of course was much reduced, but she held a good wind and she limped after the great ships with a fair chance of joining the action after they had mauled each other for a while. The *Jason* had already lost her spritsail yard — shot away or carried away they could not tell — and they knew what they had done to the *Méduse*: both the ships of the line were travelling far more slowly.

'We are well out of that,' said Jack, when at last he could come below in the twilight and drink a pot of tea. 'I never thought we should come off so easy. No killed or wounded, never a shot in the hull, only a few spars knocked away apart from the boats, and we clipped her locks finely. I thought she would blow us out of the water without so much as a by your leave, ha, ha, ha! If she had had a moment to spare she would certainly have done so. I have rarely been so pleased in my life as when I saw her run out of range, with her boom gone in the jaws.'

'What is your present intention, tell?' asked Stephen.

'Why, we must hang on their skirts as well as ever we can through the night, and if we cannot join in ourselves — which I don't despair of — we must try to bring down any ship within sight or hearing by blue lights and rockets and gunfire. There is a very fair chance of meeting with some of our cruisers, if not the Brest team itself.'

'And what of Pellworm's blow?'

'Oh damn Pellworm and his blow: we must cross that bridge when we come to it. For the moment our duty is to follow; but first I am going to have a bite. Will you join me in a cold leg of mutton?'

Following was easy enough in the first part of the night; not only did the *Jason* carry an unusually powerful toplight, but even when it was hidden by the rain and the low racing clouds, the gun-flashes showed where they were. The *Ariel* followed after them in an effulgence of blue lights, with frequent guns, and rockets twice at every bell, and at one time she was certainly gaining on them; this was at the beginning of the middle watch, when the whole south-eastern sky was lit not by the single flash of chasers but by the blaze of full broadsides, six times repeated, broadsides whose thunder reached them over the howling of the gale and reached them within two heartbeats of the blaze.

But then no more, no gleam, no flash, all swallowed up in a driving pelting rain so thick that men ducked their heads to breathe, rain borne almost flat across the deck by a wind whose voice in the rigging and over the torn sea rose to such a pitch that it would have drowned any broadside beyond half a mile. At first they thought it was a squall, but it lasted, all night it lasted; and they were obliged to admit they had utterly lost sight of the *Jason* and her chase.

'Never mind,' said Jack. 'We shall see them to windward at break of day.' Always providing the *Méduse* had not put before the wind for Cherbourg, he added to himself; for by his reckoning, based on *Jason*'s position some hours before, she should have reached the best point for a run up mid-channel, with no great risk of interception on a night as dirty as this.

'Should you not turn in, sir?' suggested Hyde diffidently. 'You have been on deck since the beginning, as well as most of last night. There is nothing we can do, with the sky as dark as pitch; and we have two hundred miles under our lee.'

'I believe I shall, Hyde,' said Jack. 'Keep her just so,' — the ship was under lower staysails, reefed forecourse and mizen, heading south-east, plunging along through a very heavy sea, the wind steady in the west-south-west — 'and let me be called at daylight, or if anything should happen before.' It was dirty weather, very dirty weather, but the *Ariel* was a fine tight weatherly little ship, a good sea-boat, and she could deal with worse than this in spite of her jury foretopmast.

Rarely had he slept so deep. He had hardly thrown off his jacket before his eyes were closing: as he lay down he could hear himself breathing, perhaps snoring, for a moment and then he was gone, gone into a strangely vivid dream in which some fool was shaking him and bawling into his ear 'Breakers under the lee.'

'Breakers under the lee, sir,' shouted Hyde again.

'Christ,' said Jack, instantly awake. He leapt from his cot and sprang up on deck, Hyde following with his jacket. There in the greyness, neither night nor yet day, white water showed broad on the larboard beam, an enormous sea breaking on a vast shoal of rocks, two cables' lengths away.

The ship was still close hauled on the starboard tack: although she was making a fair headway the wind, the swell and the making tide were all heaving her in towards the reef, broadside on. She would never stay out against such a wind even if her foretopmast were sound; he could not tack; but there was still just room to wear. 'Hands about ship. Hard a-port,' he said, and no more. The officers and men flew to their duty, the after sails vanished, the ship paid off to leeward, faster and faster towards the reef, turned on its very edge, turned through twenty points, and came up beautifully on the larboard tack heading north-north-west.

'Luff and touch her,' Jack said to the man at the wheel. 'Shiver the maincourse.' He wanted no strong headway until he knew where he was: they were either right on Ushant or the French mainland — in either case his reckoning had set him fifty miles north of his true position and far to the east — but it was essential to know which. Staring to leeward he could scarcely make out more than the dark loom of land through the rain: yet at least he did see that Hyde had done all that was proper aboard

— the carpenter and his crew stood by with axes to cut away the masts; in the bows the anchors were cleared away and ready a-cockbill; the lead was going in the mainchains, rapid casts, no chant, the depth instantly given 'Six. A quarter less five . . .'

'Breakers ahead,' roared the forecastle lookout.

Jack ran forward, surveyed the long line of fast appearing white, a second reef that barred their path to the west and the north, their way to the open sea: an unbroken line that seemed to end in a dim headland away to starboard. The reef grew clearer, and he saw rollers breaking far out into the offing, a great breadth of mortal surf. 'Fill the maincourse,' he called. 'One point to starboard.' The *Ariel* ran on straight for the white water. As he gauged the distance and the force of the wind, listening intently to the leadsman, the hands on the forecastle turned their anxious faces to his with total reliance in his judgment. Fifty yards from the turmoil he called 'Hard a-weather.' The *Ariel* shot up into the wind, paused in four fathoms, and he said 'Let go the best bower' just as sternway came on her. The anchor held. She gently veered out a cable and rode there between the two reefs, bowing the sea and the tide, a strong tide near the top of the flood. It was a respite: but if they were where he suspected it could not last long. He sent to rouse Stephen, Jagiello and the Colonel; called for a double guard on the spirit-room, for seamen loved to die drunk; ordered the galley fires to be lit. Some of the *Ariel*'s people were badly frightened, as well they might be, and an appearance of order would comfort them, to say nothing of hot burgoo in their bellies.

Already the day was coming, with light over the land: the rain stopped abruptly, the thick haze swept off the sea, and he knew where he was. It was worse than he had thought. They were in what the Navy called Gripes Bay, deep in Gripes Bay: the *Ariel* had somehow contrived to make her way between the two main reefs in the night, never touching any of the countless rocks that lay scattered between them. It was a vile bay, open to the south-west, never frequented by the ships of the inshore squadron — bad holding ground for anchors, ugly sharp rocks to cut cables, reefs wherever you looked. But he knew its waters well from fishing expeditions in small craft during calm weather when he was on the Brest blockade; and as a seventeen-year-old master's mate he had commanded the *Resolution*'s yawl when the boats of the squadron stormed the Camaret battery. He looked over the taff-rail, and there was the battery itself, a short mile away, a fort high-perched above the north end of the reef; it had been repaired of course, and presently the soldiers would wake up and open fire. Beyond Camaret lay Brest: at the bottom of the bay the village of Trégonnec with its little half-moon jetty round the fishermen's harbour at the mouth of the stream, and another strong fort. No lying there between two fires, although the shore was calm enough, protected as it was by such massive reefs; no great surf on the beach, even with such an enormous sea beating outside. But southwards there was the other horn of the bay, Gripes Point; and round Gripes Point lay salvation, the beautiful great bight of Douarnenez, where a whole squadron could lie, sheltered from the south and west and laughing at the French batteries, too far off to do any harm.

To get there he would have to work round the point. The only way of doing so was to run south, skirting the inner reef towards the rock they called the Thatcher, close in by the southern arm of the bay, and then to go about, make a short board towards the outer reef, and so round Gripes Point into safety, there to lie until the gale blew itself out and a falling tide enabled them to run clear — there was not the least possibility of weathering the outer reef, of running through the gap, at present, with the wind dead on shore. He hoped to God they would be able to go about well before the Thatcher, while there was room to wear, for there was no question of tacking right down there, where the thrust of the sea, unbroken by the outer reef, was so very much greater. But he could decide on the point of turn only when he was much nearer; in the meantime there was the question of rocks and shoals in their path. 'Do any of you gentlemen know this bay?' he asked the quarterdeck. They looked at one another: a general blankness. But before any could reply they were soaked with flying water; the fort had opened fire and the first shot pitched no more than six feet wide of the starboard mainchains.

'Cut the cable,' said Jack. 'Port your helm.'

The ship gathered sternway, turning as she went; the backed jib filled, followed by the hard-braced topsails; and after an infinitesimal pause of no motion she began to surge forward, faster and faster still, through a fresh downpour from the offing. Jack set her down the channel between the inner reef and the outer, and in spite of the shot falling all round them he reduced sail. 'Cast quick, cast quick,' he called to the leadsman: he must not run plump on to a rock or a minor reef. A ricochet from the fort knocked the ensign-staff away and skipped through the mizen topsail.

'Colours to a whip in the leeward shrouds, Mr Hyde,' he said, without looking astern. 'How I hate being fired at from the shore,' he muttered. But at least this fire was not as accurate as some he had known from French batteries; for the short time it lasted the rain-storm almost entirely hid the *Ariel*, and the artillerymen pointed their pieces at random.

On, cautiously on. He was beginning to recover the whole feel of the bay: on the starboard beam there was a rock where they used to catch gurnards, and on the bow the cluster of islets where they took crayfish at low tide — a white mass of breakers now. Presently they would pass the gap in the inner reef that the fishermen used: the spring tide would be flowing in at a furious rate.

He hauled up a point to anticipate its thrust; and as the leadsman's voice rose to a scream, 'Mark three, mark three,' the *Ariel* struck in the trough of a wave, a long deep grinding crash that made her check and stagger in her pace, trembling from stem to stern. Then she was off, running smoothly, and the leadsman cried 'Mark five, mark five, deep six, and a half six'; a long dark piece of her false keel showed in the wild water to larboard, turning and rearing as it ran through the gap to the distant shore. Grimmond hurried below.

'Cast quick, cast quick,' said Jack again. 'Cast well ahead.'

'Aye aye sir,' said the leadsman, and he whirled his long heavy plummet in an even wider circle before shooting it out.

They were out of the battery's range, and presently they would be out of the shelter of the outer reef. Its southern extremity was the point he must reach in order to wear round and run into the shelter, the safety of Douarnenez Bay; once he had reached that southern end there would be no difficulty, but of course he could only reach it close-hauled on the larboard tack and as they ran it became more and more evident that the beginning of the turn must lie far along, right down by the Thatcher itself. Nothing short of the Thatcher would bring them out. That meant there would be no room to wear, nothing remotely like it: scarcely even room to club-haul her, a perilous manoeuvre at the best of times, and here he would have to judge it to the yard. With such a wind and sea, and among such rocks, there would be no correcting any error. And the Thatcher was no great way off.

'All's well below, sir,' said the master, coming from the hold. 'A couple of foot in the forepeak, no more.'

Jack nodded. That was very far from well in such a dry ship at ordinary times, but now it did not signify. 'Mr Hyde,' he said, 'I am going to club-haul the ship when we reach that tall black and white rock. Let the sheet-anchor be cleared away: men with axes to stand by.' Then raising his voice to a hoarse shout that carried over the gale, 'Ariels: we are going about, club-hauled, when we reach the height of the Thatcher. Let every man obey the word of command on the instant and with God's help we weather the point and ride snug in Douarnenez Bay. A mistake and we drive on the rock. Do nothing until you are told, but then do it like lightning.' The men nodded, looking very grave but quite confident; he saw with pleasure that not one of them had got at the spirit-room.

Now the ship was far out of the shelter of the offshore reef and she took the full force of the sea and the gale: at this pace — and he had to bear sail — the Thatcher was five minutes away, four minutes away, the white water towering up its sheer side in solemn, thunderous, long-spaced fountains.

'What does he mean by club-haul?' asked Jagiello, clinging to the rail by Stephen's side.

'He means to drop the anchor, stop the ship's motion with its head to the wind, cut the rope, and go off in the other direction, a short way out to sea and so round the cape.'

'The rock is very close.'

'The leadsman says there is a proper depth: hear him.'

'Luff,' cried Jack, his eyes fixed on the Thatcher and the drifting kelp. 'Up staysail sheets.' And after an unbearable five seconds, 'Let go the anchor.'

All at once her bowsprit was pointing straight into the roaring gale, though the heavy seas tried to force her head to leeward. 'Up maintack . . . haul of all. Cut.'

The axe flashed down on the cable. She was almost round, in the balance. Already she had a prodigious sternway, moving straight for the Thatcher. 'Fetch a cast aft, far aft,' cried Jack to the leadsman, leaning out over the quarter-rail to judge the last possible moment, the greatest possible impetus for the full starboard helm that would bring her right round. The leadsman turned, swung with all his might: the leadline caught the bellying ensign-whip, the lead shot inboard, struck Jack down on the deck.

On his hands and knees, through the crash of the blow and the roar of the sea he heard Hyde's voice at an infinite distance shout 'Larboard all — I mean starboard,' then an all-embracing thunder as the *Ariel* struck the Thatcher full on, beating her rudder and staving in much of her stern.

He was on his feet — a momentary glimpse of Hyde's appalled deathly face — and he saw the ship broadside on to the sea. 'Brail up, clew up mizen and main: foresail sheets aft,' he cried.

Grinding and grinding again over rock, the good *Ariel* brought her head right before the wind and he drove her over the narrowest part of the inner reef with what steering the foresail alone would provide.

He was still at a great distance, very far removed, but all his mind that was clear felt with the ship and after the seventh great shattering strike he knew her back was broken amidships. Yet with spring-tide near its height she did not hold fast, but drove on and on through breakers that reared up to her tops.

In the calmer water beyond the reef she still swam, she still steered; but it could not last long. 'Guns overboard,' he said. With their weight gone she would stay afloat long enough for him to run her ashore. A few minutes later, with the wind and the sea and the tide heaving her in towards the mouth of the river he told the officers to fetch their commissions and see to their affairs: then he beckoned Stephen and they went below: the water was already shin-deep in the cabin. 'The Colonel must shift into a Marine's uniform and pass for a private,' he said. 'Do you agree?' Stephen nodded. Jack said, 'I will give the order,' and he gathered up the lead-covered signal-book, his dispatches and private papers, and his sword, told the steward to pack what he could, and went back on deck. He threw the signal-book, his dispatches and his sword overboard, spoke to the Marine officer about the Colonel, and returned to steering the poor heavy wreck to the shore.

For some reason he was perfectly confident that she would not go to pieces, but would bring them to land; and she behaved beautifully to the last. A final heave on the starboard sheet brought her wallowing up against the jetty at the height of the tide, with the water gurgling at her hatches. All they had to do was to step over the rail to the waiting company of soldiers and the small silent crowd.

Chapter Ten

In these twenty years of war quite a number of Royal Navy ships had been wrecked on the coast of Brittany, and some indeed had been taken; the authorities at Brest were used to the situation, and without undue triumph they installed the *Ariel*'s officers in a disused nunnery, her men in the lower parts of the castle, deeply lined with straw.

Men so exposed to the caprices of the elements might be expected to develop a philosophical attitude, and before this Stephen had seen his shipmates accept the unkinder strokes of fate with a fine equanimity; but even so he was surprised to see how quickly they recovered their spirits on this occasion and put a good face on adversity. It is true that since their ship had not been taken they had not been pillaged; what little they had been able to save they still possessed, and this softened the blow, since they were able to round out the sparse French rations with better food and wine than ever the *Ariel* had afforded them. On the other hand, once they found they were not to be robbed or starved they complained bitterly about the quality of the tea; and on Jack's first visit to the men it was represented to him that this here French bread, full of holes, could not nourish a man: if a man ate holes he must necessarily blow himself out with air like a bladder, it stood to reason. They did not much care for the oatmeal either, probably harvested green and parched in the ear: nor the soup.

Among the young men in the nunnery cheerfulness returned with the sun that shone on Brest from a clear calm sky within twenty-four hours of their miserable journey from Trégonnec, and with it their naval sense of fun. The commissary charged with drawing up a correct official list, which included among other things their grandmothers' maiden names, dates and places of birth, received some strange answers, delivered in sober, lugubrious tones, so strange that the port-admiral summoned Captain Aubrey. 'I refuse to believe, sir,' he said, 'that all your officers but one are descended from Queen Anne.'

'I am sorry to tell you, sir, that Queen Anne is dead,' said Jack. 'Common decency, therefore, forbids me to make any comment.'

'It is my opinion,' said the Admiral, 'that they have replied with a culpable levity. Such parents as the Emperor of Morocco, Creeping Jenny, Guy of Warwick, Sir Julius Caesar . . . You may say that the commissary is only a mere civilian, which is profoundly true; but even so I must ask you to invite them to treat him with a proper respect. He is a servant of the Emperor!'

Jack did not seem very deeply impressed and in fact the Admiral's voice lacked full conviction. He looked at his captive for a moment and went on, 'But now I come to a far more serious matter. One of your Marines, Ludwig Himmelfahrt, has escaped. His clothes have been found in the privy.'

'Oh, a sad shatterbrained old fellow, sir: a supernumerary. We only took him aboard to play the fife when the hands were at the capstan. I doubt he is even on the ship's books — he would not appear among those that have to be accounted for. Nevertheless, sir, I must observe that even as a nominal soldier it was his duty to escape.'

'Maybe,' said the Admiral. 'But I hope you will not attempt to imitate him, Captain Aubrey. I do not care greatly about a half-witted supernumerary, particularly if he was not on the muster-roll — though he must certainly be found — but with a post-captain, an officer of your distinction, sir, the case is altered; and I warn you that at the least attempt you will find yourself incarcerated at Bitche. At Bitche, sir, and incarcerated.'

Jack felt that he was on the verge of a flashing piece of repartee, of one of the best things he had ever said in his life: 'then indeed I should be bitched', or 'that would bitch my chances, I am sure', or something more brilliant still; but the want of a true colloquial link between the English bitch and the French chienne baffled him; the anticipatory smile faded, and he only said, 'Oh, as for that, sir, I dare say I shall be your guest until the end of the war. Let us hope that it will not be so long delayed that I wear out my welcome.'

'I am sure it will not,' said the Admiral. 'The Emperor is carrying all before him in the north. The Austrians are crushed.'

'I have been threatened with Bitche,' said Jack, returning to the nunnery. His meaning was instantly clear, for Verdun and Bitche had been the chief topic of conversation for the last five days, except for a certain amount of talk about the progress of the war as it could be gathered from the *Moniteur* and about the young woman who brought Jagiello's meals. Verdun was the town where the prisoners of war were kept; Bitche the fortress where those who tried to escape were confined. Both were well known by rumour as very disagreeable places in the far north-east of France, cold, wet, and expensive, but scarcely anyone in the service knew them at first hand, for since in principle Buonaparte refused to exchange prisoners in the traditional way, and since in fact very few were exchanged, almost all who went there never came back. Yet among those few was Hyde, who as a senior midshipman had escaped first from the one and then from the other with three companions, eventually reaching the Adriatic on foot.

They listened to his accounts with the utmost attention, which restored some small part of his shattered self-esteem — he had been the only one among them too low, too miserably unhappy, to give the commissary the usual facetious answers: his details had been plain, dull, and correct. Now Jack asked him to tell them about the fortress once again, with particular reference to the best means of escape, and once again Hyde described the towering sandstone crag, the covered ways, the bomb-proof excavations, the extraordinarily deep well: 'As for escape, sir, the great thing is money, of course, and a map and a compass; dried beef and biscuit and a warm coat for when you have to lie up by day, and very stout boots; but the great thing is money. It can do almost anything, and even a guinea goes a long way, English gold being at such a premium here . . .' Jack smiled: he had a fair amount in his pocket, a surprising amount, quite enough to keep the *Ariel*'s hands in modest comfort for their journey; and he knew that Stephen concealed an inconvenient weight of guineas in his bosom, the funds taken to the Baltic in case of need and entirely untouched. 'A really good knife and a marline-spike, or at least a fid, come in very handy,' Hyde continued, 'and a —'

'A young person for Monsieur Jagiello,' said the guard, with a grin. He stood away from the door, and there was the young person, holding a cloth-covered basket, blushing and hanging her pretty head. The others walked away to the window and talked in what they meant to be a detached, natural way; but few could help stealing glances at the maiden, and none could fail to hear Jagiello cry, 'But my dear, dear Mademoiselle, I asked for black pudding and apples, no more. And here is foie gras, a gratin of lobster, a partridge, three kinds of cheese, two kinds of wine, a strawberry tart . . .'

'I made it myself,' said the young person.

'I am sure it is wonderfully good: but it is much more than I can ever afford.'

'You must keep up your strength. You can pay for it later — or in some other way — or however you like.'

'But how?' asked Jagiello, in honest amazement. 'By a note of hand, do you mean?'

'Pray step into the passage,' said she, pinker still.

'There you are again,' said Jack, drawing Stephen into another room. 'Yesterday it was a thundering great patty, with truffles; and tomorrow we shall see a wedding-cake for his pudding, no doubt. What they see in him I cannot conceive. Why Jagiello, and the others ignored? Here is Fenton, for example, a fine upstanding fellow with side-whiskers that are the pride of the service — with a beard as thick as a coconut — has to shave twice a day — as strong as a horse, and a very fair seaman; but there are no patties for him. However, that is not what I meant to say. The Colonel is off.'

'I know it,' said Stephen, who had visited the castle with the *Ariel*'s surgeon.

'I thought you might,' said Jack. 'You do not seem unduly concerned.'

'I am not,' said Stephen: and after a moment, 'You have not seen him at his best. At sea he is out of his element; he talks too much and you might even take him for a mere blateroon. But I do assure you, my dear, that as a guerrillero he has not his match, a true fox by land. He will glide down a hedge like a serpent, and while you are beating about the bushes, peering into the ditch, there he is beyond a haystack, a long mile before you. I have known him make his way from Tarragona to Madrid with a hundred ounces of gold on his head, and there cut a traitor's throat as the man lay asleep in his bed. No, no: he is well supplied with money; he is rich in experience; he will be over the frontier before we reach Verdun.'

'I beg your pardon, sir,' said Hyde at the door, 'but our dinner is on the table.'

They ate their meals in what had been the nuns' parlour, an austere room, scarcely changed but for stouter bars at the windows, a judas-hole at each of the outer doors and a number of English inscriptions: J.B. loves P.M.; Bates is a Fool; How I wish Amanda were here; Laetitia, none prettier; J.S. master's mate, aetat. 47. And now their dinner was spread: it came from the best establishment in the town, recommended by the Admiral, whereas Jagiello had chosen the cheapest cookshop; yet it made a poor show compared with his — only a couple of bass, two pairs of fowls, a saddle of mutton, half a dozen side-dishes, and a floating island.

'The mutton was tolerable,' said Jack, making the island revolve, 'though it lacked red-currant jelly. But the French may say what they please — they have no notion of pudding, grande nation or not. This is not even a flummery: it is mere show and froth.'

Stephen raised his eyes from his plate, and behind Jack's head he saw the judas darken. A single eye appeared: it looked upon them at length, barely winking, expressionless, all-seeing. After a while it was succeeded by another, a blue-grey eye, whereas the other had been dark. These eyes watched them alternately throughout the rest of the meal, which consisted of brandy; and although he did not turn his head to make sure, Stephen was morally certain that the other judas was occupied too, since it gave a different view of the room. He was not altogether surprised therefore when Jack and he and Jagiello were called to the Admiral's office, nor at the change in the Admiral's attitude, which had been kind hitherto, if not positively friendly.

At some distance from the Admiral's desk sat a middle-aged civilian in a shabby black coat and a fairly white neckcloth; he had grizzled hair and dark eyes; his face was vaguely familiar to Stephen. He took no part in the interview but watched attentively, as though from a great way off. The Admiral himself concealed his embarrassment behind an appearance of rigour and formality, but he did not conceal it well. He asked Jack a series of obviously prepared questions about his voyage — where from, where to, course followed, date of sailing, nature of convoy and so on.

Jack's manner at once became as stiff and formal as the Admiral's, rather more so indeed; he looked coldly across the desk and said, 'Sir, I have produced my King's commission; I have stated the number of the *Ariel*'s crew. By the laws of war no captured officer is required to do more. With the greatest personal respect for you, sir, I must decline to reply.'

'Note down that answer,' said the Admiral to his secretary, and turning to Stephen, 'Are you the gentleman who was recently invited to address the Institut?'

'I regret I cannot satisfy you, sir,' said Stephen. 'My reply must be the same as Captain Aubrey's.'

They had a moment's uneasiness about Jagiello; but the young man was no fool. He repeated their words with an equal firmness.

'I have to inform you that your replies are not satisfactory,' said the Admiral. 'You must therefore proceed to Paris at once for further enquiries.' He rang, and told the orderly to fetch their belongings.

'At once, sir?' cried Jack. 'But surely I may see my men before I go? I have not yet seen to their victualling — I appeal to you, sir, as an officer and a seaman — I must have at least a word with them, and give them something to bear their charges. I appeal to your own example, sir: a captain cannot leave his men in the lurch.'

'There is no time,' said the Admiral. 'The carriage is waiting. I have my orders: if I do not receive satisfactory replies, you are to be taken to Paris.'

'Then at least, sir,' said Jack, bringing out his purse and laying it on the Admiral's desk, 'at least you will have the kindness to order this to be delivered to them — to a responsible man named Wittgenstein, with instructions to share it out fairly in the course of their march.'

The Admiral glanced at the civilian, who shrugged. 'It shall be so, Captain,' he said. 'I wish you good day. Monsieur Duhamel will show you to the coach.'

During the days and nights of their journey Stephen turned the situation over in his mind. He had plenty of time to do so, since Duhamel's presence prevented all free conversation, while for his part the Frenchman uttered scarcely a word. It was not that he was unpleasant or authoritarian or harsh, and although he was certainly taciturn and reserved he gave no impression of hostility as he sat there in his corner, looking vaguely at the landscape or their numerous, well-mounted escort, but rather of detachment, as though he lived on another plane, contemplating them as objectively as a natural philosopher might contemplate the animalculae in his microscope. Now and then Stephen caught Duhamel's eye upon him and he thought he detected a certain secret inner amusement, an understanding as of one professional for another caught in a very difficult position indeed: but the knowing black eye would glaze over at once and return to its watching of the various provinces they traversed. Duhamel seemed immune to boredom, unwearied by their long stages, above human weakness except at meal times.

At the outset he suggested that it would be much simpler for all concerned if they were to give their parole not to attempt to escape during the journey — a mere formality, since the coach was guarded by a whole troop of horse — and they dined and supped at the best inns in the towns they travelled through, a galloper being sent ahead to reserve a private room, to order particular dishes that varied town by town, and to desire that stated wines should be ready to accompany them. Duhamel did not eat at the same table, nor did he depart from his impenetrable reserve, but he did send over particularly successful dishes — lamb's sweetbreads in malmsey, little balls of tripe a man might eat for ever, boned larks in a pie — and presently they took to relying wholly on his judgment, although his judgment ran to an extraordinary number of courses, which he ate up entirely, wiping his plate with a piece of bread, a look of quiet satisfaction on his face. He was a spare man, but he seemed unaffected by the quantity he ate and drank twice a day: no sign of a disordered spleen or pancreas, no hepatic disturbance, no heaviness from repletion. It was a remarkable sight; it was remarkable food; and after two of these feasts (for they were no less) Jagiello's spirits, oppressed by his elders' silence, began to revive and he sang quietly to himself. After another he toyed with a key-bugle, the gift of a lady at Lamballe, until a gleam of sun induced him to lower the glass with the intention of blowing a salute to the sky.

Duhamel had been sitting in an apparent abstraction, digesting his turkey-poult, but the window was not half way down, the possible means of escape for a slim agile youth was not yet open, before he had a revolving pistol in his hand, full-cocked and pointing straight at Jagiello. Stephen noticed that it was painted a dull, unshining grey. 'Sit down,' said Duhamel.

Jagiello sat down abruptly. 'I was only going to sound a salute,' he said in a startled voice, adding, with rather more dignity, 'You forget I have given my parole.'

The gleam of extraordinary ferocity faded from Duhamel's face, being replaced by a sceptical and disillusioned look. 'You shall blow it during halts,' he said. 'Not in the coach. These gentlemen may wish to reflect.'

They had little else to do, other than sleep. Jack was gifted that way: not only had he a great deal to make up, but the enormous meals he ate in obscure competition with the unconscious Frenchman weighed down his eyelids. They weighed down his liver too, and upset his internal economy: even before they left Brittany most of the sauces were based on cream by the pint; in Normandy it was worse, and their halts became even more frequent. Although they travelled with two chamber-pots under the seat Jack's modesty could not do with less than a hedge, or at least a capacious bush, and the disgusted postillions had to draw the coach into the side every few miles or so.

Then at Alençon Duhamel's judgment failed him. As he walked into the kitchen of the inn his keen eye perceived a tub of freshwater crayfish, and although they had not fasted long enough to purge themselves of the filth upon which they had been regaling he ordered them to be boiled at once. 'Very lightly boiled — just seized, you understand — it would be a crime to spoil their flavour, such fine fat beasts.'

Stephen's reflections had left him with little appetite; but Jagiello, who did not feel the need to reflect, ate several score, and Jack, muttering 'that no Frenchman should outdo him' kept pace. In his already weakened, upset condition he became so quickly ill, so obviously and transparently disordered in the middle of an empty road that at last Duhamel suggested that Dr Maturin should do something for him, should prescribe physic, or take some appropriate measures. Stephen had been waiting for this with mounting impatience: 'Very well,' he said, writing on his knee. 'If you will have the goodness to tell one of the soldiers to take this to an apothecary, I believe we may travel on in something more nearly resembling comfort.'

Duhamel looked at the cabalistic scrawl, considered, and agreed. A trooper galloped off and galloped back again with a horse-sized enema and a number of bottles, some large, some very small. The journey continued; there were no more sudden urgent halts, no cries of 'there is a bush ahead'; Jack dozed most of the way under the influence of his physician's favourite tincture of laudanum, a powerful opiate whose abuse in time of great emotional stress had very nearly put an end to Stephen's career, but which he still considered the most valuable substance in the pharmacopoeia.

Stephen was happy to see the laudanum bottle, for although he no longer indulged he liked to have his tincture by; and when, a little short of Verneuil, first Jagiello's and then Duhamel's iron bowels succumbed to the crayfish he gave them each a dose. He could at the same time have put an end to Duhamel, for he had also renewed his store of sudden death and in one minute phial he had enough to deal with fifty Duhamels and plenty to spare; but with such an escort it would have served no good purpose and in any case he had never, as a physician, intentionally injured any man: he doubted that he could bring himself to it, whatever the extremity.

They rolled on through the Ile de France, three of them somnolent and fasting, and he returned to his reflections. One great disadvantage was the fact that he had been out of touch with Europe for some time and he had little acquaintance with recent developments in French affairs, particularly in those to do with the various branches of intelligence. He did know of course that the French services outdid even the English in their multiplicity, their jealous rivalries, and their struggle for power and control of the secret funds. The army and the navy had each their own, so did the Great Council, the foreign ministry, the ministries of the interior, of justice, and of the police, none wholeheartedly trusting any of the others, to say nothing of those virtually autonomous bodies, the descendants of the *secret du roi,* charged with the surveillance of the rest and of one another, watchdogs guarding watchdogs so that at times half the nation seemed made up of informers. He did know that Talleyrand and Fouché and Bertrand were nominally out of office, but he did not know how much influence they still in fact retained nor what agents still worked for them, though he believed their name was Legion. Where the real power lay at present he could not tell: nor did he know whose prisoner he was.

But he was tolerably certain that if he were in the army's hands they would torture him. That was also possible in the case of Fouché's successor, if only from revenge — the people in that ministry had suffered much from his activities — but with the soldiers it was probable. The supreme military argument was superior force, physical force, and in many services, not only the French, this led to the use of torture: Stephen had undergone the process once, though not to the extremity, and he dreaded a repetition. He had held out at Port Mahon, but he had been younger then, less battered, and he had the strongest immediate motive for doing so — the direct preservation of the Catalan resistance organizations, no less. Now he was not certain how he would behave: courage was far from constant in any man and extreme agony could reduce him to a shrieking, spiritually dominated animal, willing in some cases to make any concession whatever for a moment's relief. He hoped he would bear it; he thought it likely, particularly with the saving grace of anger and contempt; but he was glad, heartily glad, that in the dark-green phial he had a sure way out.

He was by no means as strongly attached to life as he had been in the days of Port Mahon, when apart from his political activities his whole heart was taken up with Diana; but even so he was unwilling to leave it in the infinite squalor of a torture-room, among the vile excitement of the operators and the flood of hatred — for torturers were obliged in self-justification to hate their victim and obviously the hatred was returned. Diana Villiers . . . at the time of Port Mahon they had not been on terms, she having bolted with Richard Canning; but it was extraordinary what a stay she had been to him — the pole that held his needle to the north and gave its pointing a significance that it had lacked since her reign came to a sudden end.

He thought of her much as they approached Paris. She would surely be there, at the Hôtel de La Mothe, rather than in the country. It would take a great deal to move Diana from the most fashionable shops in the world after her long abstinence, and although he was certain that she would never, never part with her great diamond, a fortune in itself, her other jewels would allow her to run riot for years on end. Her connexion with him, as far as Paris was concerned, was tenuous in the extreme — that of a travelling companion, physician and patient, no more — and even if it were known to the police, which he doubted, her living under the protection of La Mothe would preserve her from anything but formal enquiries which she knew how to deal with. In his opinion the reputation of the French police, except in criminal affairs, was exaggerated; he had found them rather slow and inefficient, timid where the rich were concerned, hide-bound by form, hampered by their rivals, and often corrupt.

The traffic increased on either hand. His thoughts returned to the possible reasons for their present position, the possible lines of defence. His own arrest was only too comprehensible, but this treatment of Jack and young Jagiello seemed to have little meaning. Unless . . . his mind ran along a series of hypotheses, none really convincing.

After Versailles, where the traffic became thicker still, Duhamel locked the coach doors from within. 'Oh Lord,' said Jack, starting from his doze, 'I shall have to get out.' 'So shall I,' said Jagiello.

Duhamel hesitated, fingering the key and looking out of the window, for the same imperious urge was upon him too: no, no, it was impossible. The late sun gilded an avenue crowded with carriages, passers-by on either side, and never a bush, never the least shelter to be seen. He called to the postillions to go faster, to the escort to clear the way well ahead. 'It will not be long now,' he said anxiously — his first entirely human utterance in this journey — and sank back into his corner, his hand pressed to his labouring belly, his pale lips tightly closed.

Why arrest Jack? Stephen could not see it. He remembered the universal howl of execration that had greeted the imprisonment and the almost certain murder of Captain Wright in 1805; and poor Wright was only a commander, whereas Jack was a fairly senior post-captain: no very great man perhaps, no admiral, but quite important enough to preserve him from ill-treatment unless they had some unusually convincing pretext. For his own part, Stephen was not unknown in the scientific world; he had nothing like Davy's European reputation, but even so . . . if only he could advertise his presence, that would be a certain protection: although in his case a pretext would be far easier to find. Always providing they really knew who and what he was. He reflected with some satisfaction that they could not reproach him with any breach of strict neutrality during his visit to Paris; but his satisfaction did not last for long. The pretext was the thing, and a little perjury, a little forgery, would soon produce it: the Duc d'Enghien had been shot on false documents, and he was a very, very much more important man than Stephen. The pretext: dictatorships were absurdly sensitive to the public opinion they continually outraged; they always had to be in the right, to be morally impeccable: and that was one of the reasons why those who had been much mutilated in their interrogation were rarely allowed to live, whether they had given their information or not. How much did they know in fact? And what was meant by *they?* He turned over every faint indication, the Admiral's embarrassment, Duhamel's behaviour to them, the present image of the war as presented by the *Moniteur*, by the countenance of the people he had seen, the scraps of conversation he had overheard; but now the coach had long since crossed the river and part of his mind was taken up with following its course through the lamp-lit streets of Paris. The choice of their prison would tell him a certain amount. Duhamel gave a stifled groan.

They passed the turning that would have led them to the Faisanderie, and Stephen nodded; at least they were not General Dumesnil's prisoners at present. On without crossing the river to the Conciergerie, on past the Châtelet, and then at last, sweeping in a strong left-hand turn that produced another desperate groan, they drew up in the dark courtyard of what could only be the Temple, although it seemed all wrong in the obscurity: lop-sided, obscurely deformed. The Temple: thoroughly ambiguous as a prison; but scarcely army, at all events.

Their entrance into the grim ancient fortress was unlike any that Stephen had ever known. Duhamel had his door open before the carriage stopped, and followed by Jack and Jagiello, who trampled on Stephen and broke his larger bottle in their haste, he ran into the immense vaulted guard-room where those charged with receiving the prisoners sat among scaffolding and pails. With irresistible impetuosity they rushed past the deputy-governor, his secretary, the turnkeys and ran on, pale and earnest, down a dark corridor, Duhamel a good length ahead.

Stephen was left by a heap of ancient stones among the wondering guards. 'What is the matter with Monsieur Duhamel?' asked the deputy-governor, standing there with a list in his hand.

'I believe he has an urgent need,' said Stephen. 'Pray, sir, what are they doing to the poor old Temple?'

'Alas, sir, they are pulling it down at last,' said the deputy-governor; and then, looking inquisitively at Stephen, 'I do not believe I have the honour of your acquaintance,' he said.

'That is soon repaired,' said Stephen with a bow. 'My name is Maturin, at your service.'

'Ah, Monsieur Maturin,' cried the deputy-governor, looking at his list. 'Just so. Forgive me: I had taken you for . . . Give yourself the trouble of going with these gentlemen for the necessary formalities.'

Stephen had been in several prisons, but they had all been underground, and when, after the necessary formalities, which included a thoroughly professional search, he and his companions were led away it seemed to him unnatural to walk up flight after flight of worn stone stairs. Yet up they went, up and up, and along an echoing corridor to three communicating rooms, two with pallets, one with a bed, all dimly seen by lantern-light, and there they were left in the darkness.

After a long and black but airy night — a cruelly disturbed night for Jack, an anxious one for Stephen, a night peaceful only for Jagiello, whose brisk young bowels had quite recovered after the last upheaval — the grey creeping dawn gave them the first clear notion of their quarters. Three little very dirty rooms leading into one another, each with a barred window looking out on to a towering great blank wall on the other side of the dry moat, and each with a judased door on to the corridor. So many doors and windows in so small a space so high up were enough to ensure a strange complication of draughts, but they were not all, since the first room had still another door in the left-hand wall, blind and immovably bolted on the far side, as well as a corbelled projection jutting from the tower, a primitive jakes or privy dating from the Templars themselves, through whose open base the wind came howling in whenever it happened to be in the north or east.

It seemed that until recently the rooms had been inhabited by a single man, a prisoner of some distinction; for there was a reasonable bed in the first room and a wash-hand-stand with a tap from a cistern under the leads, while he had taken his meals in the second, and the third had been his study or music-room — there were still some tattered books in a corner, and a disjointed flute — and judging by the greasy marks in the deep-cut window-seat that he and no doubt other generations of prisoners had left, it was here that he had spent most of his time. This was the only window from which they could see much, the others being little more than shafts in the great cold thickness of the wall; but here, by craning out against the bars, they had a view of the moat below, the wall beyond, and of a file of corbelled privies stretching away on the left hand, each with a strong growth of vegetation below it, favoured by some six hundred years of enrichment.

This was their view on the first morning, and having craned Stephen said that they were in the Courcy tower, probably on the side facing the rue des Neuf Fiancées, the side away from the great tower.

'The great tower of what, if you please?' asked Jagiello.

'Why, of the Temple. The Temple, where the King was imprisoned,' said Stephen, 'and most of his family.'

'The Temple, where they killed poor Wright,' said Jack in a sombre voice, and he gave the guard a sombre, dangerous look when the man came in, rattling his keys, to ask whether these gentlemen wanted the ration or whether they preferred to send out. The search had removed such dangerous things as their razors and Stephen's surprising store of money; the searchers had not found his sudden release, nor could they have done so unless they had searched his vitals; but they had given a receipt for all the rest, stating that the prisoner might draw on the sum for food and approved comforts: spirits were not allowed, nor any publications other than the *Moniteur.* These gentlemen might have the ration, the prison ration, said the guard (a melancholy man) or they might send out for their victuals. If they chose to send out, Rousseau — tapping his pendulous middle-aged belly — was at their service, for a modest, a very modest consideration. The gaoler was a slow, heavy man, but he knew to a penny the sum that had been taken from the prisoners; there were rich pickings to be had here, and his air was as nearly civil as he could make it. Besides, there was no real ill-nature in his vague, thick-boned face, though his spirits were obviously very low indeed.

'I should like the ration,' said the penniless Jagiello.

'Nonsense,' said Stephen, and to Rousseau, 'We shall certainly send out. But before that, I must ask you to tell the surgeon that the gentleman here is in urgent need of his attention.'

Rousseau slowly turned his head to Jack, who was indeed most ghastly pale, and contemplated him for a while. 'We have no surgeon, sir,' he said at last. 'The last left three weeks ago. And to think we once had seven; and our own apothecary. Oh the pity of it all.'

'Then you will present my best compliments to the deputy-governor, and tell him I should be grateful for an interview at his earliest convenience.'

The governor's convenience was far earlier than Stephen had expected. Rousseau came back within minutes and led him, between two soldiers, down the many flights of stairs. The turnkey's spirits were still very low, but at one particular corner he stopped to point out a hollow cut into the stone, an inverted shelf. 'That is where we always used to rest the coffins, before taking the awkward turn,' he said. 'Mind your step, sir. And to think we once had a coffin-maker of our own, busy every day the good God made.'

The governor's approach was stiff and formal, but it was by no means harsh or authoritarian and after a while Stephen thought he detected something almost conciliatory, something of the nervous uneasiness he had noticed elsewhere in

France, a perhaps not altogether conscious feeling of no longer being quite certainly on the winning side. The governor regretted the absence of an official surgeon, and agreed that outside advice might be called in. 'Though since you are yourself a physical gentleman,' he said, 'I will have the drugs sent for at once, if you wish to prescribe.'

That did not suit Stephen's book at all. 'You are very good, sir,' he said, 'but in the present case I should prefer a second opinion: in these circumstances I do not choose to take the responsibility myself. Captain Aubrey is a very influential man in his own country, where his father is a member of parliament, and I should be most unwilling to have to answer for any unfortunate event. I had thought of calling in Dr Larrey . . .'

'The Emperor's surgeon, sir?' cried the governor, staring. 'Do you speak seriously?'

'We were students together, sir, and he was present when I had the honour of addressing the Institut earlier in the year,' said Stephen with the simplicity of truth, and he observed that the blow went home. 'But since I see in the *Moniteur* that he is spending the rest of the week at Metz, perhaps the local man will do for the moment.'

'There is a Dr Fabre at the end of the street,' said the governor. 'I will send for him.'

Dr Fabre was very young, newly-installed, very shy, very willing to please: he came at once, and for some reason, perhaps connected with the prison's prestige, the governor saw fit to stun him with Stephen's eminence. Fabre had not actually attended Dr Maturin's lecture at the Institut he said as they walked upstairs, but he had read an account of it; and he had been amazed by the constellation of scientific and medical luminaries present, including his former professors Dr Larrey, Dr Dupuytren . . . He had the honour of being known to Monsieur Gay-Lussac, he whispered, just outside the door.

He examined the patient, agreed with Dr Maturin's diagnosis, agreed with the proposed remedies, hurried off to compound them himself and returned directly, bearing bottles, pills, and boluses. They talked for a while before he left, mostly about the Paris medical and philosophical world, and Stephen showed away in a somewhat disgusting fashion, speaking of his publications and naming the great men he knew, and saying as they parted, 'Should you see any of my friends, dear colleague, pray give them the good day from me.'

'I shall, I shall,' said the young man. 'I see Dr Dupuytren for example every Tuesday at the Hôtel Dieu; and sometimes Dr Larrey, from a distance.'

'You do not happen to know Dr Baudelocque, the accoucheur, by any chance?'

'Indeed I do. My wife's brother married his sister's niece. I can almost call him kin.'

'Ah? I consulted with him when I was last in Paris, leaving my patient in his hands, an American lady. There may well be some difficulty of presentation, the result of a long sea-voyage. He was not altogether easy in his mind, I recall. If you should happen to see him, be so good as to ask him how she does — it was an interesting case. And when you come to see our dysentery here on Friday, please bring me half a dozen of Michel's finest glass ampullae.

'I am glad that is done,' said Stephen, listening to the footsteps as they faded down the corridor. 'It was odious, and I wonder that decent young man did not revolt; but at least there is now much less likelihood of our being quietly shuffled off.

Never was there such a talkative, intermarried, clannish band as the Paris physicians, and once our presence is known . . . Now swallow this good bolus, my dear, and you will feel better tomorrow: you may even have a little of our coffee, of the coffee that we must now put in hand.' Rousseau returned from leading Dr Fabre away, and Stephen said to him, 'Certainly we shall send out. The question is, where? This gentleman,' — meaning Captain Aubrey — 'must have his new-laid egg, his gruel and rice-water fresh and fresh; and for my part I like my coffee hot.'

'There is no difficulty,' said the guard. 'I know a little place not a hundred yards from here: Madame veuve Lehideux, cooked dishes at all hours, choice wines.'

'Then let us by all means send to the widow. Fresh milk and plain crumb-bread for these gentlemen, coffee and croissants for me: particularly strong coffee, if you please.'

Rousseau took no notice of this, but pursued the one idea already in his head. 'Some clients like to send out to Voisin's and Ruhl's and such places; some clients like to fling their money out of the window. I do not wish to impose my views on any client: no one can say that Rousseau has imposed his views on any client; and tastes differ. The last gentleman here and he was a very high gentleman too sent out to Ruhl's, whatever I might say, and what happened? He died of a pneumonia in that very bed,' — pointing to it and indeed patting the counterpane. 'Died the afternoon you came in: I dare say you still felt it warm, sir, which reminds me I promised him a board for the shit-hole pardon the expression, the last one fell out he always was an awkward companion and grew worse with the rheumatism fairly bent double at the end may he rest in peace.'

'Then let us send to Madame Lehideux,' said Stephen.

Rousseau ploughed straight on: 'I do not say it is the Emperor's table; I will not deceive you, gentlemen. It is only an honest cuisine bourgeoise, but such a civet de lapin!' — kissing his thick fingers — 'such a truly velvet poule au pot! And the great point is, you get your dishes hot. I always say, food must be hot. It is only a small place, but it is not a stone's throw from here: it is in the rue des Neuf Fiancées, without a word of lie; so the food can be brought in hot, if you understand me.'

'Then let us send to Madame Lehideux,' said Stephen. 'Milk, crumb-bread, coffee and croissants; and please to mention particularly that the coffee should be strong.'

The coffee came, and it was strong. Hot, strong, and wonderfully aromatic; the croissants unctuous, but not too unctuous. It was a remarkably good breakfast, all the better for being so late: certainly the best that Stephen had eaten in any of his prisons. He felt stronger, more capable of dealing with most emergencies that might arise: delation, the sudden treachery of a captured or a double agent, even severe interrogation.

He was prepared, he had long been prepared, for many eventualities; but not for neglect. It astonished him, took him quite aback, made him feel obscurely foolish, though at the same time still more deeply apprehensive. Day after day they saw no one but Rousseau bringing up their food or peering at them surreptitiously through the judas, and once a week the barber, a deaf mute; and after what was by the calendar a very short time they fell into so even a course of life that they might have been there for months. The only break in the steady pace was that early Friday when Dr Fabre returned. He viewed Captain Aubrey with approval and listened conscientiously to the effect of the potions, boluses and pills; but he was a sad young man, almost distracted, almost overwhelmed with unhappiness, for he had received orders to join the 107th Regiment of the line somewhere in the gloomy wastes of northern Europe, in a town whose name he could not even pronounce. Unless he could obtain a most improbable exemption his nascent practice was ruined. He had been hurrying about among all the influential men he knew, however remotely, in the hope of their good word. He had seen Dr Larrey, and he was most grateful for having been able to use Dr Maturin's name as an introduction to his own plea: indeed, Dr Maturin's name had been most valuable to him as he made his rounds — they all remembered him. Dr Dupuytren, Dr Baudelocque . . . They were all deeply concerned at Dr Maturin's predicament — were convinced it was an administrative error and that it would soon be set right — would make representations in the proper quarters — offered their services if there were material difficulties of any kind. And Dr Baudelocque had given Fabre a message about the American patient: his misgivings had been confirmed, and he was by no means sure that the foetus was viable.

There was a history of prolonged, violent seasickness, and that might be one of the causes; but in any event, Dr Baudelocque could not be at all confident that the lady would arrive at term.

'Just as well,' observed Stephen. 'There are far, far too many children as it is.'

'Oh, surely, sir . . .' cried Dr Fabre, who had five, with another due in a few weeks' time.

'Surely, sir,' said Stephen, 'no thinking man will deliberately entail life upon still another being in this overcrowded world perpetually at war?'

'Perhaps, sir,' suggested Fabre, 'not all children are deliberately begotten?'

'No,' said Stephen. 'If men were to consider what they were at — if they were to look about them, and reflect upon the cost of life in a universe where prisons, brothels, madhouses, and regiments of men armed and trained to kill other men are so very common — why, I doubt we should see many of these poor mewling little larval victims, so often a present misery to their parents and a future menace to their kind.'

Tears gathered in the young man's eyes; but recollecting himself he put his hand to his pocket and said, 'Here are the ampullae you asked for.'

'Thank you, thank you, dear colleague,' said Stephen, taking them carefully in their wooden box — they were for his own private use, for his more certain exit in case of need — 'I am very much obliged to you.'

'Not at all,' said Fabre, and he took his leave, saying that he doubted whether he should ever have the happiness of seeing Dr Maturin or his companions again.

They did not see him again, and the weeks flowed by in such a calm monotony that presently the charged ampullae came to seem absurd.

The long, even days were marked by a steady thumping, by the whistles of foremen, by the distant crash of falling masonry and the cries of workmen as they demolished parts of the ancient building out of sight; the nights were perfectly calm, with never a sound but the murmur of the city like a distant sea and the deep bell of St Théodule's telling the hour. No hint of footsteps overhead, no sound from either side. They might have been alone in that great tower: they might even have been at sea, as far as their isolation was concerned; and there was something nautical about their small living-space and in the way they became so soon acquainted with it. On the other hand, the quality of their food was not nautical at all, oh far, far from it.

From that very first cup of coffee, the widow Lehideux gave the utmost satisfaction; her meals quickly became part of their daily pattern, and their chief diversion. She was very willing to do her best and she sent little beautifully-written, badly-spelt notes with suggestions according to the state of the market; and to these Stephen replied with comments on the last dish and recommendations, even receipts, for the next. 'It is only a woman's cookery, to be sure,' he said, toying with a chocolate mousse, 'and I do not know that I should trust her with game; but within these wide limits, how very good it is! She must be a knowing old soul, with great experience, no doubt in excellent service before the Revolution. Perhaps something of a slut: your amiable slut makes the best of cooks.'

Their daily life, though confined and dull, might have been very much more disagreeable. It quickly assumed an ordered shape: Jack did not exactly organize them into watches, but he showed them how the place could be brought to something like naval cleanliness with nothing but the most primitive means and a mere three sweepings in the course of the day. His pupils were sluggish, inept, reluctant, even sullen at times, and they particularly disliked hanging their blankets and their pallet-beds from Jagiello's window, piling all the sparse furniture into a pyramid, and swilling the floor before breakfast; but his moral force, his conviction that this alone was right, overcame them, and the rooms grew inoffensive at least, so much so that the former prisoner's tame mouse became uneasy and disappeared for three days. It lived behind the locked door in Jack's room and it came out of its hole in time for their first breakfast: though hesitant and confused at finding its friend gone and strangers sitting at the familiar table, it had accepted a piece of croissant and a little coffee held out at arm's length in a spoon; it sat with them while they discussed the methods of dealing with the surrounding filth, and all seemed well until the unfortunate orgy of scrubbing. The mouse did come back in time, however, and Stephen noticed with concern that it was gravid: he ordered cream — cream was eminently medicinal in pregnancy.

It did not need the mouse nor her condition to bring Diana to his mind; she was there a great deal of the time; but it did tend to bring these wandering thoughts —

recollections of her in former days, riding over the English countryside with singular grace and spirit; images of her in India, at the Institut, in the streets of Paris — to a sharper focus. Diana would be well provided with cream. Would she also be provided with a lover, with a plurality of lovers? It was probable; he had scarcely known a time when it was not so, and the atmosphere of Paris was ideally suited to such things. Yet he found himself curiously unwilling to dwell on the subject; he preferred to think of the solitary huntress he had once known.

Order and cleanliness were the first things in Jack's day, but they were very far from being uppermost in his mind. Their first dinner had not arrived, the floor was scarcely dry, before he was looking about for means of escape in spite of the sickness that had made the others insist upon his taking the one good bed, while Stephen urged him to return to it.

Although the prospect was not encouraging — a sheer drop to the moat, an apparently impossible wall beyond it, and according to Stephen's recollection of a visit to the Temple in his youth, covered ways barring the moat on either hand, out of their sight — Jack found that others had been there before him: some patient hand had picked and picked at the setting of the bars in Jagiello's window, gnawing deeply but ineffectually into the stone; another had actually sawn through one of the twenty-four pieces of iron, hiding the cut with grease; indeed, an eye that searched with greater eagerness than any gaoler could find countless signs of their predecessors' passionate desire for freedom. Yet it seemed to him that most of them had set about it in the wrong way. Even if one had the tools one could not work on the bars without risk of detection; they could be seen from the judas-holes, and there was no telling when a patrol might come round: Rousseau and his mates wore list slippers, and they were rarely heard until the key was in the lock. The privy was far more promising: its projecting floor consisted of two spans of stone resting on corbels either side, with the necessary space between them; and if they could be removed the way was clear. The way down, at all events. Unfortunately they were built in the lavish medieval fashion, regardless of weight, and they were sealed into the masonry on either side with molten sulphur; but there was at least a possibility that they might be moved in time, and the discreet hanging that covered the entrance to the privy shielded the worker from view, providing all the time in the world. The difficulties would be uncommonly great however, and the place itself was very, very nasty; before exploring it farther he considered the door in the wall, the door used only by the mouse. A lever could work wonders with a door, even so massive an iron-bound, iron-studded door as this; but before working wonders it was as well to know where the door led. Stephen was of opinion that it might possibly open on to a spiral staircase in the thickness of the wall; the Templars had been much given to spiral staircases. But on the other hand it might only lead into other rooms like their own, and they would merely exchange one cage for another.

Rousseau provided no information about the door; 'it was shut' he said, 'it was not open. It was a very old door; they did not make doors like that nowadays.' It might have been prudence on his part, though stupidity seemed more likely than caution or ill-will, but they dared not press him. On other subjects he was more communicative, above all on the decadence of the Temple, 'the finest prison in France, whatever the Conciergerie might say — such clients — the whole royal family at one time, to say nothing of bishops and archbishops and generals and foreign officers, very select — no complaints, though some of them were here for years — always contented — shit-holes and running water in many of the apartments, for cells they could not be called. And all this going to rack and ruin — barely a score of clients now — that was why he could spend five minutes chatting with these gentlemen — in the good old days, with five or six in a room, he and all his colleagues were run off their feet — scarcely time for so much as good day: though it was true that they more than doubled their wages in commission from the cook-shops then, whereas now it was stark misery. Rack and ruin: the whole place was topsy-turvy, arsy-versy — governor had not been seen this last month and more — said to have resigned — deputy governor out of his wits and likely to be replaced.' As for the demolitions, his muddled account was obviously falsified by his wish that they should be kept to a minimum, but it seemed that everything except the great tower and perhaps its companion was to be swept away. Much had already gone. 'And how can you be expected to keep a prison just so in such circumstances, with workmen all over the place, disobeying the regulations?' he asked. 'It is more like a bawdy-house.'

All things being considered, the door seemed less profitable than the privy, from which free air and free-flying house-martins could actually be seen. 'Once we have shifted these stones,' said Jack, 'I shall make a rope of our sheets and reconnoitre the moat.'

He concentrated his efforts upon the jakes, therefore; but his efforts were not what they might have been. The crayfish, or rather their effects, were still with him in spite of Stephen's doses and his rigid diet: he was drained of strength and even at times of spirit. Stephen begged him to abstain from such a very noisome atmosphere. 'I do assure you, my dear,' he said, 'that if you continue to breathe the mephitic exhalations of six hundred years of misdirected filth, your escape will be by way of a coffin rather than a rope of knotted sheets. Come, let Jagiello and me take our turn at undermining the jakes, each for a stated period of the day.'

'Very well,' said Jack, with a pale smile. It was but fair to let them have their turn, although he knew very well how it would end. He had no opinion whatsoever of Stephen as a man of his hands and not much more of Jagiello: landsmen seemed born inept and in addition to that Stephen was given to dreaming, to building hypotheses rather than destroying the Temple, and indeed he dropped their only nail down through the slabs into the moat below; while Jagiello was too volatile to accomplish much. He would be set to scrape a particular patch of filth or to scratch the mortar of a given stone, and then at the end of his spell (often cut short by Jack's impatience at his fumbling) it would be found that he had dispersed his efforts over much of the privy, exploring new crevices, clearing irrelevant areas of antique dung, and once even inscribing *Amor vincit omnia* on the roof. He would do his spell cheerfully, singing much of the time, but the prospect of escape was so very, very remote that he had no sense of urgency. He quite lacked the sacred fire that had enabled Jack to eat right through one of the seven broad Roman bricks that sealed the left-hand side of the inner stone in less than five days, using one of poor Madame Lehideux's knives, ground down to a slim steel tooth: then once his spell was over he felt that his duty was done, and would return to his window-seat, there to sing in his sweet tenor or to play the flute that Jack had mended. It never occurred to him to steal hours from the night to grind away at the massive brick and stonework, and indeed neither of them ever heard Jack at his self-appointed task, a gigantic rat gnawing at its cage in the darkness with infinite patience and determination.

In the end, as he had foreseen, Jack's turn assumed greater and greater proportions; and although Stephen and Jagiello protested that he did too much, far more than his fair share, they were obliged to confess their own comparative inefficacity. So, on a day of unusual activity among the workmen below, labouring unseen but clearly heard behind the wall on the far side of the moat, Jack was in his privy, Jagiello at his window, where their newly-washed shirts fluttered from the bars, and Stephen in the middle room, lost in thought, when the upper half of the outer wall fell with a long thunderous crash. The dust-cloud cleared, and there were the roofs and garrets of the rue des Neuf Fiancées. All the visible windows were shuttered except for one, the nearest, and from this a young woman gazed at the great line of fallen stone. 'Oohoo,' called Jagiello, smiling and waving his flute: she was the first person he had seen outside the prison for weeks.

She looked at him, smiled back, made a slight gesture with her hand, and withdrew: but could be seen still watching him from within. After a while she emerged again, studying the sky, the perfectly clear and cloudless sky, holding out her hand to see whether perhaps rain were falling. Jagiello also held out his hand, she laughed, and they contemplated one another for some time with mutual satisfaction, making motions towards the fallen wall and putting their hands to their ears to show that it had made a noise in falling.

Stephen watched them steadily from a discreet point well within the dark middle window. 'Stay there,' he cried as Jack came backing out from his hole. 'Do not approach Jagiello's room. You may look from this window here. See: a female form. I believe we may have the classical situation — the captive, the maiden — it is ludicrously hackneyed. But if you appear, all is lost.'

'How do you mean, all is lost?'

'Brother,' said Stephen, laying his hand on Jack's arm, 'I am not a romantic figure, nor — forgive me — are you.'

'No,' said Jack. 'I suppose I ain't.' He peered through the central shaft, fingering his six-days' beard: it was bright yellow and all-invasive; Stephen's was black and sparse; Jagiello's face alone was smooth, as though the barber had passed that morning. The lady had returned: she was watering her pot-plants, unconscious of any gaze, and whistling gently to a dove in a wicker cage. 'Oh what a pretty creature,' he said. 'Lord, what a pretty creature,' and then in a strong, quarterdeck voice, 'Mr Jagiello, play a melancholy air. Then sing *Stone Walls do not a Prison Make*, d'ye hear me, there?'

Jagiello was still in fine voice when their dinner appeared: the young woman was watering her plants again. 'The worst has happened,' said Rousseau. 'I was afraid of it: they have started on the outer wall. Another month, and where shall we be? The finest prison in France flung down. I dare say they will put you in the Conciergerie, my poor gentlemen. No running water, no shit-holes there pardon the expression, only pots, which are low. And what will happen to me I do not know. Rousseau will be flung aside, his long services forgotten.' He put down the basket and said, 'It is immoral: it is what I call immoral.' He stared out of the window. 'Immoral. And illogical . . . illogical, that's the word. But at least you can see Madame Lehideux now. There she is, watering her flowers.'

'Let us hope they are aquatics,' said Stephen as he looked at the note lapped in his napkin, 'Or at least swamp-plants: nothing else will survive such assiduity. *If the gentlemen have any washing, mending, or ironing,*' he read aloud, '*B. Lehideux would be happy to accommodate them.*'

'Oh, we do very well,' said Jagiello. 'Captain Aubrey was so very kind as to mend my waistcoat yesterday — you cannot see the tear — and he has already shown me how to sew on buttons and darn stockings.'

'Nonsense,' said Stephen. 'These sheets are only dabbled in cold water. I like my shirts ironed; I like them to smell of lavender. Your uniform breeches with the cherry-coloured stripe do you no credit, Mr Jagiello: they need pressing. Monsieur Rousseau, pray take these shirts, these breeches and this coat to Madame Lehideux with our compliments. Tell her it will be a great relief to be shot of the shirts in particular; there is something lamentably squalid about shirts flying from the bars, and I do not let on to be either a seamstress or a laundry-maid. Say we are very much obliged to her for her kindness, particularly the young gentleman here.'

Shirts no longer flew from the window-bars, and Jagiello was in full voice, full flute, full view all day; he was excused sweeping, swabbing, scrubbing the table and chairs; he was excused all duties, and required to make himself agreeable; Jack and Stephen kept well out of sight, but as far as they could tell he seemed eminently successful. Apart from their daily letters, more and more voluminous, the two communicated by means of an alphabet held up, by singing together, and by signs. It was a laborious conversation, taking up most of their waking hours, and how the poor young lady found time to cook their meals and deal so beautifully with their clothes did not appear.

The quiet, ordered days dropped by. The mouse brought off a creditable brood. In the *Moniteur* Stephen read a categorical denial of the report, busily circulated by the now-desperate Allies, that there was a coolness between France and Saxony: on the contrary, the friendship between His Imperial Majesty and the Saxon king had never been closer, and there was not the least hint of disaffection among the valorous German troops. The Emperor, by a judicious shortening of his lines of communication, was going from strength to strength. A continual stream of brick- and stone-dust fell from the privy: small pieces of masonry were hidden in their beds: and all round them the Temple slowly crumbled away.

Rousseau grew steadily more glum and silent: it was rumoured that even the towers were not to be spared, and indeed on a Monday they saw workmen enter their part of the moat, leaving heaps of stone and even ladders by the half-demolished wall, a sight frustrating almost beyond endurance.

'Jagiello,' said Jack, 'unless you spread more canvas they will have pulled the place to pieces before we can get out. Proper flats we shall look, if we are transferred just when I have the cross-stones almost free. I must have a cold chisel, a handspike, and some line. With the right tools I could do more in an hour than in a week of scraping. I really must have the right tools. And I must have them now.'

'I will do my best, sir,' said Jagiello. 'But I doubt whether the moment is quite ripe.'

'Never mind manoeuvres,' said Jack. 'Always go straight at 'em. Things are growing very urgent indeed, and there is not a moment to lose.'

'Shall I risk everything at one throw?'

'Yes. Do.'

'What am I to ask for?'

'A cold chisel and five fathoms of one-inch line: that will make a capital beginning.'

Jagiello walked slowly into his room. They heard him playing in the window-seat.

'The soft complaining flute
In dying notes discovers
The woes of hopeless lovers,' observed Stephen.

'Oh what a damned unlucky thing to say,' cried Jack. 'I have no notion of your *hopeless* at all. The dear creature has acquiesced in the disappearance of her cutlery: why should she baulk at a cold chisel or two and a few fathoms of line! I wish you would not say things like that, Stephen.'

'It was only a quotation,' said Stephen.

Quotation or not, Jagiello came back after a long hour of silence looking pale, desperate, desolate. He shook his head, and looking across the moat they saw that the window was quite blank, its shutters closed.

'Never mind,' said Jack as they ate their supper, a supper that seemed unusually plain and sparse. 'Never mind: I shall get a purchase under the nearer stone before the week is out — never take it to heart, man; I am sure you did your best.'

'It is not that, sir,' said Jagiello, pushing his plate away and leaning over the back of his chair to hide a tear. 'It is that I miss her so. She says she will never see me again.'

They looked anxiously at the window: even its pot-plants and the dove had been taken in. A great many thoughts passed through Jack's mind, among them a pang of regret for his coat, which he had sent across to be freshened and which might now be gone for ever, leaving him in his shirtsleeves; but in view of Jagiello's distress he did not mention it. Nor did he mention the dismal prospect of having to say farewell to that splendid succession of meals. Stephen wondered very much what Jagiello could possibly have said to spoil so promising a situation, yet for the same reason he went to bed with the question still unresolved.

They saw no chink of light through the shutters in the darkness; the shutters were not opened at dawn, nor yet when the sun shone full upon them. This seemed final, for they knew — she was not always quite discreet — that it was her bedroom, and so decided a removal did away with doubt, with hope, with all but a forced and unconvincing cheerfulness.

Yet to their astonishment their breakfast came, and with it Jack's shining coat. The basket contained Jagiello's Lithuanian delight, smoked eel and slices of yellow cheese, while neatly tacked inside the coat they found a length of very strong silk cord, and a cold chisel in each pocket. Jagiello sprang from the table with a radiant face: they saw the garret window open, the lady and her pot-plants and her bird appear. She arranged the pots in the sun, and then, with a significant look and the kindest smile she took the dove from its cage, kissed it and launched it in the air.

Chapter Eleven

This was not Rousseau's time, but he could be heard clashing his keys some way off; and he had two soldiers with him. Their boots echoed in the long vaulted passage. Stephen made the necessary signal to Jack, who backed out of the privy, brushing the brick-dust from his hands.

'Dr Maturin, if you please,' said Rousseau in the open door; and cocking his ear towards the farther room, 'How the young gentleman does sing, to be sure. You would say a canary-bird.'

'Mind your step, sir,' he said at the coffin-turn.

'Wait here a minute,' said the governor's secretary at the bottom of the stairs, and as Stephen stood there between his guards he heard voices raised in disagreement on the far side of the governor's door. Most unfortunately the soldiers and the turnkey fell to discussing the weather — fine, but perhaps too fine; perhaps the prelude to a storm; certainly the prelude to a storm —

but even so he gathered that the governor was uneasy about some irregularity and that his interlocutors were trying to overcome his objections by reason, persuasion, and hectoring. They reached a compromise: 'He is to be returned before the closing of the gates, and both of you must sign for him,' said the governor's weak, anxious voice; and then, 'Come in.'

There were not two men with him but three, all soldiers: a big burly full colonel with a red, ill-tempered face, presumably Hector; a nondescript captain; and a dark, intelligent looking lieutenant in the sombre uniform of the artillery. As he walked in Stephen said 'Gentlemen, good day.' The governor and the lieutenant replied; the captain moved his lips; the colonel merely stared.

A clerk brought papers, the colonel and the captain signed, the lieutenant said to Stephen 'This way, if you please,' and they walked to a carriage in the courtyard.

The workmen had made great progress since last Stephen saw the entrance to the Temple, and now that the outer bailey was gone he would not have known the place, but for its position. The covered ways traversing the moat now stood open to the sky and the gate-house itself was no more than a disordered heap of stones, being carried away by a long file of carts.

After some disobliging remarks about 'the awkward old sod — civilians always the same — they want their arses kicking, just like natives — a whiff of case-shot every three months' which seemed to be directed at the deputy-governor, the colonel and the captain talked about their private affairs with a brutal, truly military disregard for their companions. The two were evidently related, a certain Hortense being the wife of the one, sister to the other. But even if their conversation had been much more interesting Stephen was far too taken up with his thoughts and with observing their route to pay real attention.

They crossed the river by the Pont au Change, as though their destination were the ill-omened Conciergerie; but the loud metallic voices never ceased discussing Hortense and presently they were driving towards Saint Germain des Prés. 'It will be the rue Saint-Dominique,' said Stephen to himself: 'Even worse.' At the height of the abbey the colonel stopped the coach and told his orderly to fetch a parcel from one of the little shops behind; and it was just as the man was coming back that Stephen saw Diana. She was in an open carriage, talking earnestly to another woman, an over-ornamented woman he had never met; she was bending forward to the front seat with that peculiarly supple grace that he would have known at any distance: and now they were not six feet apart. He instantly shielded his face with his hand and watched her through his fingers. She looked well, though her face was grave; surprisingly well, straight-backed, slim. He did not recognize the arms on the carriage door nor the rather flashy liveries of the footmen behind. The carriage was past in a moment, but as the soldiers' coachman moved out into the stream immediately afterwards he had it in view for quite ten minutes and from time to time he saw Diana's companion, who sat with her back to the horses, a woman on the edge of middle age dressed in the height of fashion or perhaps a little above it, good-looking in a hard, determined way, a fair example of the Napoleonic court, not Diana's style at all, at all. The carriage turned off some way short of the Hôtel de La Mothe, to a large, newly-painted house that had belonged to the Princesse de Lamballe.

It was only when he had perceived and noted this that he found how strongly he had been moved: his knees were trembling, his breath came short against the beating of his heart, and if he had been addressed he could hardly have answered in a natural voice. He mastered these outward symptoms quickly enough, but his mind was not fully at his command before the coach wheeled in under a covered archway. He had not even taken an exact account of their turnings and he was not sure where they were, though it was probable that this building and its courtyards backed on to the rue Saint-Dominique.

Fortunately they put him into a small empty room for a two hours' wait — a traditional measure to increase anxiety and distress — and as he collected his wits his emotion died away. The place was obviously military: quite apart from the soldiers moving about in the courtyard, there was a kind of scrubbed squalor common to all armies he had ever known. Conscript hands had no doubt whitewashed the lumps of slag bordering the paths and the wooden post against the pockmarked wall, but no swab, no brush had ever been applied to the filthy chocolate-coloured paint within: nor, he reflected, would any navy, even the French navy, tolerate the unwashed glass, the fetid smell, the general seediness. At one time he heard screams, but whether they were genuine or false he could not tell: such things were not an unusual prelude to an interrogation.

The same seediness, the same contradiction, was apparent in the room to which he was led at last: some of the officers were particularly gorgeous, but they sat at rickety unpainted tables and they had remarkably dirty dog-eared files before them. These tables formed three sides of a square, and Stephen was told to sit on a bench that made the fourth: it was rather like the arrangement for a court-martial. What would have been the president's seat was filled by the colonel who was so fond of kicking civilians' arses, but he looked discontented and bored and Stephen had the intimate conviction that he was a nullity, of use partly for his rank and partly, if the army intelligence people were half as subtle as their political colleagues, to induce a man under interrogation to underestimate his enemies and so betray himself. The man in real control was a major in a plain undress uniform, a man remarkable only for his cold deep-set eyes: he said, 'Dr Maturin, we know who and what you are. But before we deal with the matter of your colleagues in France we have a few questions to put to you.'

‘I am fully prepared to answer any questions within the limits, the narrow limits, of those that may be put to an officer who is a prisoner of war,’ said Stephen.

‘You were not a prisoner of war when you were last in Paris, nor were you here in the character of an officer: but leaving that aside for the moment, you are nevertheless required to give an account of your movements. Let us begin when you were the surgeon of the *Java*, captured by the American *Constitution*.’

‘You are mistaken, sir. A glance at the Navy List will show you that the surgeon of the *Java* was a gentleman by the name of Fox.’

‘Then how do you explain the fact that the description of the surgeon fits you exactly, even to the marks on your hands?’ asked the major, taking a paper from his file. ‘Five foot six, slight build, black hair, pale eyes, muddy complexion, three nails on the right hand torn out, both hands somewhat crippled: speaks perfect French with a southern accent.’

Stephen instantly realized that this must have come from a French agent in the Brazilian port to which the *Constitution* had taken them, a man who had seen his coded documents and who had evidently taken him for the *Java*'s surgeon: an understandable confusion, since he berthed with Fox and their captured dunnage had been jumbled together. The essential point was that the major's paper did not come from Boston, where Stephen was known only too well. It was perfectly possible that even with this lapse of time his doings in the States were unknown to Paris: communication was irregular — as irregular as the Royal Navy could conceivably make it — and in killing Dubreuil and Pontet-Canet he had after all destroyed the Frenchmen's chief sources of information. If the strings of their net were as tangled and out of date as this, he might hope to elude them altogether. Looking down to conceal any gleam of triumph that might show in his eyes he said that he could not be held responsible for any man's description, and that he must decline to comment.

The description was handed about, and in the interval an orderly brought a small book covered in brown paper; its size was exactly that of the Navy List. Having consulted it the major continued without any change of expression, 'You are a linguist, Dr Maturin: I dare say you also speak Spanish?'

'Catalan,' murmured his neighbour.

'The various dialects of Spanish,' pursued the major, frowning.

'You must forgive me,' said Stephen. 'I do not find the question falls within the limits I have mentioned.'

'Your reluctance to answer is significant. It amounts to a denial.'

'I neither affirm nor deny.'

'Then I think we may take it that you are fluent in Catalan.'

'On the same basis you may state that I know Basque. Or Sanskrit.'

'Let us pass to the Baltic. What have you to tell us of the murder of General Mercier at Grimsholm?'

Stephen had nothing to tell them of the murder of General Mercier at Grimsholm. He admitted that he had been in the Baltic, aboard the *Ariel*, but when asked what she had been doing there he said, 'Really, sir, an officer cannot be expected to betray the warlike movements of the service to which he has the honour to belong.'

'Perhaps not,' said a man on the left, 'but you can be expected to account for your presence there. Your name is not on the *Ariel*'s muster: her surgeon was a Mr Graham.'

'You are mistaken. My name is on the supplementary list, after the Marines, as a passenger, borne for victuals but not pay or tobacco.'

'As a goddam spy,' muttered the colonel.

Asked why he should choose to take passage for the Baltic of all places, he said that he wished to visit the northern birds.

'And may we ask what birds you saw?' said the major.

'The most noteworthy were Pernis apivorus, Haliaetus albicilla, Somateria spectabilis, and Somateria mollissima, to whom we are indebted for the eider-down.'

'I will not be trifled with,' cried the colonel. 'Birds . . . eider-down . . . by God. He needs a lesson in respect. Send for the provost-marshal.'

'There really are such birds, sir,' said a red-haired lieutenant. 'I do not believe he means disrespect.'

'Kick his arse,' muttered the colonel, moving angrily in his seat.

'Do you expect us to believe that you travelled a thousand miles to look at birds?' asked another officer.

'You will believe what you wish to believe, gentlemen,' said Stephen. 'That is the almost invariable human proceeding. I merely state the fact. I am not unknown as a natural philosopher.'

'Just so,' said the major. 'And this brings

us to Paris. Here we are on surer ground, I am afraid; and here you must expect to be pressed for satisfactory replies, for you were not protected by the laws of war. I strongly advise you not to compel us to press you to the utmost. We know a great deal, and no equivocation will be tolerated.'

'I was protected by a safe-conduct delivered by your government.'

'No safe-conduct covers spying or collusion in treasonable activities. At Beauvillier's hotel you received the visit of Delarue, Fauvet and Hersant, all of whom desired you to carry messages to England.'

'Certainly,' said Stephen, 'and I could name many more who did the same. You must know, however, that I steadily refused their requests, and that at no time did I deviate from my neutrality as a natural philosopher.'

'I am afraid that is not exact,' said the major, 'and I can produce witnesses who will confound you. But before doing so, I must have the names of your colleagues here. Come, Dr Maturin, you are a reasonable man; you must know the importance the Emperor attaches to Grimsholm and to your sources of information. You will not oblige us to go to extremities.'

'You are asking for what does not exist. I repeat, with the utmost possible emphasis, that during my stay in Paris I never departed from a scrupulous observation of neutrality as a natural philosopher.'

A single statement of the truth might have no great immediate effect, particularly in an atmosphere of such suspicion and duplicity; but its strong, unvaried reiteration delivered in a tone of complete sincerity, compelled if not total belief then at least a suspension of incredulity. Several of the officers put forward objections, advancing names, some true some false, of those who wished to communicate with England, and again and again in their questions and in Stephen's replies 'natural philosopher' recurred, like the refrain of a tediously repetitious song.

'Natural philosophers,' cried the colonel at last. 'Natural philosophers my arse: who ever heard of half Golconda being offered for the release of a natural philosopher, which is all he says he is? A hundred thousand louis. Balls. Of course he is a spy.'

There was a very short but very awkward hiatus in which the colonel, mistaking the cause, corrected his louis d'or to napoléons; the major darted a steely glance at him and called out 'Bring in Monsieur Fauvet.'

Fauvet came in: he looked unbelievably mean and the blustering, confident air he gave himself did nothing to improve it. He was accompanied by a fat man, tight in his civilian clothes, a man called Delaris whom Stephen had watched before now, a man high in Laurie's organization, operating from the ministry of the interior and the Conciergerie: he had never knowingly seen Dr Maturin and now he stared at him with a naked, avid curiosity.

'Monsieur Fauvet,' said the major, 'pray repeat your statement.'

Fauvet did so: on various occasions Dr Maturin had offered to carry messages to England; he had spoken disrespectfully of the Emperor and had predicted his early defeat; had advised Fauvet and many others to make their peace with the King while there was yet time; and had solicited a substantial fee. Fauvet was prepared to swear to this. His voice was mechanical and unassured: a very wretched witness.

'What have you to say?' asked the major.

'Nothing whatsoever,' said Stephen, 'except that I have never seen such a contemptible exhibition; I am surprised that even a civilian can sink so very low.'

Delaris whispered in the major's ear. 'No, no: no question of it,' said the major.

'You will have to arrange that with the Temple, if you can. For the moment he belongs to —' Stephen did not catch the name of his owner, but it produced a considerable effect on Delaris, who gave a low whistle. Their conversation went on for some time, in an even lower tone: but Delaris' insistence and the major's steady negation were clear enough.

'That will do for the moment,' said the major aloud. 'Dr Maturin, you will reflect upon what I have said. You have already been confounded on one important point and at your next interrogation you may be confronted with still other witnesses. Do not flatter yourself with false hopes: we know far more than you imagine. When next you are brought here, you must be prepared to speak with greater candour or to take the consequences, which, I am obliged to tell you, will be terrible for you and your friends.'

The judas-haired lieutenant who had asserted that eider-duck did in fact exist took Stephen back to the dismal room where he had waited. He remained there, looking out of the dirty window that gave on to the broad open court, and after a while he said, 'I was at your lecture, sir: allow me to say how much I enjoyed my evening. May I offer you a cigar?'

'You are very good, sir,' said Stephen, taking it and drawing the smoke in greedily.

'It grieves me extremely,' said the lieutenant, 'to see a man of your eminence in such a position. Let me beg you, sir, for your own sake and for the sake of your companions, not to persist.'

A troop of soldiers marched into the court, halted, dressed by the right, grounded their muskets with a single crash. A bent man in shirt and breeches, his arms tied behind his back, was led limping from another gate and attached to the whitewashed post: his face, where it was not bruised and tumefied, was a yellowish green. He was another man Stephen knew who did not know Stephen, a double agent who worked for Arliss: a mercenary man, but now he looked steadily at the firing-squad with an expression that raised him very high.

At the given word the muskets fired. The face burst apart in a red horror, the body jerked with extraordinary violence under the impact and then hung limp, still tied to the post. A young soldier turned, unseeing, to Stephen's window, appalled and white, and dropping his musket he vomited on the ground.

'. . . if you persist,' the lieutenant was saying — he was obviously accustomed to these scenes — 'you will be shot. If you make just a few concessions, it will be Verdun, and a reasonably pleasant confinement, no more.'

'I am deeply concerned at what you tell me,' said Stephen, 'and believe me I appreciate your kindness at its full value; but alas your argument is based on a false premise. There are no concessions to be made, no secrets to be revealed.'

On the way back to the Temple the lieutenant, his only escort now, repeated his appeal in various forms, and Stephen repeated his reply; but he had seen this form of manipulation used so often that in time his answers grew a little short, and he left his companion with a sense of relief.

'How was it?' asked Jack anxiously.

'Sure, it was no more than an ordinary interrogation, and they feeling their way,' said Stephen, sitting down and smiling at them. 'At present they are all to seek. Long may they remain so, amen, amen, amen.'

'Amen,' said Jack, searching his face for signs of ill-treatment and finding only a desire to say no more.

'We have kept you your dinner,' said

Jagiello. 'And all the wine.'

'You are the jewel of the world, Jagiello,' said Stephen. 'I could eat the best part of an ox, I find, and drink oceans dry.'

He ate voraciously, and eating he asked, with a nod towards the privy, 'How do we come along?'

'We scarcely had the heart to do anything, with you away,' said Jack, 'but if only I can get a solid purchase on the outer slab, I do not think the other should resist us long. Stephen, what is the French for a double sister-block, coaked? With a pair of them and a proper hold-fast, I could raise the Temple.'

'A double sister-block, coaked? The Dear alone can tell. I do not even know what it is in English.'

'Then I shall have to try to draw it,' said Jack. 'Without a purchase that slab will never shift.'

'Do that thing, my dear,' said Stephen. 'For my part I am going to sleep.'

Sleep he needed, being very tired; but far more than sleep he needed silence for the ideas to turn freely in his mind and form a reasonable sequence. It was clear to him that his adversaries, or someone behind his adversaries, were working on an intuition, no more: their pieces of solid information were fragmentary; they did not link together. The *Ariel* had been in the Baltic at the time Grimsholm was given up: she was the kind of vessel used for such a mission: Maturin was in her: there was something odd about Maturin and therefore a possible connexion. During his visit to Paris some one of the services, presumably Delaris's, had tried to compromise him as a matter of routine precaution, but Stephen did not think that Fauvet's words had carried the least conviction and he knew that neither Delaris nor the major could bring forward a more persuasive witness.

But there was the colonel's outburst. Although hitherto their manoeuvres had been rather commonplace, some of the soldiers were clever men; yet he did not believe they had prompted the colonel's words. The words were spontaneous, a genuine gaffe, and the implication chilled his heart. Golconda meant great wealth: who could conceivably have offered 'half Golconda' for his release? It was possible that some of his friends might have made interest with the ministry on his behalf once his capture was known: Larrey, for example, or Dupuytren. But Larrey was perhaps the most virtuous man he had ever known; in spite of a large practice and unrivalled opportunities for corruption he was extremely poor, and boundless charity would always keep him so. Dupuytren was becoming rich, but even if such a wild step should ever occur to him, which was inconceivable, he could not possibly command such a sum as a hundred thousand louis. There was no one he knew in Paris who could do so. No one apart from Arliss, his colleague in intelligence, who controlled far greater amounts; but such conduct on Arliss's part would be unthinkable — it would be against the cardinal laws of intelligence. None of his colleagues would do so, he was certain; not only would it be entirely against the laws of the service but it was also against those of common sense — an offer dangerous to the proposer, mortal to the beneficiary. In the history of intelligence no innocent natural philosopher had ever been rated higher than a protest, no agent more than an offer of exchange. Half Golconda, any fraction of Golconda, was an open confession of his value and his guilt.

He could hear Jack and Jagiello working at the stones with a far greater urgency. A steady, discreet rasping; for in spite of the thump and crash of the workmen not very far away they dared not use hammers even by day, far less in the darkness. Twice the light of the patrol passed along the judases: his ideas grew confused, rising and falling like the waves of the sea, Golconda and Golgotha merging into one another: Diana's name and image appeared in his mind. He was faintly aware of Jagiello covering him with another blanket, and then no more until they shook him awake in broad daylight.

'They have come for you again,' said Jack.

'Let him swallow a bowl of coffee quick,' said Rousseau in the doorway with his soldiers.

Stephen gulped it down, slipped his glass ampulla into his cheek, tied his neckcloth, and he was ready. He had lain in his clothes and he presented but a scruffy appearance as he walked into the governor's office: it was not elegant officers who were waiting for him there however but a solitary figure, the almost equally unkempt Duhamel, who gave him a civil good day. 'I am come partly on my own account and partly as a messenger,' he said. Stephen was a little surprised at the humanity of his tone; but he was perfectly astonished when, after a certain hesitation, Duhamel went on to speak of his bowels. They had never been the same since Alençon; the medicines the French physicians had given him had nothing like the comfortable effect of Dr Maturin's red draught, and he begged he might be told its name. At the end of a purely medical interlude Stephen prescribed for him; Duhamel made his acknowledgements, and the atmosphere took on a completely different nature.

'I now speak for my principal,' said Duhamel in a low voice, moving Stephen to the window-embrasure. A pause. 'As you are aware, the war is no longer an uninterrupted series of victories for the Emperor. There are very high-placed men who feel that a compromise, a negotiated peace, is the best means of avoiding useless bloodshed and they wish their proposals to be carried to the King and the English government. These proposals can be carried only by a man who is trusted by those in power and who has access to their chiefs of intelligence. It seems to my principal that you are ideally suited for the part.'

'What you tell me is of great interest,' said Stephen, watching Duhamel's face with the keenest attention, 'and I most sincerely hope that your principal's project may succeed — that France may be spared as much as possible. But I am afraid I am not your man. As I was telling your friends at the rue Saint-Dominique —' here he perceived a glow in Duhamel's eye — 'I am a mere naval surgeon, not even a commissioned officer. It is true that I have a certain notoriety as a natural philosopher, but that does not give me access to the great, still less to their chiefs of intelligence: there appears to be a most unfortunate misapprehension on this point.' Duhamel's face betrayed a certain inner amusement, but it became perfectly grave when Stephen went on, 'Besides, my dear sir, would the man your principal takes me for ever be so foolish as to admit his identity? Surely he would be utterly unworthy of the confidence of either side if he were to fling himself into the arms of the first agent-provocateur that accosted him — if he were to enter upon such a very extraordinary undertaking without surrounding himself with equally extraordinary guarantees? It would be mere self-murder: the man would be an ass.'

'I fully take your point,' said Duhamel. 'But for the moment let us presume that such a man were found: what kind of guarantees do you suppose he would require?'

'Do you think it really useful to discuss

these remote hypotheses? If you were to ask me about the tertian ague or the osteology of the cassowary I could give you a reasonable answer, but the mental processes of this merely conjectural being . . . I am afraid you must have embraced the soldiers' wild notion. In spite of my denials they seem convinced that I am — how shall I put it? — a secret agent.'

'Yes, yes, of course,' said Duhamel, drumming his fingers on the packet he held in his left hand. He was very much master of his countenance, but even so the extremity of frustration now showed through: and in the long interval before he spoke Stephen became more nearly persuaded of his good faith. 'I will put the position to you quite plainly,' said Duhamel. 'My principal's organization was convinced of your identity as soon as your description reached Paris from Brest. That is why you were lodged in the Temple.'

'May I ask whose prisoner I am?'

'What's in a name?' replied Duhamel with automatic caution, and then relaxing, 'Ours, for the moment. But to resume: the intention was to invite you, or shall I say the man you were supposed to be, since I see that our conversation must remain upon that level — the intention was to invite you to undertake this mission much earlier, when there would have been time to surround it with all possible guarantees. But the Emperor delayed his departure; and there were other difficulties . . . In the meanwhile Madame Gros appeared at the Prince de Bénévent's ball with a most prodigious diamond — a blue diamond — and at the meeting of the Great Council the next day her husband proposed that you should be released, displaying a sudden love for learning and a sensitivity for international scientific opinion.' Stephen felt himself grow pale and he turned aside to hide it. Of course Golconda was not only a general term for wealth: it was the name of the Great Mogul's diamond-mine. 'Gros is no fool, except where his wife is concerned; he made a very able speech — the international character of science, Cook's and Bougainville's immunity and so on — and he very nearly gained his point; but in the end it was decided that the matter should be referred to the Emperor. Now the proceedings of the Great Council are not much more secret than those of your cabinet; your value became obvious to various other bodies, and they are competing for the possession of your person. The army is particularly insistent. This too is to be referred to the Emperor; he is to decide between the claimants, and since the army connect you with Grimsholm — he is furious about that affair — they are likely to succeed. Their messenger is on his way, a particularly influential officer.'

'Did Madame Gros give any account of her diamond?' asked Stephen.

'Oh, some poor thin tale of an inheritance,' said Duhamel, brushing that aside. 'But I must tell you you are in the greatest danger. Quite apart from anything else, if the Empire falls, or even if it looks as though it were about to fall, there are men who are determined that nothing shall survive it, men who will kill without hesitation and bring everything down in the same ruin. My principal has the Emperor's order for your release —'

'How can that be? The Emperor is in Silesia.'

'Come, come, Dr Maturin,' said Duhamel impatiently, 'you know very well how your Sir Smith escaped from this very Temple in ninety-eight: even an amateur can fabricate a convincing order. So as you must see, time presses extremely. You must make up your mind. I beseech you to tell me what conditions the man we take you for would insist upon.'

Stephen stared at the packet that Duhamel was holding: a fraction of his mind observed the familiar covers of the *Naval Chronicle* and the London *Times.* The rest was analysing the position, weighing Duhamel's personality and his words, spoken or implied. There was still the possibility of a trap. His instinct was against it; but his instinct was not infallible. 'The man you have in mind,' he said slowly, 'would in the first place require some proof of good faith. He might for example ask you to give him your revolving pistol.'

'Yes,' said Duhamel. He laid it on the table. 'Take care: it is loaded.'

Weighing it in his hand and looking at the ingenious mechanism, Stephen said in a parenthesis, 'It would be too heavy for me.'

'It cocks when you pull the trigger,' said Duhamel in the same curious time out. 'The barrel revolves by itself. You get used to the weight.'

Stephen went on. 'He would insist upon the release of his companions, the restitution of the diamond, and immunity for the original possessor, with liberty to travel, if that should be desired.'

'Your man asks a great deal,' said Duhamel.

'So does your principal,' said Stephen. 'He asks Hypothesis to put his head under the guillotine.'

'Are those the minimal conditions?'

'They would be, I am sure,' said Stephen. 'But you are to observe, that I am speaking of some airy, suppositional being.'

'I cannot engage for so much,' said Duhamel. 'I must refer to my principal. I hope to God there is time — Valençay and back . . .'

'Valençay?'

'Yes,' said Duhamel, and a look of intelligence passed between them. Talleyrand lived at Valençay much of the time and the perhaps calculated indiscretion might be a further proof of good faith. 'Would you give me back my pistol? I feel naked without it, on a journey; and it would be of no use to you here or at the rue Saint-Dominique — Major Clapier wishes to see you again this afternoon. I could not refuse without exciting comment, but we have them fairly well in hand: you will be treated as an exceptional prisoner and you will be back here before sunset. I have given the strictest orders that you are to be here before sunset.' He looked at his pistol. Stephen gave it to him and Duhamel gave

Stephen the little parcel of English papers: 'I thought these might amuse your leisure hours,' he said.

'It was only Duhamel,' said Stephen in answer to the intensely anxious expression on Jack's face. 'He wanted to be dosed, and he has very humanely brought us these publications, to amuse our leisure hours.'

'Our leisure hours,' said Jack, laughing in his relief. 'We shall have quite a few of them, I believe. There is not much more I can do in there until we have our block and tackle. Jagiello's dear pretty Poupette may possibly put them in our dinner-basket.'

He took the *Naval Chronicle*, and after a little while he burst in upon Stephen's ratiocination with a fine exultant cry, 'By God, Stephen, she did it! *Ajax* came up with the *Méduse* off La Hogue and beat her into mummy in thirty-five minutes: killed her captain and a hundred and forty-seven of her people. *Ardent* and *Swiftsure* in sight to leeward . . . by God, it was worth it . . . It was worth running poor dear *Ariel* ashore.'

Stephen returned to his thoughts. More than nine tenths of his mind accepted Duhamel's words as true: was the remaining area of doubt the effect of years and years of caution and distrust, or had it a sounder basis than mere professional deformation? As time went by, he found it increasingly difficult to believe anyone implicitly. Deformation there was, and graver deformation than he had supposed. He had been wrong about Diana, for example: he had never in his heart believed her capable of love. Of friendship, surely, of fondness and even quite strong affection at times; but never love, above all not for him. Yet now there was the proof in the form of this glorious, loving, hare-brained action. He knew she valued that bauble above her salvation: and even more than that, she had put her head into a noose for him. He felt a great wave of gratitude and admiration warm his heart, and when once again Jack broke in, pacing across the room with the *Chronicle* open in his hand, Stephen looked up with an extraordinary serenity in his face.

'Look at that,' said Captain Aubrey in a low, awed voice, pointing to the page.

'Marriages,' read Stephen. *'Lately, Captain Ross, of La Désirée, to Miss Cockburn, of Kingston, Jamaica.'*

'No, no. Lower down.'

'On Wednesday, at Halifax, Nova Scotia, Captain Alexander Lushington, of the Royal Marines, to Miss Amanda Smith, daughter of

J. Smith, of Knocking Hall, Rutland, Esquire. I do not believe I know Mr Lushington.'

'Of course you do, Stephen. A great beefy hulk of a man, just like a bull. In *Thunderer*: she has not been on the North American station above three weeks. God help him. God help us all. Could you believe such a thing? Do you suppose it was all air, that baby?'

'Sure, it may well have been.'

Jack considered, shaking his head: a great smile spread over his face. 'Lord,' he said, 'I do not know I have been so relieved in all my life. Lord, I shall have such a go at that slab — I shall clap on to it so hearty now.' He disappeared into the privy, and could be heard scraping with almost reckless vehemence until their dinner came.

They searched the basket the moment Rousseau was gone, and nothing did they find. Never mind, they said, the double sister-blocks, coaked, would come with their supper.

'So this is a soupe anglaise,' said Jack when they reached their pudding. 'I have often wished to see one.'

'Not quite an orthodox soupe however,' said Stephen. 'This forms no part of the accepted receipt.' He held out the ladle, and in it there lay a little tinned-iron pulley of the kind used for washing-lines: fishing produced its pair. Jack looked at them with wonder. 'How that dear good young woman can conceivably have supposed that these could act as double sister-blocks, I cannot tell. Look — look at their pins! Jagiello, you must signal that what we need is purchase-upon-purchase. Never mind the coaking, so the sheaves run double; but the pins must be at least five times as thick as there.'

'You forget, sir, I told you she should not be here this afternoon, nor tomorrow,' said Jagiello. And in a defensive tone he observed that as far as he could tell, the pulleys were very like what Captain Aubrey had drawn.

'Why, I am no great draughtsman, it is true,' said Jack. 'But I did put a scale, you know. Is that the barber?' he asked, turning his ear towards the door. 'I should like to be trimmed, but I do loathe being trimmed by a deaf-mute. Don't you find it make your flesh creep, Stephen?'

'I do not,' said Stephen. 'And that is no barber, but Rousseau and his soldiers to take me away: I expected them. Do not be concerned,' he said, feeling for his ampulla, 'unless something unexpected should occur, I shall be back at sunset.'

'Before sunset without fail,' said the captain as he signed for his prisoner; for on this journey the captain and lieutenant were his only companions. Little unexpected occurred as they drove through Paris, although Stephen did see Dr Baudelocque as they passed the Hôtel de La Mothe; and there was little unexpected in his arrival at the backside of the rue Saint-Dominique. The only change was that soon after he had been put into the barred waiting-room overlooking the stake, the door opened and a man was thrust in so roughly that he fell sprawling on the floor. Stephen helped him up, and he sat wiping the blood from his face and hands, muttering to himself in Catalan, 'O Mother of God, Mother of God, Lady of Consolation save me.' They fell into conversation and the man, speaking heavily-accented, hesitant French, told a very pitiful tale of the persecution he had suffered for the cause of Catalan independence; but he was a clumsy fellow, an obvious plant who had not even learnt his lesson well, and Stephen grew very tired of him and of his little bladders of gore.

The interrogation that followed was of much the same mediocre quality. Major Clapier produced two people, one a sweating minor zoologist, the other a decayed official, who almost in Fauvet's very terms deposed that Dr Maturin had offered to carry messages, had spoken disrespectfully of the Emperor, and had solicited a fee; a clerk from Beauvillier's hotel followed them and quite truthfully stated that Dr Maturin had desired him to change fifty guineas for napoleons. This, said the major as impressively as he could, was a very grave offence indeed; Dr Maturin now stood convicted on all hands, and as a man of sense he must see that the only way of escaping the penalty was cooperation with the authorities. Nobody seemed to believe it however, and Stephen was hoping that he might be dismissed when after a brief silence a sharp-looking man on the left spoke up. 'Can Dr Maturin explain how it came about that a lady should offer the equivalent of at least a million for his release, if neither he nor she is a political agent?'

Stephen at once replied, 'Can the gentleman possibly conceive of any political agent yet weaned capable of such enormous folly, mortal to himself and to his colleague?'

They looked at one another. 'Then what is the explanation?' asked a captain.

'Only an insufferable coxcomb could reply,' said Stephen.

'Is it possible that the lady, such a lady, could be enamoured of Dr Maturin's person?' cried an officer — the first honest, sincere amazement that had been heard in that room.

'It is improbable, I must confess,' said Stephen. 'But you are to consider, that both Europa and Pasiphae loved a bull; and that history teems with even less eligible companions.'

They were pondering upon this; the atmosphere was almost relaxed; and Stephen had received veiled looks of wondering respect when a man came in and leaning over Clapier's shoulder spoke to him in a low, urgent tone. The major looked up with a startled expression and hurried from the room. In five minutes he returned with a companion and his face was pale with furious emotion; but Stephen had little time to study Clapier's face, for his companion was Johnson.

'That is the man,' said Johnson at once, and they both looked at Stephen with the bitterest personal hatred and malignity. Clapier stepped forward and said in a low tone, barely under control, 'You killed Dubreuil and Pontet-Canet.' Stephen thought he was going to strike him, but Clapier mastered the impulse and cried 'Take him to the cells. Take him to the bee-hive cell.'

The bee-hive cell was deep in filth and ooze and perhaps it owed its name to the hissing swarms of bluebottles and flies. It was bare, apart from some iron rings let into the wall, and Stephen stood through the ensuing hours by a barred opening at the level of the paving outside, the paving of the execution-ground, loathsome great flies settling thick upon him, their bellies cold.

Standing there he saw the sun go down, the sky turn nacreous so that the roofs beyond the court took on the sharpness of a silhouette: the pallor deepened to an exquisite violet; the outlines vanished, lights appeared and in an uncurtained room beyond the stake he saw a man and woman eating their evening meal. They ate awkwardly, because they were holding hands, and at one point they leaned over the table and kissed.

There were also stars, a sprinkling of small-dust and one great unwinking planet that sloped diagonally down the sky by imperceptible degrees, slanting past a gable before it was lost behind the roofs:

Venus perhaps. He felt the ampulla in his cheek — undying mortal sin except by casuistry — and although he had long thought prayer in time of danger indecent, prayers sang in his mind, the long hypnotic cadences of plainchant imploring protection for his love.

The sound of boots at last: light round the door: the grind of keys and in the sudden glare, the renewed buzz of innumerable flies, he made out a sergeant's guard. They marched him back to the room where he had been questioned and there, his eyes accustomed to the light, he saw a general officer, his aide-de-camp, the deputy-governor of the Temple, and the original figurehead colonel, now pale with anxiety.

'Is this your prisoner?' asked the general.

'Yes, sir,' said the governor.

'Then take him back to the Temple. Colonel, you will report to the secretary's office at eight o'clock tomorrow morning.'

It was a silent drive. The governor seemed worn, anxious, old, depressed; the aide-de-camp was preoccupied with his sword-knot, which had caught in the carriage door.

'There you are, Stephen!' cried Jack.

'There you are at last. By God, we have been so —'

Stephen held up his hand and stood for some moments with his ear to the door. 'Listen, Jack,' he said when the ancient silence had returned, 'is it possible to expedite matters, at all? Johnson is in Paris. He has identified me.'

'Is he, though?' said Jack, and picking up the candle he strode into the jakes. He had everything ready for the coming of his purchase, of blocks stouter than those which had come with their dinner, everything but the breaking of their furniture, whose wood must provide the necessary chocks and wedges; and even that he had already prepared with deep hidden cuts, made by one of Poupette's knives, nicked into a saw. The massive cross-stones of the privy lay bare, loose in their beds: their free ends were still concealed by masonry, carefully arranged, but this masonry could be swept away in a moment and the long deep slabs only waited the application of a mechanical force to raise them. With the blocks he hoped for it would be a fairly easy task to swing them silently in, one after another; he had a good hold-fast in the two lintels, and the line, though thin, was immensely strong. Even with what he had it was not impossible. 'Whip upon whip, double rove, might do it,' he said. 'It all depends on the pins.' He took the pulleys out of his pocket and looked at them again: the axles upon which the little wheels revolved were not above three sixteenths of an inch across; they would have to sustain a very great load; and in all likelihood they were no more than soft iron. 'Lord, what pins,' he said. 'What landsman's pins. But at least the sheaves are strong, and the shells don't signify.' He called to Jagiello to hold the candle and as there was not room for three in the little recess Stephen sat on the bed and watched them.

Jack was a big man, but he moved quickly, neatly, working fast with sure, knowing hands. He was extremely reluctant to cut the line, both on principle and because silk was a treacherous stuff to splice, and in time he had woven the whole into a spider's web, an extraordinarily intricate piece of rigging with cunning knots, stoppers and beckets, the whole designed to concentrate two men's strength on the raising of the left-hand side of the farther slab: although he was never still, to a watcher his work seemed endless, needlessly finical, obscure. At last, at last he checked over the whole array to make sure that all was set up with the correct tension throughout and that the resultant motion came true for a perfectly vertical lift. Then he backed out, took their best stool, broke a leg into short lengths and split them. 'Now Stephen,' he said, 'pray go in there, kneel by the crosspiece, and if it rises, whip these under it.'

Stephen crept through the web and took up his post. He heard Jack say 'Clap on to the fall, Jagiello. Haul after me, keeping time. Handsomely, now. Handsomely does it.'

Lines in all directions tightened, straightened; the quadruple strand above Stephen's head came down to his nose in a general and musical sound of stretching; the little wheels, clear in the candlelight, revolved. The strain came on, gradually stronger, stronger; the musical sound mounted and still the strain increased. 'Handsomely, handsomely,' murmured Jack, and with a sighing groan the great crosspiece rose three inches, half clear of its granite bed. 'She rises,' said Stephen as he thrust wood into the gap. The whole assemblage of lines began to vibrate, uttering the strangest quivering sound in that silence, and the stone sank back, crushing the wood. 'Something is wrong,' called Stephen.

'Belay,' said Jack. He came into the privy, took the candle, and said 'Yes: the pins have gone.' They looked at him with appalled faces. 'I shall have to unship all this,' he said. 'They are not snatch-blocks, you see.'

At half past the hour he had the wretched little pulleys free; by midnight he had driven out the broken pins and replaced them with the steel tail of a file, struck off short. 'They ain't pretty,' he said, 'but they may answer. I shall reduce the pull to the power of three, to spare the thinner one.'

The weaving once more, into a slightly different pattern this time, and before the distant clock struck one he said again, 'Clap on to the fall.' Again the whole complication of lines straightened, stretching fiddle-string taut, but this time the little wheels jibbered and squeaked as they turned and the network trembled uneasily. It gave little impression of strength. Yet as the tension rose to such a pitch that Stephen felt all must very soon give way, he saw the slab heave gently up. Up and up, and he filled the space with wood. 'It is clear this end,' he called.

'Belay,' said Jack. He came and looked

keenly at the stone. 'Very well,' he said. 'It is very well: and if the pins hold we shall do it. But I have been thinking: my plan was to walk the slab inboard, each end in turn. But that means shifting the purchase each time, and even if the pins hold I doubt we can do both slabs much before dawn. Yet if we raise and lower this left-hand end while you wedge the other, first with the cold chisel and then with stone, the right-hand end must pivot clear of its bed and fall free. The only thing is the noise of its fall. It would save some hours; it would spare the pins; but there is the noise. What do you say?'

Stephen considered. 'I have heard a good many pieces fall from the tower where they were working in the day,' he said. 'Then again, the place is almost empty. We have scarcely had a night-patrol this last week and more. I think we should risk the noise. Show me what I must do.'

Jack showed him, changed the angle of the lift, and returned to Jagiello. 'Handsomely, handsomely,' he said, and now the stone rose in a deliberate even movement, at much the pace of a seconds hand. Stephen placed his wedges under the right-hand face, said 'Lower away,' and the descending stone crept grating sideways across its bed. More wedges in the upper, the horizontal gap. 'Pull now,' he said, and as it rose so the slab also continued its sideways motion, creeping towards the edge of vacancy. Up, down: up, down. And still the sideways movement, the wedges growing larger every time.

'It is about —' he began, but he had not time to say 'to go' before there was a void where he had been staring, no stone, nothing but night air below the candlelight and a great twanging web of lines above his head, skipping up and down. Silence for a heart-beat, and then a most shocking crash below, a shattering roar that seemed to fill the room, the whole tower.

They stared at one another, never moving until for some reason Jagiello blew out the candle. Time passed. St Théodule's struck the quarter; repeated it. No other sound at all.

At length, at great length, Jack whispered 'Strike a light,' and first Jagiello and then Stephen endeavoured to do so. 'What a couple of lubbers you are, to be sure,' said Jack, showing a certain testiness for the very first time. 'Give it here.' He took the tinder-box, struck hard, blew on the living spark, lit the candle, and inspected the gap and the line. 'Six inches more, and a thin man could slip through,' he said. 'With the next we should be well away. But this time I shall pudden the bight with Jagiello's shirt, to prevent it from chafing.'

Once more the whole system changed place to bring the hoist over the inner stone, and once more Stephen watched them. Now that the gate to freedom was half open he could no longer control his heart and as the long process ran its course he felt exasperation, impatience, impotent frustration rise to an almost unbearable pitch. He was confident that the half-demolished, encumbered moat would present no difficulty and that once they were clear of the Temple they could lie up safely in any of the half dozen refuges he knew: all this, if only they could begin to move. From there he could get into touch with La Mothe and Valençay. He was as nearly as possible certain that Duhamel's proposal was genuine, but even so it would be better to be out of his power before making the final arrangements. In any case there was no question of remaining in the Temple another day with Johnson abroad. Quite apart from the question of Clapier's personal revenge, the value of the American connexion was such that he would certainly sacrifice the prisoners, taking them from the Temple by main force if need be; he could easily justify himself after the event. Only too easily. And he would surely act soon: dawn was the usual time for such measures, or a little before it. But then again, what would be the effect of Johnson's arrival on Valençay? An absurd question; for if Valençay's plan succeeded there would be no point in any American connexion, no point at all; and no concessions would be called for. It was Diana's position that tormented him: again and again he asserted that with La Mothe's protection, her wide and influential acquaintance, and her political nullity she could not be in danger, particularly as he was convinced that Johnson had only just arrived; and again and again he replied that he was only reassuring himself, that his conjectures had no solid basis. To avoid at least some part of this intolerable, incessant arguing to and fro he collected their few possessions and heaped them into a cloth bundle; he even fed the mice, that had come out from under their door, quite amazed.

'I think that will do,' said Jack at last — they had long since been speaking in natural voices. 'But we shall have to heave hearty this time: the angle is not so good, the multiplication less. I hope to God the pins bear it. Jagiello, wrap a handkerchief round your hands. Stephen, carry on.'

Now Stephen had something real to do: now just beneath him lay a rectangle of the free night: he squatted there, his pale eyes glittering, his cold chisel and his pile of wedges at hand. And as the full strain came on, Jack and Jagiello grunting as they heaved, it occurred to him that his strength, such as it was, would ease the perilous load on the pins. He straddled the crosspiece, clasped his hands beneath it and hoisted, hoisted until the stone cut into his arms on either side, until his sight was blurred with the pounding of his heart, and until he felt the slab give a releasing jerk and yield. 'She rises,' he said in a gasping croak and skipped free to set his wedges with intense blundering activity.

Jack saw him and smiled. He also saw the door, the unknown door, the mouse's door swing wide. Four men with a lantern.

'Good evening, gentlemen,' said the leader.

'Jack, do not move,' cried Stephen, for he and Jagiello were upon their spring, as dangerous as tigers. 'Gentlemen, good evening. Pray walk in.' He stepped forward and fell into the free night up to his waist.

Jack and Duhamel leapt across and plucked him out, each by a hand: they hoped he was not hurt. 'Not at all, I thank you,' said Stephen, mopping his shin — it gave him an extreme though superficial agony. 'Gentlemen,' he said somewhat sharply, 'please to state your business.'

'You will not remember me, Dr Maturin,' said the first man, advancing. 'D'Anglars: I had the honour of meeting you when I was attached to the suite of Monsieur de Talleyrand-Périgord during his embassy to London; and I believe we have several common friends.'

'I remember you perfectly, sir,' said Stephen, 'and of course I recall his Excellency with the greatest esteem. I had the pleasure of seeing him a little while ago. Neither of you has changed at all.' This was not quite true as far as d'Anglars was concerned; he was now but an aged beauty and even by lantern-light the rouge showed plain on his intelligent, lively, but ravaged face. On the other hand, Stephen did have an affectionate admiration for the Bishop of Autun, or the Prince de Bénévent as he was now styled: a pillar of falsehood, a prodigy, a phoenix of duplicity, but excellent company, and by a certain standard quite sound.

'You are too, too kind,' said d'Anglars with a turn of his person that reminded Stephen of La Mothe, who was in fact one of their common friends. 'I see you are busy,' he went on, 'but perhaps we might have a word together? You will excuse us,' he said, bowing to Captain Aubrey and Jagiello.

'By all means,' said Jack, returning the civility; and glancing beyond him Stephen observed that d'Anglars' companions were Duhamel, of course, an officer whose cloak only partly hid a very splendid uniform, and a man in black whose face, in spite of an eye-shade, he connected with the foreign ministry, the upper reaches of the foreign ministry.

They walked into Jagiello's room with the candle, now very low, and sat in the window-seat. 'Duhamel has told us your conditions,' said d'Anglars. 'We agree on all points but one. You require the restitution of the stone, the Blue Peter; and the stone alas we cannot produce immediately. But here is a pledge of its eventual restoration.' He brought out an episcopal ring set with a huge amethyst: Stephen looked at it with some curiosity but not much liking; he did not seem pleased and he did not reply. 'On the other hand,' d'Anglars went on, 'we can produce the stone's owner, ready and indeed eager to travel, as you put it.' His voice was urgent, ingratiating, uncertain. Stephen still did not answer, but turned the amethyst over and over in the candlelight. 'And as for compensation,' said d'Anglars, more confident now, 'I have draughts here on Drummond's . . .'

'No, no,' said Stephen. 'That would complicate matters, and I have always avoided complication. Tell me, what guarantees do you offer?'

'We three will go with you to the cartel at Calais, and cross to England if you wish. Our life, or at least our liberty, will be in your hands: you may carry what weapons you choose.'

'Very well,' said Stephen. 'My companions come with me, of course?'

'Captain Aubrey and young Apollo?'

'Just so.'

'Certainly.'

'Then let us go.'

As they walked back, Stephen limping, d'Anglars said pleasantly, nodding at the dislocated jakes, 'I am concerned that you should have had so much trouble; but nothing could serve our purpose more prettily: wonderfully à propos: the perfect alibi. This way, by the door.'

'Captain Aubrey, Mr Jagiello,' said Stephen, 'we will go with these gentlemen, if you please.'

Politeness over precedence at the open door, locked behind them, then down and down the spiral staircase, a long passage, a courtyard they had never seen, a wicket with two dark figures that stood aside for them to pass, then the street, wonderfully open and ordinary: two coaches and two horses led. The man in black and the cloaked officer mounted. Jack, Duhamel and Jagiello stepped into the first coach, Stephen and d'Anglars into the second, and they drove off at a steady trot through the quiet dark streets — a warm, covered night — down towards the river.

'Where do we take up the lady?' asked Stephen.

'Why, at the Hôtel de La Mothe,' said d'Anglars, surprised.

'Indeed? You are as sure as that?'

'Oh yes,' said d'Anglars, and it was clear from his voice that he was smiling.

'She has not been molested?'

'Not really. There was an American gentleman, a newly-arrived American gentleman, enquiring for a compatriot with whom he thought she might have some connexion; but she has not been molested.'

On the Pont au Change Stephen said, 'It is understood, is it not, that she will believe this release to be entirely her own doing?'

'Certainly,' said d'Anglars. 'Certainly.' And he added, 'Anything else would be folly, from our point of view.'

The rue de Grenelle, and already a few market-waggons, one piled high with flowers. The Hôtel de La Mothe, and Diana was waiting for them there in the courtyard, slender under her hooded cloak, with a group of menservants by another coach loaded with trunks. Stephen leapt out and limped up to her, she running to meet him; they kissed and he said 'Dearest Diana, how profoundly I thank you: but I have cost you the Blue Peter.'

'Oh how happy I am to see you,' she said, holding his arm. 'Be damned to the necklace: you will be my diamond.' Then, 'Stephen, you have torn your stocking — your leg is all covered with blood.'

'Sure, I just barked my shin. Tell, how do you do, my jewel? I heard from Baudelocque that you were not quite well.'

'Stephen,' she said, looking at him under the lamp, 'I did not do it, I promise you. I kept my word: I took great care: I was amazed — amazed. Dr Baudelocque said it could not be helped, upon my honour.'

'There was no help for it,' he said, nodding, 'that I know very well. Give me your hand, put your foot on the step, and we are away: with the blessing.'

Away and away, with the sky lightening on the right hand of the road. At Beaumont le Château they changed carriages in a great silent house far down its avenue of limes. Duhamel seemed to be the somewhat incongruous master of the place and he led them in to shave, to put on civilian clothes, and to breakfast. As they were trying on their coats Stephen said, 'Listen, Jack, you must know that Diana gave her great diamond to a minister's wife for our release.'

'Did she, by God?' cried Jack, motionless, one arm in his sleeve. 'Handsome — damn my soul if that ain't handsome. But Stephen, she was so pleased and proud of it — nothing finer in the Tower — a king's ransom — how can I thank her? She was always a thoroughbred, but this . . . Sophie will be so eternally grateful: so am I, upon my sacred honour, so am I.' He ran into the high gaunt echoing room where breakfast stood on a trestle-table, seized her in his powerful grasp, kissed her heartily on either cheek and said, 'Cousin Diana, I am so grateful. I am proud, oh so proud, to call you kin, as proud as Lucifer, upon my soul. God bless you, my dear.'

In their new coach, a vast machine with six horses, he said she must live at Ashgrove Cottage; neither Sophie nor he would hear of a refusal; and as they sped through Picardy they talked of Stephen at length. He was now in the leading carriage with d'Anglars and Duhamel, in close discussion of the documents he was to carry and to comment upon in London. Any plan for bringing Buonaparte down had his wholehearted support, however wild it might be; and this was very far from wild. He made suggestions for rendering it more acceptable to English feelings, but these were changes of tone or of shading, never of substance: he thought the whole proposal admirably well conceived. Keen, intelligent, analytical minds had been at work, and he cordially hoped they might succeed — that they might meet with equal intelligence in London and at Hartwell.

The same minds had worked out their route and the details of their journey, and although he had seen what could be accomplished by efficient organization when urgent intelligence had to move fast, he had never experienced anything as smoothly effective as this. Only once, three miles beyond Villeneuve, was there the slightest delay, when a horse cast a shoe; otherwise they rolled across Picardy, rolled across Artois with never an unforeseen pause. They passed columns of troops, many of them mere boys, all marching north, long lines of cavalry remounts, a siege-train, ammunition and victualling waggons, field artillery; and every time the road was cleared well before they swept by.

Stephen knew very well that most French victories had been founded on brilliant staff-work, and it was clear that the conspiracy included some eminent staff-officers; yet he sometimes felt that this perfection could not endure, that some senior general commanding an important post might require explanations and confirmation from Paris, or that some other faction that valued Johnson and his government should send after them or worse still use the semaphore telegraph whose towers he saw on every hill. But he was mistaken: they ran into Calais at high water, with the cartel, HMS *Oedipus*, in the harbour, ready to sail on the ebb; and there was even a moderate off-shore breeze.

'You will have a comfortable voyage at least,' he said, for it had been agreed that d'Anglars should accompany him, if only to make everything doubly clear to his cousin Blacas and to the titular king. 'That ship, or rather brig, is a particularly fine sailer: a good, dry, weatherly sea-boat, as we say. Furthermore, the ocean is placid.'

'I am glad of that,' said d'Anglars. 'The last time I crossed I was very dangerously ill. I was obliged to lie down.'

Apart from smugglers, the Channel knew no vessels more discreet than these cartels; they moored in a discreet, shielded part of the harbour, and when they belonged to the Royal Navy, as did the *Oedipus* of course, they were commanded by unusually discreet captains, often quite senior men temporarily detached for the purpose. Jack, sitting in the window of the private house where they were waiting to embark, was therefore surprised to see William Babbington on the quarterdeck, obviously directing proceedings; for Babbington had served under him as a midshipman and a lieutenant, and although Jack knew he had been made commander into the captured *Sylphide* — Jack had in fact written many letters and stirred up his friends to that very effect — Babbington still seemed to him remarkably young for such a position.

But young or not, Captain Babbington understood the meaning of the word discretion as well as any man in the service; and when his passengers, English and French, came aboard there was no hint of recognition in his correct, civil reception, no hint on either side. He directed a midshipman to take Captain Aubrey, Dr Maturin and the lady to his cabin, the foreign gentlemen to the gunroom: this being done, he looked fore and aft, and in a creditable imitation of Jack's quarterdeck voice he roared 'All hands unmoor ship.'

The *Oedipus* cleared the wharf under forestaysail and jib, with her topsails on the cap; she hoisted home her yards in the fairway and ran past the north buoy, wafting very gently and discreetly through the crowd of fishing-boats and coming to the outer roads in a little over half an hour. Here Captain Babbington let fall his courses and some pretty severe remarks about the sloth of the midshipmen at the larboard gaskets, a sloth that foretold the ruin of the Navy within a very short lapse of time. He had just uttered this prophecy, which he had first heard from Jack at the age of twelve, when a tall shadow fell across the deck, and turning he saw the original prophet himself, looking nervous, apprehensive, uneasy, timid, a striking sight for one who had gone into action with Captain Aubrey as often as William Babbington.

'Shall we go below, sir?' he asked, smiling uncertainly.

'Why, I believe I shall take the air for a while,' said Jack, moving aft to the taffrail. 'It is rather hot down there.'

'Carry on, Mr Somerville,' said Babbington, and he joined his former captain by the ensign-staff.

'They are at it hammer and tongs,' said Jack in a low, private voice. 'Hammer and goddam tongs. They might have been married this twelvemonth and more.'

'Dear me,' said Babbington, appalled.

The yards were braced just so, the *Oedipus* was heading for Dover over a quiet, gently rippling sea, her deck was almost as steady as a table, and now that all was coiled down and pretty there was scarcely a sound but the wind in her rigging, the distant cry of gulls, and the water slipping down her side. They were standing not far from the cabin skylight, and in the comparative silence they distinctly heard the words, 'God's death, Maturin, what an obstinate stubborn pigheaded brute you are, upon my honour.

You always were.'

'Perhaps you would like to see our figurehead, sir,' said Babbington. 'It is a new one: in the Grecian taste, I believe.'

Oedipus might well have been in the Grecian taste, if the Greeks had been much given to very thick paint, an insipid smirk, eyes fixed in a meaningless glare, and scarlet cheeks. The two captains stared at the image and after a while Jack said, 'I was never any great fist at the classics, but was there not something rather odd about his feet?'

'I believe there was, sir. But fortunately they don't show, he being cut off at the waist.'

'Though now I come to think of it, was it not his marriage, rather than his feet?'

'Perhaps it was both, sir: they might go together. And I seem to recall something in Gregory's *Polite Education* to that effect.'

Captain Aubrey pondered, staring at the dolphin-striker. 'I have it,' he cried. 'You are quite right: both marriage and feet. I remember the Doctor telling me the whole story when we lay alongside *Jocasta* in Rosia Bay. I do not mean the least fling at your figurehead, still less your brig, Babbington, but that family was not really quite the thing, you know. There were some very odd capers, and it ended unhappy. But then the relationships between men and women are often very odd, and I am afraid they often end unhappy. How do you find your martingales answer, led single like that?'

In the cabin Diana said, 'Stephen, dear, how can you possibly expect any woman to marry you when you present it as a mere matter of expediency? As something forced upon her?'

'I only said that Johnson was in Paris, that the English ports were closed against you as an enemy alien, and that you had no choice,' said Stephen, looking miserable, confused and upset. 'I have been trying to get that into your thick head this hour at least, Villiers.'

'There — there you go again,' cried Diana. 'Surely you must know, surely you must feel that any woman, even a woman as battered as I am, must look for something more — more, what shall I say? — more romantic in an offer of marriage? Even if I were to marry you, which is totally inconceivable, I should never, never do so after such a grovelling, such an utterly mundane and businesslike proposal. It is a question of common good manners, or ordinary civility. Really,

Maturin, I wonder at you.'

'Yet indeed, Diana, I love you dearly,' said Stephen in a dejected tone, looking down.

'. . . the whole point is that we save a bobstay,' said Babbington on the forecastle. His eye lifted to the upper rigging, and directing his voice aft he called, 'Mr Somerville, I believe we may set topgallantsails.'

Bosun's piping, cries of 'Lay aloft — lay out — let fall, let fall,' and the *Oedipus* spread more canvas with a smooth celerity that warmed her commander's heart, conscious as he was of Jack Aubrey's gaze. The captains were back at their martingales and dolphin-strikers when a tiny shrill young gentleman, Babbington's sister's son, came running forward and said 'Uncle William, she wants you in the cabin.' Then recollecting himself and blushing he pulled off his hat and said 'If you please, sir, the lady in the cabin's compliments to Captain Babbington and would be glad of a word with him at his leisure. And Captain Aubrey too, sir, if you please.'

They hurried aft: the marine sentry opened the door with a significant look — significant of what? — and they walked in. Babbington at once saw that his passengers were friends again: rather solemn, but strangely contented, holding hands like a happy country pair. Instantly his spirits rose. He cried 'Oh Mrs Villiers, how delightful to see you! Lord, Doctor, how very welcome you are. What will you take? I have a whole crate of champagne. Tom! Tom, there. Rouse out the champagne.'

'Captain Babbington, my dear,' said Stephen, 'when do you expect to be in Dover?'

'Oh, in two or three hours, no more, with this breeze and tide. Why,' he said with a grin, 'was you to shin up to the maintruck, you would see the white cliffs from here.'

'Then there is not a moment to lose, I have a service to beg.'

'I shall be only too happy — delighted.'

'I desire you to marry us.'

'Very well, sir,' said Babbington. 'Tom! Tom there. The prayerbook.'

'William,' said Jack in an aside, 'do you know the drill?'

'Oh yes, sir. You always taught us to be prepared for the unexpected, you remember: it comes before the burial-service. Thankee, Tom: now pass the word for my clerk, will you? Ah, Mr Adam: the log and the proper certificates for a marriage, if you please. Note the time, and stand by to give the responses. Now, sir, who gives the lady away?'

A moment's hesitation, and then Jack, catching Diana's eye, cried 'I do, as next of kin. And most uncommon happy and honoured to do so,' he added.

'Then you stand here, sir, if you please,' said Babbington, taking his station behind the mahogany table and checking pens, paper and inkpot. 'Doctor, have you a ring?'

'I have,' said Stephen, producing the amethyst.

Babbington placed them, opened the book, and in a clear sea-officer's voice, without the least hint of affectation or levity, he read the service through. Jack listened to the familiar, intensely moving words: at 'till death us do part' his eyes clouded; and when it came to *Do you Stephen* and *Do you Diana* his mind ran back so strongly to his own wedding that Sophie might have been there at his side.

'I now pronounce you man and wife,' said Babbington, closing the book; and still with the same gravity, but with great happiness showing through it, 'Mrs Maturin, dear Doctor, I give you all the joy in the world.'